'Like the chocolate at its centre, this adroitly crafted story is both deliciously bitter and heart-achingly sweet. Set in post-WWI England and Tasmania, it explores the lengths people will go to in order to try to achieve a dream. Their gritty resilience, desperate greed, soul-breaking grief and, above all, tenacious hope, are beautifully laid bare. The historical details are fascinating; the characters unforgettable. Intending to savour this book, I devoured it in one sitting. It's an absolute treat – totally enthralling and completely and utterly satisfying. It's another triumph for Mary-Lou Stephens.' —Karen Brooks, bestselling Australian author, on *The Chocolate Factory*

'One of the most beautifully written books I've read. The evocative storytelling kept me captivated. I felt as if I was alongside Catherine and Annie as they journeyed through the highs and lows of the stages of their lives. *The Last of the Apple Blossom* will stay with me for a long time.' —Tania Blanchard, bestselling author of *The Girl from Munich*

'What a cracker of a debut! A beautiful story of family and orchards, of secrets and love and forgiveness' —Victoria Purman, author of *The Women's Pages* and *The Land Girls* on *The Last of the Apple Blossom*

'Mary-Lou Stephens has crafted a taut family drama set against a backdrop of environmental and political upheaval. The crisp prose sparkles and the characters stay with you long after the story ends.

A wonderful debut' —Lauren Chater, author of *Gulliver's Wife* and *The Lace Weaver* on *The Last of the Apple Blossom*

'*The Last of the Apple Blossom* is a love letter to Tasmania's Huon Valley and a testament to the resilience of the human spirit. Mary-Lou Stephens writes evocatively about family secrets, love, sacrifice, and finding the courage to rise again after devastating loss. An engrossing and poignant story, beautifully told' —Christine Wells, author of *Sisters of the Resistance* and *The Juliet Code*

'I have long been a fan of Mary-Lou's writing, which is always evocative and compelling. What a wonderful story this is, set at such a poignant moment in Tasmania's history. I loved it' —Josephine Moon, author of *The Jam Queens* and *The Cake Maker's Wish*, on *The Last of the Apple Blossom*

'An epic story of love, friendship, secrets and betrayal, and the woman who fought sexist tradition to retain the family orchard. Set in the aftermath of the disastrous 1967 Black Tuesday fires that devastated Tasmania and the thriving apple industry, *The Last of the Apple Blossom* will uplift, and keep you guessing, until the very last page' —Jodie Miller, author of *What Does it Feel Like Being Born?*

'This beautifully told story, starting in the late 1960s Tasmania in the midst of a catastrophic firestorm, explores how change – whether wrought by disaster, transforming social mores or politics – impacts upon individuals, families and communities. Following the lives of two orchardist families across the years, it has such emotional heft and a huge heart. Timeless yet also telling an achingly familiar story to us here and now, this is an unforgettable tale of love and loss, triumph and tragedy, featuring flawed, resilient and courageous characters who will linger in your heart and mind long after the last page' —Karen Brooks, bestselling Australian author, on *The Last of the Apple Blossom*

'This big-hearted family saga deals with far more than bushfires and apple orchards – it's an outstanding historical novel about women and the secrets and burdens they carry' —*The Australian* on *The Last of the Apple Blossom*

'*The Last of the Apple Blossom* is a meticulously researched, vividly portrayed and gripping historical novel. It's an impressive debut from Stephens, making her a name to watch in homegrown fiction' —*Better Reading*

'With lush and heartfelt prose, in-depth characters and relatable plot points, *The Last of the Apple Blossom* will keep you engaged until the last page' —*The Chronicle*

'A story of family, love, tragedy and resilience, *The Last of the Apple Blossom* is an engaging, accomplished debut novel' —*Book'd Out*

'... a sweeping, big-hearted Australian family saga' —*The Advertiser* on *The Last of the Apple Blossom*

Mary-Lou Stephens was born in Tasmania, studied acting at The Victorian College of the Arts and played in bands in Melbourne, Hobart and Sydney. Eventually she got a proper job – in radio, where she was a presenter and music director, first with commercial radio and then with the ABC.

She received rave reviews for her memoir *Sex, Drugs and Meditation* (2013), the true story of how meditation changed her life, saved her job and helped her find a husband. *The Australian* called her debut novel, *The Last of the Apple Blossom* (2021), 'an outstanding historical novel about women and the secrets and burdens they carry'.

Mary-Lou has worked and played all over Australia and now travels the world slowly with her husband and writes, mostly.

Also by Mary-Lou Stephens

Sex, Drugs and Meditation
The Last of the Apple Blossom

The CHOCOLATE FACTORY

Mary-Lou Stephens

First Published 2024
First Australian Paperback Edition 2024
ISBN 9781867255659

THE CHOCOLATE FACTORY
© 2024 by Mary-Lou Stephens
Australian Copyright 2024
New Zealand Copyright 2024

This is a work of fiction. Names, characters, places, and incidents are either the product of the author's imagination or are used fictitiously, and any resemblance to actual persons, living or dead, business establishments, events, or locales is entirely coincidental.

Published by
HQ Fiction
An imprint of Harlequin Enterprises (Australia) Pty Limited (ABN 47 001 180 918), a subsidiary of HarperCollins Publishers Australia Pty Limited (ABN 36 009 913 517)
Level 19, 201 Elizabeth St
SYDNEY NSW 2000
AUSTRALIA

A catalogue record for this book is available from the National Library of Australia
www.librariesaustralia.nla.gov.au

Printed and bound in Australia by McPherson's Printing Group

MIX
Paper | Supporting
responsible forestry
FSC
FSC® C001695

For Sue, a luminous writer and a steadfast friend.
You are missed.

1

Dorothy

Late September 1921

He reminded her of Freddie, if Freddie had been allowed to grow older. The man's steps were steady despite the roll of the ship. Every movement was sure and measured. But there was something else, something she couldn't quite put her finger on. Dorothy longed to catch his eye, to see a recognition there, even though they'd never met. She dared a smile but his only greeting was a brief 'Good morning' before he bowed his head and moved on. She was left with ghosts. She had hoped it would fade, this haunting. The ocean churned behind her, but instead of leaving memories in the wake they clung to her skin like the salt air. She took off a glove, drew a finger gently below her eyes and brought the tears that lay there to her lips. More salt.

Her morning turn around the deck had lost its charm. There was a place, though, where she would feel less at sea. Heading away from the greyness of the ocean, she clattered down through the levels, thankful for her practical low-heeled boots. Below the waterline, deep within its metal hull, the beating heart of the ship lured her onwards. As she descended, the air pressed on her with the weight of heat. A sheen of sweat rose on her brow. Dorothy longed to loosen her collar and shed her jacket, but in this place of men she needed to be decorous – the line she walked was narrow. At first, she'd been unwelcome. The men were naturally wary. It was clear the superstition about women being unlucky on ships still ran like a barbed thread through their minds. A woman on deck was one thing, but here in the bowels of the ship she'd been met with dark looks and aversion. However, her thoughtful questions, curiosity and enthusiasm had won their acceptance, eventually. A man responded to interest in his work when that interest was genuine, and a widow, especially in these times, was given a respect that a single woman of her age might not have garnered.

The door to the engine room swung open and she rose to meet the wall of heat and noise with a matching burst of intensity. Here, surrounded by the power of machinery and steam, and the earth-based scent of coal, she felt more solid. Here was the gravity she needed, afloat on the roiling sea. Here she was grounded by the massive mechanism of the four geared steam turbines that powered the ocean liner far from Birmingham and the Cadbury's factory at Bournville and towards Dorothy's new life in Tasmania.

The chief engineer waved her over and her smile widened. 'Mr Broadbent,' she mouthed, more than said. Conversations were difficult in the engine room. Fortunately she would only need her eyes and her mind this morning. The chief had promised she could watch him repair a faulty generator. She longed to see his grease-stained hands at work, teasing out the problem, following his mind as it traced the links and breaks to find the solution. She would keep her mouth closed to any answers she might discover and only speak to ask questions, and those sparingly. Her place here was reliant on his good graces. The war had taken many things, but in return it had given her this – the chance to find out how things worked. And, even better – if they were broken, how to fix them.

Later that evening she had the cabin to herself for the half-hour it would take to dress for dinner. There was so little space that she and Miss Darwood had to take turns to make themselves presentable for the evening meal. Dorothy's simple dropped-waist dress was one she'd made herself, but the beading she'd sewn around the neckline added a sparkle that would suit the captain's table tonight. Someone of her station might not usually be invited to sit at his table but Mr Broadbent had arranged it after she'd asked if it would be possible. Being the chief engineer he was almost on a par with the captain, and with his appreciation of Dorothy's interest in the workings of his ship he'd been delighted to smooth the way. She brushed her dark hair into a chignon at the base of her neck, smoothed a little powder over her cheeks and added just a touch of lipstick. It was impossible to view the full effect in the small mirror above the vanity, but she was pleased by the little she could see. A soft knock at the door alerted her to Miss Darwood's presence and the fact that her allotted time was over. Dorothy checked her watch. Miss Darwood was a stickler for punctuality. There had been much to negotiate in their cramped cabin. They'd been strangers when they'd first met on the RMS *Ormonde* – two single women placed together out of necessity and practicality. They would be strangers again once the boat docked in Australia.

'Almost done.' Dorothy checked her lipstick once more, dabbed a few of the last drops in her perfume bottle to her wrists, then opened the door.

Miss Darwood's left eyebrow formed a high arch. 'A tad overdone, don't you think, dear?'

Dorothy swallowed the retort that threatened to escape. Instead she kept her lips firmly closed and stepped aside to allow the older woman access to their cabin.

Miss Darwood stopped in the doorway, stiffened and sniffed.

'It's Yardley's English Lavender,' Dorothy said. 'A gift from my late husband. Sadly the bottle's almost empty.' She'd been eking out the contents. Often she would open the bottle just to inhale the scent, remembering the late summer days with Freddie before their world changed course.

Miss Darwood gave one slow nod. 'I know it well.' She entered the cabin and closed the door behind her.

In the dining room, Dorothy's eyes were drawn towards a figure at the bar. It was the man from the deck. She hadn't seen him until this morning, and now here he was again. Her hand rose to her neck and traced the beadwork there. What would Freddie be like now? Would he have come home to her whole or would he have left a part of himself in the fields of France? She always imagined him as her dear sweet Freddie, smelling of cocoa beans and whistling jauntily as he made his way through the streets of Bournville. But on his final much-anticipated visit home from the front she had seen a change in her beloved husband – a dimming of the light within him, a restless agitation that had not been there before. At night she'd wake to find him missing from their bed. He'd tried to keep his mood jolly but she had sensed the struggle and effort it took.

The man turned, glass in hand, his elbow propped on the bar. Dorothy narrowed her eyes. There was something not quite right. He was too posed, stiff in his dinner jacket and bow tie. It was then she noticed a slight tremor in the hand that held the glass. As if sensing her gaze, he put down his drink and moved away. A finger of doubt traced its way up her spine. All was not as it should be.

4

Dorothy approached the captain's table where half-a-dozen men in black dinner jackets smoked cigarettes while taking each other's measure. Their bejewelled companions wore shimmering dresses of the robe de style with flounces and bows at the hip that put her simple gown to shame. She was certain that none of them had experienced, or even been aware, of the kind of poverty she'd known as a child. The fact that she was here at this table, let alone on this ship, was, for the most part, her own doing – a culmination of years of hard work.

'Welcome, Mrs Adwell.' Captain Johnson bowed slightly. 'Mr Broadbent has told me of your interest in my ship. A pleasure to have you aboard.'

'Thank you, Captain. The *Ormonde* is an impressive vessel.' Even though Mr Broadbent had laid the groundwork for her, she was still nervous. Her aim was an invitation to visit the bridge, an honour not even Mr Broadbent could bestow upon her. Dorothy smoothed the hair behind her right ear. She had to make a good impression. She'd noticed one of the women, with diamonds and emeralds decorating her throat and ears, grimace slightly at the sound of Dorothy's Birmingham accent. Naturally it had never been a problem at Bournville, only a few miles away from the city, but increasingly during the voyage she'd been aware of other people's reactions when she spoke. As the ship travelled further away from the only place she'd known, she realised how small her world had been.

The waiter pulled out her chair. She was seated not as she had hoped, beside the captain, but opposite and to the right. Dorothy was introduced to the men on either side of her – a portly soul with generous grey whiskers and a middle-aged businessman wearing gold cufflinks with no crest. New money, at a guess. His sparkling wife sat by his side. A knot of tension twisted in her stomach, not being used to such company. She smiled at the older gentleman and saw the sadness in his eyes. A conversation about gentler times,

before the Great War, would be best. He could reminisce and she'd
be happy to be taken on a nostalgic journey. The businessman might
be a challenge but if she asked him about new frontiers and business
opportunities she should be on safe ground. As Dorothy mapped the
time ahead her breath steadied. Having a plan in place was always
a source of reassurance.

Dorothy returned her attention to the captain. 'I believe RMS
Ormonde has an interesting history, Captain Johnson.'

The captain sat taller in his chair and projected his voice to
include the entire table. 'She was built to be a passenger liner, but
with the war … well, priorities changed. She gave proud service as a
troopship and headed to Australia several times. Even three attacks
by U-boats couldn't stop her. Then in 1919 she was refitted and
brought to the glory you enjoy today.'

Dorothy nodded attentively. The evening was off to a fine start.
'Please, tell us more.'

The bridge offered a view like none other on the ship. The Indian
Ocean was spread before them like a magic carpet. For a moment
Dorothy's attention was only on the water, the way it split and
shivered as the RMS *Ormonde* sliced her way through with the
power of her twin-screw propellers. An able seaman was on duty as
a lookout. Imagine staring all day at this panorama. It would make
her dizzy and sea blind. The officer of the watch stood to one side,
behind the wheel, ready to correct course if need be. If he objected
to her presence here, he was not making it known.

'Magnificent, isn't she?' The captain's voice was fat with pride,
and deservedly so. Last night, with the aid of wine and good food,
he'd told many stories of his life at sea. It was her eagerness to hear
more and her curiosity about the *Ormonde* that had led to this
morning's invitation to the bridge, just as she'd hoped.

'She certainly is, Captain.' Dorothy stood with her weight slightly forward and knees bent to compensate for the swaying of the ship. Over the weeks it had become habitual.

'The chief tells me you're interested in machinery and mechanics.' Captain Johnson scrutinised her.

'During the war I took on positions at Cadbury's that wouldn't normally be available to women, including operating and maintaining machinery.' More than two thousand men from Bournville had joined the armed forces and with so many positions left vacant she'd been asked to work in the conching room. Much to her surprise she'd enjoyed the experience, surrounded by the machines that ran twenty-four hours a day, mixing the cocoa mass, sugar and cocoa butter. Not only was it a fascinating process – the way the mixture changed from a gritty, bitter paste to a smooth liquid with a heady aroma – it was a welcome respite from the fiddly work of dipping and piping. She'd also spent time in cocoa pressing, as well as learning how to operate the mélangeurs – grinders with heavy granite rollers turning at different speeds to create the first stage of what would eventually become chocolate. When engineers had become difficult to find, the war demanding so many of them, she'd been asked to turn her skills to the internal workings of the machines. Cadbury's supplied chocolate to the troops and it was vital the factory continue to be productive. To the astonishment of most of the remaining men, she became as proficient with a spanner as she'd been with a piping bag. It gave her an enormous sense of satisfaction to use her mind and her ingenuity to fix something that no longer worked and restore it to use in a world where so much was broken. Her dedication had been rewarded when the new factory in Tasmania became a reality. Cadbury's, or the Firm, as the company was known to those who worked there, needed experienced and reliable employees to supervise a local workforce unfamiliar with factory work. The fact that she was knowledgeable in many aspects of chocolate production was a distinct advantage. With no ties to bind her, Dorothy had accepted the promotion to Forewoman A, one of only two such positions at the new factory and quite an honour at only twenty-four years of age. It was with a mix of excitement and trepidation that she'd readied herself for the voyage and what lay ahead.

'I know the war changed many things for women.' The captain stroked his moustache. 'Even so, such a keen eye for the way things work is unusual. You've made an impression on the chief and he's a man not easily impressed.'

Dorothy bobbed her head in acknowledgement of the praise. 'The *Ormonde*'s turbines are unlike anything I've seen. *They've* made quite an impression on me.'

The captain's chest expanded and a pleased smile lifted his expression. 'Allow me to show you where the decisions and directions are made and how.'

As Captain Johnson explained the various facets of the bridge – the chart table, the wheel, the telegraph that directed the men in the engine room, the compass and other instruments – Dorothy absorbed his words, connecting them to each element of the workings of the ship. 'It's a marvel,' she said. 'An intricate but logical dance of engineering and design.'

The captain guffawed. 'I've never heard it described quite that way, but yes, you're right, it is.'

'Sir?'

Captain Johnson turned to the officer of the watch. 'Yes?'

'It's ten hundred hours, sir.'

'Right.' He turned back to Dorothy. 'I'm sorry, Mrs Adwell, I have a briefing with the deck department. I hope I have satisfied your curiosity.'

'Thank you, yes.' She had a thousand more questions but was aware that even this short time on the bridge had been an honour.

'Well then.' He bowed slightly, stepped aside and gestured towards the door that would lead her back to the deck.

Dorothy hesitated for a moment. She longed to take control of this leviathan, to have the power to change course and speed, to turn the *Ormonde* around if she so pleased. But all she wanted to return to was a time before the war, before the world was shattered, before Freddie was lost – and that was impossible. Her future lay in Tasmania now, far from Bournville and the home they'd had together, far from the muddy trenches of France that took him from her. The RMS *Ormonde* sailed onwards.

As she stepped back onto the deck she saw the man again, leaning into the wind, smoking a cigarette. The feeling of wanting the power to change course overcame her. Dorothy moved towards him, unabashed and unashamed. He caught sight of her and straightened. In polite society she knew a woman should wait to be introduced to a man she was not acquainted with, but Dorothy's upbringing in the slums of Birmingham had been far from polite. Many years of working for the Firm had smoothed her rough edges but there were times when the brash nature of her upbringing was useful.

'Good morning,' she said. 'I've just visited the bridge. The view from there is magnificent.' She smiled into his eyes. There was space there, in those eyes, a different focus. It was something she recognised. She'd seen it in Freddie when he'd come home on leave, as if he was no longer with her, but was over there, somewhere she could never follow. She watched the man, willing him to come back to this ship, this deck, to the cigarette burning low between his fingers, and to her. Dorothy rubbed the wedding ring under her glove. 'But where are my manners? Allow me to introduce myself. I'm Mrs Adwell.'

He crushed out his cigarette and doffed his hat. 'Good morning, Mrs Adwell. Mr Thomas Moreland.' She noted the tremble in his hands before he clasped them behind his back.

'Have you been enjoying the journey?'

He turned to face the ocean, enabling her to study his profile; the slope of his nose, the lines etched around his eyes, the set of his mouth. 'Very much so.' Dorothy heard the lie in his voice.

'I recommend visiting the bridge if you can manage an invitation. It gives a different perspective.'

He nodded. 'I'm sure.'

Dorothy would not be dissuaded by his taciturn manner. 'I've also visited the engine room.'

Thomas turned back to her with an incredulous expression. 'The engine room?' At last his eyes were alive and attentive. 'Why on earth would you want to do that?'

Dorothy laughed. 'Firstly, we're not on earth.' She indicated towards the endless horizon. 'We are very much at sea.'

She was rewarded with a smile. 'Point taken,' he said.

'And secondly, I was curious about the engine and how it works.' She smiled back at him. 'I have to say, the *Ormonde*'s geared steam turbines are very impressive indeed.'

Thomas shook his head. 'Well, I never. I wasn't expecting to be talking about steam turbines this morning, especially with a passenger such as yourself, Mrs Adwell.'

'Is there a time you would be expecting to talk about steam turbines?'

He chuckled. 'You have me there.' He leant against the railing and gave her his full attention. 'Now I'm the curious one. What is it about a ship's engine that fascinates you so?'

Dorothy happily explained her work at Cadbury's, as she had for the captain and for the chief engineer before him. At the mention of the war Thomas's eyes clouded and she sensed him slipping away. She brought him back with a tale of falling over in a large puddle of warm chocolate when one of the conches had malfunctioned and how those who'd come to help had ended up doing the same. At the end of her story he was smiling again at the picture of her and her colleagues covered in melted chocolate, helpless with laughter. 'And now I'm on my way to Tasmania to help establish Cadbury's first overseas factory in Hobart,' she finished with a flourish. 'Let's hope the conches there behave themselves.'

'What a coincidence,' Thomas said. 'Not about Cadbury's or the chocolate, but I'm headed to Hobart as well, to take up a teaching position.'

Dorothy suppressed a gasp. It was as if a piece of a puzzle had just clicked into place. Freddie might be lost to her but Thomas was very much alive, with that familiar distance in his eyes and the tremble in his hands. If she dared ask, she was sure he'd tell her he too had fought in the Great War. There was a reason she and Thomas were on the *Ormonde* together and both headed for Hobart. At that moment, with the mighty steam turbines powering beneath them, and with the engineering and mechanics that made this journey possible clear in her mind, Dorothy made a promise. She would find out where and how Thomas Moreland was broken and, tracing the links and breaks to tease out the problem, she would find the solution, and she would fix him.

2

Dorothy

October 1921

The bustle of Hobart and its trams, carts and automobiles slipped behind her with a suddenness Dorothy wasn't expecting. As the train pushed on in bursts of steam and smoke, she watched the fine Georgian sandstone buildings of the township quickly give way to small industrial lots and rows of houses, then to fields, orchards and open sky. The town and its surroundings were vastly different to the closeness of the housing in Birmingham and the beautiful park-like grounds of Bournville. Here the distance stretched out lazily without structures or familiar landmarks. The orchards glowed with the pale pinks and whites of spring, whereas back home the autumn leaves would be turning the countryside to fire. Dorothy sat up a little straighter. This was her new home. She'd find her bearings in time.

At last the train pulled into Claremont station in a release of steam. Dorothy stepped onto the small platform searching for a familiar face.

'Mrs Adwell.'

Dorothy turned with a grateful smile. 'Mr Sutton. I'm very glad to see you.' Frank Sutton had travelled to Tasmania from Bournville too, as keen as she was for an adventure in a new land after the tumult of the war. Friendly but capable of restraint, Frank was a young man who had the knack of always striking the right balance. She smiled at thinking him young – at twenty-two he was only two years younger – but often she felt as though she'd been on this earth for a lot longer. For most of the war he hadn't been old enough to enlist and, like her, had stepped up at the Firm, learning how the massive machines worked and what to do when they didn't. His time had come though, and his decision was not made lightly.

'Welcome to Claremont.' Frank tipped his hat. 'It's a bit of a change from Bournville but it's early days yet.'

'How long is it since you arrived?'

'Only two weeks. I'm still getting used to it myself.' Frank gave her a puzzled smile. 'Am I mistaken, or do you sound different?'

Dorothy waved his question away. 'Must be all those weeks on the ship.'

'It's a long journey and don't I know it. You'd probably like to be somewhere that isn't moving. I'll collect your luggage and we'll have you at the hostel in a jiffy. It's not far.' Frank led the way to one of the Firm's motor lorries.

As they drove towards the hostel Dorothy had a greater chance to take in her surroundings. The maps she'd studied showed the peninsula where the factory was being built extending into the River Derwent in a shape that curiously resembled the ankle, heel and toe of Italy, but nothing could prepare her for the reality of it. The width of the tranquil river was unlike the canals and streams of Birmingham, and the majesty of Mount Wellington to the south gave a sense of protection. Over the river to the east the valley was sheltered by the wooded heights of Mount Direction and on the landward side the orchards of the Claremont township rose through the surrounding foothills until they reached steep stretches of forest timber.

'Here we are.' Frank brought the motor lorry to a halt outside a large two-storey building with a white wooden fence enclosing a garden of roses and lavender. The Firm had bought the hostel to accommodate the women who'd arrived on this southerly isle to bring an antipodean version of Bournville to life. Some of them she knew but others had been recruited from Fry's and Pascall's, the two other companies involved in this bold venture.

'The factory is just over there.' Frank pointed along the river to where the outline of the construction jutted above the peninsula.

Dorothy took her bearings. Her new workplace would be less than a half-hour's walk from the hostel, through the orchards and along the river, a walk like none other she'd taken. Her home back in England seemed even further away. Dorothy opened the wooden gate and brushed her fingers against the leaves of a lavender bush. At least this was familiar.

Frank carried her bags to the front door. 'Here's where I leave you. You'll soon discover Mrs Rayner runs a tight ship. I'm at the estate. A few of us are bunking in together until more cottages are built. Farewell for now, Mrs Adwell. Next time we meet it'll be at the factory.'

Dorothy waved him goodbye and turned her attention to the hostel. She raised the heavy door knocker and gave three sharp raps.

An older woman opened the door. Her thinness was accentuated by the abundance of hair swept up in waves and collected in an impressive bun towering atop her head. 'You must be Mrs Adwell. My name is Mrs Rayner. Come in. Mind you wipe your feet.'

Dorothy followed her into a large entranceway panelled in a dark wood. To her right a staircase led to the upper floor and beyond the entranceway was a hallway panelled in the same wood.

'All the women here are under my care,' Mrs Rayner continued. 'No male visitors. Lights out by nine pm. Breakfast is at seven sharp and tea is at six. Mrs Brown is a competent cook – I doubt you'll have any cause for complaint. The company has modernised with electric bulbs in every room, an indoor lavatory and a gas cooker, although Mrs Brown doesn't care for it. She prefers the range. Any questions?' Her lips stretched into a shape that could almost be a smile.

Before Dorothy could answer, Mrs Rayner started up the stairs. Dorothy struggled to follow with her heavy bags.

'You're sharing with Miss Harris,' Mrs Rayner said. 'She's been here almost a month now.' She opened a door into an unexpectedly delightful room. The walls were painted a pale cream and large windows gave an expansive view of the garden, the river and the hills of the opposite shore. A good-sized desk together with a chair sat under the windows, a neat stack of books and a collection of writing implements to one side.

'You'll sleep here.' Mrs Rayner indicated one of the two iron-framed beds on either side of the room. Both beds were neatly made with candlewick bedspreads.

A small vase filled with jaunty white and yellow flowers sat on Dorothy's bedside table. 'What lovely daisies. How thoughtful.'

Mrs Rayner sniffed. 'Miss Harris must have put them there.'

As part of her briefing, Dorothy had been given a list of the British workers who had already arrived in the colony and their positions. She'd never met Miss Harris, which was surprising as she was listed as a Cadbury's employee – a member of the clerical staff working in the temporary office in Hobart.

'You're sharing a wardrobe but you each have a chest of drawers.' Miss Rayner drew a finger along the surface of the desk to check for dust. 'There's a daily who takes care of the downstairs rooms and bathroom, but you and Miss Harris are responsible for your room.'

Dorothy looked about the clean, bright room. 'It will be a pleasure.' After her mother had succumbed to a fever when Dorothy was not more than nine, she'd tried to keep the two rooms her family lived in orderly, but with four brothers and a father who was drunk more likely than not, it had been a battle. And it was Dorothy who'd have to make sure supper was on the table every night, despite working a long day herself, otherwise she'd get a belting. She shuddered, glad that those days were far behind her.

'The bathroom is down the hall to the right,' Mrs Rayner continued. 'Bath times are on a roster and strictly limited. The roster is pinned to the door. Make sure you check your allotted time and adhere to it.' She sniffed again. 'There's a laundry at the back of the hostel.'

'Thank you, Mrs Rayner.' Dorothy had been at sea for six weeks and opportunities to launder her clothes had been limited.

'And mind, there are to be no male visitors to the hostel under any circumstances. I'll have none of that jiggery-pokery under my roof, thank you very much.' Mrs Rayner nodded once and left.

Dorothy reached for the chair to steady herself as the floor pitched a little beneath her feet, a physical memory of the sway of the ship. Her body, as well as her mind, would need to acclimatise to her new surroundings.

Dorothy spent the rest of the day unpacking and in the laundry tending to her clothing. Miss Harris had made room in the wardrobe with a few coat hangers to one side suggesting they were for Dorothy's use. She was keen to meet this thoughtful woman who'd already made her feel welcome.

At tea time, after a deliciously hot bath, Dorothy presented with clean hair and scrubbed skin. The smell of braising meat and boiled vegetables made her mouth water. Lunch had been a cup of tea and a slice of toast she'd rustled up in the kitchen, expecting Mrs Rayner to barge in and tell her off at any moment.

A woman with hair the colour of sand and a lined face dotted with freckles sat opposite Dorothy. 'I'm Esme Abbott. *Miss* Esme Abbott. Forewoman A. From Fry's cocoa department.' She scowled, making her appear even older. Dorothy guessed she was closer to forty than thirty. 'Now I'm supervising cocoa packing for you lot as well.'

'My lot?'

'Fry's has been around for almost a hundred years longer than Cadbury's. I'll always be a Fry's girl.'

There had been some resentment from the Fry's workers when the company had merged with Cadbury's two years earlier. The former great rivals were now one company but Cadbury's held the controlling interest. Fry's employees felt the sting of it still. To help ease ruffled feathers there were two Forewomen A in charge of the chocolate section in Hobart. One from Fry's and one from Cadbury's.

'And you must be Mrs Adwell.' Esme's mouth remained downturned. 'The skilled enrober they've been waiting for.'

Dorothy was taken aback. 'I suppose I am.' Esme must have been given the same briefing list and surely knew that Dorothy was the other Forewoman A, as well as being Head of Training in Covering and Piping.

Voices echoed down the hallway to the dining room and several women of varying ages pressed in to join Esme and Dorothy. Dorothy spotted the face she'd been longing to see.

'Ida!' Dorothy stood to meet her. 'How wonderful to see you.' She took in her friend's hazel eyes, the mousy brown hair Ida always moaned about and the familiar quirk to her smile.

Ida hugged her then stood back and rested her hands on Dorothy's shoulders. '"How wonderful to see you?" My, don't we sound posh.' Her eyes were bright with mischief.

Dorothy laughed to cover her embarrassment. During the voyage she'd made an effort to soften the edges of her Brummie accent, as the Birmingham brogue was known, not only because of the reactions of women like those at the captain's table but also because she'd been told Hobart was a conservative and class-conscious town, determined to distance itself from its convict roots. Moderating her accent would have many advantages in the new life she was hoping to build. She'd practised by imitating the rounded vowels of the first class passengers and correcting the Birmingham habit of ending 'ing' words with a k. *Something* was no longer *somethink*. *Anythink* became *anything*. Miss Darwood had entered their cabin unexpectedly as Dorothy was repeating words like *but* and *shut* with the short 'uh' vowel sound instead of the Brummie 'oo'. She'd been mortified but Miss Darwood had surprised her by not only encouraging her but also making some suggestions. She'd surprised Dorothy even further when, after Miss Darwood had departed the *Ormonde*, Dorothy had found a bottle of Yardley's English Lavender on the vanity in their cabin with a note, *In honour of your husband and his service*. She'd held the bottle to her heart and wept.

'Oh, Ida. I've missed you, bab,' she said, letting her Brummie accent shape her words. She hugged her friend again, reminded of how Ida had helped her through the darkest days of her life. After Freddie had been killed Ida had been worried for her, all alone, and had moved into the room that once would have been the nursery. Without Ida, those days and nights would've been unbearable. When the war had finally ended and the surviving men returned, she and Ida had settled into one of Bournville's newly built bungalows for single women. With so many on their own after the war, it made sense to build cottages where two women could make a home. Dorothy and Ida were different in many ways, with Dorothy captaining the women's cricket team and attending numerous evening classes while Ida preferred dancing and concerts, but they had formed a solid friendship.

The babble of voices grew as the other women crowded around the table, all curious about the new arrival.

Ida cleared her throat. 'Ladies, this is Dorothy. You already know all about her, but she don't know some of you, so make sure and introduce yourselves. And don't be shy about it.'

'They know all about me?' Dorothy whispered to Ida as they sat.

'I told them you were the best cricketer Cadbury's has ever had. I also said you were the queen of the enrobers and like clarting about with machinery.'

'Anything else?' Dorothy knew her friend wouldn't have left it at that. Ida was naturally talkative and often chatted about other people's business without a second thought. *Just being friendly and making conversation*, she'd say if challenged.

Ida leant closer. 'I thought they'd want to know about Freddie. You being a missus and all.'

Dorothy's stomach tightened. The memory of the day the telegram arrived was etched into her bones. Freddie's personal effects had arrived in a wooden box a week later. The much-creased photo of their wedding day caused her to drop to the floor and howl. He'd been buried, so she'd been told, in the muddy torn-up field where he'd died. Since then she'd heard stories of men being obliterated by mortar shells, as if they'd disappeared, quite literally, in a puff of smoke. Had that happened to Freddie, and if so would anyone have told her? No. Letting her believe he'd been buried was a far kinder thing.

'Ar, bab,' Ida said. 'Most everyone here has lost someone close.'

Dorothy smoothed the hair behind her right ear. She knew it was true.

A woman with rosy cheeks and a colourful apron covering her ample bosom emerged from the kitchen carrying a large dish. The youngest of the women jumped up. 'Let me help you with that, Mrs Brown.'

'Thank you, Bessie. There's boiled carrots and cabbage in the kitchen. Be a love and bring them in.'

When the beef stew and dumplings had been passed around and every woman had filled her plate, Dorothy was able to concentrate on her fellow adventurers. Apart from Ida, she was already acquainted with two of the women who'd travelled from Bournville. Lizzie was highly skilled at box making and packing. Margaret, previously Forewoman A in confectionery, had been promoted to Chief Forewoman of the Claremont factory and as such would be addressed as Miss Stanton from now on. Young Bessie from Pascall's had landed a position as Forewoman B.

The door opened and a stylish woman in a deep blue suit and cream shirt took her place at the table. 'Apologies, Mrs Rayner. I was held back at the office.'

'Good evening, Miss Harris,' Mrs Rayner said from the head of the table. 'You'll have to make do with whatever's left, I'm afraid.'

'Don't worry, Sarah.' Lizzie passed her the dish of stew. 'There's plenty.'

Dorothy took in her roommate's fashionably styled dark blonde waves and intelligent blue eyes. She was older than Dorothy but by how much it was hard to tell. Mid-thirties perhaps. 'Thank you for the daisies, Miss Harris. That was thoughtful of you.'

'Please, call me Sarah.' Dorothy noted there was no trace of a Birmingham accent.

'I don't remember seeing you at Bournville.'

20

'With more than seven thousand employees, I'm not surprised. And we do work in different sections.'

'Yes, that's true.' Dorothy was still curious. Cadbury's had only approached women to come to Tasmania who were highly experienced and had given years of faithful service. 'When did you start working for the Firm?'

'After the Armistice. I did think about becoming a nurse because of my experiences during the Great War, but apparently I wasn't of a suitable age.'

'You volunteered?'

'We all did our bit.'

Dorothy nodded. During the early stages of the war any spare time the Bournville women had was spent knitting vests, scarves and socks, and packing up books and chocolate for the soldiers. When it was clear the war wouldn't be over by Christmas, George Cadbury had given two of the Firm's buildings for use as hospitals. Dorothy had become one of the Cadbury Angels, volunteering to do laundry for the injured soldiers recovering there. As the war raged on, she'd joined the Bournville Nursing Division on her days off to give the full-time staff some much-needed relief – bathing and bandaging the wounded and making beds. Often, though, she thought she was of most use talking with the soldiers, listening to their stories of home and the girls they intended to marry, trying to buck up their spirits and ease their troubles. Through those heartbreaking years, it became clear to Dorothy that machines were easier to mend than men.

'I'm sure we'll enjoy sharing a room.' Sarah smiled.

'I got a room to meself.' Ida shot a look at Sarah. 'That's the prize for coming out with the rest of this lot and putting up with a horrible crossing on the *Orsova*.'

'Gawd, it was awful, wasn't it?' Esme's scowl deepened. 'Sick as dogs, the lot of us.'

The voyage had been so treacherous there had been fears that the ship had been lost with all lives. When news finally came through that it had arrived safely, Dorothy had wept with relief.

'Why didn't you sail out with the rest of us?' Lizzie asked Dorothy.

'The new enrobers,' Dorothy replied. 'I needed to learn how they worked.' It was vital she was up to speed with every aspect of the machinery. With the new factory so far away, the manufacturer wouldn't be on hand to fix any problems.

Margaret shook her head. 'I'm all for modernisation, but those fangled machines will never take the place of a skilled fork and bowl worker.'

Dorothy took another mouthful of the beef stew instead of answering. An enrober was such a clever invention with the perfect name – it did indeed enrobe the confectionery centres with chocolate in a fraction of the time it took by hand. Machines like this were the future of chocolate manufacturing. However, hand-dipping was still the mainstay of the boxed chocolate division and in her new role as Forewoman A she'd be in charge of the entire section. It would be a challenge, especially with unskilled local workers. Fork and bowl work, with the large bowls of liquid chocolate and special dipping forks, was an exacting process. Achieving the correct thickness of chocolate and ensuring there were no bubbles or drips required a skill that some could never master.

'Are you coming to town with us tomorrow?' Ida asked. 'We're still interviewing.'

'Blimey, some of the girls have been right gawbies, haven't they, Ida?' Esme and Ida exchanged a conspiratorial look.

Dorothy watched them. *Gawbies* was a Brummie expression. Why would Esme, from the home of Fry's in Bristol, use it?

Ida laughed in agreement. 'The mothers get their hopes up but they're just as bad.'

Cadbury's had a policy of visiting potential employees to check their home environment was conducive to good morals and reliable character. In some cases, though, a promising girl was employed with the hope that the opportunities for self-improvement would have a positive effect on her family. Dorothy had been grateful for the Firm's leniency when it had come to her own upbringing.

Margaret brought her napkin to her lips. 'Dorothy has a day off to recover from the journey.' She turned to Dorothy. 'You're to report to the office in town on Thursday and be given instructions then.'

'Lucky for some.' Ida gave Dorothy a teasing smile.

'If you'd like to see the factory,' Sarah said, 'I'd be happy to take you tomorrow. It's still under construction but you'll get a sense of the layout and operations.'

Sarah's invitation came as a surprise. It was as if she already understood what interested Dorothy. 'I'd like that very much. Thank you.'

'The construction is taking too long,' Esme said. The woman's scowl seemed a permanent fixture. 'Our work's going to be cut out for us when it's finally up and running. You mark my words. They'll be cracking the whip to get production up to speed.'

'We'll all be expected to do our bit,' Margaret said, pushing her spectacles back into place. 'But the Firm isn't in the habit of cracking whips.'

Esme humphed. 'Cocoa will be the first line in production. The weight will be on my shoulders.'

Bessie stood and started collecting the empty plates. 'Pascall's sweets will be the first to market though,' she said proudly. 'I'm sure it will all work perfectly.'

Esme mumbled something indecipherable while Lizzie set about helping Bessie.

A wave of exhaustion washed over Dorothy. Swaying slightly in her seat she decided to skip the spotted dick and custard. Her pillow was more enticing than pudding. 'Excuse me,' she said, holding on to the table for support as she stood. 'It's been a long day.'

'There's a washing-up roster, Mrs Adwell,' Mrs Rayner said. 'Mrs Brown leaves as soon as the pudding is served.'

'Of course. I'll help clear away and begin doing the dishes.' Her head was swimming with fatigue but Dorothy was used to long hours and pushing her reserves beyond their limits.

'Allow me.' Sarah stood and took the bowls from Dorothy. 'Let's swap turns. I'm on duty Thursday night. Would that suit?'

Dorothy smiled in gratitude. 'Thank you.'

'I'll come upstairs with you, bab.' Ida took Dorothy by the arm. 'It's been so long and we've got so much to talk about.'

As Ida steered her towards the door, Dorothy caught the look Esme shot in her direction. The woman clearly didn't like her.

In Dorothy's room, Ida sat beside her on the bed, her eyes bright and curious. 'You were quiet at dinner,' she said. 'And when you did say something it sounded as though you had a bob on yourself.' She searched Dorothy's face. 'It's a man, ain't it, got you wanting to sound like a toff? You met someone on the ship.' Ida winked. 'You know me, I'd be the last to judge, but I don't want to be the last to know.'

Much as Dorothy wanted to catch up with her best friend, just the two of them, she wasn't sure she could confide in her about Thomas. Not yet. 'There's nothing to tell.'

'Nothing? Are you sure?' She placed a hand on Dorothy's arm. 'I know you loved Freddie, bab, but he's been gone a long time now. You can't keep mooning over him.'

Dorothy shook her head slowly, as much to shake away the fatigue as to discourage Ida's questioning. 'I'm not interested in anyone else.' It wasn't quite a lie. 'Besides, none of us are allowed to get married, remember?' It was in the terms of their contract.

'Who's talking about getting married?' Ida's smile was wicked.

'Oh, Ida.' Dorothy laughed. 'You're such a tease. You don't want to be known as the type who goes round the back of Rackhams.'

'We're a long way from Rackhams now, bab. Besides, I'm not after a Bible and a carnation and getting shoved out the door like what we get when we marry.'

George Cadbury believed if a wife worked her husband could afford to be idle and what does an idle man do? He goes to the pub and drinks away his wife's wages, neglects his children and adds to the misery of society. Also, if a married woman worked she wouldn't be able to devote the proper care to her children, on which the future strength of Britain was dependent. The marriage bar was imperative to stop the fall of the Empire!

Ida stood and moved to the window. The darkness turned the glass into a mirror. Dorothy watched her face reflected there. 'I want to keep working,' Ida said. 'But I want to have a bit of fun as well. You were lucky. You got to be married and keep working.'

'Lucky,' Dorothy murmured. With the war had come the lifting of the marriage bar as the men disappeared into the hungry maw of battle. She had kept working and happily so. But she'd always thought Freddie would return. After the war the marriage bar was firmly back in place but, without Freddie, Dorothy had a career she'd never expected.

Ida turned, her mouth twisted in regret. 'Sorry, that ain't what I meant. But at least you had Freddie, even though it weren't long. It's been years now. Don't you want to have fun again?'

'There'll be sporting clubs and music and arts here, just like back home.'

Ida harrumphed. 'I didn't come here for things to be the same as they were back home. I want to do new things, meet new people. I never would've met Esme if I'd stayed back home and she's a right laugh.' She noticed Dorothy's quizzical look. 'Ar, she was a bit grumpy at dinner, but she was a lifesaver on the trip out here. Almost two months! It was horrible.'

Dorothy's mind traced over the experience of her voyage on the *Ormonde*, quickening at the thought of Mr Thomas Moreland. The last time they'd spoken was on the deck, the rain falling in sheets as the ship ploughed through heaping leaden seas. He was at the prow, drenching wet, hatless, his hair plastered flat. Her legs were steadier by then and she'd reached his side with a practised gait. They were alone. When the seas were rough, most passengers stayed in their cabins, retching into basins and buckets. Dorothy had overcome her nausea early in the voyage and relished the wildness of the ocean. Such weather strengthened her admiration for the ship and the team who crewed her. In the face of this muscular and aggressive seascape, they prevailed.

Thomas's eyes had been more present than before but what she'd mistaken for a smile at a distance proved to be a grimace once she reached his side. 'We must be mad, you and I,' he'd said.

Dorothy had leant in closer to catch his words before the wind snatched them away. Her arm pressed against his and, despite the chill of the rain, a warmth radiated between them. 'Maybe, but we're alive.'

They'd stood rocking together, the rain penetrating every layer of clothing. A rogue wave had sent her stumbling against him and he'd caught her in a firm embrace. 'Steady now, Mrs Adwell, or people will talk.'

Despite a deep and unexpected yearning to stay in his arms Dorothy had pulled away and gripped the railing for balance.

'No one would believe them if they did – that we were out in such weather, that is.'

He tossed back his head and laughed. She remembered thinking the rain must be falling into his open mouth but it was clear he didn't care. His laughter stopped as abruptly as it had begun. He murmured something about spending years in such weather but against the roar of wind and waves she couldn't be sure.

When it was time to disembark in Melbourne and transfer to the Tasmanian Steamship *Nairana* she'd craned her neck hoping to catch a glimpse of Thomas in the crowd. On the journey to Hobart she'd searched for him but he'd never appeared. She'd consoled herself with the knowledge that he was bound for Hobart and would be there in time. Their paths would cross and her plan would unfold. But now, knowing how far Claremont was from the centre of the town, she faltered.

'Are you all right, bab?' Ida was still at her side.

Dorothy forced a strained smile. 'Sorry. I'm so very tired.'

'"So very tired",' Ida imitated her. 'There you go again with your posh talk.' The sparkle in her eyes ensured Dorothy knew she was joking. 'Well, I'm knackered too. You'll find that out for yourself when you're trudging all over Hobart interviewing girls.'

'Trudging all over Hobart?'

'Ar, wear your most comfortable shoes. The tram only takes you so far.'

Dorothy's thoughts were already drifting. She'd be in Hobart. The odds of seeing Thomas were small, but there was still a chance.

3

Dorothy

Dorothy longed to pull on her breeches for the tour of the factory. They'd be more practical than a skirt or dress for visiting a construction site, but decorum said otherwise. Even though her Bournville colleagues wouldn't turn a hair, being used to her wearing trousers for walking and gardening, she'd been warned the locals might not be so accommodating. Not wanting to create the wrong impression straight off the bat she dressed in a blouse and skirt with a long knitted cardigan belted at the waist and her sturdy boots.

After a breakfast of eggs and toast prepared by Mrs Brown, Dorothy and Sarah said their farewells to the other women who were setting off on the train into town. Sarah led the way through the gently sloping garden of the hostel towards the river where sunlight through the clouds cast a steely gleam on the water. As they neared the riverbank Dorothy was startled by a raucous screeching. 'What on earth is that?'

'Cockatoos. See there.' Sarah pointed towards one of the trees by the river. The foliage was a dull green compared to the verdant elms and beeches of Bournville. Within the branches white birds bobbed and rocked, making an awful racket. 'They're nothing like the woodlarks and nightingales of home, but they have their own charm. The birds here are rather rowdy – cockatoos, parakeets and noisy miners.'

Dorothy stared at her. 'Noisy miners? You're making it up?'

Sarah laughed. 'No, honestly, I'm not. They're called noisy miners, and they're bossy with it. You'll get to know them and all the other bird life. The cockatoos are cheeky and the parakeets are beautiful with flashes of blue and green, but neither are very good singers.'

Dorothy had been told Tasmania was similar in climate to England and she'd assumed the plants, animals and birds would be similar too. 'Are there any birds I might recognise?'

'I think they might be familiar, at least in part.' Sarah pointed towards the shoreline.

Three large birds drifted on the ripples just beyond the sandy arc of the small bay. Further out many of them bent their long necks to the water. 'Are they swans?' The birds had the same shape but instead of white they were as black as ravens.

'Aren't they magnificent? Black swans are native to the colonies. Not so the starlings and sparrows that have made a home for themselves here, along with blackbirds and robins. There is a kind of swallow that Mrs Brown tells me is a native but you'll only see it in spring and summer. The clever little thing flies north for the winter.'

'North? Why? It would freeze.'

'In Tasmania everything is upside down. North is warm and south is cold.'

'Of course.' There was so much to get used to.

'Don't worry. We're all in the same boat.'

Dorothy wondered. It was clear the other women had bonded on the long and fraught trip they'd shared from England and, even though it was early days, she did feel a little on the outside. The earth moved beneath her feet as if it were the deck of the *Ormonde*. She shifted to correct her stance and instead found herself faltering.

Sarah put out a hand to steady her. 'Are you dizzy?'

Dorothy smiled in apology. 'I'm still finding my land legs. I was warned this would happen.'

'I was swaying for days. It was quite unnerving. The effect will wear off in time.'

They continued past fields and orchards heavy with blossom. Dorothy imagined they could have been on a pleasant country amble if it weren't for the growing sound of construction. The last part of the journey saw them ascending a steep but short incline to a plateau atop the peninsula where the factory was taking shape behind extensive fencing.

'Eventually this will be known as the Cadbury Estate but for now the locals still refer to it as Triffets Point,' Sarah said. 'It was the training ground for Tasmanian troops bound for the war. Some of the infrastructure the army left behind will be put to use. The old camp hospital will become the social hall. It's ironic, don't you think? The very ground we're walking on was once used for drills and target practice.'

Dorothy knew Sarah was referring to the Cadbury family being Quakers, as were the Frys and the Pascalls, and the fact that Quakers were opposed to war. The Firm hadn't stopped their employees from enlisting though; indeed the non-Quaker men were encouraged to do their bit for King and Country.

Dorothy took in her surroundings. Apart from the continual noise of construction, it was idyllic. The vault of sky above was reflected in the waters of the River Derwent surrounding them on three sides. When talking about the decision to build Bournville, the factory in the park, George Cadbury had said, 'No man ought to be condemned to live in a place where a rose cannot grow'. Dorothy could imagine roses growing at the Cadbury Estate, once all the cottages were built and inhabited.

She gazed down the river, past small coves and rocky outcrops, southward towards the township of Hobart under the majestic presence of Mount Wellington. 'It's a beautiful spot but it's a long way from the docks.'

'There are undesirable elements near wharves. And lots of pubs.' Sarah raised a perfectly arched eyebrow. 'You know how the Firm feels about such things.'

'Ar,' Dorothy said. She cleared her throat. 'Yes,' she enunciated clearly. Bournville had been built away from those undesirable elements in Birmingham, the very places where Dorothy had grown up.

'To compensate, the railway has been extended,' Sarah said. 'Everything will be delivered right to the factory, including the workers, and our confectionery and cocoa will be taken straight from dispatch to the dock. Come on, I'll show you.'

Dorothy followed her through the gate to a shed where Sarah greeted a man wearing a dusty suit and battered Homburg. 'Mr Stacey, this is Mrs Adwell, Forewoman A of the chocolate section. Please allow her access at any time.'

Mr Stacey doffed his hat. 'Good-oh.'

'Thank you, Mr Stacey.' Dorothy smiled, committing his name to memory. It was always useful to be on good terms with the gatekeepers.

Sarah pointed to several single-storey wooden buildings. 'Change rooms, shower rooms et cetera, but up ahead is the main attraction.'

As they walked closer the sound of hammering, sawing and grinding grew in intensity. A massive three-storey concrete structure with workmen crawling over every surface rose above the work-roughened ground.

'This building will be roofed by the end of the month. It's Block 2 – Pascall's. The first to be completed.'

Mr Wilfrid Pascall was arriving in Hobart soon to oversee the commissioning of the factory. Cadbury's and Fry's had been in partnership for two years but Pascall's was new to a collaborative way of working. There were some concerns, but Dorothy had only heard vague rumours.

'When Mr Pascall arrives I'm to be his private secretary,' Sarah said.

'He didn't bring his own?' Dorothy had thought a man of his importance would have his own staff.

'There was some trouble. An illness apparently. She had to return home before the ship reached Australia.'

A massive blast shook the ground. Dorothy grabbed Sarah's arm in alarm.

'It takes a while to get used to but, believe it or not, you will,' Sarah reassured her. 'There's a quarry on the other side of the factory. All the stone for the cement comes from the peninsula. The dreadful grinding noise, and most of the dust, is from the stone crushers.' She indicated the massive machines, half hidden in a haze of dust. 'Let's take a look at the rest of the site.'

They walked past buildings in various stages of completion. Scores of carpenters and ironworkers prepared moulds and manipulated, often with brute force, the metal rods used to give the concrete its reinforced strength. Sarah explained the layout, enabling Dorothy to picture it all in her mind – the flow of production, from the delivery of raw materials to processing and finally to the dispatch of completed goods by rail.

'What are those?' Large rounded sections lay end to end on the ground, made, as was everything else, of the concrete that spewed from the lofty towers straddling the building site.

'Moulded sections for the chimney. You can see the base there next to the boiler house.' Sarah pointed to the elegant two-storey brick building with arched windows. 'The concrete stack will be one hundred and twenty feet high. Quite a landmark. It's said to be the only one of its kind in the world.'

As they walked Sarah pointed out a stretch of grass beyond the factory site. 'That space is set aside for sporting grounds, something I'm sure you'll be extremely interested in.'

Dorothy shook her head with a smile. 'That Ida. She told me she'd been boasting about my cricketing skills.'

'I expect that's the reason you didn't come out earlier with the others. The captain of the Cadbury's women's team could hardly desert her teammates before the end of the season, especially when they were on such a winning streak.'

When the enrober training had been rescheduled Dorothy had been grateful she could stay on to lead her team to victory. 'I had to stay to train on the new enrobers.'

'Of course you did.' Sarah's voice was warm with amusement. 'I'm fond of cricket myself, although I've never played. I especially like the cricketing terms. Silly point and long hop are two of my favourites.'

'I'll have you know, I've never bowled a long hop in my life.'

'I'm sure of it. I'm told you're a tremendous bowler and a reliable run winner. Hopefully you'll be able to get a team together here.'

None of the women at the hostel played but Dorothy hoped she might be able to field a team with the local girls employed by the Firm. It would have to wait though. There was too much work to be done at the factory to consider putting in the time and effort needed to train a new team.

At the river Sarah pointed out the pump house at the base of a short but steep cliff. She gestured towards the Derwent. 'As you can see there's abundant water to supply the refrigerators.'

The gentle lapping took Dorothy back to the *Ormonde* – the engine room, the bridge, and the way it all worked together so ingeniously to keep the passengers safe and heading towards their destination. She had the sense that this factory, with its clever design and generous proportions, would do the same for those who worked there.

Sarah took a silver cigarette case from her jacket pocket, removed a cigarette and tapped it on the case. She glanced at Dorothy. 'A habit I picked up during the war. Don't tell Mrs Rayner. I have to sneak out of the hostel like a schoolgirl to partake of my vice.'

Dorothy laughed in surprise. Almost every man she'd met smoked but Sarah was one of the few women.

Sarah lit her cigarette. 'Have you enjoyed our potted tour?'

'The layout is impressive and the building process is fascinating.'

'Fascinating?' Sarah's smile was sardonic. 'I asked the other women at the hostel whether they'd like to view the factory site and not one of them said yes. You're the first.'

'The noise and the dust would put most people off.'

'But not you.'

'I was curious to see the construction and get a sense of the techniques being used.'

Sarah drew deeply on her cigarette and narrowed her eyes against the smoke. 'That's a rare thing.'

During the tour Dorothy had felt emboldened when Sarah encouraged her curiosity, but now she was wary. Sometimes those who didn't know her were threatened by her desire to discover how things worked. 'Then why have the press been so keen to visit?'

'That's different. The factory is newsworthy. The other women didn't see the point in visiting the site until it was completed.'

'I can understand that. How many people travel by train without the slightest knowledge of how the engine works? All they want is to reach their destination, preferably on time.'

'And yet, I expect you know how a steam engine works.'

'We can thank the Firm for that. And the war.'

Sarah studied her. 'I understand you worked in many different areas at Bournville during that time.'

'And you? Have you always worked in administration? Or have you taken on other roles as well?' Dorothy was aware she sounded defensive.

Sarah laughed. 'I'm sorry. You must feel as though I'm interrogating you. I'm a naturally curious person, like you, that's all. I hope I haven't caused offence. I'd like us to be friends.'

Dorothy softened. 'I'd like that too.' Friends would be hard to find in this isolated outpost, plus it was true, she and Sarah had certain traits in common.

'Well, then. It's agreed. It's rare to meet a woman who's interested in construction.'

'Women are hardly encouraged to think about such things, let alone talk about them.'

'Tasmanian women have had the right to vote since 1903. Even more extraordinarily, this year a woman was elected to parliament in Western Australia. We think of the colonies as backwards when in fact they're impressively progressive.'

As a British woman Dorothy still didn't have the right to vote. That privilege had only been given to women over thirty who owned property or had been to university. Dorothy knew no such women. 'Where do I sign up to become a Tasmanian?' She was rewarded with one of Sarah's melodious laughs.

'How long is your contract for?'

'Five years.'

'Perhaps by then England will have come to her senses, led by the fine example of her southern colony.' Sarah stubbed out her cigarette and put the butt in the cigarette case. She noticed Dorothy watching her with curiosity. 'Another habit I have, to escape detection – the eagle eye of Mrs Rayner.'

They returned to the path that would take them to the hostel. 'When we get back I'll freshen up and then catch the train to the office in town,' Sarah said. 'I imagine you'll be wanting to rest.'

Dorothy was restless more than in need of rest. 'To be honest, I'm tempted to return to the site later today. There are areas we didn't explore like the bean store and trades section. I'm not sure when I'll get the chance again.' To see the factory being built filled her with pride, excitement and a fair amount of trepidation. She was part of the team entrusted with the success of this enterprise. Many had their doubts. For Cadbury's to build their first overseas factory so far from home, so far away from anything, had at times seemed ridiculous. But the Firm had their reasons. A breeze ruffled the water of the Derwent and, even on this spring day, the chill reminded Dorothy of one of those reasons. The cool climate.

Sarah smiled. 'You're one of a kind, Mrs Adwell. I think we're going to get along famously.' She stopped and turned to Dorothy. 'I could help you, if you like.'

'What do you mean?'

'I heard what Ida said to you, about your accent.'

'Oh.' The promotion and move to Tasmania had lit a fire within Dorothy. There were possibilities here at the new factory that would always have been out of her reach at Bournville. Her ambition burnt bright but she knew she'd have to be accepted by the right people for it to happen. If only her distinctive accent would change naturally like the leaves in autumn, gradually shifting in colour and then falling away completely. 'I ...'

'Believe me, I understand.'

'You do?' Dorothy wasn't sure where Sarah was from, but it certainly wasn't Birmingham. Her voice was modulated and cultured.

'There are certain expectations in my area of work. I wonder if I'd have been chosen to be Mr Pascall's personal secretary if I'd had a Cockney accent? Hmm?' Her gaze was intense.

'You're from East London?' Surely Sarah couldn't have been born into the slums as she had been.

'You have ambition,' Sarah said. 'You wouldn't have come all this way to the outskirts of the world for this opportunity if you didn't.'

Dorothy went to protest – she didn't want anyone getting wind of her ultimate goal. Not yet.

Sarah held up a hand. 'I admire you for it. Unfortunately, to be taken seriously you need to sound and act a certain way. It's part of the circus. Let me help you swing on the trapeze and fly through the air. Or at least help smooth your vowels and consonants a little. And I'd love to see you shake that curious Birmingham trait of making every sentence sound like a question.'

Dorothy longed to take up Sarah's offer and yet she hesitated. 'It would be helpful, but ...'

'You'd rather nobody else know?'

Dorothy nodded. Ida's reaction hadn't surprised her. There was part of Dorothy that felt like a traitor.

'Just as well I'm good at keeping secrets then, isn't it?' Sarah linked her arm through Dorothy's again and they continued to walk along the river. Sarah laughed lightly. 'I wonder if I could pass you off as a duchess.'

'A duchess?'

'Have you seen the play *Pygmalion*?'

Dorothy smiled. 'I washed my face and hands before I come, I did.' The play had been a hit in London and its popularity had spread throughout England. The Bournville Dramatic Society had staged a production.

'You could be a real-life Eliza Doolittle. I only hope I'm not as rude as Professor Higgins.' Sarah pressed a hand to her chest in mock horror.

'The man was a bully.'

'Ah, but he achieved results.'

'I think most of the credit goes to Eliza. She succeeded despite 'enry 'iggins.'

'Oh, my dear. I think we need to start with, "In Hertford, Hereford and Hampshire hurricanes hardly ever happen."'

'In Hertford, Hereford and Hampshire hurricanes hardly ever happen.' Dorothy mimicked Sarah perfectly.

'By George, I think she's got it.' There was a gleam in Sarah's eyes. 'This will be fun. We'll make sure of it. And if ever you decide you don't want to continue, please let me know.' Her expression grew serious. 'I'd never want to be a bully like Henry Higgins.'

'I don't think anyone will ever mistake me for a duchess but if I could sound a little more like you, I'd be grateful.'

As they strolled along the path towards the hostel, Sarah guided her through vowel sounds, teaching her about diphthongs and the way they formed in the mouth and throat. It was a revelation to Dorothy and far beyond anything Miss Darwood had taught her. A small hope kindled in her chest – her ambitions might yet be realised. But still the thought niggled – what would Ida think?

4

Maisie

Maisie pulled her coat tighter in an attempt to keep out the bitter wind. Although it was spring, the weather held the ice of Antarctica in the gusts that blew along the River Derwent and through Hobart. The steep streets of the Glebe angled upwards to the small weatherboard cottage that was home. The cottage clung to the side of the hill, three-quarters of the way up, surrounded by others just like it. When Maisie was young she worried that all the houses would slide down and end up in a crumpled heap at the bottom with her and her family buried beneath the rubble. However, their house and the street, indeed the whole of the Glebe, continued to defy gravity.

Once more her gloved hand reached into the pocket of her coat to touch the newspaper clipping hidden there like a talisman. It was frail from being folded and unfolded many times and the type was smudged to the point of being almost illegible, but Maisie knew every line by heart. Cadbury's was opening a factory in Claremont – the first outside of their home base in England. The article described the new factory as well as plans for cottages, sporting fields and a social hall, but most importantly it contained details of how to apply for one of the many jobs on offer. When Maisie had first read those words, a mix of sensations had risen within her – excitement tinged with fear. Dare she let herself hope? Now she shivered, not from the cold but from anticipation and nerves. Once word had got around of the pay and conditions the factory was offering, competition for the Cadbury's jobs was fierce. Maisie was determined to make one of them hers.

She opened the front door to be met with a blessed rush of warmth.

'There you are.' Mother's face was bright and intense. 'Quick now. Change into your Sunday best. Mrs Adwell will be here within fifteen minutes.' She hurried Maisie into the house. 'I was worried you wouldn't be able to get the afternoon off.'

Interviews for the Cadbury's jobs were being held during the week and, most oddly, at the prospective employees' homes. When Maisie had asked for a half-day off, she'd been unable to lie but she couldn't quite tell the truth either in case she jeopardised her job for the possibility of a new one. She said she was needed at home for the afternoon and left it at that. It was known that her mother hadn't been well and no further questions were asked.

While Mother put the kettle on the hob in readiness for a pot of tea and laid out the best cups and saucers, Maisie changed her dress and fixed her hair as best she could. They met in the parlour, both unable to settle.

Mother startled at the knock on the front door. 'Punctual,' she said and hastened to answer it.

Maisie stood, nervously twisting her fingers. She eyed the old lounge suite, sagging in places with a few stray horsehairs sticking out. At least the antimacassars were freshly laundered. She took a breath and steadied herself. Surely anyone applying for a job at Cadbury's wouldn't be posh. The recruiters would be used to houses such as theirs.

Mother ushered their guest into the parlour. The woman wore a navy blue suit belted at the waist, a wide-brimmed hat, black stockings and well-polished boots. In one hand she carried a flat leather bag. Everything about her was contained and quietly confident.

'Mrs Adwell, I'd like you to meet my daughter, Maisie. Maisie, this is Mrs Adwell from Cadbury's.' Mother's voice was higher pitched than usual. She was nervous too. It wasn't often a stranger came to their home, let alone one who held the possibility of well-paid, steady employment.

'Nice to meet you, Maisie.' The woman's voice had a kind of lilt to it.

'And you, Mrs Adwell.'

'Would you like a cup of tea?' Mother hovered near the door.

'That would be lovely, thank you.' The way Mrs Adwell said 'lovely' sounded more like 'loovely'. Maisie had heard a few different accents in Hobart but this was one she couldn't place. Mrs Adwell enunciated her words carefully as if she was forming each syllable from nothing and creating it just for that moment.

'Won't be a moment.' Mother hurried down the hallway.

Mrs Adwell put down the bag and removed her gloves and hat. Maisie was immediately jealous of the smooth dark sheen of her hair drawn back in a neat bun at the back of her neck. Without thinking, Maisie touched her own wild locks. Trying to tame them with pins and a ribbon was a thankless task. Not that she'd ever complain. She'd inherited her father's hair – thick and with a mind of its own. She was glad to have something of his as a remembrance.

'Shall we sit?' Mrs Adwell indicated the worn lounge suite.

Maisie perched on the edge of the couch with her hands in her lap. She'd imagined Mrs Adwell to be something like the headmistress at school, aged and brittle, instead she was little more than a handful of years older than herself.

Mrs Adwell pulled a folder from the leather bag. 'Please, tell me a little bit about yourself.'

Maisie hesitated. Mrs Adwell must have seen her application form, surely? It had the details of her age, schooling and employment.

'What do you like to do in your spare time?' Mrs Adwell prompted. 'Do you read, play an instrument or do sport?'

Maisie lowered her head. She might as well give up now. She hadn't realised the kind of person Cadbury's wanted to employ – the kind who had spare time. 'I help my mother. She takes in laundry, ironing, mending and suchlike.' Her voice had no substance to it, breathless with nerves and tinged with shame. 'I also look after my little sister when needed.' She risked a glance at Mrs Adwell. 'I do like to read though, if I get time.' The truth was most nights she couldn't keep her eyes open long enough to read and the few books in the bookcase were her father's and not to her taste.

Mrs Adwell smiled. 'I like to read myself.' She looked to the notes in her folder. 'It's you, your mother, younger brother and little sister in the house?'

'Yes, Andrew works at a tannery and Lily's still at school.' Thinking of Lily, Maisie couldn't help but smile. Her sister was such a bright girl with a craving for knowledge as big as the sky. Maisie's fervent hope was that Lily be able to stay in school and eventually continue on to the University of Tasmania, housed in the ornate sandstone building surrounded by gardens only a street away from where they lived. Lily was forever telling her the subjects she would study there – archaeology, palaeontology, physics, law, medicine, English literature, biology, astronomy; the list was endless and changed every week. There had been some objection to female students attending University House in the past but they had been overruled. Women were welcome to study, but would Lily ever have the chance? Mother was grateful for the war widow's pension but it wasn't enough to support a family of four. Everyone had to earn their keep. It was a shame that in a little less than a year Lily would have to give up her schooling and get a job, just as Andrew had and Maisie before him.

'Your father is deceased?'

'He was killed at the Western Front in 1916.' Maisie had been almost eleven when the Great War was declared, thirteen when that fateful dispatch arrived. The light had snuffed out in Mother's eyes. Every day since then seemed veiled in grey.

Mrs Adwell inhaled sharply. '1916?' Her face was pale, her lips tight.

'Here we are.' Mother bustled in with a tray, set it down and began to pour the tea. 'Milk? Sugar?'

'Just milk, thank you.'

'And Maisie made some shortbread.' Mother offered the plate.

'It looks delicious.' Mrs Adwell selected a piece and placed it on her saucer. 'Now you're both here, I'd like to go over a few details.' She put her cup and saucer on the table and referred again to her notes. 'Maisie. That's your christened name? It's not short for Margaret?'

'We liked Maisie,' Mother said. 'It's cheerier than Margaret. Friendlier, if you know what I mean.'

'It's a delightful name,' Mrs Adwell said. 'Maisie, you're eighteen, is that right?'

'Yes.' Maisie bobbed her head.

'Just turned. Her birthday was in August,' Mother added.

'That's a little older than most of the girls we'll be employing in covering and piping, but not to worry, a little maturity can be an asset. You've had several domestic positions. Can you tell me why you left them?'

'They were just temporary. And …' Maisie faltered. After Father was killed, an income was more important than school. It had been almost five years now of menial tasks, domestic service and doing for others.

Her mother stepped in. 'With the war and all, people found they couldn't afford permanent help. And afterwards too. That's why we were so thrilled when Maisie got a job at Brownells department store.'

'Aren't you happy there?' Mrs Adwell's voice was gentle.

Maisie wasn't sure what to say. The job at Brownell Brothers hadn't been the step up she'd hoped. Her days were still full of sweeping, dusting and mopping. The girls with prettier eyes, daintier hands and hair that wasn't quite so wild were given the cherished positions behind the counters. The days were long and the pay was minimal but it could be worse. Andrew worked long hours at the tannery for a pittance and came home filthy and reeking. At only sixteen he already looked as if he were a man in his twenties. 'I'd prefer to work at Cadbury's. I've read about Bournville in the paper and how Cadbury's want to do the same thing here.' In truth the idea of working in a factory was foreign to Maisie. One of Andrew's friends had an apprenticeship at the zinc works. His talk of the enormous machines, the heat and noise sounded more like hell than a place of employment. Cadbury's would be different though, she was sure of it.

'It will take some time for the Cadbury Estate to be on a par with Bournville.' Mrs Adwell's expression grew serious. 'And I've got to be honest, Maisie, you'll be doing the same thing every day and it can be tiring.'

Maisie was used to dusting the same shelves every day, scrubbing the same floors. Nothing could be more monotonous than that. 'I'm used to hard work.'

'She is. She's used to hard work,' Mother repeated.

'I'm sure.' Mrs Adwell took a sip of her tea. 'Mrs Greenwood, are you regular churchgoers?'

Mother nodded primly. 'Yes, we're Church of England and attend St David's Cathedral every Sunday.'

Maisie fingered the collar of her dress. Church was always a must, no matter how much washing, ironing and mending there was to do. Neatly spruced up after their Saturday night bath in the hip tub by the range, the Greenwood family would dutifully walk the twenty minutes to St David's Cathedral in town. The soaring vaulted ceiling and the grand stained-glass windows served to lift Maisie's spirits even when there was snow on the mountain and the sharp wind blew drafts of icy air between the pews. In between prayers and hymns Maisie admired the hats, frocks and furs of the well-heeled women at the front of the church. Everything about them glowed with the sheen of wealth. Maisie's Sunday best was dull in comparison and the woollen dress itched. Whenever she wore it she was reminded of John the Baptist and his hair shirt of penitence. Even now, sitting in the parlour, she resisted the urge to scratch.

'And Maisie, how are your teeth?'

'Pardon?' Maisie frowned at the unexpected question. She'd only ever had one tooth that worried her and Mother had taken care of it with a pair of pliers. Maisie shuddered at the memory.

'Her teeth are excellent,' Mother said.

'At Bournville we have several dentists on staff as well as doctors. Good health is important to the Firm and that includes good teeth. Cadbury's can't have people missing work because of a toothache.'

Ever since Mother had taken to her mouth with the pliers, Maisie had been vigilant about cleaning her teeth. The toothpowder was an added expense and needed to be eked out, but the memory of those pliers and the pain was inducement enough. 'I have no problems with my teeth.'

Mrs Adwell pulled out a pencil and a loose piece of paper from the sheaf she carried. 'Now, Maisie, write your name, address and age on this piece of paper in the space provided then answer the few simple questions below.' She turned to Mother. 'Mrs Greenwood, I'd like to see more of your home, if I may.'

Mother rose to her feet. 'Of course. It's not grand but it is cosy.'

Maisie's thoughts raced to the piles of ironing and mending in the kitchen. Would Mrs Adwell think less of them because of the work her mother took in for mere pennies? What would she think of their meagre possessions, the paucity of their larder? She took heart knowing their small home was as neat as a pin from top to bottom. She and Lily had scrubbed, dusted and polished in anticipation of Mrs Adwell's visit. Maisie had promised her little sister as much chocolate as she could eat if she helped her gain a position at Cadbury's. Lily's hands had flown with cloths and buckets. Never had Maisie seen her more diligent in getting into every nook and corner.

'This is the girls' bedroom.' Mother's voice echoed down the hallway. Maisie was glad Lily was at school this afternoon. Her curiosity would have derailed the interview. She would have asked more questions of Mrs Adwell than Mrs Adwell could ever ask of them.

Maisie turned her attention to the piece of paper. The pencil was almost new and neatly sharpened. She filled in the allotted spaces in careful cursive writing and then turned to the questions. The few mathematics problems were easily solved with simple division and the basics of addition, subtraction and multiplication. The general knowledge questions were all about Britain. Maisie couldn't help but wonder how Mrs Adwell would fare with questions about Australia and Tasmania.

46

'It's a charming cottage.' Mrs Adwell returned to the parlour with Mother. 'Owned by the Church, you say.'

'Yes. The Glebe is Church land. The Anglican Church was first to establish housing here and the Presbyterians followed ten years later. We have a ninety-nine-year lease and reasonable rent, for which we're grateful.'

'The arrangement reminds me of Bournville, although the first houses were on leases of a little longer.'

'How much longer?'

'Nine hundred and ninety-nine years.'

'Goodness me, just like owning a house really.'

'There is the option to buy and the costs are kept as low as possible. In time it's hoped the Cadbury Estate here will operate on the same model.' Mrs Adwell turned her attention to Maisie. 'Have you finished the questions?'

'Yes, Mrs Adwell,' Maisie said; aware she'd replied in a slightly sing-song way reminiscent of the school room, she bit her lip, wishing she'd just replied 'yes'.

Mrs Adwell laughed lightly. 'I do feel like a school ma'am when handing out these tests.' She took the proffered paper from Maisie and read it quickly. 'Good, good. Your handwriting is lovely.'

Maisie ducked her head. 'Thank you.' Lily had insisted she improve her handwriting after a mix-up over a shopping list. Maisie had always had an affinity for mathematics but the written word was not her forte whereas her sister's lettering was impeccable. They'd sat together at the kitchen table while Maisie practised her penmanship. 'One day you'll be able to write beautiful love letters to your beau,' Lily had said. 'And he'll be able to understand them.' Maisie had laughed along with her, then it was back to the ironing. No beaus had appeared as yet.

'Do you have any questions, Mrs Greenwood? Maisie?'

Maisie had many questions but didn't want to ruin her chances of employment. In her experience silence and compliance were prerequisites for any job.

'Maisie? I think there's a question there.' Mrs Adwell smiled, encouraging her to speak.

'I was wondering about Dairy Milk chocolate ...' Maisie wanted to swallow her words as soon as she'd uttered them. She was committed now to asking the question even though it was trivial and would sound selfish. 'When will we be able to buy it again?' Her father used to come home early from work on Christmas Eve and invite her to dip her hand into his jacket pocket. There would always be a small block of Cadbury's Dairy Milk hiding there. It had been years since she'd tasted it. Every Christmas she searched the shops for her favourite chocolate to no avail. It was as if it had never existed.

'Many people have been wondering the same thing,' Mrs Adwell said. 'That's one of the reasons Cadbury's is opening a factory in Australia. It won't be long before Dairy Milk will be made right here in Tasmania with Tasmanian milk.'

Maisie's shoulders relaxed slightly. She hadn't made a fool of herself. She even dared hope she might help make Dairy Milk one day, if she got a job at the factory.

Mrs Adwell placed the folder back in her bag and reached for her hat and gloves. 'Thank you for your hospitality. It was lovely to meet you, Mrs Greenwood, and you, Maisie. You'll be informed by post if your application is successful.'

'Thank you, Mrs Adwell.' Maisie's skin tingled in anticipation. She'd check the letterbox every day.

Mother escorted Mrs Adwell to the front door where they said their goodbyes then returned to Maisie. 'That went rather well, I think. We'll add Mrs Adwell to our prayers tonight.'

Maisie knew better than to bargain with God. It didn't work. She and her mother had prayed endlessly when her father went to the Great War. Even so, maybe God would listen to this one selfless prayer. If she got a job at Cadbury's, her little sister would be able to stay in school and Mother could work a little less. And then there was the chocolate. Without Father, Christmas treats consisted of dried fruit, some boiled sweets and the ever-reliable Christmas pudding. But maybe this Christmas would be different. Maisie crossed her fingers and sent an early prayer heavenward.

5

Dorothy
21 October 1921

With a jaunty burst of speed, the train climbed the curved gradient to where Dorothy, Ida and their fellow employees waited on the Cadbury's platform. It was the perfect weather to show off the beauty of the location, surrounded as it was by blue river reaches, sun-bathed hills and blooming orchards. The women stood in their Cadbury's whites, all the better to be recognised as employees and guides for the 500 visitors invited to this special day. Further along the platform the directors of this new enterprise stood waiting to greet the more distinguished guests.

'Don't see why we have to play guides to a mob of snobs and moochers,' Ida complained. 'Can't remember seeing that in my contract.'

'Aren't you just a little bit excited?' Dorothy asked. The day's much-anticipated event had been planned in great detail. The guests began to alight from the train the Firm had hired for the day. 'Look, there's the governor and his family. The archbishop is next to him.'

'Oh, lah-di-dah. I've got enough work to do without having to play nice to this lot.' Ida tossed her head in the direction of the gathering crowd.

Dorothy heard echoes of Esme's complaints in Ida's words. She shook off a trace of annoyance and instead concentrated on the crowd. She recognised the premier from his photo in the *Mercury*. Other members of the government were present along with important businessmen, most of them accompanied by their wives. All of them held a copy of the illustrated souvenir booklet published especially for the occasion.

After welcoming the dignitaries, the visitors were separated into groups by the directors, and with a background cacophony of stone being crushed, the clanking of metal and the screech of timber saws, the tour commenced.

Ida brushed some cement dust from her white uniform. 'The ladies won't be so pleased getting this muck on their finery. It's barmy to keep them machines running during all this clarting about.'

Ida had a point. The roaring stone crushers poured out their streams of graded metal, filling the air with a dusty haze, but pressing deadlines meant they'd stop for no one, not even the governor. The Firm hoped to be manufacturing by Christmas. How it was going to happen she couldn't tell. 'We'd better split up. Make ourselves useful.'

Ida snorted in annoyance but moved towards the other side of the large group. Dorothy approached some visitors who were reading one of the descriptive placards attached to the building – a useful touch when there was so much to explain about this massive undertaking. The Chairman of Directors, who usually resided in Sydney but had travelled to Tasmania for this special day, called for attention and the group shifted towards him.

'Two of the factory blocks are now almost complete in readiness for the machinery that waits at Constitution Dock,' he said, raising his voice against the ongoing racket. Dorothy was only able to hear some of what he was saying. 'Steam and gas mains are being connected … progress is being made with the additional blocks … three concrete mixing plants are in continuous operation.'

Dorothy had studied the plans for the entire factory. Mr Moresby in the site office had objected but she'd told him it was official business. 'I'm one of the tour guides for the governor's party and need to have this knowledge at my fingertips.' It was stretching the truth but had done the trick. Thanks to her studies, Dorothy could envisage the completed six blocks, five of them three storeys high and linked by arched bridges. It was hard to believe that hundreds of employees would, in a matter of months, be creating delicious chocolate and confectionery on this site. The screech of a grinder nearby brought her back to the reality of her surroundings. This was still a work in progress, no matter how impressive it might be.

As the tour moved on a woman approached Dorothy in Block 2, where workmen were giving a smooth finish to all the curves and edges.

'I haven't seen one square corner,' the woman said in a cultured voice. 'It gives the interior a strange appearance. Why are all the columns and corners rounded?'

'To make cleaning easier,' Dorothy said, doing her best to smooth her accent. 'It stops particles lodging in corners that would encourage ants and other vermin. Cadbury's takes pride in its hygienic standards.'

'Most admirable.' The woman smiled and moved away.

In the boiler house one of the directors, Mr Cooper, was holding court. While he expounded on the emphasis the company put on healthy working conditions, Dorothy lingered in the trade section with the latest and improved drills and lathes. She longed to pick them up and feel the heft of them but resisted as the group continued on to one of her favourite buildings, the bean store. The roof was of terracotta Marseilles tiles that added a warmth to the place and the walls were made of hardwood, a happy change from all the concrete. The large doorways in the eastern wall opened on to a long railway platform.

'As you can see,' one of the male employees said to a group of guests, 'the platform is protected by this verandah roof, designed especially to keep goods dry in case of inclement weather.'

'We certainly get a lot of that,' a visitor said with a wry grin.

At one end of the spacious building temporarily installed machinery whirred as men shaped tins and boxes for cocoa and chocolates. It was more for show than anything else, giving visitors an example of the work in a factory where nothing was being produced as yet.

Another of the well-dressed women turned to Dorothy. 'How does this compare to Bournville?'

Dorothy was momentarily dazzled by the woman's beautiful coat, a pale aqua that draped gracefully from the woman's shoulders almost to her ankles. Not the thing to wear to a work site but perfect for a fine spring day. Dorothy shifted her gaze to the machinery. 'At Bournville, on one line alone, half a million cocoa tins are shaped a week.'

'Half a million a week. Goodness me.'

Dorothy didn't mention that, even when complete, the Claremont factory would produce only one tenth of Bournville's output.

A call to order marked the beginning of the speeches and the delights of the afternoon tea, spread out in a space that would eventually be filled with hundreds of sacks of cocoa beans. The Chairman of Directors began by talking about the dependability of the Firm's products and the happy relations they had with their staff. He then introduced Mr Pascall, who stepped forward and graciously acknowledged the applause. Sarah stood close behind him, keenly observing both him and the crowd.

Next, the governor declared that as true Tasmanians they were all directly interested in the efforts of the associated firms. 'No more beautiful site could have been selected than that determined upon in the garden State. Governments and individuals alike—' His speech was interrupted by an explosion from the quarry, or it could have been a detonation from the excavation of one of the new building sites. Dorothy's attention was drawn to a sharp movement to her left. She was riveted by a shock of recognition. It was Thomas, she was sure of it. But why was he here? She skirted the crowd, edging closer, but when she reached the spot where he'd been, he was gone.

Once the explosion stopped reverberating the governor continued. 'Governments and individuals alike might be handicapped by financial difficulties, but the sight of the steadily rising buildings is an indication of what is possible. With Tasmanian hydro-electric power and the Firm's brains, the State will assuredly boom in the not far distant future.'

A thunderous applause greeted his remarks but Dorothy had no time for promises and rhetoric. Thomas was here. She scanned the crowd but saw no trace. Had she imagined it? No. She was certain. Dorothy made her way outside. A man, his hat drawn down over his eyes, slumped against the far wall. Thomas. She walked slowly towards him, remembering how he was affected by sudden movements. He turned to her as she approached. 'Mr Moreland.'

He tipped his hat with a shaking hand. 'Mrs Adwell. You find me indisposed.'

'I'm surprised to find you here at all.' She stood at a small distance. 'What brings you to Cadbury's?'

'I'm known to Mr Cooper as well as several members of staff. We meet together on Sundays.'

Ah, that explained his presence. He was a Quaker. Theirs was a religion without clergy, rituals or hierarchy of any kind. On Sunday mornings, while others went to church, Quakers gathered in meeting rooms to sit in silence, only speaking if moved by God. Dorothy had attended a few meetings at Bournville but had felt out of place. Her upbringing had been very different to that of the quiet, dignified men and women.

'Also a sense of curiosity,' he continued. 'Something I'm regretting at the moment.' His fists were clenched and yet his hands still shook. Another blast would be disastrous.

'Would you like to see the estate?' The cottages were a small distance from the construction site and even further from the quarry – it would be quieter there. 'A few of the cottages are already occupied. It'll be rather pretty when it's finished but it's not quite Bournville yet.'

'Thank you.'

Dorothy led him away from the battered ground of the factory towards the rolling green. 'I didn't see you on the *Nairana* during the trip to Hobart. Did you stay in Melbourne for a while?'

'Yes.'

Dorothy waited for him to say more but was met by silence. She smiled politely. 'And how are you finding Hobart?'

He cleared his throat. 'Not quite as I'd been led to believe.'

'In what way? The climate, the population, the school?' Dorothy stopped herself. On the *Ormonde* she'd learnt to keep her questions to a minimum – too many and he'd nod politely and take his leave. 'I'm sorry,' she said. 'I'm being nosy. Please, forget I asked.'

He said nothing but remained by her side. Dorothy wondered how he was faring. If his students were rowdy she could imagine he'd have some difficulty. She kept her thoughts and her questions to herself as they made their way to where the cottages were laid out in a pleasing arc. 'The cottages have every convenience, including electricity in all the rooms.'

'How extravagant.' His smile was weak but she was glad to see the shaking in his hands had settled. 'It costs a week's wages just to keep one bulb burning back home.'

'The reasonable price of the hydro-electricity is one of the main reasons Cadbury's came here.' Dorothy had been delighted at the convenience of flicking on a switch when she'd arrived at the hostel. Some of the other women, including Esme, complained the light was too bright but Dorothy was happy to leave the fiddly kerosene lamps behind.

'At Bournville, we were encouraged to grow vegetables in the plots behind our cottages. It's the same here in Claremont.' She pointed out the rows of young vegetables in the backyards.

'Do you live here?'

'No.' With so few cottages available she'd be living at the hostel for some time. 'I live nearby, with the other women who've come out from England.'

'Ah, so the men have the cottages and the women bunk together, eh?' His voice had a lightness to it.

The Firm had thought it best, for the women's care and protection, that they be housed together under the care of a matron. 'It's nice to have company. Also, many of the men have families and need more room.' Dorothy pointed to their left. 'Over there, by those trees, will be a playground for their children.' At present it was a scrappy piece of grass but she'd seen the plans for a sandpit and swings. 'There are sports grounds too – so much room for a child to run around in the fresh air.' Growing up in the crowded tenements of Birmingham, she hadn't seen a green field until she'd started working at Bournville.

Dorothy glanced at Thomas. His breath was even and the worry had lifted from the lines around his mouth.

Thomas shifted his weight, looked towards the river and then back to the cottages. 'It would be liberating to live here by the river. Nothing can be built on the water to hem a person in. All that space. A man can breathe here.'

Away from the dust and noise of the construction site it was true. Even when the factory was at full production and workers, families and sporting clubs filled the area, there would always be the expanse of the Derwent surrounding them on this piece of land – the chocolate peninsula. She shifted her attention to the hills, bathed now in the fading sunlight. Thomas followed her gaze.

'It is a beautiful spot,' he said. 'But nothing like home. The light here is completely different. It has an edge to it. Everything is so clear. It would be mid-autumn in England and the leaves all shades of orange and red.'

'We'll be celebrating Christmas in the middle of summer. It's very strange.'

'Traditionally Quakers don't celebrate Christmas.'

'Or Easter,' Dorothy agreed. 'Except when it comes to selling chocolate.'

Thomas laughed with a genuine warmth. 'One must make some allowances.'

For a moment their eyes met and held. Dorothy's heart expanded with a kind of joy. She felt less tethered to the earth. 'Thomas,' she whispered.

He looked away and cleared his throat. Instantly gravity reasserted itself and Dorothy was again firmly grounded. 'You've seen where I work, or will be once the factory's up and running. May I ask about your teaching position?'

Thomas clasped his hands behind his back. 'The Friends' School is a fine establishment.'

Dorothy nodded. The Quaker school in North Hobart.

'However, I'm not certain teaching and I are a suitable match.' His voice was subdued. Dorothy longed to lean in to hear him better but held herself back in case it stopped him from divulging more. She barely dared to breathe. 'After the war, well, I wasn't the only one who needed to convalesce. And then jobs were scarce.' Thomas put his hands in his pockets and hunched his shoulders. 'I was offered a position out of kindness, I suspect.' He cleared his throat again. 'It was thought a change of scenery would be just the ticket.'

Dorothy had hoped for the same thing. A new start. A grand move that would sever the chains of memory, grief and regret. And then there was her promotion and a pathway forward to her grand ambition. When she'd seen Thomas on the *Ormonde* another ambition had stirred within her. Surely the fact that he was standing here beside her now was part of this unfurling of a new life. The sound of voices in the distance alerted her to an approaching tour group. 'The speeches must be over.'

The frown returned to Thomas's face, deeply etched and solid as the cement in the factory walls. He doffed his hat, 'Mrs Adwell,' and strode away, edging around the cottages out of sight of the approaching crowd.

6

Dorothy

'Ee-yar,' Ida called out to Dorothy. A group of dignitaries had gathered around the first of the cottages with one of the directors explaining the details of the Firm's philosophy on housing and community, giving Ida and Dorothy a few moments together. 'I thought you, of all people, would've lapped up the governor's speech, instead you scarpered.'

'I needed to go to the lav.' The lie tripped off Dorothy's tongue with ease. It was best to keep things simple. She still hadn't mentioned Thomas to Ida and didn't know if she would. Her relationship with him felt too tremulous, too ephemeral, as though if she spoke about him he would cease to exist.

'You didn't miss much. After the gov had stopped gasbagging, Mr Pascall had a go. Them men love the sound of their own voices.'

Dorothy laughed with her friend, all the while keeping an eye out for Thomas. She wondered whether he'd skirt around and join the group from behind. After the director wrapped up his talk Dorothy nudged Ida. 'We'd better get on with it.'

Ida grumbled but they mingled with the crowd, answering questions until it was time for the guests to depart. From the appreciative chatter, Dorothy suspected that during the days and weeks to come word would pass around town of this model factory, of the grand details and the small touches, of every corner rounded and the spectacle of the chimney. Finally the train pulled away in a shroud of smoke and steam, its whistle ringing out a cheerful hoot.

'Thank goodness for that,' Ida said. 'I'm famished. Those cakes looked delicious but that mob chobbled the lot.'

Dorothy linked her arm in Ida's as they set off for the hostel further along the river. 'At least we don't have to cook our own tea, bab. I'm glad there'll be food on the table tonight that wasn't prepared by us.'

'There'd better be some pudding. I need something sweet after today.'

'I'm sure Mrs Brown will have whipped us up something fortifying after our busy day.'

'Fortifying? Gawd love you. You sound as highfalutin' as the governor.'

Dorothy bit her lip. Often it was as though she had two personalities and sometimes her juggling act slipped. While interviewing the girls, Dorothy focused on the tips Sarah gave her, but around Ida and at the hostel Dorothy tried to make sure her Brummie accent came to the fore. With a start she realised she'd naturally spoken with her more refined accent with Thomas this afternoon. When they'd first met her accent had been pure Brummie. What must he think of her?

At the hostel Dorothy and Ida freshened up and made their way to the dining room where a babble of voices rose and fell.

'Waste of bloody time, if you ask me.' Esme was holding court. 'And money. All that tea and cake and putting on a special train. I'm amazed the company can afford it.'

'What do you mean?' asked Lizzie.

Esme puffed herself up. 'I've heard this whole thing is costing more than they thought and there's no denying it's running behind schedule. We was supposed to be training the girls by now and at full production by Christmas.' She shook her head. 'Never going to happen.'

'If it fails, where does that leave us?' There was a note of panic in Lizzie's voice.

A ripple of anxiety and whispered questions circled the table as Ida and Dorothy took their places.

'There's no need to worry,' Margaret said, her voice even and placating. 'The Firm has every confidence that, even given the change in the estimated start of production, the factory will be turning a profit in the allotted timeframe.'

'What a lot of gobbledygook,' muttered Esme. Nevertheless, the anxiety within the group eased and the women tucked into their meal of lamb and vegetables.

The mood improved even more when Mrs Brown placed a large golden syrup pudding on the table accompanied by jugs of custard. Dorothy savoured a spoonful of the warm, sticky dessert and sighed with contentment.

A knock on the door interrupted the chatter and Mrs Rayner rose to answer it. She returned with a quizzical expression on her face.

'A letter for you, Mrs Adwell.' She put the envelope beside Dorothy's bowl. 'Delivered by a messenger boy. Most unusual.'

Dorothy picked up the envelope, aware that the women had fallen silent and were watching her with open curiosity. All except Sarah, who kept eating with her usual restraint and perfect manners.

A pressure built in her chest. Could the letter be from Thomas? After their conversation he knew where she lived. Was this an invitation to meet?

'Ain't you going to open it?' asked Ida, her eyes keen with interest.

Much as she longed to excuse herself and open the letter in the comparative privacy of her room, Dorothy slipped her fingernail under the seal. Inside was a single sheet of paper, the writing a neat cursive.

Dear Mrs Adwell,

I watched you today in the bean store. What a shame you left before we had a chance to talk. I do hope to see you again. I believe you have something of great value.

Yours sincerely,

An admirer

'What does it say?' Ida leant over in an attempt to read the letter.

Dorothy stared at the words, a cold chill creeping up her spine. The letter wasn't from Thomas, but it was from someone who might have seen them together. Whoever had written the letter had 'watched' her.

'Let me see.' Ida took the sheet of paper from her hands. Dorothy's impulse was to grab it back but didn't want to make a scene.

'Ooh err.' Ida chortled with delight. 'Dot has an admirer. Get this. *I believe you have something of great value, yours sincerely, an admirer.*' She waved the piece of paper at the transfixed faces around the table. 'Not even one month in the colonies and Dot has a beau. Perhaps those naysayers were right when they said we'd all be married before our contracts were even halfway done. Our Dot here might lead the charge.'

Dorothy forced a laugh. 'Don't be silly, Ida. I haven't even met the man. It's probably some kind of mistake. Yes,' she reassured herself, 'he's mistaken me for someone else.' He'd been watching her though and that was unnerving.

'You're right. It must be meant for someone else. What do you have of great value?' Esme sneered. 'Nought that I can see.'

'I beg to differ.' Sarah had finished eating her pudding and laid her spoon in her bowl with a delicate and precise movement. 'Clearly this admirer has great discernment.' She looked straight at Esme with an unflinching gaze.

'Great discernment, eh?' Esme mocked Sarah's cultured tones but it was all bravado with no force behind her words. There was an air about Sarah that caused even Esme to defer. 'Well, that's me back in my box.'

Ida's eyes flicked between Esme and Sarah. A small frown pulled at her mouth for a moment and then her smile returned. 'We're all just a bit jealous, ain't we? We don't have a fancy man writing us love letters. Well, not yet, anyways.' She gave the letter back to Dorothy. 'Just having a bit of a laugh. It is a bit funny, innit?'

Dorothy folded the letter carefully and put it back in the envelope. 'Yes, most odd.'

'It's queer that he knows your name,' Bessie said, her bright eyes questioning Dorothy.

Dorothy's fingers tightened on the envelope. The paper was taut and unyielding but if she twisted it and found the right angle, it would tear.

Sarah folded her serviette and placed it on the table. 'I dare say a few prudent questions would reveal all our names to those curious enough to ask. Each one of us was mentioned in the *Mercury* when we arrived on the *Nairana*, as are all new arrivals. Our identities are hardly a secret.'

Bessie nodded thoughtfully but her eyes were still on Dorothy and the letter.

Sarah stood. She picked up her bowl in readiness to take it to the kitchen. 'It's been a long day. Good evening, ladies.'

Dorothy felt Sarah's eyes on her. She looked up and saw an invitation there. No, more of a directive. A small tilt of Sarah's chin, indicating the door and the stairs beyond to their room, was discernible probably only to herself. She was aware that the other women around the table were still focused on her and, more especially, the letter.

'Yes,' Lizzie agreed. 'Quite a day. Lordy, all that walking and talking and not even a cup of tea to wet our whistles.'

'Reminded me of my days in service, it did,' Esme moaned. 'Them upstairs who think they're better than us. I didn't go work for Fry's to be looked down on by the likes of them.'

'Those people still think of us factory workers as skivvies though, don't they?' Lizzie said. 'Not much better than kitchen maids.'

Dorothy winced. She'd been lower than a kitchen maid. From the age of ten she'd spent the early mornings in the cold, dank boot-hole of a big house in Birmingham, polishing shoes and boots till her hands ached. The pay was a pittance but sometimes the cook would take pity on her and give her a piece of bread. It was always stale, but Dorothy had been grateful.

'Those toffs can think what they like,' Bessie said. 'I'm a forewoman now and proud of it.'

'True,' Lizzie said. 'We're all here because we're good at what we do. The best, actually.'

A murmur of agreement ran around the table as the women pushed their chairs from the table. George Cadbury Junior himself had approached Dorothy with the offer of promotion to emigrate to the colony. They needed her skills and expertise, he'd said, and she was honoured to accept.

After they'd cleared the dishes, Margaret and Bessie remained in the kitchen to deal with the washing and drying, while Lizzie, Esme and Ida made their way to the parlour.

'Are you joining us, Dot?' Ida asked.

'Not tonight. I'm very tired.' She was aware of Sarah waiting in their room.

'Too much excitement, eh?' Ida nodded towards the letter in Dorothy's hands.

Dorothy had hoped to throw it, unnoticed, into the embers of the range in the kitchen. The chance had not arrived. Instead she still clutched it, worrying one corner of the envelope with her fingers. 'Yes.' She managed a half smile. She was glad, now, the letter wasn't from Thomas. Her elation would have been obvious and caused endless questions from the other women.

'Ar, bab. See you in the morning.'

Upstairs, Sarah sat on her bed, waiting. 'Come, sit,' she said, patting the space beside her.

Dorothy sat, the letter still clutched in her fingers.

Sarah held out her hand for the letter. 'May I?'

Dorothy handed it to her.

Sarah examined the envelope closely. She traced the handwritten letters of Dorothy's name on the front, then carefully turned it over. She slipped the single piece of paper from the envelope and held it out in front of her as if it might speak to her. She turned the paper one way then the other.

Dorothy watched with a distant curiosity. She wished the letter had never been delivered.

'This man was watching you,' Sarah said. 'He knows who you are and where you live.'

Dorothy suppressed a shiver. 'It would seem so.'

Sarah remained silent for a moment and tapped the letter with a manicured nail. Sarah didn't use nail polish, that would be a step too far, but Dorothy had observed the care she took of her hands, buffing and filing her nails. For the factory girls there were only two requirements – clean hands and short, neat nails. Hands were tools of work, that was all.

'*I believe you have something of great value,*' Sarah quoted. 'Do you have any idea what he means?'

Dorothy shook her head. 'None.'

'Are you sure?' Sarah's voice was gentle but there was a pressure behind it.

Dorothy forced a smile. 'Ida's right. It's from a cheeky local lad who's hoping to get lucky. I wouldn't be surprised if Ida receives a similar letter soon, or Bessie.' It was the only explanation.

Sarah folded the letter and placed it back in the envelope. 'I think we should hold on to it. As you say, he may well be an admirer. Who knows, you might fall in love. Let's keep the letter safe.' She rested her hand on Dorothy's. 'Next time he could well send you flowers and, heaven forbid, chocolates.' Sarah laughed in her melodious way. She shifted on the bed to face Dorothy. 'You look peaky. A good night's rest will do you the world of good.'

Dorothy was soothed by Sarah's caring manner. A faint memory of being tucked into bed by her mother flitted through her mind and was dismissed with a small sense of loss. Instead she went through the stages of her bedtime ritual. By the time she returned to their room from her nightly ablutions there was no sign of Sarah, or the letter.

7

December 1921

Maisie was tired and footsore when she arrived home after ten hours on her feet. The weeks leading up to Christmas were frantic at Brownell Brothers and everyone's nerves were frayed. Even after the store finally closed its doors and the other girls had rushed off home, Maisie still had the floors to scrub. How wonderful it would be to take off her shoes, rub the aches that collected at the bottom of her big toes and put on her slippers, but she'd barely had time to shrug off her jacket when Mother called out.

'Maisie? I need you to deliver the ironing to Mrs Tate in Aberdeen Street.'

Maisie arranged her face into a smile before she entered the kitchen. As always it was crowded with other people's clothing – shirts, blouses, trousers and dresses. Mother sat at the table, a needle and thread darting through the sheer seam of a chiffon blouse. 'I have to get this done by early tomorrow. Mrs Shields has her

67

morning tea.' She looked up at her daughter, her eyes creased with worry and fatigue. 'I've kept your tea warm.'

'Thanks, Mother.' Maisie bent down and kissed her cheek. She picked up the basket of ironing. Andrew would be in the lean-to out the back that served as his bedroom, exhausted and filthy from work – a state unsuitable for delivering the freshly washed and ironed clothes. 'Is Lily doing her homework?'

Mother tsked. 'More like reading one of those books she wastes her time with. The sooner she turns fourteen and gets a job the better.'

Maisie bit her tongue. The joy that had filled the house when the letter arrived from Cadbury's announcing Maisie had been successful had faded when she'd raised the subject of Lily now being able to stay in school. Mother had refused to budge despite the fact that Maisie would be making more money once she started work at the factory in January. But Maisie hadn't given up. There was still time before Lily's birthday next year to change her mother's mind.

She laid the basket in the hallway outside the bedroom she shared with her younger sister. Opening the door she knew the scene that would greet her – Lily curled up on the small bed, immersed in a book, with the cat purring beside her. 'Hello, Lily.'

Her sister looked up. 'Did you know an insect is an animal? I thought only things with fur or hair and warm blood were animals – like Blackie.' Lily rubbed the cat under his chin and the purring increased. 'But even creatures with cold blood, all the reptiles and all the insects, they're animals too.'

Maisie sat on the side of the bed. 'I must admit, I can't really think of an insect as an animal.'

'But it is. We're all animals. You, me, Blackie, the spiders in the outhouse.' She giggled. 'All of us.'

'What are you reading?'

A stricken expression clouded Lily's eyes as she hurried to hide the book under the bedclothes.

'Oh, Lily, did you "borrow" another book from school?' Her sister had been in trouble for this before. *'The encyclopedias are for all the students, not just Lily,'* her teacher had said.

Lily sat up straight and thrust out her bottom lip. 'No one else ever looks at them. They just sit there getting dusty. I wish we could have a set of our own, but when the salesman comes knocking Mother always sends him away.'

'Darling Lily.' Maisie stroked her sister's hair, so unlike her own. It lay flat in auburn sheets, smooth and shining in the light of the bedside lamp, as if their mother had ironed it to perfection. 'You know you're not allowed to bring any of the encyclopedias home. What about the idea of reading them at lunchtime? Didn't we agree that that would be best?'

Lily turned her head and mumbled something to Blackie.

'What was that?'

'The other children at school.' Lily kept her chin down.

'What about them?'

'They tease me. They call me names.' Lily's bottom lip wobbled.

'What kind of names?'

Lily squirmed. 'They call me a bookworm.' She looked up at Maisie with shimmering eyes. 'I'm not a worm.'

'No, you're not. No ordinary worm, that is. A bookworm though? Well, that's special. Didn't you tell me insects and reptiles are animals? That would mean a worm is too. We're all animals, that's what you said. So, you're an animal who loves to read. That sounds pretty good to me.' Maisie tickled Lily on the stomach. 'I'm proud to know such a magnificent bookworm.'

Lily squealed with delight. 'I am a magnificent bookworm.'

'Yes, you are. There's no shame in loving to read. Make the most of the time you have to do it.'

'I could read all weekend if we had a set of encyclopedias.'

'I know.' Maisie had discussed it with their mother. The money wasn't there, and besides, Mother had said when Lily started work there'd be no need or time for encyclopedias. 'But you have to take that one back to school first thing tomorrow morning. Get there early if you can.'

'So I don't get caught?'

Maisie took a breath. She was loath to encourage deceit in her sister, but Lily had been warned more than once. There would be consequences this time. She gently touched Lily's cheek. 'So you don't get caught.'

A hot, restless wind followed Maisie all the way home, grabbing at her skirts and teasing out her hair. She was grateful Christmas Eve had fallen on a Saturday, meaning only a half-day at Brownell Brothers, but even so that afternoon the hill to their small cottage seemed steeper than ever. She knew piles of ironing waited for her at home. Her mother's customers would need their damask tablecloths and serviettes starched and crisply ironed for tomorrow. The rest of Maisie's day would be spent in the steamy kitchen bending over a hot iron and then running around the dusty streets delivering the snowy linens. Tomorrow there'd be church and then the big family dinner – roast lamb and vegetables with plenty of her mother's special potatoes, finely coated in seasoned flour and baked in lard until crispy. The Christmas pudding had been hanging from a hook in the pantry for weeks now. On Christmas Day it would boil away merrily on the range until her mother placed it proudly on the table along with a jug of creamy custard. Maisie's mouth watered just to think of it.

When she opened the gate, pushing it back on squeaky hinges, Lily flung open the front door and rushed to meet her. 'Oh, Maisie. Thank goodness, you're here.'

'What is it? What's wrong?'

'Mother.' That's all Lily could say before breaking into a sob.

Maisie raced inside, not knowing what would greet her. In recent months Mother had become clumsy. Her eyesight was failing, along with her health, and the quality of her work with it. Burns and scalds marked her hands and arms from the ironing. Despite her thimble she'd often prick herself when mending clothes in the lamplight. The mending brought in more money than ironing but only if her work was up to the mark. Some of the posher clients had already gone elsewhere.

In the kitchen Mother lay on the floor, her face pale as death. The air was close and hot with the heat of the range adding to the stifling summer day.

'I was telling Mother about the eruption of Mount Vesuvius and the ruins of Pompeii.' Lily's face rumpled and the tears began again. 'I was saying how bad I'd feel if Blackie was burnt alive by lava and turned into a statue and she fainted. It's all my fault.'

Maisie knelt and placed her cheek against her mother's mouth. A slight breath brushed her skin. Mother was alive.

'I put a pillow under her head so she'd be comfortable. I thought she'd wake up but she hasn't,' Lily wailed. 'Did I do the wrong thing?'

'You didn't do anything wrong.' Maisie kept her voice calm even as the panic rose within her. She should ask Lily to run for the doctor but the little money they had spare had gone on dried fruit for the pudding and small fripperies of presents.

'Lily, run next door and ask Mrs Perkins if she has any smelling salts.' Maisie prayed it was only a fainting fit. Mother's breath was shallow and her skin as white as the sheets that hung around them in the kitchen.

Maisie wet a clean rag with water and pressed it to her mother's forehead. 'Please, Mother, please, wake up.'

Mrs Perkins bustled in with Lily trailing behind her. 'Oh, deary me. Oh, deary, deary me.' She tsked and lowered herself slowly to the floor with the aid of the edge of the table. 'This was bound to happen though now, wasn't it? What a burden your mother has carried for so long. Three kiddies with no father. It isn't right. It's a cruel, cruel world.' Mrs Perkins took a handkerchief from her pocket and dabbed at her eyes, although there was no sign of tears. There was a whiff of sherry about her.

'Do you have any smelling salts, Mrs Perkins?' Maisie forced a polite tone to her voice.

'Oh, my dear, dear girl. Sal volatile won't cure what ails your poor, poor mother. Too much grief, too many children, too much work.' She sighed dramatically and shook her head.

Maisie bit her tongue. Mrs Perkins had five children and a husband who worked away on the hydro-electricity scheme. Her two youngest boys ran wild most days. But for all that she was a kindly neighbour, especially when her kindness would glean her some gossip.

Lily pushed forward. 'I have them. Mrs Perkins gave them to me.'

'For the best, I thought. I've had a bit of a Christmas Eve tipple.' She placed her index finger to the side of her nose and her eye twitched as if she was going to wink and then thought better of it. 'Would hate to break the bottle.'

'Thank you, Lily.' Maisie waved the smelling salts under Mother's nose. With a sharp intake of breath her mother opened her eyes.

'Maisie?' She struggled to sit up. Maisie put an arm around her as support.

'You fainted, Clara.' Mrs Perkins bellowed as if Mother was deaf not ill. The sherry fumes hit Maisie with the power of a distillery.

'Val?' Mother's eyes widened. 'What are you doing here?'

'It's Christmas Eve. I thought I'd pop over and spread the good cheer.' Mrs Perkins chortled and heaved herself onto one of the kitchen chairs.

Maisie forced a note of reassurance into her voice. 'Let's get you off the floor and make you a nice strong cup of tea.'

'I'd love one of those too, if you don't mind, dearie.' Mrs Perkins settled herself at the table. 'And some shortbread too, it being Christmas Eve and all.'

'Fainted?' Mother looked around with an air of being somewhere she didn't recognise as Maisie eased her gently into her chair.

'It's all my fault,' Lily sobbed. 'I was talking about Pompeii and people being turned into statues. It upset you.'

'Oh, Lily.' Mrs Perkins pursed her lips and shook her head. 'What nonsense you spout sometimes. People being turned into statues? Well, I never.'

'But—'

'Lily.' Maisie interrupted her. 'Fetch the biscuit tin from the pantry please, and put out the cups and saucers while I make the tea.' The knowledge her little sister gleaned from the encyclopedias she devoured often startled even her. She'd learnt to accept it but sometimes others found Lily's enthusiasms unnerving. Maisie poured the tea while keeping an eye on Mother, who sat confused and apologetic. Mrs Perkins pulled the plate of shortbread closer.

Lily asked to be excused and returned with her copybook from school. Maisie knew what was inside, rows of perfect sentences in Lily's exquisite writing with nary a blot or splodge to be found.

'What's this?' Mother asked as Lily joined them at the table.

'I was saving it for tomorrow, but I think now might be a better time.' Her eyes darted nervously towards Mother. 'To make up for Pompeii.'

'Lily, darling,' Mother said, her voice an exhausted sigh. 'You did nothing wrong.'

Lily opened the copybook to the very back page. The inside back cover was filled with her writing, small and neat, including several lists denoted by asterisks. 'I copied this from the encyclopedia at school,' she said. 'I didn't want to forget any of it.'

Mrs Perkins harrumphed. 'I didn't come over for a lesson. By the time I turned eleven, I was happy to see the back of the schoolroom.' She put an entire piece of shortbread in her mouth and reached for another.

Lily smiled shyly at Maisie. 'It's part of your Christmas present. You'll be working at Cadbury's soon and I thought …' Maisie waited. It was unlike Lily to be shy. 'Well, maybe you'd like to know the history behind it.'

'Oh, Lily.' Maisie put her hand to her heart.

'History?' Mrs Perkins slugged down the dregs of her tea and picked up another piece of shortbread. 'Time for me to go. Hope you're feeling better, Clara.' She turned to Lily. 'Bring the salts back on Boxing Day. Hopefully your mother will have no further need for them by then.' She heaved herself out of her chair. 'I can see myself out. History?' She shook her head and muttered to herself as she swayed down the hallway.

'It's only a brief history,' Lily said, once Mrs Perkins had closed the door behind her. 'The Mayans thought cocoa was the drink of the gods, the Aztecs used the beans as currency.' Her eyes lit up. 'The Spanish brought it to Europe and the British loved it so much they opened chocolate houses where people would drink hot chocolate. They didn't work out how to make chocolate bars until much later.

I've written it all down here.' Lily tapped the rows of tightly written words.

Maisie marvelled at her little sister's endless love of knowledge. What a waste it would be to have it bludgeoned out of her by the drudgery of the working world.

'It sounds very interesting,' Mother said, smiling wearily, 'but I must get back to work.' She touched her forehead and looked around vaguely. 'The ironing.'

'A good lie-down is what you need.' Maisie stood and helped Mother to her feet. 'Let's get you to bed.' Mother began to protest but Maisie wouldn't allow it. 'I'll finish the ironing. Lily and I will deliver it. I'd rope in Andrew too when he gets home from his shift, if he wasn't always so filthy from the tannery.' She smiled, forcing some lightness into her voice. 'If he gets anywhere near the linen we'd have to wash it again.' Andrew's job paid so little that Maisie had encouraged him to apply for a job at Cadbury's too, but he wasn't willing to take the risk. Jobs were hard to find. Better to have the bird in the hand, he'd reasoned.

'I can help with the ironing too, you know I can,' Lily chimed in. She often helped with simple things like handkerchiefs and pillow cases and could manage the serviettes. Maisie would take care of the fiddlier blouses and shirts.

'And you can tell me all about the history of chocolate while we work. You see, Mother, we have it all in hand.'

'Just a little lie-down then,' Mother acquiesced. 'I'll be right as rain in a jiffy, I'm sure.'

Maisie supported her to the bedroom, helped her out of her apron and shoes and settled her on the bed. Before she closed the bedroom door, Maisie looked back at the small crumpled form lying there, eyes already closed, face grey with exhaustion. If only Father were here to take care of Mother, to take care of them all. Maisie shivered despite the warmth in the air. There would come a day, sooner than she'd hoped, when she would be the head of the household, fretting over the price of milk and bread, worrying about bills and rent, taking care of her mother as if she were the child. It would be worth it though to see Andrew married with a family of his own and Lily fulfil her potential. Maisie would be the spinster aunt, the one who took care of others. There were many like her since the war, but she felt it deeply, especially now. She closed the door gently and let out a breath in a steady stream to still her racing heart. In only a few more weeks she'd be a Cadbury's employee. Her stomach knotted at the thought. At first she'd been thrilled to be one of the chosen ones but now the weight of responsibility was on her shoulders and there was an added urgency. The new job with Cadbury's must work out, it had to.

'Maisie?' Lily called out from the kitchen. 'The iron's hot.'

'Coming.' Maisie straightened her shoulders. 'I'm looking forward to hearing all about the history of chocolate.'

8

Dorothy

Christmas Day dawned hot and still. It was odd to wake after sleeping under only a sheet when back home Dorothy would have been snuggled beneath layers of woollen blankets. Mrs Rayner had told them that sometimes there was snow on Mount Wellington on Christmas Day. Dorothy would've liked a reminder of home, no matter how brief, but snow didn't eventuate. Instead, after attending the service at St Alban's in Claremont, the women enjoyed a full Christmas dinner with all the trimmings – a stuffed goose, roasted vegetables, a well-seasoned plum pudding and fruit cake covered with marzipan and royal icing – in the stifling air. They ate, dabbing at their perspiring faces with their handkerchiefs. Dorothy was glad she'd had the foresight to pack two day dresses in light cotton before she'd left Bournville. Esme hadn't been so wise and spent her evenings sewing a summer dress and grumbling to anyone who'd listen about the insufferable summer when they'd been promised mild and clement weather.

'I know the seasons are all topsy-turvy here,' Bessie said, 'but a little respite from this heat would make for a jollier Christmas.'

Mrs Rayner's nod carried the weight of her local experience. 'Knowing Hobart, the weather will turn and we'll be eating Christmas leftovers with sleet battering the windows and a bitter southerly roaring up the valley.'

It was true. The weather here was changeable, going from cold wind and rain to hot sun and then back to cold within the space of a day or even an hour. Dorothy was glad the heat had fallen during the holiday break. In future, if the temperature climbed this high, the factory would have to shut down to protect the chocolate.

After dinner they gathered in the parlour to open the presents from home that had been hidden away under beds and in wardrobes for this day. Dorothy hadn't expected anything in the post. It had been years since she'd last seen her brothers. Mere months after the Great War was finally over one of them had tracked her down to tell her their father had died from Spanish flu and asking for money for the funeral. The disease had spread through England killing many thousands. Someone happily eating kippers at breakfast could be blue with death by teatime. The forethought of the Cadbury brothers in moving their factory out of the city and into the park-like grounds of Bournville was much praised, as was their insistence on good hygiene, healthy food and lots of exercise. The chocolate companies had always emphasised the health-giving properties of their products. During the pestilence the belief that a cup of cocoa drunk three times a day served as a protection against disease became even more popular. All in all, Bournville employees fared better than most. Against her better judgement Dorothy had given her brother money, although she suspected he'd spent it at the nearest pub once he'd got back to Birmingham. She'd heard nothing from her family since.

Among the presents under the Christmas tree were beautifully wrapped gifts from the Cadbury family for their chocolate pioneers – thoughtful, practical presents like sewing kits and yards of cloth, pillow slips and handkerchiefs. Dorothy was delighted with the gift Ida gave her – a framed cross-stitch of a pretty village covered in snow.

'The only white Christmas we'll be seeing for a while, bab,' Ida said.

Dorothy gave Ida a small brooch in the shape of an English swallow set with four blue stones. 'To commemorate all the miles we've travelled.'

'Oh, Dot.' Ida hugged her. 'It's beautiful.'

Mrs Rayner's prediction didn't eventuate. Boxing Day burnt as bright and hot as the day before. The waters of the Derwent glistened in invitation from Dorothy's window. Not far from the hostel was a sandy cove fringed with trees. It was perfect for a cooling dip on days such as these. Knowing how to swim was a requirement of employment with the Firm. Dorothy wondered if that would be the case here, on the peninsula surrounded by water. It would be an entirely different proposition learning to swim in the river rather than the men's swimming baths, with its diving board and waterslide, or the heated indoor girls' baths on Bournville Lane.

In the parlour, Lizzie was attempting to cool herself with a small Chinese fan while Ida, Esme and Bessie lounged listlessly, their cheeks flushed with heat.

'I'm heading to the beach for a swim,' Dorothy said. 'Who'd like to come with me?'

Bessie's eyes lit up. 'I'll come.'

'Me too.' Lizzie flicked her fan closed.

'That makes four of us,' Ida said. 'What about you, Esme?' Ida looked to Esme who'd hardly registered Dorothy's presence.

Esme gave a small shake of her head. 'Walking down the hill in the heat, to get covered in sand and them horrible sticky flies, just for a splash in the water and then have to walk back up the hill again and wait in line for a shower bath to wash it all off? I'd rather just have the shower bath.' She waved a hand at Ida. 'You go though. Leave me here all on me own.'

Dorothy would be happy to do just that but she noticed Ida hesitate. 'Come on, bab,' Dorothy said. 'It'll be fun. And you never know, some of the local lads might be there, sunning themselves and showing off their skill at the Australian crawl.' The beach was popular with the locals on a sunny day off. Families gathered with picnics, children squealed and splashed in the shallows and the young men who worked on the farms and orchards did indeed enjoy showing off to any of the young women nearby.

'Well, if you put it like that.' Ida's eyes gleamed. 'I'll go and get changed.'

Dorothy smiled. Ida could never resist a bit of fun.

Esme huffed. 'I guess I'd better come too then.'

On the walk down the gently sloping path to the river, Esme insinuated herself between Ida and Dorothy, dominating the conversation with talk of Fry's and Christmas back home, but once they were at the beach she sat in the shade of a tree while the others swam in the cool river water.

'What a blessed relief,' Lizzie said.

Dorothy wondered if she was referring to the water or to the fact they had escaped Esme for the moment. Only a few weeks earlier Ida had invited Dorothy to the pictures and Dorothy had said yes, expecting it to be just the two of them. It wasn't until she was standing on the front steps of the hostel pulling on her gloves that she discovered Esme was accompanying them. More and more Esme was becoming Ida's shadow. But now she had Ida to herself. She splashed her playfully. 'Race you to the point.'

Ida laughed and splashed her back. 'You know I'm going to win.'

They both swam with a strong breaststroke, the way they were taught at Bournville. Dorothy was in the lead but the thought of Esme waiting on the sand caused her to slow. How easy it would be to make Ida happy by letting her win. By the time they reached the point Ida was the clear winner. Her friend's triumphant cheer was reward enough for Dorothy.

Once the festive season was behind them, the women returned to work – the others to interviewing prospective staff and Dorothy to the factory. A delivery from England awaited her in Block 1. She passed through the factory gates to be met by the constant hammering, sawing and crushing of stone. Her curiosity had drawn her back many times over the previous months. Now that the enrobers had arrived from England she had no need to find an excuse to be here. Her duties included setting up the machines, even while the factory was being built around her.

In Block 1 she ran her fingers along the side of one of the packing crates.

'Won't be long now.'

Dorothy turned at the sound of a male voice. Frank Sutton. Dorothy couldn't help but smile at the sight of him. 'Ah, our sporting hero. I hear you scored a century on Saturday.'

Frank tried to look bashful but Dorothy could see the smile twitching at the corners of his mouth. 'It was an easy pitch.'

Frank was one of the stars of the newly established Cadbury's cricket team. With so many construction workers it hadn't been difficult to field teams – football through the winter and now cricket. 'You led us to victory.' Dorothy tried to subdue the envy in her voice.

'I have every faith you'll be fielding a women's cricket team next season.'

'I hope so. Perhaps I'll find some recruits, once the local girls have settled in.' She missed the familiar feel of the ball between her fingers, the bat in her hand and the camaraderie of her team. It would be almost a year before she'd have the chance to captain a team again and then only if the local girls were keen.

'Let's take a look at the enrobers.' Frank turned to the row of packing crates.

It was strange to be in a factory without the aroma of cocoa and chocolate, sugar, milk and the roasting of cocoa beans. The powerful smell had taken getting used to when she'd first started work at Bournville. Here she was surrounded by the sharp scent of rough stone and cement. 'I miss the smell of chocolate, don't you? Never thought I'd say so, but I do.'

'The cocoa presses have arrived along with the conches. The roasters are ready to go. I know the delays have been frustrating but we'll have you breathing in the scent of home before too long.' Frank levered a piece of wooden planking from one of the crates.

'I'll be glad when the sawdust and rock dust is a distant memory.'

'Even when production is up and running they'll still be working on Blocks 4 and 5.'

'Well, at least the beautiful perfume of Cadbury's Dairy Milk will overpower it all.' Dorothy helped pull away the packing material.

'Now, Mrs Adwell, you know that won't be happening for a while yet.'

'More's the pity.' Cadbury's had an arrangement with Fry's that meant Fry's chocolate would be the first off the production line. 'I'll have to be content with these clever enrobers then.' She ran a hand over the machine they'd just unveiled. She knew every bolt, belt and bearing intimately. The cleverness of the mechanics that carried the centres through a constant flow of chocolate and the engineering that allowed the excess chocolate to be reused was ingenious. It wouldn't be long now until she was showing some of the girls she'd recruited how to operate them.

A crash of wood and a sharp cry pulled Dorothy's attention to the other end of the building where two workers had been removing formwork from the concrete. She and Frank rushed towards the scaffolding. The planks had given way at one end. One of the workers lay on the ground moaning while another crouched beside him.

'What happened?' Frank asked.

'Buggered if I know.' The crouching man glanced up and, seeing Dorothy, mumbled an apology for his language.

'Are you hurt?' Dorothy asked the man on the ground.

'It's me ankle, missus, it's paining me.'

'What's your name?' Frank asked.

'Horrie. Horace Crosswell.'

Frank knelt by the man's feet. 'Are you in pain anywhere else, Horrie?'

He shook his head. 'Nope, don't reckon I am but that ankle hurts like the devil.'

'Let's get this boot off and see what the trouble is.' Frank began undoing the laces.

Dorothy admired Frank's soothing tone and the way he handled Horrie with gentleness and dignity. If she was ever injured, Frank was the one she'd want by her side. She turned her attention to the co-worker. 'Mrs Adwell,' she said, by way of introduction.

'Jack Taylor.' He frowned and turned towards the scaffolding. 'Don't understand it. We was up on this all day yesterday without a worry. The under-foreman himself was about the scaffolding three or four times. We did some heavy work and all.'

'And today?'

'Horrie and I were just doing this bit here.' He pointed to a section of the wooden formwork. 'We'd already dismantled the one beside it. See?'

Dorothy nodded. 'And you didn't notice anything odd about the scaffolding?'

'Like I said, it was fine yesterday. We didn't feel the need to check it this morning. Horrie and I erected it ourselves. We know what we're doing.' A note of defensiveness rose in his voice. 'Never had a problem until now.'

Dorothy examined the two fallen planks. They were still secure at one end but the brace that secured the other was broken. 'You were up there together?'

'Yeah, missus. This scaffold was solid, I'm telling you.'

'Mrs Adwell.' Frank called her. 'We should take Horrie to the site office and get him looked at. I don't think the ankle is broken but he won't be working for a couple of days at least.'

'There goes me wages,' Horrie grumbled. 'And with me missus and eleven kids to feed.'

'Eleven children,' Frank said as he helped Horrie to his feet. 'A cricket team.'

'That may well be, except five of them are girls.'

'That's not a hindrance when it comes to cricket, is it, Mrs Adwell?' Frank grinned at Dorothy.

'None at all, Mr Sutton.'

At the site office Horrie sat with his leg propped up on a chair. Mr Moresby fussed around him while the men stood to one side. 'Hot water,' he said. 'We'll bathe the leg, then disinfect it.'

'We'll need to strap that ankle,' Frank said.

'Yes, yes,' Mr Moresby muttered as he tended to the injury. 'I know what I'm doing.'

'I'm sure you do,' Frank said, without a trace of rebuke.

'We'll strap him up and send him home,' Mr Moresby said. 'You'll be right to catch the train, hey, Mr Crosswell?'

'I'm not sure if the train is the best idea,' Dorothy said. Horrie's face was the colour of milk despite the warmth of the day. 'I'll see if someone can drive him home.'

'You do what you like, love,' Mr Moresby said, disdain dripping from his words. 'Horrie's all right. Good strong man like this is fit enough to catch the train.'

She exchanged a look with Frank before venturing outside to the main entrance. Within minutes a motor lorry approached the gates. She waved it down and made arrangements for the driver to take Horrie home.

'Thanks, Mrs Adwell,' Jack said on her return. He turned to Mr Moresby. 'I'll find the foreman and tell him what happened.'

'Good. I'll make a note of the incident in the log book.' Mr Moresby finished wrapping Horrie's leg and tied off the bandage.

Outside Dorothy and Frank watched the motor lorry leave the site, with Horrie safely inside.

'You would've done a much better job,' Dorothy said. 'That bandage was woeful. It'll come loose within the hour.'

'As long as he stays off that leg he should be all right. But with eleven children I don't like his chances.'

'Horrie will be looked after. The Firm is good at taking care of their own.' At Bournville the workers were provided with sickness, death, old age and unemployment benefits.

'That's true.' Frank rolled his shoulders as if to ease some tension there. 'We'd better get back to those enrobers that fascinate you so much.'

Dorothy laughed. 'I've noticed you're pretty keen on them too.' She and Frank had trained on the new enrobers together at Bournville. Within hours it had been clear Dorothy was as capable as Frank in diagnosing and fixing any problems. To his credit, Frank had never found it threatening. In fact he'd encouraged her. 'Always helps to have a twelfth man, or woman, in your case,' he'd said, in reference to her cricketing prowess. She'd never forget his support when so many men, returned from duty and dismayed by the fact that women had done their jobs while they were gone, had reacted very differently.

On the walk back to Block 1 Dorothy took in the landscape – the trees and even the grass they walked on was still so foreign to her. She missed the forget-me-nots and cornflowers, primroses and buttercups that blossomed in the grounds of Bournville during the English summer. 'What do you miss most, about home?' she asked Frank.

Frank hesitated for a moment and looked up into the almost cloudless blue. 'My brothers. But I'd already been missing one of them for years.'

'That war.'

'That war.'

They walked on, not needing to speak, understanding each other perfectly.

9

Maisie

Late January 1922

As the train turned from the main line towards the Cadbury's factory, Maisie's eyes were immediately drawn to the massive chimney. The sheer height of it intensified the unease in her stomach. Excited as she was to be starting her new job, her doubts resurfaced. What if she wasn't good enough? What if she couldn't get the hang of factory work? Mother's health was little improved and Lily's fourteenth birthday loomed like a dark cloud. She had to succeed in this job. Maisie closed her eyes for a moment as if by doing so she could block out such thoughts. A hiss of steam and the clanking of brakes jolted them open again.

'Here we are,' Pearl said. She was a sweet girl of fifteen years who'd sat next to Maisie when the train had stopped at Newtown. The carriage had been almost empty at the Hobart station but with every stop the numbers had grown until about thirty girls, all of them eager and chatty, surrounded her.

They bundled out onto the platform. The factory buildings loomed large and purposeful, connected with arching walkways high above the ground. Maisie caught a glimpse of water through the gathering throng and turned towards the river and, in the distance, Mount Wellington. Before that day she'd only seen the mountain from the Glebe or in town, where the rock columns of the Organ Pipes stood tall and majestic. Here the mountain was in profile and presented a completely different view. Its massive sloping hulk was a stranger to her. With a shock she realised she'd never been so far from home. Now, after only a little more than half an hour by train, she was in an entirely different world.

At the far end of the platform Mrs Adwell called the girls to her like a mother hen. Maisie followed as she led the group to a wooden building, one of several in a row.

'This is your change room,' Mrs Adwell said. 'Your uniforms and caps are inside. There are lockers for your clothing and belongings.' She opened the door and ushered them inside.

The change room was light and airy with benches, lockers and clothes hooks in neat lines. Once they'd changed, the group gathered outside. All dressed in white, they reminded Maisie of angels in a nativity play. All they needed were wings and haloes.

Mrs Adwell checked that none of them were wearing make-up, jewellery or hair pins. 'We don't want any foreign objects or matter in the chocolate,' she explained.

They moved to the next wooden hut, which contained lavatories, shower baths and basins. 'You must wash your hands when you first arrive in the morning. I'll be checking hands every day before work begins. In addition, make sure you wash your hands after you use the lavatory. No exceptions.'

After their hands were scrubbed clean, Mrs Adwell pointed out another of the buildings. 'This is the female dining hall. Male and female dining is segregated. There will be no intermingling.'

One of the girls uttered a disappointed 'Oh' and a few others giggled.

At the train station earlier this morning, Maisie had been surprised to find herself guided into a carriage that was strictly for girls only. There was even a matron to make sure the men kept to their carriages and the girls to theirs.

'Don't worry,' Mrs Adwell continued. 'There'll be other opportunities to meet your male co-workers.'

'Huzzah,' another girl cried.

'Gertie, please keep your enthusiasm in check,' Mrs Adwell said with a sharp look. 'And tuck your hair into your cap.'

'Yes, Mrs Adwell.'

Maisie turned to see who had spoken. Golden haired and with rosy cheeks, Gertie looked like a cherub. Gertie rolled her eyes and arranged her hair as instructed. She noticed Maisie watching and winked. Maisie smiled back.

Mrs Adwell led them through the main entrance where the girls were dwarfed by the massive buildings surrounding them. A heady scent of sugar, citrus and berry, mingled with the aroma of toffee, caramel and butterscotch drew them forward. Maisie breathed in the magical mix of enticing smells. It was better than Christmas or any of her birthdays.

'This is Block 2, where Pascall's products are made.' Mrs Adwell indicated one of the massive cement structures. 'You'll meet the Pascall's girls in the dining hall at lunch. Say hello and make yourself known. We like to think of Cadbury-Fry-Pascall as one big family.'

'Golly.' Gertie had edged closer to Maisie. 'I'm one of seven kids. I was hoping this job would get me away from being in a big family.'

A few of the girls tittered.

Mrs Adwell turned her attention to Gertie. 'Is there something amusing you, Gertie?'

'No, Mrs Adwell.' Gertie's lips betrayed a suppressed smile.

'Right. Then let's get on. You'll be working in Block 1 but before we head to the covering and piping section I want you to get an understanding of how chocolate is made.'

As they entered the building, the heavy air slammed into Maisie like a tram. It wasn't as she'd imagined a chocolate factory to smell – sweet and delicious. Instead it was harsh and bitter.

Gertie screwed up her face. 'This place stinks,' she said over the constant rumble of machinery. 'I might have to wear a peg on my nose.'

Mrs Adwell called out, 'Follow closely, girls, and don't touch anything.' Maisie noticed the determined set of her shoulders and the way she held her jaw. It must be tricky for a woman not much older than herself to be in charge of so many girls.

Their first stop was at the cocoa bean roasters, large revolving drums where men shovelled in the cocoa beans with spades and others turned them with long paddles. The roasters roared and rattled as the beans tumbled over and over. The group leant in close to catch what Mrs Adwell was saying.

'After roasting, the beans are cracked into nibs.' Mrs Adwell led them through the heat and cloying scent of the beans to an area where the noise intensified even further. 'These grinders liquify the nibs and turn it into what we call mass, as you can see here. Mass is the basis for all our cocoa and chocolate products.'

A brown stream poured from the machine to be collected in a trough below the spout. It might have looked like molten chocolate but it smelt nothing like it. The acidic scent burnt Maisie's nostrils.

Mrs Adwell directed them onwards through the factory, past more machines, troughs, pipes and men in white overalls tending to them all. One of these men stood beside a tall metal structure, which thankfully was not emitting any steam, heat or noise. Next to him was a stack of large brown discs.

'Good morning, Mr Sutton.'

'Good morning, Mrs Adwell. Good morning, ladies. Welcome to Cadbury's.'

A few of the girls giggled and batted their eyelashes. Maisie had to admit he wasn't bad to look at. His dark hair had a fetching wave to it and his nose was finely proportioned. His teeth were a little irregular but his smile was genuine.

Mrs Adwell cleared her throat to regain their attention. 'Mr Sutton, could you explain the workings of this particular machine, please.'

'I'd love to, although, as you can see, it's *not* working at the moment. But not to worry, I'll have the press up and running again in no time.' He tapped the machine with the spanner he held in his hand. 'In the meantime I'll just have to *tell* you how it works. To make cocoa, the mass is squeezed by this press to release the cocoa butter. It trickles into a funnel here.' The funnel was positioned above yet another trough.

Maisie never thought making chocolate would involve so many troughs, pipes and machines. Her treasured memories of carefully opening the paper wrapper and then delicately folding back the foil from her Christmas chocolate were at odds with what she'd seen.

'Excuse me.' One of the girls raised her hand. It was Pearl. 'Why do cocoa beans need so much done to them before we can eat them?'

'That's a very good question,' Mr Sutton said.

Pearl blushed and looked at her feet.

'You might not know this, but cocoa beans aren't like the beans we eat with our mutton and potatoes. They're actually the seed of the cocoa tree. Imagine eating a cherry pit or an apple seed. Would you want to do that?'

The girls giggled. A few of them tried to swish the skirts of their white uniforms before discovering the utilitarian clothing wasn't designed for flirting.

'Fresh cocoa seeds are very unpleasant in taste. They're fermented before they reach us but even so I wouldn't recommend you eat one. How anyone came up with the idea that something delicious might be made from them is beyond me, but I think we're all glad they did, aren't we?'

The girls agreed with enthusiastic nods while Maisie couldn't help but think Lily would have something to add from all her reading about cocoa pods and chocolate.

'Mrs Adwell will show you what happens next, but I guarantee you, without sugar and a lot more grinding and mixing, chocolate would taste more like vinegar than the delicious treat we love.'

'Yuck,' a few of the girls muttered.

'Yuck indeed,' Mr Sutton agreed. 'Now, if you'll excuse me, I need to adjust this cocoa press or our latest trial will be held up even more than it has been already.'

'I'm sure you'll have it working in no time.' Mrs Adwell turned to the girls. 'Mr Sutton knows how to fix every piece of machinery in the factory.'

'As does Mrs Adwell.' He lowered his head towards her in the equivalent of a small bow. Maisie noticed the look that passed between them. It was clear they knew each other well.

'Not quite all,' Mrs Adwell said. 'Thank you, Mr Sutton. We appreciate it, don't we, girls?'

The girls responded with the schoolroom sing-song chant of 'Thank you, Mr Sutton,' reminding Maisie how young most of them were. It could be Lily here, in this group of girls all dressed alike in their white uniforms.

'Because we're only doing trial runs at this stage, many of the machines won't be operational, but you'll get the general idea of what's involved. Follow me.' Mrs Adwell led them past areas that, once the factory was in full swing, would be crowded with workers. 'No dawdling, girls,' Mrs Adwell called behind her. 'We have a busy day ahead.'

Mrs Adwell halted beside a large round contraption. 'This is where the sugar is added to the mass, along with some cocoa butter. The machine is called a mélangeur and it acts, in a way, like a flour mill, except the process takes a lot longer. In time the mixture turns into a dough-like consistency, so much so that it can be removed with a shovel.'

'A shovel?' one of the girls asked with a grimace. Maisie sympathised. More troughs and now shovels.

'The operator rests the shovel here,' Mrs Adwell pointed to the base of the machine, 'and the mixture simply mounds up onto it. Such a clever piece of engineering, as all the machines in the factory are.'

Maisie was curious. Mrs Adwell had told them that this floor was a male domain and they wouldn't be allowed here after this morning, yet she knew so much about all of these machines. Mr Sutton had said she could fix them too. The thought daunted her. If she was to move up the ladder as she hoped, would she need to know all these things?

The girls followed on into an area filled with yet more odd-looking contraptions – long lines of metal containers, each with pipes and spouts, and metal arms. Only two of the machines were working, their metal arms circling endlessly, tended by a man dressed in white.

'Mrs Adwell.' He raised a hand to his forehead in greeting before busying himself at the other end of the row of machines.

'Gather round, girls. This is the last process before the chocolate is pumped upstairs to be moulded into bars and used for covering and piping.' The girls crowded around, lured in part by an aroma more delicious than they'd encountered so far. Mrs Adwell touched the side of the machine with a kind of fondness. 'These are called conches. This is where the magic happens. If you sampled the chocolate at the beginning of the process it would be bitter and gritty, but by the end, a wonderful change occurs. The taste of the chocolate mellows and the texture becomes beautifully smooth.'

Mrs Adwell drew them in closer to show them the mechanism. A large roller pushed the chocolate from one side of the trough to the other. Both ends of the trough were curved and the thick liquid moved over and under the roller in a constant motion. The endless back and forth combined with the smell of chocolate was hypnotic. If not careful, Maisie could find herself slipping into an almost trance-like state.

'Upstairs now, girls.' Mrs Adwell called them to attention. As they followed her up to the next floor the noise and heat dropped away, but the pervasive scent of warm, earthy chocolate accompanied them. The first floor was almost deserted with very little activity. Mrs Adwell pointed out various aspects as they walked through the space. 'Compressor, to get rid of any air bubbles, tempering machines, moulds for chocolate bars, shaking tables, cooling chambers and wrapping stations.'

After the bustle and noise of the ground floor, the relative silence was eerie. The massive space of curved corners and rounded columns all painted white reminded Maisie of the cathedral, in a way. Once the factory was fully operational it would feel very different, she was sure.

'Why aren't many people working in this area?' Maisie asked.

'We're still batch testing and doing trial production runs. Plus the latest batch of chocolate isn't suitable for moulding. It's been prepared with more cocoa butter to make it flow easily for covering and piping. Speaking of which …' she gestured towards another set of stairs, 'it's time to begin your training.'

Upstairs, they arrived in a long light-filled space with large tables lined up in even rows. Tiered racks ran the length of each table and trays of chocolates waited at every workstation. The girls let out a sigh of anticipation almost in unison. Here there was a much more subdued scent of chocolate, one that Maisie could accommodate happily.

Mrs Adwell called for their attention. 'From tomorrow onwards I expect you to be here at your workstation by eight am sharp. Today you'll be assessed for your aptitude with piping. At the start of each working day your hands will be checked for cleanliness and warmth. Surprisingly the temperature of your hands will vary from day to day and you'll be allocated tasks accordingly.'

Maisie waited in line with the others. When it came to her turn Maisie held out her hands and Mrs Adwell checked her palms and fingernails and then gently pressed her fingers and then her fingertips between her own. It was the strangest sensation.

'Nice and cool, Maisie. Perfect for wrapping when the time comes, depending on how the training goes.'

After their hands were checked most of the girls sat on wooden stools at their assigned positions. Mrs Adwell instructed them on how to hold the bag, how to stop the tip from dripping or smudging and the various patterns to be piped on the different chocolates. The other girls were given the task of filling the piping bags from the large pots of melted chocolate. Mrs Adwell's actions were assured and swift while the trainees struggled to keep up. She was patient as she repeatedly corrected their technique. Some of Maisie's lines looked more like swirls and the dots like squiggles. Before long her hands began to ache. She longed to scratch an itch on her nose but they'd been told not to touch their faces while they were working.

When her piping bag was close to empty it was hard not to blob and smear the chocolates.

'Take a pause, girls,' Mrs Adwell said in a commanding voice. 'Here's a good example of what to avoid.' She held up Maisie's piping bag. 'See how low the chocolate is in the bag? Ask for a new bag before the level gets to here.' She pointed to a place just above where the level was in Maisie's bag.

A blush of shame crept up Maisie's neck at being singled out in front of the others. Mrs Adwell handed her a full piping bag and smiled. 'Thank you for serving as a useful example, Maisie. That's how we learn.' She gave the briefest of nods and moved on. 'Back to work, girls.'

After a full day of piping some of Maisie's chocolates looked acceptable and others were a disaster of smudges and blobs. When Mrs Adwell inspected her work she expected to be sacked on the spot. Instead, she merely nodded and moved on.

'Attention, girls.' Mrs Adwell stood in front of them. 'Tomorrow's training will be fork and bowl work, which might be where you're suited. If not, positions in wrapping and packing will be available soon. I'm hopeful we'll have enough chocolate to give one of the enrobers a trial run tomorrow as well.'

'Excuse me, missus.' A voice piped up from the back. 'What's an enrober?'

The expression on Mrs Adwell's face lightened. Maisie thought she noted a trace of pride. 'An enrober is a very clever mechanical device for covering the confectionery centres in chocolate. I'll explain how it works tomorrow. Any other questions?'

'What kind of chocolate have we been using today?' asked a small fair-haired girl whose uniform was smudged in chocolate as was her mouth. 'It don't taste like what I thought it would.'

Mrs Adwell regarded the girls. 'Are there any of you who didn't taste the chocolate?'

Many hands shot up but as Mrs Adwell turned her gaze on them, most of the hands wavered and were slowly lowered. Maisie hadn't been able to resist. Just a small taste. She'd accidentally piped chocolate on her thumb and had licked it off without thinking. It had none of the dark smoothness of Bournville chocolate or the delicious creaminess of Dairy Milk.

'Any thoughts?' Mrs Adwell's eyes weren't unkind but they were sharp. Maisie's heart dropped when her gaze landed on her. She'd rather not stand out from the group but she was keen to please Mrs Adwell. 'Maisie?'

'It's not Bournville,' she said, hesitantly.

Mrs Adwell nodded, encouraging her to continue.

'It's definitely not Dairy Milk.'

'No, it's not.'

'When will we be working with Dairy Milk, Mrs Adwell?' another of the girls asked.

Mrs Adwell's gaze shifted towards the bank of large windows. The light they allowed in was necessary, Maisie had discovered through the long day, to enable the girls to see clearly, especially when it came to piping fine lines. 'All in good time. Fry's chocolate bars will be the first in production.'

Maisie's shoulders slumped. The longed-for taste of her favourite chocolate would remain nothing but a yearning for now. The memory of her father, the Christmas Eve treat and the times when their family was happy, slipped even further away.

10

Dorothy

February 1922

Dorothy sat facing Sarah in the privacy of their bedroom. Her lips and tongue, even her jaw ached a little. But it was worth it. She could hear the change in her accent. Over the past months, with Sarah's patient tutelage, the Brummie was fading from her voice.

'I think that's enough for tonight,' Sarah said. 'Your elocution is coming along very nicely.'

'Thanks to you.' Dorothy was beginning to feel comfortable with these strange sounds in her mouth. Even so, she was still careful to sound more like a Birmingham girl when she was around the other women. Especially Ida.

'Accept the compliment, Dot. You must always take credit for your endeavours. It helps when making your way in the world.'

'Well, then.' Dorothy stood and curtseyed. 'Thank you very much, Miss Harris, for your words of praise.'

Sarah laughed. 'That's more like it. We'll have another lesson tomorrow evening but after that I'll be away for two weeks. I still expect you to practise though.'

Dorothy sat. 'Where are you going?'

'Mr Pascall has meetings with the Chairman of Directors in Sydney and with agents in Melbourne. I'll be taking notes, writing letters, arranging appointments, all the usual bits and bobs. I'm looking forward to seeing Sydney though. Rather more exciting than Hobart.'

'I'm sure.'

'You'll have your own kind of excitement right here though – our room all to yourself, and if you keep it quiet you could take my turn on the bathroom roster as well as your own.' Sarah laughed lightly. 'Have yourself a nice long bath.'

'Great idea.' Dorothy tried to match Sarah's lightness of tone and failed. She would miss Sarah dreadfully.

'The timing of this trip couldn't be better as far as I'm concerned,' Sarah said. 'Remember the accident with the scaffolding? The one you and Frank Sutton witnessed?'

'We didn't witness it exactly, just the aftermath.'

'There's to be an internal inquiry. The Firm wants to make sure all safety measures were followed. If I was here I'd have to take notes. It would be too tiresome for words.'

'An inquiry? Will I be called on?'

'It's been decided as both you and Mr Sutton were there only one of you is needed to give an account. Guess which one?'

'I couldn't possibly.' Dorothy rolled her eyes. Of course a man's testimony was preferable to a woman's.

'Usually I'd object to that kind of bias but honestly I think you're better off out of it. It will be a dull day of pontificating by a room of men full of self-importance.'

'Sounds dreadful. I'll be much happier in the factory with my girls.'

'How are they coming along?'

'Some are doing well. Others seem so young it's hard to believe they're fourteen.' She'd barely been thirteen when she started work at the Firm but she'd lied about her age for so long she'd almost forgotten it herself.

'The Firm likes workers with no factory experience. It means they aren't set in their ways. No bad habits to be broken. Had you worked in a factory before?'

'No.' From the age of eight it had been scrubbing on her knees, her hands raw from the caustic soda, mucking out stalls and all the other filthy jobs no one else wanted. Working in the boot-hole had been a step up. 'None of the girls I've interviewed have worked in a factory. From what I've been told there aren't many factories here.'

Sarah nodded. 'It's one of the reasons the Firm chose Tasmania. That and the lack of industrial action.'

Dorothy was aware of the strategy. It wasn't only the cool climate, the cheap hydro-electricity and the abundance of fresh milk that had cemented the Firm's decision. There had to be something else to make up for the fact that Tasmania was a difficult proposition in terms of freight. The workforce was it.

Sarah shifted forward slightly. 'You were in the bean house last year at the special event when the Chairman of Directors said that Cadbury's have always stood for their happy relations with all those working with them.'

Dorothy nodded warily. She'd left shortly after his speech to look for Thomas. Had Sarah noticed?

'Have you been happy?'

'Very much so.' As a girl she'd heard how well Cadbury's looked after its staff and had been determined to get a job there. She'd turned up at the office in her least patched dress with two good references from her previous employers. The Cadbury's recruiters had wanted to visit her home but after she'd told them her mother had long since passed, they relented. When they'd offered her a job it had felt like a miracle. She suspected the Quakers' charity had much to do with it, but even so she'd been grateful ever since. After her mother had died she'd been taught she was worthless, both at home and at work, until the Cadbury's job changed her and her life. 'And you?'

'The workers here at the factory. Do you think they're happy working for the Firm?'

Dorothy was aware Sarah had dodged her question but moved on. 'I haven't had much contact with the men, except for Frank Sutton, but from what I've seen they all seem content, except for Mr Moresby in the site office.'

Sarah gave a sly smile. 'Yes. He is a mean-spirited little man with an overblown sense of his own importance. He'd be better suited in another position, preferably tucked out of the way. The pump house perhaps.'

Dorothy laughed. Sarah could be wicked sometimes.

'And the girls? Are they happy?' Sarah asked.

Dorothy was aware of the growing pressure at the factory. The girls were struggling with the unfamiliar work and long hours. She'd hoped to recruit a greater percentage of older women who were familiar with routine and, she had to be honest, monotony, but the marriage bar excluded many of them and the war had made widows of others whose days were full of struggle – taking care of their fatherless children and finding work where they could in the corners of their days. Dorothy had met many desperate mothers in the course of the recruitment – all of them pushing their daughters forward, almost demanding they be employed in this factory of hopes and dreams. In contrast, Maisie Greenwood and her mother had exhibited a quiet dignity, despite their circumstances. She couldn't help but feel an affinity with the girl. Maisie's father and her Freddie had died in the same godforsaken trenches of the Western Front in the same year. She wondered if they'd met or at least passed each other in the blood-soaked mud of France. She hugged her arms hard across her chest to quell the ache that blossomed there – the shrapnel in her heart.

Sarah watched her with inquisitive eyes. 'A penny for your thoughts.'

Dorothy brought her focus back to Sarah. 'When the factory is at full production, more than half the workers will be women and girls. The fact that they're not familiar with factory work mightn't be the advantage the Firm was hoping for; only time will tell. As for their happiness?' Dorothy shrugged. 'They have a job and that's better than the alternative. Plus working with chocolate is still a novelty. I'd say, for the most part, they're happy.'

Through the open window, beyond the sloping gardens of the hostel, the river reflected the pink-tinged clouds of sunset. The twilights were long here in the summer. Already there'd been days much hotter than she'd ever experienced in Birmingham. Inside the factory the large windows were perfect for illuminating the workspaces but there had been complaints from the Pascall's girls. The combination of the heat from boiling sugar and the sun pouring through the glass had made the working conditions too hot to bear. Sarah had been well aware of the situation. Changes were made and the complaints stopped.

'Why are you asking about the happiness of the workers?'

Sarah tapped her fingers on her skirt then, as if she'd become aware of what she was doing, stopped. 'Curiosity, that's all. I'm stuck in the office all day in town. Hopefully it won't be too much longer before all the clerical staff move to the offices on site, but until then I have no idea how morale is at the factory, especially with these delays.'

'The directors have said they're pleased with the progress.' Despite their encouraging words, Dorothy knew there was tension. They'd hoped to be in production by Christmas and here they were, halfway through February. Pascall's toffees, butterscotch, mints and fruit bonbons would soon be on shelves around Australia, but the chocolate division lagged.

'Yes, that's what they've said.' Sarah stood. 'I'm going for a walk in the garden to enjoy the last of the evening breeze.' A wicked smile danced on her lips. 'I'll also enjoy a cigarette away from Mrs Rayner's watchful eye.'

Dorothy sat in the growing gloom. She'd become accustomed to having Sarah near. Hers was the first voice she heard when she woke and the last before she went to sleep. The elocution lessons, their secret, had formed a bond between them. She already felt Sarah's absence stretching out before her. It would be a lonely two weeks.

A few days after Sarah had left for Sydney Dorothy joined the other women in the parlour. The Firm had provided a piano for the women's entertainment and they spent many nights gathered around it singing popular music hall tunes. Ida's rendition of 'Burlington Bertie from Bow' was always a favourite, especially when she drew a moustache on her top lip with a piece of charcoal and pretended to twirl it. Tonight the women were singing 'I'm Henery the Eighth, I Am' as Dorothy entered. Lizzie was at the piano while Esme led the women with gusto, swaggering about with a grin that transformed her features, belying the surliness of her usual expression. Dorothy glimpsed another side of Esme during these evenings, an Esme she could possibly like if given the chance.

Ida beckoned her over and linked her arm through Dorothy's without missing a note. Her voice was not the prettiest but the tone was true and she did love to sing. Back at Bournville when they'd both been youngsters in the chocolate wrapping room, Ida would often get the whole lot of them singing. The supervisors didn't mind, in fact they'd encouraged it and often joined in. Dorothy recalled Sarah's question, *Have you been happy working for the Firm?* Cadbury's had always wanted the factory girls to be happy.

The song ended, Esme took an exaggerated bow and the women, including Dorothy, applauded with enthusiasm.

Ida joined Lizzie at the piano, whispered in her ear and then turned to the group. 'At Bournville, back in the day, Dot was known for one song in particular. She hasn't sung it for a good long while, but she promised me when we got to this island down the bottom of the world she'd give it a whirl. We've been here for months now and I reckon it's time.' Ida smiled at Dorothy, her eyes bright with anticipation. 'Dot?'

Dorothy smoothed the hair behind her right ear. Much as she was hesitant, it was time she delivered on a promise to her friend. Ida stepped aside and Dorothy took her place by the piano as the other women settled into their chairs in expectation. Lizzie looked up at her from the piano, a question in her eyes. Dorothy nodded. The music began and she started to sing. The words and the notes came to her as easily as they had when she and Freddie were courting. She closed her eyes and imagined herself back at Bournville at one of the many concerts, Freddie in the back row, the equivalent of the cheap seats, eyes bright with love.

'*The boy I love is up in the gallery,*
the boy I love is looking now at me.'

The song transported her with its yearning and joy wrapped up in the happiness of love and the anticipation of a future together.

'*I haven't got a penny, so we'll live on love and kisses,*
And be just as happy as the birds on the tree.'

A tear made its way from eye to cheek. As the women applauded Ida returned to Dorothy's side. 'Oh, bab, I didn't mean to make you cry.' She pressed a handkerchief into Dorothy's hand.

'All part of the performance, I'll be bound,' Lizzie said. Her voice was warm and tinged with sympathy. 'You have a beautiful voice.'

'Passably good,' Esme grudgingly agreed.

'Bravo,' Bessie said. 'I think your singing is wonderful.'

'There you are.' Mrs Rayner stood at the doorway looking at Dorothy. Mrs Rayner had dined out this evening. Dorothy hadn't seen her since breakfast. 'A letter arrived for you this afternoon.'

Dorothy took it from Mrs Rayner's outstretched hand and examined the envelope. There was no stamp, no postmark, just a neat and faintly familiar cursive addressing the letter to her.

'It was in the letterbox with the afternoon post but it couldn't have been delivered by the postman without a stamp or he'd've asked for money.' Mrs Rayner waited expectantly for Dorothy to open it.

'Thank you, Mrs Rayner.' Slowly she edged a fingernail under the sealed flap. The letter inside was short, more of a note, but the content sent a chill through her.

Dear Mrs Adwell,

I'm sure you know about the internal investigation into Mr Crosswell's unfortunate accident. His fate could have been so much worse. Imagine if he had died. You have something of great value and it would be a shame to lose it.

Yours sincerely,

An admirer

Dorothy tightened her lips. All the women were focused on her and the letter.

'What is it?' Ida asked. 'What does it say? Who's it from?' She pressed closer.

Dorothy folded the letter to hide its contents. She couldn't reveal the threat it contained. Her mind raced to concoct a lie. 'It's just a memo from the Firm about the internal investigation into the scaffolding incident. It confirms I won't be called on to give a statement.' She put the letter in her pocket.

Mrs Rayner humphed. 'No wonder there was no stamp. Must have been sent by messenger.' Her curiosity assuaged, she turned and left.

'I thought it might have been another letter from a potential beau.' Ida pouted. 'A memo? How dull.'

'I'm sure you're relieved you don't have to go to a boring inquiry,' Bessie said. 'Let alone give a statement.'

Esme sneered. 'Don't know what you were doing sticking your nose in other people's business in the first place.' Any warm thoughts Dorothy had for Esme dissolved, leaving her with a familiar antipathy.

'Mind now, Esme,' Margaret said. 'We all know Dot was supposed to be in the factory dealing with the enrobers. It's not her fault the man fell from a scaffold right in front of her.'

'Was it right in front of her?' Esme muttered. 'Or did she go stickybeaking?'

Dorothy bristled. 'What was I supposed to do? Leave an injured man there on the ground, in agony?'

'The way I heard it there was another man there with him, and Frank Sutton too.' Esme pursed her lips. 'You should've left well enough alone, I reckon.'

'Leave off, Esme,' Ida said. 'If it weren't for Dot the poor bloke would've been sent home on the train.'

Esme narrowed her eyes at Ida. 'You gotta choose your battles. Remember that.' She stood and stalked out of the parlour.

Dorothy was rattled by the exchange. No matter what she did, Esme always goaded her but tonight her words had an added edge. 'I had to help,' she said to Ida. 'I had to do something.'

'I know, bab. That's you, always wanting to fix things. But you know what they say, no good deed goes unpunished. You were lucky not to be dragged into the inquiry.' Ida brushed off her dress as if brushing away the unpleasantness. Her features shifted into a wide smile as she turned to the other women. 'What about another song?'

Dorothy tried to sing along as Bessie led them in her favourite, 'Don't Dilly Dally on the Way', but her mind was on the letter in her pocket. She longed to show it to Sarah and to discuss with her the truth of what it contained. But Sarah was many miles and many days away.

11

Dorothy

The following weeks went by in a flurry of training and batch testing. The letter continued to play on Dorothy's nerves. She tried to push the thought of it away but it was like one of the annoying blowflies that sometimes got trapped inside the parlour or dining room, constantly buzzing in her mind.

When she arrived at the hostel after another long and trying day, Margaret called her aside. 'I think this will be of interest to you. The result of the internal investigation about the scaffolding incident has been announced.'

'What was the decision?'

'No blame is attachable to anyone. Cadbury's was not at fault. I'm sure it's a relief to you, as it is to the Firm.'

'Thank you, Miss Stanton.' Dorothy didn't feel relieved. The niggle in her stomach remained.

'Miss Harris has returned from Sydney. She's unpacking as we speak. Please remind her tea will be on the table at six.'

Dorothy rushed up the stairs. Sarah was home at last – the one person she could talk to about this dratted letter. Sarah was hanging a blouse in the wardrobe. Her suitcase sat on the bed, half unpacked.

'Welcome home.' Dorothy took an awkward step forward. Her impulse was to embrace Sarah but she faltered, not knowing how Sarah would respond. 'How was your trip?'

'It was mainly boring business matters.' Sarah returned to her suitcase and shook the creases from a dress Dorothy hadn't seen before.

'New dress? There must have been time for shopping in between the boring business matters.'

'I popped into David Jones when I had a spare moment in Sydney. What a magnificent department store. All the latest fashions.' She held the dress against her body. 'I needed something new for the prime minister's upcoming visit to the factory. What do you think?'

The day dress was in a dusky pink and the calf-length skirt was detailed with panels of a darker pink pattern that was repeated on the sleeves and neckline. 'It's lovely.'

'How marvellous to be able to buy a new dress and not feel guilty. Remember those austerity posters during the war?' Sarah struck a pose. '*To dress extravagantly in war time is worse than bad form, it is unpatriotic.*' She laughed. 'What a relief those days are over.'

'Indeed. But we all had to do our bit.'

'Yes, we all did our bit.' A shadow crossed her face, then Sarah brightened. 'I thought I might be too old for pink, but this particular hue is so sophisticated.'

'And I shall be wearing my Cadbury's whites, as usual.' Dorothy sat on the chair with a feigned weariness.

'Oh, Dot, forgive me.' Sarah draped the dress over her suitcase and sat opposite her. 'Here am I twittering away like a debutante. To be honest, it was wonderful to be on the mainland. Even though

I was working most of the time, I did manage some sightseeing – the tall buildings, the throngs of people, the stunning beauty of Sydney Harbour; it was a dizzying whirl. I shall settle down again soon, I promise, and be back to my level-headed self.'

'I'm afraid I'm in need of your level head right now.'

'Why? What is it?'

'Another letter.' She passed it to Sarah, relieved but also excited to finally share it with her.

Sarah opened it, read in silence and then put it back in the envelope. 'Interesting.' She placed it on the desk next to Dorothy.

'Interesting?' Sarah's response disappointed her. 'You don't think the letter is a veiled threat?'

'Maybe, but it could read like the first letter. An admirer expressing a genuine concern.'

'*Such a shame about Mr Crosswell's accident.*' The words were burnt into Dorothy's memory. '*His fate could have been so much worse. Imagine if he had died. You have something of great value and it would be a shame to lose it.* That sounds like a threat to me.'

'Hmm.' Sarah frowned. 'He, if it is indeed a he, has been very careful.'

'You think it might be a woman?' The thought had never crossed Dorothy's mind.

'May I?' Sarah gestured for Dorothy to give her the envelope. She examined it. 'Once again, no stamp and no postmark.'

'Mrs Rayner said it was in the letterbox with the rest of the afternoon post, but it must've been delivered earlier.'

'Mrs Rayner gave you both letters, didn't she?'

'Yes.'

'Did you see or hear a delivery boy when the first one was delivered that evening?'

'Yes, remember? It was teatime, we were all in the dining room and there was a knock on the door. Mrs Rayner went to answer it.'

'Ah, yes, that's right. Well, that counts her out then. Unless she has an accomplice.'

'Mrs Rayner? You certainly can't suspect her?'

'Suspect everyone. We learnt that during the war. Have you done anything to put her offside?'

'Have you seen her handwriting? It's definitely not a match.'

'You're right. I think we can eliminate Mrs Rayner as a suspect.' A smile danced at the corners of Sarah's mouth.

Dorothy bit back her annoyance. Sarah wasn't taking this seriously. 'Yes, I think that's a safe bet.'

Sarah must have picked up the irritation in her tone. Her expression became one of concern. 'I'm sorry for being flippant. This letter worries you, doesn't it?'

'I think both the letters are meant to unnerve me. Why, I don't know. But it's worked.'

'Let me have another look.' Sarah scanned through the letter again. 'The trouble is there's nothing here that can be construed as a direct threat. The words can be read just as they are, a fervent hope from a keen admirer. We should wait. If it is a threat, he'll make a move at some stage.' Sarah's eyes were distant as if her mind was somewhere else, whirring through the possibilities.

Dorothy had no desire to be a pawn. Or bait. 'What makes you so sure?'

Sarah returned her focus to Dorothy. 'You're aware of the spies that infiltrate the Firm back home.'

'Yes.' Competition between the chocolate-makers was fierce. Spies posing as employees constantly tried to steal secrets, manufacturing techniques and recipes from rival companies. Cadbury's had become highly protective of its recipes and chocolate-making processes to the extent of employing detectives to keep an eye on the workers. She wasn't sure how much her girls back at Bournville knew about it, even though it had been reported in the newspapers. Dorothy had been kept informed because of her position as a Forewoman B.

'And you know about the agreement Cadbury's has with Fry's, that Fry's chocolate will be manufactured first.'

'Of course.'

'It's strategic in many ways. To most people it looks like a move designed to appease Fry's but the Firm wants to hold back. They need to know the lay of the land – to see whether spies will infiltrate the factory here as they do back home.'

'Is that why Dairy Milk is being delayed?' Dairy Milk's domination of the market had sparked a frenzy of activity from the chocolate spies. The manufacturing process was off limits to all but the most loyal workers. Strict and punitive confidentiality agreements had been put in place, and the recipe itself was kept in a vault.

'It's too much of a risk, not only because of the British companies but also the local confectioners like MacRobertson's and Hoadley. They've become used to having the lion's share of the market. Naturally they're hostile to three giants of the confectionery industry setting up in their territory. Think what they could do if they got hold of the Dairy Milk recipe.'

'Hostile?' The hairs on the back of Dorothy's neck prickled.

Sarah leant forward in a conspiratorial manner. 'Not only that, Pascall's might be after it as well.'

A shocking thought crossed Dorothy's mind. 'Is that why you were given the position as Mr Pascall's private secretary? To keep an eye on him?' Before his promotion, Wilfred Pascall had been the manager of Pascall's chocolate section for many years.

Sarah laughed lightly. 'You have an overactive imagination, Mrs Adwell. Mr Pascall's previous private secretary was genuinely unwell and couldn't complete the journey from England. I was asked to fill the position, being the most senior secretary.'

'I'm sorry. It's just we were talking about spies and—'

'It's all right.' Sarah waved her apology away. 'With all those spies sneaking about at Bournville, it's easy to get carried away.' She stood. 'I'm ravenous. I must finish unpacking before the other women eat all our tea.'

'It's Mrs Brown's fish pie tonight. I'll save you a slice.' It was one of Sarah's favourites.

As Dorothy descended the stairs to the dining room, she thought over their conversation. Sarah had assuaged her concerns in some ways and heightened them in others. The most worrying one being that, despite her belief to the contrary, they hadn't left the chocolate spies behind at Bournville.

When Dorothy had committed to coming to Tasmania, she knew her work would be cut out for her. A brand-new factory staffed with girls unfamiliar with the work would see her capabilities stretched to their limits. What she hadn't expected was the enormous interest in the enterprise from all quarters and how that would impact on her days. Every business association, school group and politician, including the prime minister, wanted to visit the factory. This morning over one hundred men from all around the country, in Hobart for the conference of Associated Chambers of Commerce, were the Firm's guests, along with their wives. Once again Dorothy had been asked to put aside her normal duties to act as a tour guide. She wasn't alone – Ida had been roped in as well, along with several of the men.

After the group had seen the boiler house, Mr Cooper gave a short speech about how the factory would employ at least 600 Tasmanians once it was at full capacity. When the round of applause faded, one of the visitors stepped forward.

'I have a question about your Babcock and Wilcox boilers. I thought the factory ran on hydro-electric power. Isn't that one of the main reasons the company chose Tasmania, because of the cheap hydro-electricity?'

'Good point,' Mr Cooper answered. 'Hydro-electric power will be the main motive force, but steam is also necessary for certain purposes.'

Dorothy sensed someone standing very close behind her. 'I heard the government gave you free electricity,' a low voice muttered.

She tensed. Surely he wasn't speaking to her.

The man edged even closer. 'Free electricity, paid next to nothing for the land, and no duty on the machinery you're bringing in. It's a disgrace.'

His voice was so quiet that his words must be meant for her ears alone. Dorothy took a step forward to gain some space between them and turned. He was of medium height and dressed, as were all the men, in suit, tie and hat, but his Homburg was pulled down well over his eyes. The only visible feature was his mouth.

He sneered. 'Special treatment, all kinds of incentives, anything to get you foreigners here.'

Dorothy bristled. 'I beg your pardon?' It was assumed that any visitors would be excited about the factory. Instead this loathsome man was trying to intimidate her.

'It's the local confectionery companies that are going to suffer. You lot come out here with all the back-door deals the government has given you and undercut the Australian firms. The local confectioners have worked hard for years to establish their markets. This will destroy them.'

Dorothy's heartbeat quickened. Sarah had talked about this very thing. He must be involved somehow with one of the companies she'd mentioned, MacRobertson's perhaps. 'If you have concerns, I suggest you take them to one of the directors.'

His laugh was a mocking bleat. 'I don't think they'd like what I have to say. Mark my words, there'll be trouble.' He turned on his heel and pushed his way through the crush.

Dorothy stood, stunned, and watched him go. The crowd moved around her but she remained, her mind racing. Who was he and why had he targeted her?

'Bab,' Ida called out. 'What are you doing just standing there like a gawby? We're off to the bean store for the next part of the tour.' She beckoned her and strode off.

Dorothy followed the group, but her thoughts remained with the man. He'd been intimidating, threatening even. The thought stopped her in her tracks. Could he be the one who'd written the letters? Instantly she was on her mettle, searching him out in the crowd. All the men wore similar suits and hats. She tried to recall his features but all he'd revealed was his mouth and part of his nose. To add to that, their exchange had been so unexpected – shocking even – the small glimpse she'd had was a blur.

Throughout the tour Dorothy scanned the crowd for the man but every time she thought she'd spotted him she couldn't really be sure. Even if she was, what could she do about it? If she confronted him he'd deny her accusations. No one else had heard their conversation, he'd made sure of it.

When the group reached the Pascall's section, it was Mr Pascall's turn to give a speech. As always at these events, Sarah stood slightly behind him dressed in a smart tailored skirt and jacket, looking perfectly at ease. Mr Pascall then invited the guests to test the caramels, toffees and a host of other sweets that had made his firm world famous. The crowd wasn't shy and filled not only their mouths but their pockets. Dorothy hoped to talk with Sarah but she never left Mr Pascall's side.

At the end of the tour came more speeches. Dorothy took the opportunity to watch the crowd, hoping for a glimpse of the man. The president of the conference was first to speak. 'We are all delighted with the wonderful progress,' he said. 'The metal market might fail, and the bottom fall out of the produce market, but knowing the taste of the Australian public, nothing is more certain than that the future of this industry is very sweet indeed.'

The crowd laughed in appreciation. Dorothy made her way to join Ida to get a different view of the crowd.

The president continued. 'When a company is prepared to spend from £300,000 to £500,000 in a venture, as our hosts are doing, they take a very big risk, and they thoroughly deserve the success which everyone wishes them.'

When the applause died down a mischievous sparkle lit his eyes. 'I noticed all the jaws were working during the tour, but not the tongues. In fact I told Mr Wilfred Pascall, in strict confidence, that he should change the name of his confections to Lady Quieteners.'

Ida rolled her eyes. 'It was the men who were chobbling the toffees, much more than the wives,' she whispered.

The Chairman of Directors, in Hobart for meetings, was next to take the floor. He made the usual niceties of thanking the president for his kind tribute and the Chambers of Commerce for the honour of visiting. Then he cleared his throat and shifted his stance. There was something about the change in his countenance that made Dorothy instantly alert.

'There is one thing I would like to say.' He eyed the crowd. 'In case some of you haven't read the mainland trade papers on the subject, Cadbury-Fry-Pascall are in gross conspiracy with the State Government and Federal Customs to establish our industry here.'

A shocked stillness fell upon the gathering. Dorothy was appalled by his words. It was just as the horrid man had said. Was it true? Had the Firm received under-the-table deals to establish the factory?

The chairman smiled and relaxed. 'Why, everyone has gone out of their way to bestow gifts upon us.' He raised his hands in mock wonderment. 'The State Government has even given us a railway, free.'

The crowd laughed as did Dorothy, as much in relief as anything else. He was joking.

'As for the land,' he continued, 'I don't know where we got that but I suppose someone must have given it to us also.' He chuckled.

The laughter grew but then his expression grew grave once more. 'In all seriousness, I want to stress that Cadbury-Fry-Pascall has asked for nothing more than it is entitled to and has not received anything more than anyone else. Cadbury-Fry-Pascall does not want the people of Tasmania to look on us as outsiders. We are, are we not, all British.'

At these words Dorothy watched the crowd. Surely the man who was so angry about foreigners invading Australian shores would take umbrage at this and betray himself. But no, the only response from the crowd was a cry of 'Hear, hear,' and more applause.

After the visitors left on the special train the company always supplied for such events, Ida linked her arm through Dorothy's. 'Ee-yar, bab. Another tour over. Another group of men who love the sound of their own voices. Lady Quieteners? I reckon there's more of a market for Boring Speech Quieteners.'

Dorothy laughed. 'That's true. My ears need a rest after all those speeches. I'm going to sit by the river for a while. How about you?'

'I'm going back home, to rest my weary feet and see what Mrs Brown is cooking for tea. Hopefully she's making her famous apricot pudding and I'll get to lick the bowl.' She gave Dorothy one of her mischievous smiles. 'Tara-a-bit.'

'Tara-a-bit.' Dorothy repeated the Brummie farewell and waved Ida goodbye, grateful for some time to collect her thoughts. Even though the sun was low in the sky, there was still warmth in the air and plenty of time to get back to the hostel before dark. She wandered to the riverbank to the spot where a large rock formed a natural seat and replayed the course of the afternoon – the words the man had said to her and the rebuttal the Chairman of Directors had given at the end of the tour. The chairman's defence of the company had been well executed but even so the accusations must be commonplace for him to have to make such a speech. The crowd had cheered but clearly there were some who thought differently.

Dorothy had been led to believe that the Firm would be welcomed with open arms. After all, it was providing employment and an economic boost to Tasmania. But Sarah was right. There were some who didn't want them here and those, like that man, who'd make trouble. Was that what the letters were about? Were they meant to intimidate her so that she'd think twice about staying? She picked up a pebble and tossed it into the river, watching the ripples disperse in ever larger circles. How far would those ripples travel? Would they reach the bank of the opposite shore, or travel down the Derwent to Hobart? Would they, by some miracle, cross the ocean to England and then through the system of rivers and canals to Birmingham and Bournville? She picked up another pebble. When she left Bournville she'd known her life would be very different in Tasmania but she hadn't expected this sense of isolation. The factory was miles away from Hobart, hundreds of miles away from the thriving cities Sarah had described on the mainland, and thousands of miles away from home. There were few opportunities to meet other people and the sense of camaraderie she'd expected to grow among the women in the hostel hadn't eventuated, at least not on the level she'd hoped for. Even her friendship with Ida had begun to feel tenuous. She was aware of a growing bond between Ida and Esme but was at odds to understand it. Thank goodness for Sarah. Apart from their friendship, Dorothy had come to depend on her in ways she could never have imagined. She let the pebble fall to the ground. Later this evening, when they were alone in their room, she'd tell Sarah she was almost certain the man who'd sent the letters was a member of the tour. Dorothy stood, brushed off her hands and turned towards the hostel. She had a plan and Sarah was the only one who could help her.

12

Maisie

The girls lined up in nervous rows under the scrutiny of Mrs Adwell. She was being especially strict about their appearance and cleanliness. 'Remember, girls, the prime minister is not royalty, you don't need to curtsey.'

Gertie whispered in Maisie's ear, 'But I bet he'd like it if we did.'

Maisie shushed her while suppressing a smile. Gertie was getting a reputation for being cheeky but Maisie couldn't help liking her.

'If he addresses you, which I doubt, you're to call him prime minister, is that understood?'

'Not Your Highness then?' Gertie asked. The girls laughed.

'No, Gertie, not Your Highness.' Mrs Adwell raised a stern eyebrow then turned her attention to the group. 'Now, all of you, settle down.'

Mrs Adwell's accent was plummier than usual. Maisie had noticed it shift and change through the past few weeks. She'd also noticed Mrs Adwell's accent take on a lilt more like its original form when she was with the other Bournville women in the factory or the dining hall. It was a curious thing.

'He'll be touring the factory, accompanied by his wife and daughter,' Mrs Adwell continued. 'The premier will also be with him, and the mayor.'

'Golly,' Gertie whispered to Maisie. 'What a lot of toffs. They'll all feel at home in Block 2.'

'Pascall's? Why's that?' Maisie whispered back.

'Because that's where all the toff-ees are.' Gertie giggled and Maisie hid her burst of laughter by pretending to cough.

'What is it, girls?' Mrs Adwell's keen eye fell upon them.

'We're just a bit nervous, Mrs Adwell, with all these posh people coming in today,' Gertie said. 'Our piping might come out as shaky squiggles.'

'Then you'll both be filling piping bags today.'

'Sorry,' Gertie mouthed at Maisie. The two of them would be at the beck and call of the other girls. If they weren't quick with a freshly filled piping bag there'd be trouble.

Maisie shrugged to show there were no hard feelings.

Mrs Adwell went along the line of girls doing her daily hand check but when it came to Maisie's turn Mrs Adwell surprised her. 'Maisie, you'll be on the enrobers this morning.'

'Pardon?' Truth be told, Maisie would've been a lot happier filling piping bags. The enrobers were strange machines that made most of the girls skittish, never having experienced anything like them. When it had been Maisie's turn she'd listened carefully, watched closely and got on with the job. It wasn't difficult, just a bit fiddly to get the centres lined up properly on the wire trays before they rumbled on their way through the waterfall of chocolate.

'With the prime minister here today, it's important to make the best possible impression. I'm putting you girls where your skills are strongest. Maisie, you've shown great aptitude with the enrobers. We'll only be running one of them today, as an example for the prime minister, and you'll be in charge.'

'Me?' Maisie was horrified.

'I have every confidence in you. I'll set up the enrober and make sure it's running properly before I leave to accompany the prime minister's entourage through the covering and piping division. We'll end with a demonstration of the enrober.'

Maisie's heart sank at the thought of being in charge of the intimidating machine while Mrs Adwell was elsewhere in the factory.

'Right then.' Mrs Adwell nodded once as if sealing the deal and moved on.

Word reached the enrobing department in a rush of excitement – the prime minister had arrived and was beginning to make his way through the different areas of chocolate production. Maisie's pulse raced. The demonstration of the enrober was to be his last port of call, designed to illustrate the future of chocolate making. Maisie steadied herself. She had to set a good example to the four other girls assigned to the enrober. Two of them fed the centres into the machine and two at the other end used fine metal implements to press, prick or swirl a pattern on each of the covered chocolates before Maisie removed the trays to place them in racks to cool. She was also responsible for the smooth running of the operation and helping where needed. Although all of them were clearly nervous, the process was working as it should. Maisie eased her shoulders to release the tension there. They just needed to do as they'd been instructed and soon this trial would be over.

A horrible grinding noise broke Maisie's concentration. She'd never heard anything like it, not even downstairs where the cocoa beans were ground into liquid. Confused, she looked up from her work to see the enrober shudder to a standstill. Maisie stared at the machine in mute terror. The other girls turned to her with frightened eyes.

'What should we do?' Pearl gasped.

Maisie tried to think. She'd been taught how to use the enrober and how to correct small mishaps, but not what to do if anything major happened. This was major. Maisie forced herself to focus. The prime minister was probably in the conching area by now, which meant he still had the moulding and wrapping department, the fork and bowl section, and the hand piping room ahead of him.

She turned to Charlotte, who was wringing her hands and on the verge of tears. 'Do you remember Mr Sutton? He was in cocoa pressing when we did our tour and talked to us about how bad cocoa beans taste before they're turned into chocolate.'

Charlotte nodded, blinking. 'He was lovely.'

'I need you to run and find him.' She remembered Mrs Adwell saying Mr Sutton could fix any of the machines in the factory. He'd said the same about her but with the dignitaries heading towards Mrs Adwell's department she wouldn't be able to help.

'Where will he be?' Charlotte's voice trembled.

'Go to the mélangeurs. Someone there will know where he is.'

'But we're not allowed in there.'

'This is an emergency. If anyone objects, tell them to come and talk to me. Quickly now.'

Charlotte skittered off and Maisie turned her attention to the enrober. The other girls hovered nearby.

'Could we try and get one of the other machines going?' Pearl asked.

'There's not enough time. We'd have to redirect the chocolate through the pipes and I don't know how to do that.' There were so many things she didn't know. 'I'm sure once Mr Sutton gets here he'll fix it in no time.'

Maisie tried to start the mechanism again. Nothing. She checked the belts for snags and blockages but couldn't spot any. Chocolate slowly dripped onto the centres in the machine. All of them would be ruined. Thank goodness the chocolates that were already covered were all right. They'd make a pretty offering to the dignitaries when they arrived. The ongoing batch trials meant there were always plenty of chocolates for guests as well as the staff. Maisie had never thought she'd tire of the taste of chocolate but after a month of working at Cadbury's she was becoming blasé. Lily was always excited though when Maisie came home with a few chocolates.

Maisie glanced at the clock on the wall, the second hand ticking ever onwards. Where was Mr Sutton? She stared at the enrober, willing it to give up its secrets. The trouble was there were so many moving parts that weren't moving at the moment. She bobbed down to look under the contraption. Perhaps something had become dislodged.

'Right, what seems to be the problem?'

Maisie startled, banging her head on the side of the enrober as she stood. Blinking away sudden tears, she faced Mr Sutton. He was calm but concerned.

'Are you all right? Miss ...?'

'Greenwood. Maisie Greenwood.' Maisie resisted rubbing the sore spot on her head. 'I'm all right, Mr Sutton, but the enrober isn't. There was a grinding noise and the whole thing came to a stop.'

'Ah.' Mr Sutton moved to the side of the machine. 'Right.' He began to tinker with the cogs and wheels of the mechanism. 'One of the cogs has jammed ... yes, here it is.' He talked as he worked. 'I just need to align it. And this nut here ...' He used a small spanner to tighten the offending nut. 'There we go.' He stepped back, took a clean rag from his overall pocket and wiped his hands. He turned to Maisie. 'Would you do the honours, Miss Greenwood?' He indicated the switch.

Maisie turned it, hoping with all her might that the enrober would start. The machine juddered, rattled and then began behaving as it should. A flood of relief made her momentarily dizzy. Mrs Adwell had put her trust in Maisie. If she'd failed, and she'd come close, she might have been permanently relegated to filling the piping bags.

'Thank you, Mr Sutton.' Tears of gratitude pricked at her eyes. 'You've saved the day.'

Mr Sutton smiled. 'Hardly. I should have double checked. There's been so much to do today for the prime minister's visit, I don't know whether I'm coming or going.'

Mr Sutton was very different from any young man she'd met before. He had a steady air about him that was reassuring. 'Can you stay? Just in case it happens again?'

Mr Sutton's smile faded. 'I'm sorry, Miss Greenwood.' He looked genuinely remorseful. 'But the enrober should run perfectly for the rest of the day. This is what test runs are for. To iron out the faults.'

Maisie pressed her lips together What a pity this fault had to make itself known today, of all days.

'Maisie?' Charlotte called. 'I need help getting the centres lined up.'

'Of course.' Regretfully she left Mr Sutton's side. 'Thank you again.'

He gave her a smile and headed off to work another of his miracles elsewhere in the factory.

In the dining hall at lunchtime all the talk was of the prime minister's visit. Charlotte told the others of the near disaster with the enrober and how Mr Sutton had saved the day.

'Oh, Mr Sutton,' sighed a few of the girls, one of them even placing a hand to her heart.

'Your knight in shining armour.' Gertie winked at Maisie. 'What a shame he doesn't have a white steed. I suppose his white overalls will have to do.'

Maisie kept her head down and focused on her lunch.

'Mrs Adwell did all the talking when the PM came to look at the enrober,' Pearl said. 'She knows an awful lot about how everything works. She impressed him no end, as did the enrober.'

'As much as Mr Sutton impressed you, Maisie?' Gertie teased.

'I was very grateful,' Maisie said. The enrober had worked perfectly for the rest of the morning, thank goodness. Without Mr Sutton it would have been a disaster. She'd like to thank him again but she'd have to come up with a reason to search him out. The separate dining halls for men and women made an accidental meeting almost impossible.

'I heard the prime minister spent a lot of time in the Pascall's section,' Pearl said.

'Yes, I heard that too,' Gertie said. 'Let's find out why.' She called one of the Pascall's girls over to their table and made a space for her to sit down. 'This is Helen. We catch the train together.'

'Hello.' Helen smiled and nodded at her attentive audience.

'Tell us all about the PM,' urged Gertie. 'Why was he in your part of the factory for so long? Was he flirting with you?' She nudged Helen's arm.

Helen laughed. 'He was eating caramels. Lots of caramels. It was so funny. He'd get asked a question but couldn't answer because he had one in his mouth so he'd chew really quickly, answer the question, then pop another in. I've never seen a man eat so many caramels! Then he had the nerve to tell everyone, including the journalists, that he'd eaten so many he didn't want to see another caramel for weeks.'

'Oh, dear,' Gertie said. 'We all know what tomorrow's headline is going to be, don't we?'

The other girls looked at her with wide eyes. 'What?' Charlotte asked.

Gertie raised her hands and pressed the air for each word as she said it. 'Prime Minister Never Wants to Eat Another Pascall's Caramel.'

Helen punched Gertie's arm lightly. 'Oh, Gertie, you are dreadful.'

Maisie laughed while some of the younger girls looked perplexed. 'She's joking,' she explained.

'Actually, I think the journalists were rather impressed.' Helen tilted her head to the side with a smug little smile. 'I mean with Pascall's being in full production and all.' She pouted dramatically. 'What a pity Cadbury's is dragging its feet. It would've been such a let-down for the prime minister, don't you think?' She looked around the table with an innocent expression.

The girls' faces dropped. Everyone had been working as hard as they could.

'Oh, Helen.' Gertie's expression matched her friend's, wide-eyed and innocent. 'How wonderful it is that Pascall's sweets are so easy to make. I mean anyone can make toffee and caramels at home, can't they? But chocolate? Has anyone ever heard of being able to make chocolate at home?' She looked around the table. 'No?'

Maisie sat back, enjoying Gertie's performance. She'd wanted to rush to Cadbury's defence and to reassure the girls who looked so crestfallen, but Gertie was doing a much better job of it.

'I didn't think so,' Gertie continued. 'There are so many processes involved, complicated processes.' She leant towards Helen, who, it must be said, was taking Gertie's teasing in good humour. 'So complicated, not to mention detailed, intricate and prone to disaster.'

Gertie cocked an eyebrow at Maisie. 'Why even today we've heard about the enrober causing no end of problems.'

Maisie played along by nodding gravely. 'It's true. Everything about making chocolate is so very *complicated*. From the roasting of the beans, to the cracking and winnowing, the grinding to make cocoa mass. There's the mélangeurs and the conching that goes on for days. Covering and piping take skill and I haven't even started on the wrapping and boxing.'

Gertie threw her hands up in mock horror. 'You see, Helen. So complicated.' She lowered her hands and patted her friend on the arm in a patronising fashion. 'But toffees? Anyone can make a toffee.'

Helen nodded with a slow sarcasm. 'Thank you for explaining it to me. I see now that making chocolate is very ... complicated. Which is why this is such a miracle.' Slowly she drew something from out of her pocket and placed it on the table.

Gertie gasped in mock horror. 'Traitor. Get rid of that chocolate immediately.'

'Oh, I will. I'll make it disappear completely.' Helen's eyes gleamed with mischief. 'By eating it.' She slowly unwrapped the bar of MacRoberton's Old Gold chocolate, broke off a piece and popped it in her mouth. 'Mmm. Delicious.'

Maisie watched with curiosity. Old Gold was extremely popular, especially since Dairy Milk had disappeared from the shops. She'd tried it one Christmas but it hadn't appealed.

'Honestly, Helen, why on earth would you bring chocolate to a chocolate factory?' Gertie asked.

'Because I don't work in a chocolate factory,' Helen replied. 'I work in a factory that makes toffees and caramels, which anyone can make at home, as you have so kindly pointed out.'

'But there's always chocolate available in the dining hall, for free,' Charlotte said, genuinely puzzled. 'Why would you buy it?'

'Ah yes, the mistakes, the trial batches and the practice runs. I did try some once. To be honest, I didn't care for it. All that work, all those complicated stages, and that's the result?' Helen waved her hand dismissively. 'Hardly worth the effort.' She broke off another piece of Old Gold and chewed it slowly.

'It's Fry's chocolate,' Maisie said. 'Not Cadbury's.' She felt a loyalty to Cadbury's even though she was disappointed they weren't making Dairy Milk yet.

'I must say, Helen,' Gertie turned to her friend, 'I do like a Fry's Chocolate Cream.'

'To each their own.' Helen shrugged. 'But I'm a patriot. I much prefer the confectionery that's made here on our own shores. The Poms have nothing on our chocolate or sweets. Old Gold isn't Australia's favourite for nothing. And what about Hoadley? Who doesn't love a Violet Crumble, eh?'

'Ooh, I do love them,' Pearl squeaked, then bit her lip with a guilty expression.

'I agree, Helen,' Gertie said with a poker face. 'About everything you've said.'

Helen looked at her in surprise. 'You do?'

'Absolutely. Us Australians make much better sweets than the Poms. I mean, just look at Allen's. Their sweets are all dinky-di Aussie, and, as you've just told us, are far superior in every way to Pascall's.'

Maisie couldn't help but be impressed. If Gertie and Helen had been playing chess, this would be checkmate in Gertie's favour. A range of expressions crossed Helen's face as if she was battling to decide how to respond. It must be clear to her she'd been outwitted. Finally Helen slapped her hand down on the table. 'You're too clever by half, Gertie Thompson. Well played indeed. But I'll have the last laugh.'

'In what way?'

'I'm only working here to save money to move to Melbourne as soon as I'm old enough.'

'Why would you move there?' Maisie asked.

'I'm going to get a job at MacRobertson's.' Helen bit into her final piece of Old Gold.

'MacRobertson's?' Gertie exclaimed. 'Why haven't you told me about this before?'

Helen glanced at the girls around the table then looked over her shoulder and back again. She quickly swallowed her mouthful of chocolate. 'I was going to keep it under my hat and now I'm asking you lot to as well.'

Maisie could see the worry in Helen's eyes. She'd been backed into a corner by Gertie's quick wits and had spilt the beans in an attempt to regain the upper hand. Now she was regretting it.

Helen spoke in almost a whisper. The others leant in to hear. 'My dad says MacRobertson's is the way to go. Much better than the muck made in this factory. The only reason the Cadbury's mob is here is because of all the tariffs us Aussies put on the Poms.'

'What's a tariff?' asked one of the younger girls.

'It's kind of like a wall that stops things from coming into Australia,' Maisie explained. She'd read about it in the old newspapers that were dropped off with Mrs Collin's ironing. Before cutting them up for the outhouse she always read the main stories, scanning them for any mention of Cadbury's.

'A wall?' Charlotte asked.

'Yes, it makes things made in other countries more expensive so it's hard for us to afford them. That way we're forced to buy locally made things.' It was one of the reasons her favourite chocolate had been impossible to buy. She found it hard to like a government who'd deprive people of their small pleasures.

'Our stuff is better anyway.' Helen tucked the Old Gold wrapper into her pocket. 'My dad says we don't need any of that inferior rubbish from overseas.' She pushed back her chair and stood. 'It's been lovely, ladies. Good luck with the chocolate.'

Maisie watched her return to the girls at the Pascall's table. Helen said something that made them laugh and look over. She was probably saving face at the expense of her girls. Her girls? Maisie looked around the table at the young faces, most of them only a few months older than Lily. While Helen had been talking, a need to protect them had risen within her. She'd been pained to see the hurt and confusion on their faces. They'd been so excited about the prime minister's visit and Helen had robbed them of it. 'What a morning,' she said, pasting a bright smile on her face. 'I know the prime minister and all the other dignitaries were very impressed with everything they saw today.'

'Really?' Charlotte's voice was tentative.

'Yes. We should all be very proud.'

'Too right,' Gertie said. 'Anyone who says different is just jealous.' She leant close to Maisie and lowered her voice. 'I don't actually like Helen all that much, she's always going on about what her dad thinks. Some of it is rather unpleasant but she agrees with it all.'

A tightness in Maisie's chest eased a little. She'd thought Gertie and Helen were best chums. 'I'm glad. I don't like her much either.'

'But I know who you *do* like.'

'Who?' Maisie was happy to play along.

'Mr Sutton.' Gertie gave her a quick wink and, before Maisie could respond, stood and addressed the table. 'I'll see you lot back in the land of covering and piping. Remember, if you need your piping bag filled, I'm at your beck and call. But first, the loo.' With a grin she saluted and marched away.

13

Dorothy

March 1922

Dorothy caught up with Sarah as they made their way up the stairs to their room after a day's work. 'How did you go comparing the guest lists?' When Dorothy had talked to her about the incident with the man from the Chambers of Commerce, Sarah had agreed to Dorothy's plan to track him down. Dorothy was certain he was responsible for the letters and therefore must have been at the first tour of the factory back in October.

'I haven't had much luck, I'm afraid.' Sarah opened the door to their room, looped her handbag over the back of the chair and shucked off her shoes. 'There were no two names the same on the invitation list from last year and the Chambers of Commerce visit.' She sat on her bed and rubbed her toes. 'These dratted shoes do pinch a bit.'

Dorothy sucked in her cheeks. She'd been so certain. 'Not even two names that were similar?'

'It confirms what I suspected. I don't think the man who spoke to you is the same person who wrote the letters.'

'Why not?' Dorothy sat down beside Sarah.

'The letter writer prefers to stay in the shadows. It wouldn't suit him to approach you in public. The man from the Chambers of Commerce was nasty, there's no doubt, but from what he said to you I don't think he's local. From Melbourne most likely, where the main confectioners are, and looking to stir up trouble. A horrible toad of a man, but not our letter writer – he definitely has his feet on the ground here and has more style.'

'Is that what you call it? Threats and intimidation. Style?'

'I'm sorry you've been targeted but I'm not surprised.'

'What do you mean?'

Sarah studied her for a moment as if she expected Dorothy to answer her own question then gave a small shrug. 'You're a strong, independent woman in a position of importance. You've got where you are through hard work, intelligence and grit. You should be proud.'

Sarah's words were almost overwhelming No one had ever described Dorothy in such a way. It was all she could do to utter a breathy, 'Thank you.'

'It makes me wonder what other ambitions you harbour.' Sarah's voice was languid. She'd tossed off the remark almost carelessly. Even so, Dorothy stiffened. It was as if Sarah knew her too well.

'I was hand-picked to come to Tasmania and given a promotion to Forewoman A; isn't that enough to fulfil anyone's ambition?'

'You tell me.'

Dorothy hesitated. The words were on the tip of her tongue. When George Cadbury Junior had asked her to consider coming to Tasmania it was as if a dazzling future had opened up before her. She could see her destiny. A brand-new factory required a brand-new board. She knew she'd have to bide her time, prove her worth and be strategic, but eventually she hoped to achieve her ultimate desire. Dorothy Cadbury was the only woman on the board at Bournville, but without the aid of a certain surname Dorothy had no chance. But in the colonies? That was a different matter. She pressed her lips together. It was too soon to give voice to such a grand ambition. It was one she'd have to keep close and nurture until the time was right. 'I think so, yes.'

'Well then, congratulations on achieving your dreams.' Sarah's voice was warm but Dorothy was aware of an undertone of disbelief. Sarah stretched her neck and stood. 'Time to put my uncomfortable shoes back on and head down for tea, don't you think?'

'Ladies, I have an announcement.' Margaret addressed the women as they finished their corned beef and white sauce. All faces turned towards her. Margaret had become more officious over the past months, was often curt and appeared ill-rested. She began her announcement but was interrupted by an almighty shriek. Lizzie shot up, her chair toppling behind her, and pointed at the wall behind Margaret's head.

Bessie's mouth dropped open in horror. 'It's a monster. A horrible big hairy monster.'

Margaret stood and slowly backed away from the wall, her face pale and tight. Dorothy was spellbound. She'd never seen a spider so large. It was easily as big as her hand. The brightness of the electric bulb illuminated it perfectly – its long hairy legs, the bulbous abdomen – as it crawled along the dining room wall.

'What is that thing?' Ida gasped.

'Another reason we should be paid more,' Esme grumbled. 'We were warned about the snakes but they never told us about the spiders.'

Mrs Rayner stood, cool as a cucumber, and walked to the kitchen door. 'Mrs Brown, could you please come to the dining room? We have an unwelcome visitor.'

'Reminds me of a boyfriend I used to have.' Ida laughed but her attempt at humour fell flat. The other women remained transfixed by the spider.

Mrs Brown emerged wielding a broom. 'Where is the little blighter then?'

Mrs Rayner pointed to the beast.

While they watched on, Mrs Brown encouraged the spider onto the brush of the broom where it began to crawl down the handle towards her. Lizzie screamed again and Bessie whimpered into a handkerchief clutched in her hand.

'Don't worry. A spider like that won't kill you,' Mrs Rayner said.

'You mean there are spiders that will?' Bessie gasped.

Dorothy watched a thin smile stretch Mrs Rayner's lips. The woman was enjoying this.

'No reason to fuss,' Mrs Brown said as she carried the spider-laden broom towards the kitchen. 'I'll pop him outside in the back garden. Plenty of insects there.' She disappeared through the kitchen door.

'I would've killed it,' Esme said. 'It'll only come back inside.'

'I'll never go into the back garden again,' Bessie said with a shudder.

Lizzie clutched at her heart. 'I won't sleep a wink tonight.'

'It's all right, girls, it's gone now.' Mrs Rayner sat back at the head of the table and replaced her serviette in her lap. 'Now, I believe Miss Stanton was making an announcement.'

Pale faced, Margaret cleared her throat, as the women settled back at the table still eyeing the walls nervously. 'Thank you, Mrs Rayner.' She took a sip of water. 'Four new women are joining us within the next fortnight. They sailed from home last month and the voyage has been uneventful so they're expected to arrive on time.'

'I wonder if they've been warned about the giant spiders,' Ida muttered.

Margaret continued, her voice becoming firmer and more confident. 'With more local girls being employed there's a greater need for their work to be kept up to the exacting standards the company expects.'

Dorothy had already lost some of her girls to other areas. Their covering and piping hadn't been up to par and they'd been moved to box making, wrapping or packing.

'Where are they going to stay?' asked Lizzie.

'They won't want to stay here once they hear there are monsters crawling the walls,' Ida said.

'If they get cottages and we don't there'll be trouble.' Esme had already complained to the directors – the men who'd come out from Britain lived in the cottages on the estate and she demanded the women should too. Ida and Lizzie had supported her. Dorothy had kept her opinion to herself. If anyone was given a cottage it would be Margaret and then she'd have to decide which of her forewomen she'd share it with. If Margaret chose her, Esme would be impossible to deal with.

'No. No cottages. The new arrivals will live here, at the hostel.'

'But where? There are no spare rooms,' Lizzie said.

'Gawd, I know what's going to happen,' Esme whinged. 'We're going to have to double up, aren't we?'

Margaret nodded. 'You can choose to share your room with one of the new arrivals or you can decide among yourselves who you'd like to bunk in with. Sarah and Dorothy, as you're already sharing, you can remain as you are or make an arrangement to share with someone else.'

Dorothy immediately looked to Ida. It would be like old times. She tried to catch her eye but she was fiddling with her fork.

'Dibs on sharing with Ida,' Esme said, turning to her. 'We make a good team, don't you think?'

Ida looked up at Dorothy for a moment then back to her fork. A sad little smile flitted across her lips. 'Ar, we do.'

Esme eyed Dorothy with a smug expression.

Dorothy willed herself not to betray her feelings as a wave of melancholy rose in her heart. For a moment it was as though she was back on the *Ormonde*, the deck shifting beneath her as she left her old life and friendships behind.

'I'm more than happy to keep our arrangement, Dot, if it suits you.' Sarah smiled at her with the kindness that was evident on the first day they'd met.

Dorothy was grateful for the lifeline. 'Yes, it does.' Despite the pain of Ida's rejection there were many benefits to sharing with Sarah, not least of which were her elocution lessons – the lessons she kept a secret from Ida. And then there was the second letter, another secret she'd kept from Ida but not Sarah. With a jolt she realised she was as responsible as Ida for the changes in their friendship.

'And who will you be sharing with, Miss Stanton?' Esme's voice held none of the respect it should for their Chief Forewoman.

'My room is small. There's no space for an additional bed.' Margaret dabbed her mouth with her napkin.

'I see.' Esme's tone said it all.

That left Bessie and Lizzie, and as one of the new arrivals was known to Bessie from Pascall's, it was agreed Lizzie would share with one of the other newcomers.

'As long as I don't have to share my room with a spider,' Lizzie shuddered, 'I don't mind.'

The following morning Dorothy had hoped to walk with Ida to the factory, just the two of them, to try to mend the distance that was growing between them, but when she went to find her Esme stood in her way.

'Let's you and me have a little chat, eh?' Esme's voice held no room for argument.

Dorothy followed her outside to the garden where Esme led her between the rows of fruit trees, away from inquisitive eyes and far enough from the hostel that their voices wouldn't be heard.

'You weren't there when she needed a friend, but I was.' Esme propped her hands on her hips.

'You're talking about Ida, I presume?'

Esme's mouth turned down in disgust. 'Hark at you and your fancy words. That's part of the reason she's gone off you. All the airs and graces you bung on. She used to talk about you all the time. Dot this and Dot that. But now ...' Esme's smile was cruel. 'Now, she don't hardly mention you at all.'

Esme's words stung but Dorothy refused to betray it. It was clear she and Ida weren't as close as they used to be, but Esme was part of that problem. She'd wedged herself between them.

'It was me that looked after her on the *Orsova*,' Esme continued. 'We looked after each other. It was hard enough being the only one from Fry's ...' She faltered as if she knew she'd exposed a weakness.

Dorothy acknowledged Esme would have needed friends, being the outsider that she was, but Bessie was an outsider too, coming from Pascall's, and she was pleasant to everyone. Bessie felt no need to pit people against each other to stake her claim on a friendship. Dorothy waited, curious to see how Esme would save face.

Esme jutted out her chin. 'Then we got here. They told us Tasmania was just like England but it ain't. Not the trees or the animals nor those horrible screeching birds. It ain't nothing like home. We had to stick together, see? And we did. I looked out for Ida, just like I did on the boat. You,' her eyes flashed, 'you're just interested in looking out for yourself.' Esme moved closer, using her height to advantage. 'I'm a better friend to Ida than you'll ever be. You stick with that lardy-dardy Miss Harris and we'll all be better off.'

'Is that a warning?' Dorothy clenched her fists. She might be shorter than Esme but she could give as good as she got in a scrap.

'Take it like you hear it. I'm just letting you know.' Esme smirked and walked away humming 'I'm Henery the Eighth, I Am' to herself.

Dorothy glared after her, her fists still clenched. At least now she knew what she was dealing with.

14

Maisie

April 1922

Mrs Adwell pulled a small spanner from her uniform pocket and tightened one of the many nuts on the enrober. Maisie stood beside her, watching her work.

'You see here, Maisie?' Mrs Adwell pointed to the nut. 'The vibrations of the enrober often loosen these. You can screw them up tight but over time the endless motion works them loose.' She handed the spanner to Maisie. 'Your turn. See how tight you can make it.'

Maisie hesitated. 'This one here, Mrs Adwell?'

'Yes.'

Maisie took the proffered spanner and tightened the nut.

When she was done, Mrs Adwell checked her work. 'Perfect. That should hold for a good while. Remember what I showed you. If this belt moves out of alignment you'll need to check these points here and here. Usually it will be as simple as tightening the nuts with this small spanner.'

'What's all this, then?' Maisie turned to find Mr Sutton watching on with amusement. 'Are you trying to do me out of a job, Miss Greenwood?'

Maisie stammered and blushed, almost dropping the spanner.

'Don't you mind our Frank, Maisie. He does like to tease.' Mrs Adwell shook her head at him in friendly reproach. 'Just a few minor tweaks, Mr Sutton. Nothing worth bothering an important engineer like yourself.'

'You know better than anyone how to keep these machines running smoothly.' Mr Sutton patted the enrober. He smiled at Maisie. 'If Mrs Adwell trusts you with a spanner around her precious enrobers, you must be very special indeed.'

Maisie shuffled nervously and looked anywhere but at him. Mrs Adwell eyed her with curiosity then turned her attention back to Mr Sutton. 'We have everything sorted here, but thank you.'

'Well, then.' He touched a finger to his forehead in farewell. 'I'll be off. There must be some machines around this factory that still need my expertise.'

'If you have any trouble with them, you know where I am,' Mrs Adwell said with a sly smile.

'Indeed I do, Mrs Adwell. And I know where you are too, Miss Greenwood, with your handy spanner.'

'Oh, I, um, this isn't my spanner.' Maisie chided herself for sounding like such a foolish young thing. Mr Sutton's presence made her feel a mixture of emotions she couldn't quite define.

'Isn't it?' He cocked his head, looked at Mrs Adwell and then back at Maisie. 'I'm not so sure about that.'

'Off you go, Mr Sutton.' Mrs Adwell shooed him away.

He gave a little bow before walking away. 'Farewell, ladies, until we meet again.'

After he'd gone, Maisie offered the spanner back to Mrs Adwell, but she refused to take it. 'That's yours now. I can always get another from the trades shop.'

Maisie left the spanner hovering between them. 'I'm sorry, Mrs Adwell, I don't understand.'

'It's time for you to step up, Maisie. I think you have all the attributes of a supervisor. You've shown a remarkable ability with the enrobers and displayed quick thinking during the prime minister's visit.'

Maisie's mouth dropped open. 'Me? Are you sure, Mrs Adwell?' A tremble of nerves danced in her chest. She'd never been given a position of responsibility before.

'With more workers coming on board, the Firm has asked me to keep an eye out for potential supervisors among the local staff. I'm certain you're up to the task. You're a few years older than most of the girls and I know they look up to you. Your duties will include teaching the new girls how to use the enrobers, inspecting the work for neatness and quality, and ensuring everyone works quickly and efficiently with as little wastage as possible. There'll be a small pay increase.'

Maisie's stomach tightened. Despite her misgivings, Mrs Adwell believed in her and a pay increase would make all the difference. 'Thank you, Mrs Adwell.'

'Another thing. The Firm will be starting evening classes soon. I highly recommend them. The Cadbury family are great believers in education, so much so that at Bournville the younger employees attend Day Continuation School once a week as a condition of their employment until they turn eighteen.'

Maisie frowned. Surely she'd misheard. 'I'm not sure I understand. Are you saying if someone starts work at fourteen they can still continue with their education?'

'Yes, indeed – they must.'

'And Cadbury's provides that education?'

'Not only that, the Firm pays them for the time they spend at the school.'

This was unheard of. Maisie's mind whirled with thoughts of Lily. If the worst came to pass and Lily had to find a job, with Cadbury's at least her education could continue in some form. 'When will Day Continuation School begin here?'

'All things in time, Maisie. There are other matters that need to be put in place first, including the evening classes. I do hope you'll sign up for them. Your prospects would improve greatly if you do. In time we'll not only be needing more supervisors but forewomen as well.'

It was as if Maisie's world had been turned around, all with a few words from Mrs Adwell. A forewoman? In charge of a whole section? She didn't think she'd dare. The Bournville women were formidable. They had mountains of knowledge and experience, not to mention confidence. But Mrs Adwell had said if she took advantage of the classes, and she would, then she might become a forewoman. If she did, then Lily could definitely go to university and Mother could finally rest. One step at a time. First she had to prove herself as a supervisor. Maisie firmed her resolve. She wouldn't fail. 'Thank you, Mrs Adwell. I won't let you down.' Nor would she let Lily down, or Mother. She straightened her shoulders to balance the weight that settled there.

Maisie washed the dishes while Lily dried. Mother sat mending a blouse for Mrs Medhurst, her chair pulled up to the dying embers in the range. The evenings had turned cold again. Summer had come and gone and the winds from the Antarctic made everyday life a little more difficult. Fortunately for Maisie, the walk to and from the train station wasn't long and at Cadbury's the train pulled up right outside. She enjoyed the warmth and bustle of the factory, the other girls were friendly and Gertie in particular was fun. But now, with her promotion, she wondered how much that would change.

'My girl, a supervisor,' Mother said proudly as she stitched. 'You've only been working there a matter of months and all. Just think of where you might go, given a year or two.'

Maisie hadn't mentioned Mrs Adwell's words about future advancement to Mother. That was a hope she held tight to herself. She scrubbed the mutton fat from the pan. 'I have to prove myself in this position first.'

'You'll end up the boss of the entire factory.' Lily waved the tea towel in an expansive arc. 'And we'll go and live there and eat chocolate for breakfast, lunch and tea, and all the minutes in between.'

Maisie laughed. 'I think even you'd get sick of chocolate if we did.'

'Would not.' Lily returned to the dishes in the rack. 'I wish I could get a job at Cadbury's.'

Maisie's stomach dropped. 'But then you wouldn't have time to read and learn.' She hadn't told Mother or Lily about the Day Continuation School. She didn't want to give Mother any excuses to pull Lily out of school and, besides, it wasn't up and running yet. 'How would you find out about Egypt and Mesopotamia if you were working in a factory all day?' Lily's latest fascination was the ancient histories.

'You said they had evening classes. You said you might be late home a couple of times a week if you went to them and asked Mother if that would be all right. I know, I heard.'

'Oh, Lily, an hour or two's learning after a long day of work in the factory isn't the same as being in school where you get to learn all day. I thought you wanted to go to university.'

Lily twisted the tea towel in her hands. 'I do, but Mother said—'

'Don't go filling her head with silly notions, Maisie.' Mother looked up at them from her mending. 'You started work at fourteen and Lily will too. As you've told me, many of the girls at the factory are the same age as our Lily.'

'Yes, and they've lovely girls, well, most of them, but they don't have the keenness of mind that our Lily has. Factory work is dull and repetitive and I think Lily could do much better.'

'Aren't you happy there?' Mother asked.

Maisie sensed the trap and sidestepped. 'I've been made a supervisor because I'm older than most of the girls, more mature. At fourteen Lily won't have the same opportunities.' Maisie put down the scourer and wiped her hands on her apron. She moved to sit beside her mother. 'I've just been given a pay increase—'

'Which is all well and good but it's not much.'

'—and there's the scholarship. I know Lily's going to win it, I do.' The scholarship would pay for Lily's tuition at one of the independent schools in town.

'The test wasn't very hard,' Lily said matter-of-factly.

'She'll still have to earn her keep.'

'We'll come up with a way. Please, Mother, give it some thought.' Maisie wanted to say more about the possibilities that would open up for Lily if she continued with her education but held her tongue. Ever since Edith Cowan had been elected to parliament there was a sense that more opportunities would become available to women, but Mother had told her she was sick and tired of hearing about Mrs Cowan.

Mother huffed and went back to her mending. 'We'll wait and see about the scholarship first.'

Maisie rose with a small sense of relief. She knew Mother was as proud of Lily as she was. It was the endless grind of finding money to pay the bills that wore her down.

Andrew came rushing in through the back door bringing the cold air with him. 'There's a big fire down in Melville Street. You can see it from the backyard. Come and have a look.'

'That'll be the sawmill, no doubt.' Mother eased herself out of her chair with a slow groan.

The four of them stood in the backyard exhaling little puffs of steam and watched as sheets of flames danced around the buildings down the hill. The sound of men shouting and the bells of the fire trucks racing to the scene cut through the distance and cold night air.

'I'm going down to have a closer look.' Andrew turned to them. 'Who's coming with me?'

'Me,' cried Lily. 'I want to go.'

'No, Lily.' Mother pulled her close. 'It's too dangerous. We can watch it from here.' She coughed, rummaged for a handkerchief and then coughed again.

The sound put Maisie's nerves on edge. 'Let's get you inside, Mother, back in the warmth.' She wrapped an arm around her and helped her into the cottage.

Lily followed. 'Please, can I go? I'll stay back from the flames, I promise.'

Mother nestled back into her chair. 'It's too dangerous. It's the sawmill, as I thought. With the amount of timber there, the fire could spread. There are buildings with shingle roofs in every direction and just a spark would see them go. Up here we have the best view in Hobart and are nice and safe.'

Andrew came back in from the lean-to, thrusting his arms into his coat. 'I probably won't need this it'll be so warm down there.'

'I'd rather you didn't,' Mother said.

'I'll be careful.' He kissed her briefly on the cheek and was out the front door.

Lily yawned. 'Another boring night at home then. I'm going to read in my room.'

'There's still drying up to be done.' Mother's voice held a hint of exasperation.

'I'll take care of it.' Maisie would rather Lily read and keep learning. Hopefully it would dispel any thoughts of her working at Cadbury's.

Mother tsked. 'You spoil her. She should be pulling her weight. Her stitching is poor and her ironing skills leave a lot to be desired.'

Maisie turned back to the dishes. The water had cooled and a scum of mutton fat coated the surface. She pulled the plug, scrubbed the sink then picked up Lily's discarded tea towel and began drying the plates. Was it a crime to want her sister to have a better life? Lily would have to grow up soon enough. Maisie had her hopes pinned on the scholarship and Mother relenting, but would that be enough? 'Give me Mr Medhurst's shirt,' she said to Mother. 'The cuffs are easy enough to mend. I'll take it to Lily and show her how it's done.'

'Take this swatch for her to practise on first.' As Mother handed over the shirt and swatch she looked up at Maisie with tired eyes. 'It's for the best, you know it.'

Maisie nodded, keeping her mouth firmly closed. She walked down the hall to the bedroom she and Lily shared. 'Lily, lovely Lily, I have something even more exciting for you on this Saturday night.' She pushed open the door expecting to see Lily's face looking up at her from the pages of a book. Instead she was greeted by Blackie, who stretched and yawned before curling back into sleep. 'Lily?' Was she hiding under the bed? No. In the wardrobe? No. Maisie rushed to the parlour. Not there. Their mother's bedroom? 'Lily?' Not there either.

'What is it?' Mother called, then broke into a cough.

Maisie came back to the kitchen. 'It's Lily. I can't find her.'

'What?'

'She didn't come back through the kitchen, did she? Maybe she's in the outhouse.' Even as she said it, Maisie knew it was impossible. The cottage was so small, Lily could never have snuck by.

Mother struggled to her feet. 'She's followed Andrew. That girl! Honestly, her curiosity will be the death of her.'

'Don't worry, I'll go after her. I'll keep her safe, I promise.'

Maisie rushed down the hill, almost stumbling in her haste, and took the most direct route through the streets of Hobart. It was the way both Andrew and Lily would have come. She hoped Lily had caught up to Andrew and he was making sure she didn't come to harm. As she neared Melville Street the smoke thickened, hitting the back of her throat with a stinging acridity. The light of the flames cast the street in a red glow. She searched for her brother and sister but the gathering sightseers crushed against her. The residents of Melville Street also crowded the streets, carrying their most precious possessions away from danger. Maisie pushed through the throng, calling out for Lily and Andrew, frantically searching for any sign of them. Firefighting equipment lined the road opposite the inferno and as Maisie edged her way closer she saw more clearly the firemen with hand reels and hose pumps battling against incredible odds.

One of the onlookers leant towards her the better to be heard. 'They reckon the mill's gone, the factory, boiler house and stables as well, not to mention the stores of wood. Biggest fire I've ever seen.'

His words added to Maisie's fears. 'Have you seen my brother? He's about this high.' Maisie raised her hand above her head. 'He might be with my little sister who's about this high.' She lowered her hand to Lily's height.

The man shook his head. 'Can't say I have.'

A cry went up as part of the office building collapsed and the walls of fire forced the firefighters back. They continued to play the water against the flames from the other side of the street. Men, stripped down to their singlets, helped the firefighters with hoses and buckets. It was the kind of thing Andrew would do but surely not if Lily was with him. The flickering light from the flames made it hard to make out people's faces. The roar of the fire and the shouts of the firemen combined with the bangs and cracks of the building's collapse created a hellish cacophony. Despite the heat, a cold sweat beaded on Maisie's brow. Andrew and Lily would've definitely come in this direction. Had she passed them in the crowd and not seen them? If Andrew had arrived ahead of Lily and volunteered to help, would Lily have followed him closer to the fire? 'Lily. Lily Greenwood.' The scream rose in her throat as a desperate wail. Tears sprang unbidden. She turned in circles, not caring if she looked like a madwoman. She was mad, mad with fear for her little sister – her infuriating, fascinating, clever little sister. 'Lily. Where are you? Lily Greenwood.'

'She's over there,' a man close by yelled over the heads of the crush. 'If'n your name's Maisie Greenwood, that is. I heard her calling for you.'

'Where?'

He pointed up the road. Maisie searched for her sister's face in the crowd. 'Lily? It's Maisie.' She pushed her way through the press of bodies. 'Lily?'

A woman shoved past her yelling, 'Have you seen my bedding? Has anyone seen my bedding?'

'Your bedding?' a man grunted.

'I put the whole of the bedding on the street in case our home went up in flames. Now it's gone. Some filthy mongrel has carried it away.'

Maisie continued her search but it was like swimming upstream. The sightseers wanted to get closer to the site of the disaster while

Maisie was desperate to get to where the man had pointed. 'Lily Greenwood, where are you?'

'Up here, Maisie.' It was her brother's voice. She struggled through the crowd towards it.

'Maisie, over here.' Lily was perched on Andrew's shoulders, safely back from the worst of the fire.

When she reached them Andrew gently lowered Lily to the ground. 'You're getting a bit too heavy for me,' he said as he rumpled her hair. 'Sorry, Maisie, she caught me up and I couldn't make her go back home. I figured she'd be safer with me than anywhere else.'

'I must have walked straight past you.' In her haste and fear Maisie had missed them.

'We were closer to the fire before,' Lily said proudly. 'But when things started crashing down I thought it was safer to be up here.'

Andrew raised an eyebrow at Maisie and she knew what it meant. Andrew had thought it was safer further up the road away from the fire and had managed to convince Lily it was her idea.

'Thank goodness you're both all right, but, Lily, you scared the wits out of Mother. I'm taking you home right now.'

Lily pouted. 'I want to stay here. This is the most exciting thing that has ever happened.'

'Here come the police,' said Andrew.

Maisie lifted her head to see a row of policemen pushing the sightseers back. The surge reached them and Maisie grabbed Lily's hand before they became separated. 'The show's over, Lily. Time to go home.'

'Maisie's right,' Andrew agreed. 'We've had enough excitement. You'll have lots to talk about at school on Monday.'

Lily seemed pleased at the thought. 'They won't say I'm a boring bookworm when I tell them I was at the fire.'

Maisie sensed a hesitancy in Andrew. 'Are you coming?'

He looked back at the fire, his body stretching towards it. 'I could help.'

'Yes, you could. And you could die. You're more help alive. Come home with us so Mother doesn't suffer a sleepless night worrying about you as well.'

He took a deep breath. 'You're right.' Maisie knew he felt responsible for the wellbeing of their family as much as she did. Even though she was the oldest, he was the man of the house.

A shout rang out as another part of one of the buildings collapsed. A shower of sparks whirled into the dark skies.

'It's better than Guy Fawkes night,' Lily squealed with delight.

'It'd be best if we left right now.' Maisie pulled at her hand.

When they arrived home, Maisie expected Mother to be angry. She might even give Lily a hiding. Instead, she pulled Lily close and kissed the top of her head. 'Don't you ever run off like that again.'

Lily squirmed for a moment and then relented into Mother's embrace. 'I won't.' She looked up with bright eyes. 'But it was very exciting.'

'Exciting, my eye,' Mother chided. 'There's nothing exciting about me having a heart attack because of your disobedience.'

Lily hung her head. 'Sorry, Mother.'

'Now go and wash your face. You too, Maisie. You look like a couple of urchins.'

'What about me?' Andrew's teeth flashed white against his sooty face.

'My son, we're used to you looking like a chimney sweep.' Mother patted him on the shoulder and made her way to bed.

15

Dorothy

Dorothy was back in the close-packed tenements of her childhood; every lamp, every candle and every hearth a fire hazard. Flames caught, running wild through the maze of cramped rooms and hovels. Dorothy tried to escape but each turn was a dead end blocked by fire. There was no one to help her. No one to save her. The smoke was choking – she couldn't scream or call for help.

She woke in a tangle of bedclothes, the scent of smoke lingering. The room was unfamiliar – not Birmingham nor her bedroom at Bournville. She threw back the coverlet. The night was cool but she was damp with sweat. It wasn't often her dreams took her back to the tenement where she grew up – two rooms, four brothers and a drunkard for a father. It would've been better for all of them if it had burnt to the ground.

Slowly her eyes adjusted to the dark. A desk and chair by the window. A sleeping form in the bed opposite. Her heartbeat steadied. She was in the hostel at Claremont. She was safe. Dorothy slipped out of bed, careful not to wake Sarah, and crept silently to the bathroom where she splashed her face with cold water. Her skin was pale in the mirror, her eyes wide and dark.

Margaret folded the letter after reading the details to the women gathered at the breakfast table. Overnight a fire had destroyed the Crisp and Gunns sawmill in Hobart, the one the Firm had contracted to build the formwork and mouldings for the factory. The letter from Mr Cooper had been delivered especially this morning to inform her of the news. 'So there we have it. Yet another delay.' Margaret put the letter on the table beside her plate with a scowl so fierce Dorothy was surprised the offending missive didn't burst into flames itself. Dorothy's nightmare must have been triggered by the fire. It had been large enough that a hint of smoke had reached them all these miles away.

'Blimey, this is a great to-do our first week here.' Anna was one of the new arrivals, a Forewoman B in box making from Cadbury's.

The women who'd journeyed with her nodded in agreement. Bertha and May were both experienced confectioners from Cadbury's, and Agatha was Bessie's compatriot from Pascall's.

'Do we know exactly how much of the Cadbury's contract work was destroyed?' Lizzie asked.

'Cadbury-Fry-Pascall,' muttered Esme. 'It said so, right there in the letter.' The fact that none of the new arrivals were from Fry's had aggravated Esme's ill temper even further. She'd become increasingly tetchy at the factory becoming known colloquially as Cadbury's. The enterprise was a consortium of three companies, she kept reminding people, not just one.

'I'm sorry, Esme,' Lizzie said. 'Do we know exactly how much of the Cadbury-Fry-Pascall contract work was destroyed?'

'Not at this stage, no.' Margaret frowned, intensifying her worn and worried expression.

Bessie leant towards Agatha. 'It won't affect us at all.' Even though Agatha was many years older, they'd already formed a strong bond. Bessie had suffered from homesickness and Dorothy suspected Agatha would become a mother figure to her. 'Everything at Pascall's is fully operational and has been for some time.'

'There's a meeting with the directors tomorrow morning,' Margaret said. 'I'll be informed of the extent of the damage then.' She turned to Dorothy. 'I'll be in town all morning, if not the entire day. You'll be in charge in my absence.'

Esme took a sharp intake of breath and Dorothy braced herself for the inevitable outrage.

'It should be me,' Esme said, her face white with anger. 'After all, I am Forewoman A too.'

Margaret's sigh carried all the frustrations of the past months. 'For goodness sake, Esme. It's for one day, if that.'

'It's all right, Miss Stanton.' Dorothy kept her voice steady. 'Esme can act in the position.' There'd be other opportunities, she was sure. Esme glowered at her but Ida shot her a grateful smile.

Margaret pushed back her chair abruptly. She stood and glared at both Dorothy and Esme. 'I will not be told what to do by either of you, do you understand? My decision is final.' She almost slammed the door behind her.

Margaret's dramatic departure left them all slightly dazed. Dorothy decided it was best to leave her be for now. She'd knock on her door later to make sure she was all right.

Sarah picked up the letter and scanned it quickly. 'There'll be a slight delay to some of the new building work but current production will continue on schedule.'

'Miss Stanton didn't seem so sure,' Ida said. 'How can you be? It's all gone up in smoke.'

'I've seen the plans and construction schedules and am aware of the mouldings and other finished work that was destroyed in the fire. I can't see anything's been lost that's essential to our current production timeline.'

Dorothy wondered again at the extent of Sarah's knowledge. She seemed well across every aspect of the Firm's business. When asked, Sarah said it was in the nature of her work. She took dictation, typed up the letters and took the minutes at meetings, so of course she knew what was happening at every level.

'Why didn't you say so when Miss Stanton was here?' asked Lizzie. 'She seemed right upset.'

Sarah raised her hands in defence. 'I hardly had a chance.' She looked square at Esme.

'What?' Esme objected.

'Cadbury's,' she emphasised the word, 'will ensure the items destroyed in the blaze are manufactured by another company with all due haste.' Sarah's gaze softened as it shifted to the other women. 'Plans will be back on track in no time and production won't be delayed.'

Dorothy stood before Esme could object yet again. 'I, for one, am not hanging about moping. It's our one day off and I intend to make the most of it. Excuse me.'

Upstairs it wasn't long before Sarah joined her in their room. Dorothy got straight to the point. 'Do you think the fire was targeting the Firm?'

Sarah gave a small shake of her head. 'I don't think so. The university lost valuable work as well. If I were investigating the fire I'd be looking at rival sawmills and manufacturers rather than someone who wants Cadbury's to be inconvenienced. That being said, sawmills are always at risk of fire.'

'Margaret was more upset than I expected.'

'Yes. It's worrying.' Sarah frowned slightly. 'Never mind that.' She returned her focus to Dorothy. 'I wouldn't be surprised if you received another letter in the near future.'

'In relation to the fire?'

'Exactly. Whoever it is, they're trying to rattle you. I expect the next one will hint at how easy it would be to burn the hostel down.'

Dorothy shuddered. The images from last night's nightmare flashed through her mind. 'One day they might make good on their threats.'

'They'll definitely make a move at some stage but I seriously doubt they'll set fire to the hostel. No, it'll be more subtle than that.'

'That's good to know.' Dorothy hardly felt reassured.

'You say you don't have any enemies.' Sarah eyed Dorothy. 'I think Miss Esme Abbott might be in the running for that vacancy.'

Dorothy thought on it. Esme would certainly enjoy undermining her. 'I think she's more bluster and spite than anything else. Besides, have you seen her handwriting?' It was no better than a scrawl.

'True, but best to be careful. Women like her are like squeaky gates – if they complain long and loud they get the oil. You, my dear Dorothy, are the stoic type who battles on without complaint. It could be your undoing.'

'What do you mean?'

'You were willing to give up being Chief Forewoman for the day just like that.' Sarah snapped her fingers. 'Just because the gate squeaked.'

Dorothy didn't know whether to bristle or laugh. The image of Esme as a squeaky gate was one she'd think of every time the woman complained. It was Ida, though, who she'd thought of when she'd capitulated so quickly. Part of her still longed for the closeness they used to have. By pleasing Esme she'd reasoned she would please Ida. Sarah might see it as weakness, a mere sentimentality. 'I've risen up the ranks to Forewoman A. I'm no pushover.'

'And will be Chief Forewoman, if only for a day. At the heights you're at now, the air is thinner. Be aware of that.'

'Thanks for the warning.' Dorothy stood. She'd be glad to get away from the hostel for a few hours. 'And now I must get ready to go.'

'And I must get ready to do absolutely nothing.' Sarah lay back on her bed with a smile as wide as the Cheshire cat's. 'I do love Sunday mornings when all you girls traipse off to church and I have the place to myself.'

Dorothy could understand why Sarah never went to church. During the war many people's faith had wavered. There was a time when Dorothy had felt abandoned by God but even so there was a kind of comfort in the rituals and hymns of the church service. When everything was uncertain and the world was falling apart, at least there was one place where nothing changed. But church wasn't where she was heading that day.

The Quaker Meeting House in upper Murray Street was an attractive sandstone building with pilasters and a pediment in contrasting white. Dorothy pushed open the gate into the small garden filled with the rhododendrons and camellias she was familiar with. She approached the large wooden doors with some trepidation. It had taken her many weeks to gain the courage to come here. She hoped it would be worth it. In the entrance hall men and women gathered in respectful silence. Dorothy followed them through the arched doorway into the meeting house. Inside, the ceiling was domed and the room flooded with the light from large windows. The beautiful but simple room reflected the Quaker values and beliefs as she understood them. There was no stained glass or altar, no pulpit or church organ, no men in robes. Quakers believed that the light of God was in everyone, not just an ordained few, which meant women had the same right to speak and be heard as men. In all her years of churchgoing, Dorothy had never seen a woman in the pulpit or behind the altar but in the meeting house at Bournville women rose and spoke if the spirit moved them just as often as the men.

A brief look around the room confirmed the presence of many Cadbury's workers and their families. She caught the surprised expression on Frank's face and smiled demurely. He quickly cast his eyes downwards. If she'd told him of her plan to come he'd have asked questions she had no ready answers for.

As the last arrivals were seated and the silence grew, disappointment settled deep in Dorothy's bones. Thomas had told her he attended these Sunday morning meetings and yet there was no sign of him. The minutes slipped away and a restlessness grew in her. She wondered if, as she was here, she might concentrate on the God within as the Quakers did. She searched for a spark of goodness and tried to imagine a light inside, pulsing in time with her heartbeat. She'd thought her heart had broken forever when Freddie's light had been snuffed out, but like every other woman who'd lost a husband, a son, a brother or a father, she'd pressed on against the weight of grief. The cold sensation of a tear crawling down her cheek brought her back to the meeting house, the windows, the dove-grey walls. It had been almost six years. It had been no time at all.

The door opened, accompanied by the sound of swishing cloth as someone snuck into the meeting house and sat down. She resisted for a moment but then raised her eyes. The sight of him hit her hard. Thomas looked harried and careworn as if he'd aged many years instead of the months since she'd last seen him. His eyes were downcast and she took the chance to study every feature of his face: the creases bracketing his mouth, the wrinkles around his eyes and the furrows on his brow. Her gaze fell to his hands and there it was, the slight tremor. A surge of anguish swept through her. This man, this good man, had been ruined by an evil war.

The silence remained. Dorothy was glad of it. The space gave her time to compose her thoughts. After the meeting she'd make conversation with the members and bat away Frank's questions with a practised hand. The opportunity to spend time with Thomas would arrive and if it didn't, she would make it so.

Dorothy bided her time for almost an hour after the meeting. Conversation was easy because all the talk was of last night's fire. Dorothy distracted Frank from his questions with a casual, 'I've been to meetings before,' and left it at that. She caught Thomas's eye on more than one occasion and the pull towards him was strong, but she resisted. Even Quakers' tongues could wag. When it became obvious she could linger no longer she bade her goodbyes to the few remaining and wandered slowly through the small garden. At a camellia bush she paused and inspected the leaves.

'What are you hoping to find?' The voice was the one she'd been waiting to hear.

Dorothy feigned nonchalance and kept studying one leaf in particular. 'Any sign of disease or pest infestation.' She'd known nothing of plants until she'd moved to Bournville with its garden plots and allotments. Growing flowers and vegetables and tending fruit trees had been another mystery that, in time, had divulged its secrets to her.

'And?' Thomas stood beside her and peered at the leaf.

'Nothing.' She turned and smiled up at him. 'It is, I'm happy to report, perfectly healthy.'

'And you? Are you in good health also?'

'I am, thank you, Mr Moreland. And yourself?'

'Apart from my tardiness this morning, I'm well and in better circumstances. I'm soon to be a colleague of yours, Mrs Adwell.'

Dorothy startled at the news. 'A colleague?'

'Indeed. I've been offered a position at Cadbury-Fry-Pascall and begin within the week.'

'A position?' She was aware she was echoing him but could manage nothing more.

'In administration at first, but when the facilities are up and running I'll take on the role of supervising the evening classes.'

Dorothy battled to restrain her smile to one of an appropriate nature. 'That's wonderful. Congratulations.' Thomas working for the Firm was better than anything she could have hoped for. 'I took many of the evening classes at Bournville.'

'How interesting. What subjects did you take?' He smiled awkwardly. 'Sorry, I don't mean to pry but it would be helpful to know the range of classes available at Bournville.'

'Quite a variety, from mathematics and science to economics and English.' She stopped short at telling him about the psychology classes. Dorothy had been fascinated by the science of mental life and observable behaviour but some people regarded it as hogwash. 'I also studied industrial administration, which included industrial law, general factory management and business finance. It was over two years, twice a month in the winter months.' During the cold evenings her ambition was fed by the fuel of those classes. In summer her spare nights were spent at cricket training feeding her ambitions for a winning season.

Thomas laughed. 'I don't imagine a course of that scope will be taught here in the near future but you've given me something to aim for. I'll teach the basics to begin with and build the curriculum in time. I'm looking forward to seeing the hall where the lessons will be held.'

'It's scrubbed up well.' The old camp hospital had been refurbished and was already in use, including the billiards room and a reading room. The remaining space would be used for dances organised by the social committee, of which Ida was a keen member, and the classroom where Thomas would teach.

A loud sound like a gunshot echoed down the street. Dorothy flinched and put a hand to her heart as the offending motor car puttered past. 'I thought there'd be fewer automobiles and more horse and carts here, but no.'

She turned to Thomas. The tendons in his neck stood out in taut ropes and his hands shook wildly. 'I'm sorry, Mrs Adwell.' He squeezed the words out between gritted teeth. 'I ...' He removed his hat and wiped the sweat gathering there.

'Come, sit down.' Dorothy guided him to a wooden bench at one side of the garden. His body was tight as wire. She took his hat, the brim in danger of being crushed by his claw-like grip, and placed it beside her on the bench.

He balled his hands into fists and pressed them to his eyes. 'I can't ...'

'Let's sit here for a little while on this lovely Sunday morning.' Dorothy kept her voice low and soothing, her hand on his arm as a steadying presence. 'We're perfectly safe here and can stay as long as we need.'

'But I ... I have ...' He brought his hands away from his eyes and looked at her with a pain that pierced her right through.

'You're safe. It was noise. Only noise.' Her gloved hand smoothed the wool of his jacket. 'You're in Hobart. The war is over. There are no bullets here, no bombs.'

'You … you know?'

Dorothy nodded. 'I'm familiar with shell shock. I volunteered at the Cadbury's hospitals and my …' Her voice failed. Freddie had battled to hide the symptoms but, in that one brief week they'd had together before he was sent back to the front, the nightmares had given him away. He never admitted to being anything other than fit for duty, such was the shame he'd felt. His symptoms had been mild compared to the cases she'd seen and tended to at the Cadbury's hospitals. So many men had returned with war trauma, damage that no operation, bandage or medicine could fix. After all the horrors they'd endured, she thought it a wonder, not that men came back with their minds in tatters, but that any men came home sane at all.

'My life is not what it was.' His legs jiggled restlessly as if they wanted to bolt but his jaw had relaxed a little. He unclenched his hands and ran them down his trousers as if to wipe away the fear in them.

'But perhaps it could be better than it is.'

'I don't know how.' He turned to her with such desperation the breath caught in her throat.

'Let me help you.'

He shook his head. 'There's no help to be had. I'm more fortunate than those who've been locked up in asylums or who were charged with desertion or cowardice and shot dead by our own side. It was suggested I leave the city and live in a place with space and fresh air, hence this rather drastic move. It hasn't turned out the way it was hoped.'

'I'd like to try, if you'll let me.' She'd done her best to help the men at the Cadbury's hospital. Towards the end of the war she'd heard of a hospital in Devon that was having great success with their treatments and she'd written requesting information.

Thomas looked away. 'Can you turn back time? Can you stop the assassination of Archduke Franz Ferdinand and everything that happened as a result?'

'No. But I would like to help you.' She touched his hand. His fingers were long and elegant, unlike Freddie's work-callused ones, but the look in his eyes was familiar.

He withdrew his hands. As she had feared, she'd been too presumptuous. 'I'm sorry, Mrs Adwell. I'm afraid I'm a lost cause. Even my—'

'Thomas?' a man called out from the front portico of the meeting house.

Thomas startled and quickly stood up. 'Excuse me. I must take my leave. I'm lunching with a friend.'

'Of course.' She stood and handed him his hat. 'I'll see you next Sunday.'

'You'll be coming to meetings regularly?' A slight expression of confusion crossed his face.

'I think so, yes.' It was too late for Freddie but not for Thomas. Perhaps next Sunday she could convince him to accept her help. 'I attended meetings at Bournville. The quiet is a change from all the prayers and hymns of church.'

'Well, until then, Mrs Adwell.' Thomas doffed his hat.

'Mr Moreland.' She bobbed her head in farewell. From her secluded spot in the garden she watched as he joined his friend and walked away from the meeting house. 'Until next Sunday, Thomas,' she murmured.

When Dorothy returned to the hostel Mrs Rayner was waiting for her. 'The others were back from church hours ago.' She gave Dorothy a suspicious look. 'Your dinner is cold. You'll find it under a cover in the kitchen. Miss Harris put it aside for you.'

'Thank you, Mrs Rayner.'

'And a letter arrived for you.' Her mouth curved down in disapproval. 'Two letters arriving by messenger on a Sunday. It's very odd indeed.'

Dorothy hid her surprise. Sarah had been right. 'May I have it?'

'Miss Harris said she'd look after it for you. She's in your room.' Mrs Rayner gave her one last disdainful look and returned to her parlour.

Ignoring her hunger pangs, Dorothy rushed upstairs. Sarah was writing at the desk when she walked in. 'You have the letter.'

Sarah carefully covered her writing with blotting paper and put it to one side. She turned towards Dorothy. 'I do indeed. It's just as we suspected.'

'You opened it?' Dorothy sat on her bed and eased off her shoes. She'd worn her good shoes, the t-straps with the small heels, instead of her usual boots or lace-up Oxfords. She'd wanted to make a good impression at the meeting house but had regretted her choice on the walk from the railway station.

Sarah opened the desk drawer and pulled out the letter. 'You can read it yourself but it's just as we thought.' She unfolded the letter. '*Such a pity the sawmill burnt down,*' she quoted. '*You have something of great value. It would be a shame for it to go up in flames.*'

Sarah handed it to Dorothy. 'I had hoped to accost the messenger and find out who'd sent it, but he was long gone by the time I knew about the letter.'

Dorothy read the words written in that same distinctive writing. A shiver ran through her.

'I hope I wasn't presumptuous in reading it,' Sarah said. 'It's just that I consider these to be our letters now.'

Dorothy found Sarah's presumption comforting. She wasn't in this alone. 'You predicted this one. It's more yours than mine.' She handed it back to Sarah.

'That's a relief.' Sarah folded the letter back in its envelope. She looked into Dorothy's eyes. 'Does this worry you?'

The fact that this person was watching her, knew where she lived and what she did, was unnerving. 'You've told me whoever is writing them will make a move at some stage. That worries me.'

'Don't let it rattle you.' She leant forward and put her hand on Dorothy's. 'This man is a coward. He will not best us.'

The warmth and pressure of Sarah's hand was reassuring and yet the memory of the nightmare was still with her – the flames, the choking smoke and the growing panic of there being no escape.

16

Dorothy

After a particularly trying day at the factory, Dorothy retreated from the gossip and chatter in the parlour and retired upstairs with a book. She was happily ensconced on her bed when Sarah came in, her hair swept up in a towel.

'What are you reading?' Sarah settled on the chair opposite, unravelled the turban and began to dry her hair. '*How to Be a Good Quaker*?'

Sometimes it was hard to tell when Sarah was joking or serious. There was a sparkle in her eye though that gave her away. 'It's one of the books the Firm supplied. I'm sure there'll be a Quaker reference in it somewhere.' Along with the piano, Cadbury's had provided reading material for the women's entertainment and edification. The books were more of the latter and less of the former and as such Dorothy was one of the few women who read them.

'Ah, but a book is just words and, as they say, actions speak louder than words. Your actions have certainly sparked some interest.'

'Why? What have I done?'

'People have been asking questions about you in the office. Imagine my surprise when I was told you went to the meeting house on Sunday.'

'Oh.' Dorothy had hesitated to tell Sarah because of the inevitable questions that would arise. When she'd gone to the occasional meeting back home it had never been a matter for discussion. She was a fool to think it would be the same here, where the Quaker community was so much smaller.

'Even Mr Cooper is impressed. I pretended to know you were going, of course. I hope the surprise on my face didn't give me away.'

'It was a spur-of-the-moment decision.' Dorothy thought fast. 'I'd planned to go to church with the others but after all the fuss about the fire, I craved the silence of a Quaker meeting. At Bourneville I attended some meetings. They have such a calming effect.'

Sarah draped the towel over the back of the chair. 'Well, no matter your motive, you've made quite the impression – not only for attending the meeting but for your conversation at the gathering afterwards.'

Dorothy struggled to remember what had been talked about, apart from the fire. She'd been so distracted by Thomas's presence she was astounded she'd been able to make intelligent conversation at all. 'It would've been rude to leave without making people's acquaintance.'

'Indeed.' Sarah picked up the hairbrush from her bedside table. 'I find myself inspired to make a similar spur-of-the-moment decision next Sunday.'

Dorothy battled to keep her expression neutral. Her plan to spend time with Thomas again after the next meeting would be impossible with Sarah there. 'You're going to the meeting house?'

'Maybe.' Sarah began nonchalantly brushing her hair.

'But what about your Sunday mornings and having the hostel to yourself?'

Sarah raised one shoulder in an elegant shrug. 'I too crave the calming effect of a Quaker meeting.'

Dorothy's heart sank. Her plan had seemed so perfect at the time.

'Although I do wonder ...' Sarah stopped brushing her hair.

Dorothy leant forward, hoping Sarah would change her mind.

'Once word gets out I imagine Esme will want to join us, given her ambitions.' She smiled then, in her wicked way, and Dorothy realised Sarah was teasing. 'And Margaret, of course, will want to cement her position. Oh dear, Dot, I do believe you've started a trend.'

Dorothy laughed in relief. 'You have no intention of going to a meeting, do you?'

'And give up my lazy Sunday mornings? Absolutely not.' Sarah put down her hairbrush. 'Although I must admit you've made such a good impression on the directors I'm a teensy bit jealous.' Sarah joined Dorothy on her bed. 'It was a rather clever move.'

'But honestly, I didn't go to be clever or ambitious. I went because I felt the need.' That much was true. She had needed to see Thomas.

'I believe you. Even so, you'll be remembered and who knows what will happen in the future. It's always good to be top of mind, don't you think?'

A flutter stirred in Dorothy's stomach. She'd done many things out of ambition but this hadn't been one of them. Interesting that it had had the unintentional effect of shoring up her position.

'Good news.' Sarah's eyes lit up. 'The fire hasn't delayed the completion of the office building. We move the furnishings in next week and the week after we'll be happily installed, all working at the same site together. Won't it be grand?'

'That's wonderful.' Coupled with the knowledge that Thomas would soon be working in administration, this was good news indeed.

'We'll be able to walk to work together.' Sarah bumped her shoulder playfully against Dorothy's.

'I can visit you in the office. I'm always interested to see how different departments work.' Knowing where Thomas spent his days and the kind of environment he worked in would help Dorothy come up with strategies to help him in his daily life.

'That's one of the things I love about you, Dot. You find everything interesting.' Sarah picked up the book Dorothy had been reading, flicked through a few pages and feigned a yawn. 'Even this.'

The following Sunday, Dorothy waited for Thomas to notice her leaving after the meeting. She inclined her head towards the garden bench outside to let him know she'd wait for him there. As the minutes ticked by and he didn't join her, her confidence melted away. Had she fooled herself that they'd formed a kind of bond on the *Ormonde*? But then for him to be so open about his troubles last Sunday, she was sure that friendship had been strengthened. She tightened her coat as the coolness of the autumn day echoed the chill of her growing disappointment. At least, as Sarah had told her, attending the meeting house was good for her career – coming here hadn't been a total waste of her time. But she'd been so sure Thomas had been put in her path for a reason. Dorothy stood. Mrs Brown wouldn't have to keep her dinner warm. She'd be back at the hostel in time after all.

'Mrs Adwell. Leaving so soon?'

Dorothy's heart leapt at the sound of Thomas's voice. He stood, hat in hand, looking at her with an expression she couldn't decipher. 'Mr Moreland. I could stay a little longer.'

'May I join you?' He nodded towards the garden bench.

'Please do.' She sat at one end, leaving plenty of room between them, wondering how she could repeat her offer of help without causing him embarrassment. It was one thing when he was vulnerable and in need, quite another to talk of such things while he was composed and controlled.

Thomas cleared his throat. 'Over the past week I've been thinking about our ... exchange last Sunday. Firstly, as a Quaker, I feel the need to explain why I was involved in combat during the war.'

'Not to me. Many of the Bournville Quakers decided to bear arms. Even one of the Cadburys themselves enlisted.' Egbert Cadbury was a war hero, honoured with a Distinguished Flying Cross for his bravery as a fighter pilot. Quakers who had been in combat were not as rare as those who'd handed out white feathers believed. Quakers might be pacifists but they weren't cowards.

Thomas's brow furrowed. 'Even so, the Great War caused disruption within the Quaker world.'

'Every man had to follow his own conscience. The war was unlike any other the world had ever seen. I hope you don't think I judge you for your decision. I'm sorry if others have.' The thought that he'd suffered the horror of war for the greater good and then was condemned for his choices made her heart ache.

'Thank you for your understanding.' He shifted slightly and cleared his throat again. It was then she realised he was nervous. 'I've been considering your offer of last week.'

Dorothy hardly dared to move. She yearned for him to say yes.

'I must admit I am in need of ...' He puffed out a breath of air. 'How can I explain this? You see, my wife ...'

A sharp coldness hit Dorothy like a slap. She steeled her expression to hide her shock and dismay. He was married. He'd never mentioned it before, she was sure of it. Her mind raced to grapple with this information. She reminded herself that her aim was to help him and had been from the start. What did it matter if he was married? She steadied her breathing. 'Please, go on.' She waited, hands clasped together in her lap, the fierceness of their grip teetering on the verge of pain.

'Things were very difficult at home, after the war. My wife tried to understand. I followed all the doctors' advice and guidelines and she helped as best she could, but after a year and then two went by and nothing changed, her patience grew thin.' Thomas looked away. 'When one of the doctors suggested a change of scenery might help, she was enthusiastic about the idea of coming to Tasmania.' He gave a small bitter laugh. 'I assumed she'd come with me, but she thought it best if she and our son remained at home for the time being.'

'You have a child.' Dorothy's voice was soft, hardly more than a sigh. A wife was one thing, but a son?

'He's a fine young chap.' Thomas's face lightened for a moment before a familiar shadow crossed his eyes. 'I'm afraid I scared him at times, not that I ever meant to. I couldn't admit it to anyone and certainly not to the doctors, they'd have me put away.'

Dorothy took a sliver of hope from his words. 'You've admitted it to me.'

'I feel as though you understand. You're the only one who's seen me at my worst and still respects me. I hope I can trust you.'

'You can.' She let out a slow breath. He might be married but he'd let her into his confidence and for that she was grateful.

'My wife has said they will join me out here once I'm settled. Meaning once my ... condition is under control. I've been doing everything I can but I never know what's going to set it off or when. My affliction is so often seen as a sign of cowardice or emotional weakness, as something to be hidden and denied. I try to conceal it as best I can, but I see men look at me askance when my hands tremble or my jaw locks. I wonder if they think it's catching, this weakness of mine.'

'You're one of the bravest men I've met, Thomas Moreland. You haven't given up. You've moved across the world to become a better man.'

'And yet it hasn't worked. You said you could help. Will you, Mrs Adwell? I miss my son. I hate to think of him growing up without me.'

The plea in his voice almost undid her but a battle raged within. If she helped him and he improved, his wife and son would join him and her time with him would be over. Her selfish thoughts dismayed her. He was married. He had a son who needed his father. He was asking for her help, and that's all she'd ever wanted, wasn't it? Dorothy took in his furrowed brow and the pain in his eyes. The ache in her heart reminded her of what was at stake. 'It would be an honour.'

17

Maisie

May 1922

Stepping into the role of supervisor was like being flung into the air with no idea quite where the ground was. Maisie found herself tentative and apologetic, afraid the girls would dislike her when she told them what to do. Mrs Adwell had instructed that those under Maisie's supervision must now address her as Miss Greenwood. It made Maisie squirm. She'd hoped the girls would be happy for her, and some were, but others were resentful. They rolled their eyes and whispered behind her back. Thank goodness Gertie wasn't under her charge, instead she was happily ensconced in the piping department. Her skills had improved and she liked the work. Maisie would often sit with her at lunchtime but it was strange to have some girls at the table call her Miss Greenwood and others, like Gertie, call her Maisie. Lately she'd taken to having her lunch outside even though winter was only a month away.

She'd found a place by the river where a large rock formed a natural seat. The constant flow of the river and the ever-changing surface of the water usually had a soothing effect but her thoughts churned over the problems of chocolate consistency, centre placement, speed and efficiency and how on earth to get Ruth, who was being deliberately churlish, to pull her weight.

'Good afternoon, Miss Greenwood. It's a lovely day.'

Maisie turned to see Mr Sutton. He'd often stop by the enrobers during his rounds to make sure they were working properly and to tease her about the little spanner in her uniform pocket, but this was the first time she'd seen him outside the factory, and alone. Flustered, she stood and smoothed her uniform. 'Good afternoon, Mr Sutton.'

'I think we can dispense with the formalities, don't you? When we're away from the factory, at least. Please, call me Frank.'

Maisie was taken aback. 'I'm not sure I could.' He'd been working for Cadbury's for years and was in a position of some authority. Calling him by his Christian name would be disrespectful.

'Forgive me. I've been overbold.' He touched a finger to his forehead in a gesture of goodbye and stepped away.

Maisie chided herself for being such a fool. She liked him, he might even like her, and here she was as good as giving him the cold shoulder. 'Frank,' she called after him.

He turned with a smile. 'Miss Greenwood?'

'Please, call me Maisie.' She clasped her hands behind her back to hide her nerves.

He walked back towards her. 'Glad to make your acquaintance, Maisie.'

The way he said her name sent a delicious shiver up her spine. There was kindness in his eyes and something else that she couldn't place. A sadness perhaps? Her heartbeat quickened. No doubt he'd suffered as all the other young men who'd been sent to fight in the Great War had suffered. For so many sadness was a weight they carried every day.

'A penny for your thoughts.' Frank's eyes crinkled with an inquisitive smile.

Maisie pushed away her melancholy to focus on the delicious fact that she and Mr Sutton were now on a first-name basis. 'I'm thinking how lovely this is.'

His eyes never left hers. 'And I was thinking the exact same thing.'

She smiled shyly. It was like a dream.

Frank turned to look across the water to Mount Wellington. The silence stretched out.

'I'm slowly getting used to seeing the mountain from this side,' she blurted. What a stupid thing to say. He would think her a dimwit.

'It's the view I'm most familiar with,' he said. 'Which side are you used to?'

'The one I think of as the front. It's the side you see from town.'

'You live in town?'

'Yes, at the Glebe. We have a lovely view of the mountain from our front steps and backyard. Our street is so steep you have a good view of it from anywhere, really.' She was gabbling. She should have stayed quiet and demure.

He turned to her. 'I'm intrigued. May I call on you one Sunday and see your view of Mount Wellington?'

'Oh, you can see the same view from anywhere in town really. The Queen's Domain is a lovely spot.' Maisie groaned inwardly. He wanted to call on her and in her nervousness she'd ruined it.

'I haven't had much practice at this kind of thing and clearly I'm not very good at it.' Frank cleared his throat. 'Maisie, if I may, I'd like the honour of calling on you. I could take you to the pictures in town, or on an outing, perhaps on the tourist steamer to Browns

River, depending on the weather. Some of the other chaps have taken the trip and speak highly of it.'

Maisie tried to catch her breath. The world dipped and tilted. It was as if she was on the merry-go-round at the regatta.

'I'm sorry,' he said. 'I'm rushing you.' His features fell into resigned lines.

Maisie tried to form a sentence. She'd never been asked out before. She'd seen the pretty girls at Brownell Brothers meeting their beaus after work on a Friday night. Here at Cadbury's the girls' whispers and giggles about boyfriends sometimes made her envious. Now, here was Frank Sutton, asking to call on her, and she could hardly speak. 'Mr Sutton, oh, I'm sorry, Frank,' she stammered, 'I would very much like to go on an outing with you. Thank you.' She sounded so formal and stiff. And stupid. He was bound to change his mind and tell her he'd made a horrible mistake.

To her surprise his smile was wide and genuine. 'Shall we say this Sunday?'

She nodded, mute. His enthusiasm was overwhelming.

'I'm always in town on Sunday mornings. Let's say I come to your house at two pm. Would that suit?'

Maisie thought of her mother and the piles of ironing and mending. If she came straight home from work on Saturday, did as much of the ironing as she could and then worked on the mending that evening, she could clean the house before church the next day. 'That would be lovely.'

Maisie rushed to clean up after Sunday dinner while Mother watched on from her chair with a bemused expression and Lily rolled her eyes at Maisie's orders. Andrew, wisely, kept well out of it. When Mother had asked him to chaperone he'd said, 'Times have moved on. Maisie's been out working for the past four years. I think she knows how to take care of herself.' He'd turned to Maisie. 'However, I expect him to ask my permission if he plans to marry you.' He'd grinned like an idiot before heading off to catch up with some mates.

'He'd better be worth it, this young man of yours,' Mother said as Maisie checked the room for anything out of place. 'Just remember, a married woman is not allowed to work, outside of the home, that is.'

'Mother! It's a bit too soon for that kind of talk.' Frank might decide he didn't like her after all and that would be that. Oh, but she hoped not.

The longed-for knock on the door sounded at exactly two pm. That would be his military training making him so punctual.

'Here he is.' Lily rushed to the parlour to peek through the curtains.

'Lily,' Maisie whispered as she followed. 'I wish you wouldn't.' Her little sister's enthusiasm usually lightened her heart but for once she'd rather Lily was more subdued.

Maisie and Lily sat dutifully in the parlour while Mother welcomed Frank into their home.

'For you, Mrs Greenwood.' He presented a posy of flowers to Mother, who tried to hide her delight. He made polite conversation, and even managed to make Lily laugh. Maisie relaxed a little – clearly both Mother and Lily were taken with him.

As Frank and Maisie stepped out into a light drizzle with strict instructions from Mother to have her home by five, he turned to Mount Wellington. 'You're right. The mountain looks completely different from here. More majestic. And the geological feature at the front is fascinating.'

'That's the Organ Pipes. They're dolerite columns.'

'The Organ Pipes? How imaginative, but yes, I can see why.' He opened a large black umbrella. 'If you take my arm we can both shelter under here.'

Maisie hesitated. Mrs Perkins peeked out from behind her curtains. No doubt the whole neighbourhood would soon know about this development. As the drizzle became a little heavier Maisie linked her arm through his. The neighbours would talk anyway, she might as well give them something juicy.

As they walked they made small talk about how steep the street was, the railway station being so close to her home, the apple boats at the wharves and out on the river waiting to dock, and what a pretty town Hobart was – wedged between the mountain and the wide expanse of the Derwent. On their way to the Bijou Theatre in Melville Street, they passed by the scene of the sawmill fire. Frank stopped short at the sight of the blackened wreckage. 'It's worse than I imagined.'

Maisie shuddered remembering that night, grateful there'd been no loss of life. The demolition work and clearing of the site only served to illustrate just how devastating it had been.

'The brigade did a good job of containing the fire,' Frank said. 'I read the reports in the newspaper.'

'I'd never seen anything like it and I hope I never do again.' Maisie remembered all too clearly the massive walls of flame.

Frank's face dropped. 'You were here? For goodness sakes, why?'

'My little sister is too curious for her own good. I had to fetch her back home.'

'Your mother must have had hell's own needles worrying about you both.'

'My brother kept her safe and we returned home with not so much as a singe mark.'

Frank tucked her arm more closely to his side. 'I hate to think of you in any kind of danger.'

Maisie was overcome with a piercing sense of gratitude. With so many young men gone and with her family to support, she thought she'd live her life without having a man by her side, a hand to hold and, she ducked her head to hide her trembling mouth, a beau to kiss. She took a shaky breath and presented Frank with a smile. 'And what about you? Where did you grow up? Do you have brothers and sisters back home?'

'My parents and younger brother are back at Bournville. We grew up there. Our father has worked for the Firm all his life, still does. I followed in his footsteps, as did my little brother.'

'You grew up in Bournville?' Maisie stopped in surprise and envy. 'It must have been a dream come true.' Local newspaper articles had described Bournville as a factory in the park and a model village, catering to everything its workers could ever need or want, including musical and theatrical productions as well as sports and other outdoor activities. 'Bournville sounds like a fairytale from what I've read – a wonderful kingdom where everyone lives in harmony and is looked after by a loving and generous king.'

Frank laughed. 'That's not a bad description, except you've left out the bit where everyone works hard to earn their living.'

'Why did the Cadburys build all of that for their workers?' Maisie found it hard to understand an employer who'd go to such lengths. It certainly hadn't been her experience in any of her previous jobs.

'Ah, well, do you know much about Quakers?'

Maisie chewed her lip. She knew the Cadburys were Quakers but she didn't know anything really about their religion. Now her ignorance shamed her. Embarrassed, she deflected. 'I've always wondered why the Quaker school in North Hobart is called The Friends' School.'

'The name Friends comes from Jesus's remark, "You are my friends, if you do whatever I command you." The Quakers are officially known as the Society of Friends, but Quaker stuck right from the very beginning. As to Bournville, Birmingham has many problems so when the Cadbury family became wealthy, George Cadbury came up with the idea to move the factory out of the city and into the countryside. It's proved so successful Cadbury's is hoping to do the same thing here.'

'Then I could live in a fairytale too.'

Frank laughed. 'Yes, you could.'

When they reached the theatre, Maisie and Frank joined the queue for tickets and, even though they were out of the rain, Frank kept her arm in his. Maisie was acutely aware of the warmth of his body. It was exciting but also terrifying. Large photos of Mary Pickford, Gloria Swanson and Douglas Fairbanks Senior lined the walls of the foyer. Maisie glanced at the poster for *The Sheik* starring Rudolph Valentino. When Maisie had told Gertie she was going to the pictures, never mentioning she'd be accompanied by Mr Sutton, Gertie insisted she must see *The Sheik*. Gertie had swooned over Rudolph Valentino and was envious of Agatha Ayres, not only because she got to kiss him but also because of the beautiful gowns she wore. The more Gertie had talked about *The Sheik* the more Maisie realised she could never see it. Lily would want to know all about the film and Mother would listen with interest. How could she tell them about a sheik who steals a woman, keeps her captive and forces himself upon her? Charlie Chaplin was a much wiser choice. She had a soft spot for the Little Tramp and there'd be nothing in his film she'd be embarrassed to describe to her little sister.

'Do you go to the pictures often?' Frank asked.

'I've only been a couple of times.' Both times had been with Lily and Mother as a treat. The huge moving pictures on the screen had been shocking at first and Mother had flinched several times but overall it had been a wonder. Mother had told her at the time that the Bijou had started life as a temperance hall. Now Maisie watched the people around her, chatting, laughing and buying confectionery from the counter and wondered what the temperance movement would think. The idea of it made her giggle.

'What's amusing you?' Frank asked as the queue inched slowly forward.

'I was thinking how different it would've been when this theatre was a temperance hall.'

'A temperance hall? Really? In a way that's fitting.'

'How?'

'Here we are, two Cadbury's employees, in an old temperance hall. There aren't any pubs at Bournville. Quakers believe strongly in temperance. Actually, that's how they became involved in chocolate to begin with.'

Maisie was tempted to nod and agree as if she knew what he was talking about but her curiosity got the better of her. 'How did the Cadburys become involved in chocolate?'

'It wasn't only the Cadburys. Many Quakers saw that alcohol was ruining lives and families so they started selling hot chocolate and cocoa as a healthy, and cheaper, alternative. It caught on.'

'When did they start making chocolate bars?'

'Quite early on, but the chocolate was gritty and bitter. Some clever Swiss fellow came up with ways to improve it and the English factories started doing it too. Even then, the milk chocolate was rather chalky until George Cadbury Junior perfected the recipe for Dairy Milk after years of trial and error and no small expense. It was worth it. Almost as soon as it was released in 1905 it outsold every other chocolate.'

'It's always been my favourite.' She pulled away slightly to look at him more closely. 'You know a lot about the Quakers. Does it rub off on you, working for Cadbury's?'

The queue moved on but Frank didn't step forward. Instead he turned to face her. 'I am a Quaker, Maisie. I was at the meeting house this morning where I am every Sunday morning.' His eyes searched hers.

'Oh.' She'd assumed he'd been at church. Up until now her ignorance of his religion hadn't been important. Now it mattered most of all. He'd quoted the Bible, so clearly Quakers had Christian beliefs, but Catholics believed in God and read the Bible and Mother would never let her step out with a Catholic. Indeed she would expressly forbid it. Would Frank being a Quaker be a problem for her mother? Was it a problem for her?

'Excuse me,' said the man behind them in the queue. 'Could you move up, please?'

'Yes, of course.' Frank stepped forward and Maisie followed. They remained side by side, without touching, as they neared the ticket counter. He turned to her, tension in his jaw. 'Do you still want to see the picture with me? I'll pay for the tickets but if you don't want to sit with me, I understand.'

There was sorrow and a kind of resignation in his expression. Guilt gnawed at Maisie. Her reticence had caused him pain. He was a good man, she knew it. She also knew her brother was right, times were changing. Did it really matter if Frank was Church of England or not? How could she work for a Quaker business and yet refuse to keep company with a Quaker man? And then there were her feelings for him. She liked him very much. If need be she'd deal with her mother later. 'I would like to see the picture with you.'

His entire body relaxed. 'Thank you.' His smile returned and she couldn't help but smile too.

Maisie had no experience in matters of the heart but she dared believe that his relief at her answer might mean he liked her too. Later in the dark, as *The Kid* lit up the screen in front of them, when his hand brushed against hers she didn't pull away.

18

Dorothy

22 May 1922

The scent of wood, leather and beeswax was a change from the powerful aroma of chocolate, but even here in the Firm's boardroom the air was redolent with roasting cocoa beans. Dorothy stood in her uniform, surrounded by the directors and the senior staff. Part of her hoped Thomas might attend and part hoped not. The shock of finding out he had a wife and son still lingered. She'd resolved not to ask about them and fortunately he was reticent on the subject. She would never know their names, the colour of his son's hair, or how he and his wife met. Such details would only twist the knife in her heart.

A brief glance around the room confirmed he wasn't present, which wasn't surprising. Thomas hadn't been involved in the long process of getting the cocoa and chocolate divisions up and running, unlike Margaret standing beside her and Esme at the other side of the room. Sarah stood beside Mr Cooper, stenographer's pad in hand.

When Mr Pascall had returned to England, Sarah had taken the position of Mr Cooper's private secretary. It was one she relished. He was, as a Bournville man, naturally more involved with the Cadbury's side of things. 'He started as an office boy at Bournville,' Sarah had said. 'And now he's a director. One has to admire that kind of gumption.'

Mr Cooper called the room to order. 'I'd like to congratulate all of you for a job well done. There have been difficulties and delays, and I acknowledge all of you for your patience and diligence. Today is a landmark day. Today we celebrate the first of our cocoa and chocolate products rolling off the line and heading to market.'

A cheer erupted. Men slapped each other on the back and shook each other's hands. Esme's expression didn't change – it was as sour as ever. Dorothy shifted her attention to Margaret. 'Congratulations, Miss Stanton.'

'Thank you, Dorothy. It's been a long road and more difficult than predicted.' Dorothy noted the greyness around her eyes behind the spectacles. If she'd been a friend she would have asked what ailed her but the distance Margaret had kept for a while now had become a deep chasm.

Mr Cooper called for attention once again. 'It's been six years since any fresh consignments of our famous Cadbury's chocolates have been available in Australia. Now all states are assured of high-class chocolates and sweets as fresh as when they left the factory. We know there are customers waiting eagerly for our products. Today the waiting ends.'

There was another mighty cheer. Mr Cooper picked up a newspaper from the boardroom table. 'Now, if you'd please indulge me, I'd like to read from today's *Mercury*.' He straightened the paper with a snap. '*Samples of the sweets have been forwarded to this office, and the quality is quite up to the standard we expected would be reached under the perfect conditions produced by nature and science at Claremont.*' Mr Cooper lowered the newspaper. 'We expect similar glowing reports from newspapers and magazines all around the country.' He turned to Sarah and she handed him a telegram. 'I have here a telegram from George Cadbury himself. It reads, *You have made the Firm proud. Congratulations to my chocolate pioneers.*'

Once the final cheers had died down Sarah beckoned Dorothy to follow her to her desk. 'There are a few things Mr Cooper failed to mention,' she said in a low tone. Her desk sat just outside Mr Cooper's office and although he was still in the boardroom and the likelihood of anyone else overhearing was slight, it was clear she didn't want to take any chances. 'Now our products have gone to market, I expect some kind of pushback.'

'What do you mean?' This was the first Dorothy had heard of such a thing.

'Without the tariffs, our Australian products are being put to market at a substantial reduction on our English equivalents. Similar packaging, equal quality, as you heard in the *Mercury* report, but at a much lower cost.'

'That sounds reasonable.'

'There'll be pressure on other brands, other manufacturers here in Australia, to reduce their prices too.' There was an edge to Sarah's voice.

'If everyone reduces their prices the customers benefit. As long as we're not running at a loss, I don't see a problem.'

'Remember the man from the Chambers of Commerce?'

Dorothy shuddered. 'Yes.'

'Think of his resentment towards Cadbury's being here. What did he say? That we were getting free electricity and other benefits.'

'The Chairman of Directors scotched all those rumours in his speech that afternoon. They were lies and speculation.'

'Be that as it may, those lies were printed in the mainland trade papers. That man also said it was the Australian companies that would suffer. He's not the only one who regards us as foreigners trying to take over their patch.'

'The chairman also addressed that issue. He said we're all British.'

Sarah tapped her fingernails on her desk. 'I think that was a mistake.'

'Why? Everybody cheered, the entire Chambers of Commerce.'

'From what I've heard, many Australians think differently. The Great War forged an independence of spirit. There's a feeling that it's time to break free of the yoke of Britain and be truly Australian. As a result, some view us as being invaders.'

'Invaders.' Dorothy was horrified. 'We're here to help the economy. To provide jobs.'

'Interesting you should mention that.' Sarah pushed a newspaper towards her, folded to a particular page. 'Read this.' She pointed to a small article.

WORKERS FOR HOBART

London, Mon.

Bristol messages state that Fry's, Cadbury's and Pascall's, which have combined to start a new factory at Hobart, are sending out 1,000 workers.

'That's absurd,' Dorothy said. 'Who'd believe such rubbish? The cost alone of sending out one thousand workers from Britain would be exorbitant.'

'Who'd believe it? Every Australian who reads this. The same press release has been sent to all the newspapers in Australia.'

Dorothy looked at the article again. 'It's come from Bristol, the home of Fry's. Do you think they're behind it?'

Sarah shook her head. 'The resentment from Fry's since the merger is still strong – we have Esme to thank for the constant reminder – but no, I don't think Fry's is responsible for this. In my opinion it's a clever case of misdirection, which is much more worrying.'

'But by whom? And why?'

'The Australian confectioners have had the market here to themselves for many years. They see us as a hostile force. A war is brewing, you mark my words.'

An uneasiness settled on Dorothy's skin. 'But surely the directors have refuted the claims in this article.'

'I took the dictation and typed up the response myself.' Sarah picked up a sheet of paper from her desk. 'The company, an *Australian* one,' she read, 'has a policy of using Australian labour and Australian materials whenever possible. Less than thirty employees were brought out from England to teach the Australian workers, who now total over one hundred, and whose number will be quickly added to as the building is completed. In total the English experts will number thirty-two, the last of whom are expected to arrive next week, and are the only non-Australians in the factory. It is not the intention of the company to import any more, despite statements to the contrary.'

'Well, then. That should stop the scandalmongering in its tracks.'

'The damage is already done. Throw plenty of mud and some of it is sure to stick. I fear this is only the beginning.' Sarah glanced up at the sound of approaching footsteps. Dorothy turned to see Mr Cooper approaching.

'A fine speech this morning, sir,' Sarah said. 'I was just congratulating Mrs Adwell in particular on a job well done. Mrs Adwell is, as you know, Forewoman A of the chocolate division and Head of Training in Covering and Piping. She's also in charge of the new enrobers we're all so proud of.'

'Ah, yes, Mrs Adwell. A pleasure.' Mr Cooper bobbed his head in a small bow. 'I've heard wonderful reports about you and your department. Keep up the good work.'

'Thank you, Mr Cooper.' They'd met before, many times. Dorothy wondered at Sarah's enthusiastic introduction.

'We need more employees of your calibre and diligence. I hope you're unearthing future supervisors from among the local girls.'

'Indeed, I am, sir. One of them in particular is very promising and is already working as a supervisor.'

'Excellent.' He turned to Sarah. 'Come into my office. I'll amend the press release to include that detail – local workers already rising up the ranks.' He nodded again at Dorothy. 'Mrs Adwell.'

'Mr Cooper.'

He walked into his office. Sarah picked up her notepad and leant closer to Dorothy. 'I have more news. I'll tell you tonight. By the way, your elocution was spot on with Mr Cooper. He's very impressed with you, I can tell.' She raised an eyebrow at her in a knowing way, followed Mr Cooper into his office and shut the door behind her.

When Dorothy joined the other British women at lunch, Esme was holding court. Dorothy would prefer to eat outside than listen to Esme's familiar complaints but the weather had turned nasty and her favourite spot by the river would be an unpleasant mix of rain and wind.

Esme directed her attention to Bessie. 'All this bragging about Cadbury's this and Cadbury's that, when it's Pascall's that was first to market.'

'That's true.' Bessie's eyes widened. 'By rights I should have been at that meeting this morning.'

Ida looked up as Dorothy sat in the chair beside her. 'Ooh, here she is. Our other Forewoman A,' Ida said. 'What do you think?

Should Bessie have been at the meeting having tea and cakes while the rest of us were working?'

'It was a celebration of the first products from the chocolate section going to market. I'm sure Pascall's had a similar celebration that didn't involve us. Am I right, Bessie?'

'Well, yes, but—'

Esme scowled at Dorothy. 'You always have an answer for everything, don't you?'

Dorothy gritted her teeth. She really must find another place for lunch when the weather was unpleasant. It was enough that she had to put up with Esme at the hostel.

'Where did you get to anyway, after the meeting?' Esme asked. 'I went straight back to cocoa packing but I didn't see you hurrying off to your precious enrobers. Them machines are going to take our jobs, I tell you.' She muttered 'traitor' under her breath.

Something in Dorothy snapped. Sarah's talk of war and hostilities had upset her more than she'd realised and Esme's continued carping was the last straw. 'You'd have us going back to the dark ages, I expect. Or even further. Why, I'm certain even the wheel would have met with your displeasure. The industrial revolution changed everything, for better or worse, but given what Cadbury's has achieved, I'd say it's for the better.'

'Cadbury's! Always Cadbury's.' Esme flung up her hands.

'Oh, get used to it.' Dorothy glared at Esme. She'd been polite to the woman for way too long. 'Fry's is little more than a subsidiary. If Cadbury's hadn't merged with Fry's it would no longer exist. The company failed to modernise and was in danger of extinction. It's through innovative practices, including the use of machines, that Cadbury's has continued to succeed. Succeed to the point of taking over your precious Fry's.'

Esme gaped like a landed fish. The other women looked aghast, except for Lizzie who disguised her smile by dabbing her mouth with her napkin.

Ida got to her feet and gestured for Dorothy to do the same. 'Come on, bab. Let's get some fresh air.' She guided her towards the long railway platform beside the bean store where they'd be protected from the worst of the weather. 'You're not doing yourself any favours, you know, ragging on her like that.'

'I'm sorry, but it's so tiresome to hear her go on constantly about how Fry's is better than Cadbury's. Today was a day of celebration and she ruined it for everyone.'

'Did she? She didn't ruin it for me. For me it's just another working day.'

'It was a small gathering. A cup of tea, a piece of cake and speeches. Knowing how much you detest speeches, I thought you'd be happier not to be there.'

'Not that I had a choice.'

'Neither did I.' Dorothy was growing impatient. 'Why did you call me all the way out here just to tell me you're annoyed at not hearing speeches?'

'Because it ain't about speeches, or cake. It ain't even about Esme. It's about you.'

'Me?' Dorothy frowned.

'I was looking forward to coming to Tasmania with you.' Ida's smile was tinged with sadness. 'Remember how we prattled on about all the adventures we'd have? But then you stayed behind with the enrobers while I spent six horrible weeks being tossed about on the ocean without you. Esme was there though, with a bucket and a cool flannel. She weren't bothered that I was a Cadbury's girl and she was Fry's. We were in it together, battling the weather and an ocean that was trying to kill us. Make no mistake, we honestly thought we were going to die. Esme was beside me, through all of that. It should've been you, Dot, but it weren't. Your precious machines were more important.'

Dorothy recognised the echoes of Esme's rant in Ida's words. A dull heaviness descended. 'I had no choice.'

'You were so excited about them enrobers, and your cricket finals. More excited about them than coming out with me. And then, after you arrived, you took up with that hoity-toity Sarah.' Ida shook a finger at her. 'And if you say you had no choice one more time, I swear I'll smack you one.'

'But—' Dorothy was shocked by Ida's words and at the vehemence behind them.

'Shut it. I'm talking now. Not you, with your made-up airs and graces. You told me you were Brummie through and through, but you ain't. You're ashamed of your accent, otherwise why would you go changing it? You sound stupid if you ask me. The other girls think so too.'

'Meaning Esme.' A simmering anger mixed with remorse in Dorothy's chest.

'Meaning all of us. You're ashamed of us and the way we talk. We ain't good enough for you any more. But those highfalutin' types you want to be like, they ain't never going to accept you. Remember what it was like growing up in Birmingham. Cadbury's and Bournville might make it feel like we're all the same but it ain't true. There's us and there's them, and they'll never accept you in a rain of pig's pudding, no matter how much you bung it on.'

Dorothy stared dumbly at Ida. It was as if the friend she'd been so close to had never existed. The vicious class divide of Birmingham hadn't been as evident at Bournville. George and Richard Cadbury weren't toffs. They were businessmen who'd done it tough. The brothers had pulled the Firm out of debt after their father struggled, and together they'd built the company to something far greater. They'd never forgotten the workers who helped them achieve it – the factory in the garden was evidence of that. Dorothy knew she should apologise if she was to salvage any scrap of her friendship with Ida, but this bitterness, which had clearly been fuelled by Esme, was too much. 'We came out here to create a factory from nothing. It was always going to be hard work. I won't apologise for doing my job. And I won't apologise for wanting to better myself. Just think, if John Cadbury hadn't wanted to better himself neither of us would be here in Tasmania. It's not a bad thing, Ida, wanting to be better.'

'Better? Now you're saying you're better than us.' She sneered. 'You and Sarah deserve each other. Her accent is as tinpot as yours.' Ida scrutinised her with sharp eyes. 'What's her game, anyway? And why did she stop in the hostel with us? She should've been put up in a boarding house in town with the other office types instead of catching the train to and fro every day like a navvy. When we arrived we all jumped at the chance to have our own rooms but someone had to share and Sarah was dead keen on bunking with you for some reason so—'

'You made a choice. A room of your own. Then when everyone was told they had to share, you chose Esme.'

Ida's face hardened. 'Esme spends more time with me than you have for a long time. You don't even come to church any more. Every time I ask you to the pictures or on a day trip like we used to, you turn me down with some excuse or other.'

Dorothy couldn't deny it. Recently when she'd gone out with Ida, Esme had always tagged along, watching her with beady eyes and doing her best to exclude her from the conversation. Ida always seemed oblivious. These outings left Dorothy restless and in need of a comfort she wasn't sure how to find. But when she returned to the hostel, Sarah would offer her an apple picked fresh from the garden orchard or she'd have freshened the flowers in the vase on Dorothy's bedside table, making her feel welcome and, yes, even special. It had been a good while since she'd felt that way with Ida.

'I've been so busy.' Sharp guilt needled Dorothy. She made time for Thomas, any chance she had. Last Sunday afternoon had been spent with him, safely tucked away from curious eyes, talking over his fears and concerns. At the time she'd been torn between longing and duty. The more they spoke, the more her feelings deepened towards him, feelings that weren't hers to have. But she couldn't tell Ida any of that. She couldn't tell anyone, not even Sarah, especially now she knew Thomas was a married man.

'We've all been busy,' Ida said. 'Worked off our feet. Some of us are wondering why we bothered coming all the way out here. It ain't the same as at home. Everything worked proper back there – supervisors, trainers, technical forewomen. Here there ain't enough of us who know what's what. Most of the local girls don't have a clue. How the first chocolate has come off the line is a bloody miracle. It's hard, Dot, it's just too bloody hard.' Ida's bottom lip trembled and she impatiently dashed away a tear. 'We're stuck down here at the bottom of the world, far away from everything. I thought at least I was here with my best friend, but … ' She waved her hands in a gesture of defeat.

'Oh, bab.' Dorothy went to hug Ida but was shrugged off. They stood, facing each other like two boxers in the ring exhausted by nine hard rounds.

Dorothy smiled in sadness and resignation. 'Everything you say is true.' She'd assumed production would run as smoothly as it did at Bournville, but it had taken years to perfect the systems and training. She'd been a fool to think it would be the same here at Claremont. 'We've all been struggling to make it work. I'm sorry I've been so distracted. My mind's been on other things.' Even now, with their friendship teetering on the brink, Dorothy hesitated to tell Ida about the letters and the veiled threats they contained. She wasn't sure how Ida would react, or what she'd do with the knowledge. In all likelihood she'd tell Esme and then everyone would know. 'I'm sorry.'

A look of determination hardened Ida's face. 'Sorry don't cut it. Esme's going to do something. She's demanding a pay rise. We were promised more money once production started. We want what's owed us. Pascall's lines have been on the market for months and our Bessie ain't seen a shilling more in her pay packet.'

'I see.' Dorothy could only imagine how Esme's whining would go down with the board. The squeaky gate. She couldn't help but smile.

'What are you smiling about?' Ida bristled. 'This is serious stuff. She don't like you, you know, but she's doing this for all of us, even you.'

A small barb pierced Dorothy's heart. Nothing was turning out as she'd hoped. Yet. The journey was far from over. Diplomacy was needed here. 'I'm smiling because Esme is a woman of strong beliefs and isn't afraid to voice them. I'll thank her for her efforts when I see her.' She was aware her voice had taken on the plummy tone she tried to avoid when with Ida, but it didn't matter now she knew what Ida really thought and who'd put those ideas in her head.

Ida cocked her head to one side. 'Really?'

'Truly.' Dorothy grasped Ida's hands briefly. 'Now, we'd better get back to work. Shall we walk together?'

'All right.' Ida seemed unsure but Dorothy linked her arm through hers as they walked towards the factory with the scent of cocoa heavy in the damp air. Dorothy would love to pretend that everything was just like it had been back home, with her and Ida sharing a life and a friendship, but she realised now that Bournville had been the glue that kept them together and, as Esme had reminded them many times, they weren't at Bournville any more. Things had changed irrecoverably between herself and Ida, and she accepted it wasn't entirely Esme's fault. If Dorothy had wanted everything to stay the same, she should never have come to Tasmania.

At tea that evening, Dorothy was polite and spoke only when spoken to. She watched the other women interact and observed where their allegiances lay. It was clear Esme had developed quite the following with her talk of better pay for all. Dorothy was as disappointed as the other women that the promised pay rise hadn't eventuated but she was sure it would once the factory was in full production. Besides, if her ambitions played out the way she hoped and she was appointed to the board, she'd be in a position to make sure all the women were treated fairly, not only those who'd come out from England but the local girls as well. But those plans would take time. Until then, she'd keep her cards close to her chest. She was sure if Esme got wind of her aspirations, she'd do everything she could to scuttle them. So instead Dorothy was careful to thank Esme for her efforts, and while Ida seemed pleased, it only caused Esme's scowl to deepen.

Upstairs in their room, Sarah turned to her with a quizzical expression. 'You were subdued at tea.'

'It's been a long day. Besides, why bother trying to get a word in when Esme's on a roll.'

'Indeed.' Sarah flopped on to her bed. 'All her talk about pay rises. She's complained to the directors before, you know.' She laughed. 'Mr Cooper would never say as much, but he's had enough of her griping.'

'Haven't we all.'

'And yet you were so polite to her this evening.' Sarah gave her a questioning look.

'Like I said. It's been a long day. I've already had one run-in with Esme today.'

'I see. So, a tactical retreat this evening.'

Dorothy bit back a sigh. She was tired of the war references that had made their way into everyday speech. The day had been especially trying.

'Come sit beside me.' Sarah had a conspiratorial smile on her lips. 'I have some good news. I've been dying to tell you but thought I'd better wait until we were alone. It's bound to cause a ruckus, especially given Esme's complaints about accommodation.'

'She's not the only one who feels that way.' Dorothy sat next to Sarah on her bed.

'Be that as it may, now the office has moved here to Claremont ...' Sarah paused and lowered her voice, 'I've been offered a cottage.'

Dorothy stiffened. Esme, Ida, Lizzie and even young Bessie had all moaned about the fact that the men had cottages and they didn't. Even after Esme had complained to the directors, nothing had changed, and yet here was Sarah telling her she had what they all wanted. Ida was right. The divide would always be there. Us and them. She was glad she'd been polite to Esme this evening and that her friendship with Ida, although hanging by a thread, wasn't completely severed. Once Sarah moved into a cottage, Dorothy would have to work hard to restore her bond with the others. She'd let her friendship with Sarah blind her because she thought she could rely on her. Instead she'd been discarded. Well, at least Ida would be happy.

Sarah frowned. 'You don't look pleased. I thought you would be.'

'I'm surprised, that's all. I didn't think any of us would be given a cottage.'

'Two of the smaller ones are ready. The plan was to give them to single men. However, it was pointed out that as the majority of the confectionery workers are women and as the senior female staff are responsible for the most labour-intensive sections of the factory, consideration should be given to an equal division of the new cottages.'

'And who pointed that out to the directors?' Dorothy asked, knowing exactly who.

'Rest assured, it was not Esme.' Sarah's smug little smile set Dorothy's teeth on edge.

'But you're not a forewoman, and you're not responsible for any of the confectionery workers. How does that argument work in your case?'

Sarah pouted in a show of hurt. 'I'm senior staff. I have many responsibilities. And I can be very persuasive. But to assuage your doubts, I was told I was to share with Margaret.'

'Miss Stanton?' That made sense. Margaret was the Chief Forewoman and had been at Cadbury's the longest.

'But she declined.' Sarah's eyes widened at the wonder of it.

'Why?'

'Several reasons. One is that she wants to keep an eye on everyone here at the hostel, but the main reason, I'm sure, is that she'd prefer to stay in the company of Mrs Rayner. You must have noticed. They've become great pals.' Sarah raised a knowing eyebrow.

It was true. Margaret's responsibilities as Chief Forewoman put her in an uneasy position, one that demanded respect from the other women in the hostel, not friendship. Dorothy understood it was professional etiquette, but it had made Margaret's life here at this isolated outpost even lonelier. Over the months she'd slowly withdrawn from the other women – having meals with them but otherwise spending her time in her room or with Mrs Rayner in her private parlour. It made sense that the two would become friends, both of them being in a position of responsibility and of a similar age.

'And here's where my news becomes very good news indeed.' Sarah's excited smile returned. 'I've been given the choice of which forewoman I'd like to share with.'

Dorothy's palms grew clammy. She dared to smile. 'And you've chosen Esme because you love the sound of a squeaky gate.'

'I was tempted.' Sarah's lips twitched. 'It was a very difficult decision, but I knew how much she'd hate living on Bournville Crescent and I didn't want to upset her.' Her melodious laughter broke through the pretence of seriousness. One of Esme's many complaints had been that the first street on the Cadbury Estate was called Bournville Crescent. 'So, I chose you. Just imagine it, Dot, the two of us setting up house in a brand-new cottage. The freedom we'll have. No more bathroom rosters for a start. We'll have to cook our own meals, but I'm a dab hand in the kitchen and the cottages all have gas cookers – no more mucking around with coal or wood. And if we can't be bothered cooking, we'll have chocolates for tea.' Sarah reached for Dorothy's hands, her eyes bright. 'Please say yes, Dot. Please do.'

A mix of gratitude, excitement and apprehension flooded through Dorothy – gratitude that Sarah had chosen her and excitement at the prospect of living in a cottage with a room of her own. She'd tried not to dwell on how much she'd missed it, but the thought of being independent again, living outside the confines of the hostel, made her feel as though her life in Tasmania was truly beginning. Dorothy squeezed Sarah's hands. 'Thank you. Yes.'

Sarah leant over and hugged her then pulled back and put her hands on Dorothy's shoulders, her eyes gleaming. 'I'll make sure you never regret it.'

But part of Dorothy already did. Cold tentacles of dread threatened to strangle her happiness. She'd be hated by the other women in the hostel, Esme would make sure of it. But more than that, moving into a cottage with Sarah would finally spell the end of her friendship with Ida.

19

Maisie

June 1922

Much as she was reluctant to admit her shortcomings, Maisie could avoid it no longer. 'Excuse me, Mrs Adwell. I wonder if I might have a word.'

'What is it, Maisie?' Mrs Adwell gave Maisie her full attention.

'Could we …?' Maisie indicated they walk a short distance away from the enrobers.

Mrs Adwell nodded and they moved out of earshot of the others. 'What's troubling you?'

'I'm sorry, Mrs Adwell. You've put such faith in me but …' Maisie shifted awkwardly. She needed to hold on to her job, her family was reliant on her wage, but she couldn't pretend any more. She steeled herself. It was better to be honest now than face humiliation later. 'The truth is I don't think I'm a very good supervisor. You might be better off giving someone else the position.'

'And why is that?' Mrs Adwell folded her hands in front of her.

'It's just that …' Maisie lost her nerve. She wanted to impress Mrs Adwell. She had from the first day they'd met. 'I'm probably just being silly, but …'

'Let me guess.' Mrs Adwell fixed Maisie with a look. 'You'd rather be friends with the girls than supervise them. They have to call you Miss Greenwood, which makes you uncomfortable. You don't want to offend them, so you find it difficult to correct their work, and you're even a little afraid of them.'

Maisie gasped. All of it was true. 'How did you know?'

Mrs Adwell's smile was kind. 'Because it is a very common response. Girls like to be liked, so much so it often stops them from reaching their potential. I see a lot of potential in you, Maisie. However, if you'd rather be liked by girls who'll drop you as a friend on a whim, move to a different department or leave the factory altogether, than be a supervisor, I understand.'

Maisie opened her mouth to speak but Mrs Adwell raised a hand to stop her. 'You have a younger sister. Lily, I believe.'

'Yes, Mrs Adwell.'

'With Lily, I'm sure there are certain things she must do and you have to make sure she does them. She accepts your direction and does what's expected.'

Maisie worried at her lip. 'Not all the time.'

'And then you reprimand her, gently. It's the same here in your role as supervisor. You're not the girls' enemy. You're here to help and support them, which will make their work easier. But in the end, you're in charge.'

'Forgive me, Mrs Adwell, but you make it sound so simple.' It was clear she'd have to toughen up. Any idea of being friends with her fellow workers would have to be forgotten.

'Do you know why I chose you to be a supervisor?'

'Because I'm older than most of the others?'

'That's part of it, yes. You're good with the younger girls, probably because of your relationship with Lily. I understand it's trickier with the others. Some of them are the same age or older than you. However, you have attributes they don't – adaptability, cleverness, the ability to think on your feet and honesty. I admire you for coming to me with your concerns, even though it may have meant losing your position. So many other girls would lie themselves into a tight corner. Believe me, Maisie, you have everything you need to be a supervisor.'

'Thank you, Mrs Adwell.' Maisie's fervent hope was that her forewoman's faith in her wasn't misguided.

'There are certain things we can put in place to make it easier for you. Are there any of the girls you can rely on?'

'Mary is a good worker and more mature than the others.'

'Good. I want you to think of Mary as your assistant. Give her more responsibility. You need someone on your side to back you up with the other girls. Encourage Mary to think of being a supervisor herself one day.'

'How do I give her more responsibility?'

'Who's taking the tray of chocolates to the office?'

'Either Charlotte or Pearl.' Every morning one of the girls left the tray on top of a filing cabinet in the office and the clerical staff helped themselves to the chocolates throughout the day.

'I want you to do it from now on. Leave Mary in charge while you're gone and see how she goes. I imagine she'll rise to the challenge and be loyal to you in return. Once the others see you have support from one of their own they'll be less inclined to give you trouble.'

Maisie's nerves settled. Mrs Adwell's idea could work.

'I'll also introduce you to the other supervisors. You're not alone, Maisie. You can support each other, exchange practical knowledge and generally make the experience an easier one.'

Relief untied the knot in Maisie's stomach. She could now see a way forward to keeping her position and the extra money it brought her family. 'Thank you, Mrs Adwell.'

'You're a supervisor now, Maisie. Don't be scared to do what's required. Also, take advantage of the evening classes. You'll meet other like-minded girls there.'

'What's all this then?' Frank appeared, a broad smile lighting up his face. 'Mrs Adwell, Miss Greenwood.' He nodded at them both. 'Is this a private meeting of the Enrobers Society or can anyone join in?'

'Your timing is impeccable, Mr Sutton,' Mrs Adwell said. 'We've just completed all the items on the agenda.'

'Mr Sutton.' Maisie ducked her head, unsure of how to act with him in front of Mrs Adwell. The warmth in her cheeks threatened to betray her. For the first time in her life she was in love and she dared to think Frank Sutton might feel the same. Every day he made sure he came by to ask how the enrobers were behaving. Sometimes he'd slip her a note, other times a small flower that she'd tuck in her pocket, hoping to preserve it until she got home to press it between the pages of a book. Often they'd meet for lunch by the river, eating their sandwiches side by side. They talked about many things. Maisie was curious about England and Bournville, and Frank wanted to know all about her life and Hobart. She'd kept their friendship quiet from the other girls except Gertie, who was thrilled. Maisie had sworn her to secrecy but even so she knew it wouldn't be long before word got out.

'How are you, Miss Greenwood, on this fine morning?'

'Well, thank you, Mr Sutton.' She couldn't look at him, not with Mrs Adwell standing right there.

'Those enrobers behaving themselves?'

'Yes, thank you, Mr Sutton.' Her cheeks grew hotter with each exchange.

'And what brings you to this neck of the woods, Mr Sutton?' Mrs Adwell's voice held a note of knowing, or was it Maisie's imagination?

'Doing the rounds.'

'I see.' Mrs Adwell sounded very sceptical indeed. 'Well, I must be off.' She nodded to Maisie. 'Put in place the changes I've suggested and we'll talk again in a week.' She turned her attention to Frank. 'Do your rounds include the fork and bowl section? If so, you can walk with me.'

'No need for me there. No machinery.'

'But there are pipes and suchlike. One never knows when they might need attention.'

Maisie's hands grew clammy. Mrs Adwell was teasing him.

'What's that noise?' Frank put a pantomime hand to his ear. 'I do believe I hear a conche calling me.' He shrugged. 'Machinery! What can I say?'

'There's always something that needs your special touch.' Mrs Adwell's smile faded and her expression grew serious. 'Just be careful what you touch, Mr Sutton. There are always consequences.'

'Indeed I will. No need to worry.'

'Make sure of it, Mr Sutton.' Mrs Adwell nodded to them both and departed.

Maisie had listened to their exchange with a growing anxiety. 'Are we in trouble?' she whispered once Mrs Adwell was out of sight.

Frank's gentle smile reassured her. 'Mrs Adwell's known me since I was a young lad. She might only be a few years older than me but she thinks it's her duty to give me a motherly warning, that's all. As forewoman, she has a responsibility towards you.'

'But still, we need to be careful, don't we?'

'Why, Maisie? We aren't doing anything wrong. Which reminds me, have you heard about the dance the social committee is putting on next month?'

Maisie had heard of little else. The girls were atwitter about it. 'Yes, I have.'

'Would you like to go with me? The Firm's putting on a special train. I can come into town and escort you here, then make sure you're safely home at the end of the night.'

Maisie's hand flew to the pulse that raced at her throat. They'd arrive together, dance together and leave together. Everyone would know they were a couple. 'Is that what you really want?'

'More than anything.'

'Then yes, I'd love to go to the dance with you.' Maisie swayed a little.

Frank reached out a hand to steady her. Her skin flamed at his touch. 'Are you all right?'

She looked up at him. 'Yes.' She had never felt more alive.

He moved as if to kiss her cheek then stopped as if only just remembering where they were. 'I really do have to check on the conches. I'll see you tomorrow.'

Maisie smiled as she watched him walk away. He liked her. He really did. Going to the pictures was one thing, and their lunches together were another, but going to the dance together? That made it official.

Maisie put Mrs Adwell's suggestions in place and enjoyed her daily break from the enrobers to take the tray of chocolates to the office knowing that Mary was running a tight ship in her absence. Mrs Adwell had been right. The more troublesome of the girls had settled down now Maisie had an ally. She was on her way to the office now with a tray of chocolates in her hands when a deep voice stopped her.

'You must be the most popular girl in the factory.'

Maisie steadied the tray. 'Pardon?'

He was dressed in white overalls, leaning casually against the wall of the office block, smoking a cigarette. His accent was Australian so he was a local employee. 'I see you walking by with your chocolates every day and I think to myself, the paper pushers must love her, a pretty girl bringing them treats.'

Warmth crept up her neck to her cheeks. Frank had told her she was pretty but a stranger never had. She'd only ever been treated like an ugly duckling at Brownell Brothers. She dared to study this stranger. He was older than her, older than Frank too. His dark hair was slicked back and parted at the side and his eyes had a Rudolph Valentino look. He even made the white overalls look dashing. 'Would you like one?' She proffered the tray. 'I'm sure they wouldn't miss it.'

He pushed himself away from the wall, extinguished his cigarette beneath his heel and stepped towards her. 'Don't mind if I do.' He examined the selection then looked into her eyes. 'What's your favourite?'

'I'm partial to the Turkish Delight. Second from the bottom with a piped swirl across the top.'

'That sounds exotic.' He picked one up delicately between two fingers, as if it were the most precious thing in the world. Maisie's stomach fluttered as he slowly bit into it and closed his eyes as if in rapture. 'Mmm. Delicious.' He licked his lips.

'I'm glad you like it.' Maisie's words came out half choked.

'Yes, you must be very popular indeed.' His lazy smile made her feel as though she herself had been wrapped in chocolate.

'I must be getting on.' She had to leave before she melted. 'It was nice to meet you.'

'I'm sure we'll see each other again. Oh, but where are my manners.' He made a small bow. 'Percy Bates, at your service.'

'Maisie Greenwood.' She bobbed her head and hurried off, her mind all muddled at the strange encounter.

Percy Bates was true to his word. More often than not he'd be waiting for her outside the office building. She'd offer him a chocolate and he would eat it with a slow delicacy. He was different to the other local men who worked in the factory – he seemed more of a man of the world, but when she asked him where he was from he gave her a vague 'here and there' and left it at that. But he seemed fascinated by her and asked her many questions in his languid way in the few moments they had together.

On a bright cold day, Maisie approached the office block with anticipation. The sky was a pure, crisp blue stretching out to touch the hills in all directions. There was no breeze, and the aroma of chocolate hung heavily in the air. Maisie's pace quickened. Would Percy be there? She always looked forward to seeing him, even though a nagging guilt accompanied her anticipation.

There he was, leaning against the wall with a cigarette between his fingers and a smile on his lips. They did their dance of greetings and the offering of a chocolate or two.

'Don't you have work to do, Percy?' They'd been on a first-name basis almost from the start. 'How do you get away every day, just as I happen to be walking by?' Maisie had been curious for a while but only now had the courage to ask.

'Pure coincidence.' Percy winked and flashed her a smile. 'Or pure luck. I feel lucky every time I see you.'

'Lucky because you get a couple of chocolates.'

'Oh, I can get chocolate anytime.' His voice had an undertone that made her knees tremble, although she wasn't sure why. 'But you, you're special.'

Maisie lowered her chin to hide the blush that crept up her neck. 'I'd better be going.'

As she made to leave Percy called her back. 'It's not just the clerical staff you're popular with, is it, Miss Maisie Greenwood?'

'What do you mean?'

'I must confess, I was hoping to see you at lunchtime yesterday.' He looked away and then back at her. 'You'd mentioned that you often like to have your lunch by the river. I searched you out but what did I find? You were keeping company with one Mr Frank Sutton. You looked very cosy together, the two of you.'

The nagging guilt solidified into a heavy lump in her chest. In her conversations with Frank she'd never mentioned Percy, and Percy had never asked her if she had a beau. She'd done nothing wrong and yet it felt like she had.

Percy studied his fingernails. 'How well do you know Mr Sutton?'

There was a slight sneer in his tone when he said Frank's name that made her defensive. 'We're friends.'

'You know he's a Quaker then?'

'Yes.' Her feeling of unease strengthened.

'So, you know about the Quaker beliefs?'

'A little.' All she knew was what Frank had told her.

'I'm surprised you're not worried about being seen with him.' Percy's eyes narrowed.

'Why would I be?' Everyone loved Frank. The younger girls still giggled and blushed when he was around. Mrs Adwell thought very highly of him and she was no fool.

'You told me your father died in the war.'

Maisie nodded. Percy asked her so many questions. Some of them were personal but it seemed the most natural thing in the world to answer them, even the ones that made the tears well in her eyes. He was always so kind. So sympathetic. But at the moment he was being neither.

'Many brave men did their duty and many made the ultimate sacrifice, but not Frank Sutton.'

Maisie rocked back as if he'd hit her. She stared at Percy, unable to speak.

'I'd be asking him how many white feathers he was given. He'd have quite the collection, I'm sure.'

During the war Maisie had seen women in the streets of Hobart searching out men to give a white feather. After her father had died she was tempted to join them even though she'd only been thirteen. She'd been blinded by grief and longed to do something, anything to take the pain away. She watched the women hand out feathers, not just to able-bodied young men, but even to those who'd been injured. Some men objected, saying they were exempt from service, but still the women scorned them. Other men turned out to be soldiers on leave, for goodness sake, but the white-feather brigade didn't care. As Maisie's grief had abated to a low ever-present thrum, she saw these women in a different light. They felt powerless, like her, and scared, but their fear had turned to spite and self-righteousness. They would be better off knitting socks and sending care packages than persisting with their spiteful, pointless acts. Even so, the fact that Frank might not have served in the war was a stab to her heart. 'Are you saying he's a coward?'

'It's not up to me to say anything. Frank's the one who should tell you.' Percy sighed. 'I'm sorry, Maisie. It seems Frank has been holding back some vital information.' He gave his customary little bow and walked away.

20

Dorothy

'Come and look, Dot – we have our very own bathroom.' Sarah beckoned from down the hallway. 'No more roster.'

Sarah's excitement was hard to resist. It had been less than two weeks since Sarah had first told her about the cottage and now here they were, moving in. Dorothy joined her to admire the brand-new tub and shower bath. 'It's wonderful.' She'd studied the plans and blueprints before they moved in – Tasmanian oak floorboards, King Billy pine window frames, vertical boards both inside and out, and the walls and ceiling filled with wood shavings to keep the winter chill at bay – however, being inside the cottage was a different thing altogether. It smelt of fresh paint and new carpet and everything shone with a pristine light. With a sharp pang she was reminded of the day she and Ida had moved into their small cottage at Bournville.

'What's wrong?' Sarah asked. 'You look as though someone walked over your grave.'

In a way they had. As she'd feared, Ida had been upset at the news of the cottage and Esme had fuelled the flames of resentment, not just with Ida but with the other women at the hostel. Dorothy was glad the cottage was close to the factory. As she no longer felt welcome to lunch with them, it was a simple thing to have her midday meal at home. 'It's nothing. I was just reminded of my cottage at Bournville.'

'The one you shared with Freddie.' Sarah nodded wistfully and Dorothy didn't correct her. 'I feel the same.'

Dorothy was instantly curious. Sarah spoke so little of her life back in England. 'You had a cottage at Bournville?'

'Not Bournville, no.' Sarah drifted towards the living room and Dorothy followed, hoping to pick up crumbs of information. Sarah ran a hand along the mantelpiece, examined her fingertips and gave a satisfied nod.

'And you lived there with someone?'

Sarah shook her head as if clearing her mind. 'Don't mind me, reminiscing like a melancholic. Today's a happy day. Let's take a look at the kitchen.' By the time Dorothy reached the kitchen, Sarah was already exploring another part of the cottage. 'Oh, Dot,' she called out. 'We have our own laundry too!'

It only took them a few days to settle into their new home. The Firm provided furniture as part of the rent and the few possessions they'd brought with them were unpacked in no time. Stocking the larder and mastering the gas cooker took a little longer but to Dorothy's delight Sarah was a very good cook. In the garden, though, Dorothy would be working alone. Sarah confessed to having not the slightest interest or aptitude.

That Sunday, Sarah smoked a cigarette and watched Dorothy digging in one of the vegetable beds in their backyard. Now they had their own yard and a fenced one at that, Dorothy was at last wearing her breeches. She was still reticent to wear them while out walking due to the conservative nature of the locals, but gardening in skirts had never made sense to her.

'You haven't gone to the meeting house today,' Sarah teased. 'Have I been a bad influence on you?'

Dorothy smiled. 'I'm always open to new experiences and sleeping in on a Sunday morning is certainly one of those.' Dorothy didn't feel the need to go to the meeting house as often, now that Thomas was working at Claremont. 'Besides, spending the day in the garden under God's blue sky, digging in God's good earth is a kind of church, wouldn't you say?'

'I'll take your word for it.' Sarah sniffed the air. 'I thought you were planting vegetables. Why does everything smell of cocoa, even here?'

'That's the cocoa bean husks. They make excellent compost and mulch for the garden.'

'Well, I never.'

Dorothy saw a chance to unearth a little about Sarah's past. She leant on the spade. 'Didn't you ever do any of the gardening at your cottage back home? Deadhead a rose or do a little weeding?'

'I was never gifted in that department. Arthur—' She stopped abruptly. 'Watching you is thirsty work.' Her laugh was brittle. 'I'll get us both a glass of apple juice. Best I've tasted. I can see why they call Tasmania the Apple Isle.'

While Dorothy waited for Sarah's return, she mused on who Arthur might be. A brother perhaps, or a cousin. Died in the war, most probably, given how reticent Sarah was to talk about him. Dorothy turned back to the garden. Even though she worked with chocolate all day and the estate forever smelt of cocoa, she savoured the deep earthy scent of the bean husks. She'd lived almost half her life surrounded by these aromas. They were part of her soul. She dug into the soil once more. It may not be much as yet, but one day this garden would flourish.

After a job well done, Dorothy peeled off her gardening gloves, left her Wellington boots by the laundry door and made her way to the kitchen. She found Sarah surrounded by bowls, measuring cups and canisters of flour, sugar and cocoa. 'So this is what you've been up to.'

'It's a recipe I haven't tried before. Chocolate Vermicelli Gateau. The cake and icing combined use almost half a pound of butter.' Sarah's brightness sounded forced. 'Extravagant, I know, but I thought it'd be the perfect way to celebrate our new home.'

'It sounds delicious.' Dorothy took two glasses from the cupboard. 'Would you like a glass of apple juice? Apparently it's the best you've tasted.'

'Oh, I'm sorry.' Sarah looked up with a contrite expression. 'I forgot.'

'I'm joking. It doesn't matter, truly.'

Sarah pushed a wisp of hair from her cheek with the back of her hand. 'While I was watching you in the garden I was reminded of how I felt after the war. Utterly useless.' She nodded at the chaos on the kitchen table. 'I had to do something.' She picked up the tin of cocoa and put it down again. 'The war was horrible, truly dreadful, but at least there was important work to be done. Then it was over. We thought our lives would be better, brighter – we were the victors after all – but instead there was nothing but struggle and rationing. It was such a crushing let-down. I often wondered what it was all for. The war, that is.'

Dorothy placed the glasses on the table. 'I felt the same.' After the air of victory had dissipated she'd been left with a gnawing sense of disappointment. Life was harder than before. There was no work for the men who'd fought so bravely. Returned soldiers begged on the streets. Even the upper class with their country estates struggled and many had to sell up. It was as if everything was cracked and in danger of falling to pieces forever. What was the point of Freddie's death, of anyone's death? What had the war achieved except more poverty? 'It's one of the reasons I'm here. When I was asked to come to Tasmania to help set up the new factory, I had a sense of purpose again for the first time in years.'

Sarah's expression lightened. 'It was the same for me. I knew there'd be challenges and problems but that made me even more determined.'

'Lord knows, we've had more than a few challenges.'

'And it's been worth it. I feel alive again after the drudgery of England, don't you?' Sarah's eyes were alight with a kind of zeal.

'Even so, there was a lot we loved back home and had to leave behind.' Dorothy's curiosity made her forward. 'Sarah, who's Arthur?'

Sarah's smile faded. 'Oh, don't worry about that. All in the past.' She fussed with the ingredients on the table. 'The past is gone. We're building a future together, you and me, and I'm making a spectacular cake to celebrate. So much butter! Thank goodness rationing has gone by the by.'

Dorothy watched her. 'Yes, thank goodness.' Sarah's reaction made one thing clear – Arthur was neither a brother nor any other relative. If he was, Sarah wouldn't have avoided the question.

The weather turned with a chill that made Dorothy glad for the warmth of the factory. Cadbury's was at its best in winter, with the steam pipes to keep the chocolate molten ensuring her workers were comfortably toasty. It was different in the packing and wrapping department where coolness was a necessity. Autumn had come and gone but without the riot of colour she'd been used to at Bournville.

Dorothy missed the turning leaves; the vibrant reds, golds and browns of the elms and oaks. Here the trees stayed the same mottled hues of green. She'd been told the wattles put on a magnificent show of yellow blossoms later in the season. It would bring some colour to her first winter in Tasmania.

Dorothy wrapped her scarf high around her face to protect her cheeks from the bitter wind as she hurried towards the cottage. The tentative bond she and Thomas shared had strengthened over the weeks since he'd been working for the Firm. When they could, they met by the river, conversing in a manner that would never arouse suspicion if overheard, but it wasn't enough, not if Dorothy was going to be of real use. It had taken several attempts to persuade Thomas to join her at the cottage for lunch but finally she'd been successful. She'd instructed him to walk along the riverbank to the north of the factory then up to the cottage and enter through the back gate. If they arrived and left at different times, and used different paths, no one would be the wiser.

At the cottage she laid out plates, knives and napkins on the dining table. Lunch was simple fare – cold meat, cheese, fresh bread and pickles. She'd also made chocolate tarts last night, much to Sarah's delight. A tentative knock at the back door brought her senses into sharp focus. Thomas was here. Dorothy smoothed the napkin beside his plate, the linen stiff with starch, then moved to greet him. He stood just inside the portico, his hat in his hands. His expression held a hint of nervousness.

'Good afternoon, Thomas. I'm glad you could make it.'

'I hope no one saw me.' He glanced back over his shoulder.

'I'm sure no one did.' She understood his concern. They were in new territory with this visit to her home. Dorothy ushered him inside, took his hat and gestured for him to follow her. 'Can I take your coat?'

'Thank you.'

She hung his things on the hallstand near the front door. 'I wonder if we'll have snow,' she said on her return. 'Being our first winter here, I have no idea what to expect.'

'There's been some talk of it in the office – freezing winds from the Antarctic, much snow on Mount Wellington but very little settles in the town.'

'That's a shame. If we're going to be cold we should at least be able to build snowmen.'

Thomas laughed lightly. 'Indeed.' He turned to the dining table. 'This is quite the spread you've laid on.'

'Nothing fancy but I do hope you like it. Please, take a seat.'

Over lunch they talked about the new arrivals from Britain and how they were settling in, the small changes to Dorothy's workload now that more local girls had become supervisors and the evening classes that were due to start soon. 'English and mathematics to begin with,' Thomas said. 'I hope to include other subjects such as the histories, but we must walk before we can run.'

Dorothy folded her napkin and turned her full attention to Thomas. She'd planned to use their time together productively and the lunch break was slipping away. 'I've been reading about a treatment for shell shock.'

Thomas pressed his lips together. 'Yet another treatment. Does it involve eating porridge every day, finding a hobby and getting plenty of rest? All of them were recommended by my doctors and none of them worked.'

'Apparently this one does. The article states hypnosis is being used to great effect.'

'Hypnosis?' Thomas frowned. 'Would you have me cavorting about on stage like a fool?'

'Not that kind of hypnosis.' The mesmerists of the stage were popular for such acts but the hypnosis she'd studied as part of her psychology classes was a very different kind. 'There's a hospital in Devon where they've been treating shell shock with hypnosis and persuasion, along with occupational therapy, for some years. The results are very encouraging.'

Thomas spread his hands on the table. 'I'm sorry, Dorothy, I can't come at the thought of being hypnotised and as for "persuasion", how can that be of any benefit?'

'Hypnotism has been used by doctors in various fields for many years, but I understand your hesitancy. May I make a suggestion?' Dorothy didn't want him to leave today without giving him something that might help. 'When you begin to feel anxious, think of a place where you feel safe. A place where you're happy and at peace.' She lowered her voice. 'It could be a memory or something completely imaginary. Breathe deeply, slowly in and out. Close your eyes if possible and stay there for as long as you can.'

Thomas shook his head. 'I don't think it'll make the slightest difference. I don't mean to offend, but it sounds like codswallop to me.'

'Codswallop or not, there's only one way to find out.' Dorothy wasn't surprised by his reaction. She'd read about resistance in the studies from England. 'It might help.'

'To be honest, the greatest help you give me is just this, being able to talk to you openly and without judgement. I've seen doctors back home who've told me all I need to do is gain a sense of proportion, that health is largely a matter of our own control. I left their offices feeling worse than before. I apologise if sometimes I seem ungrateful but I despair that I'll never be free of this.'

'That might be true; you may never be free of it.' Dorothy wasn't going to make false promises. If she did she'd destroy any trust he had in her. 'But if together we can ease your burden, even lessen the effect somewhat, then I'd call that a victory, wouldn't you?'

He lowered his head to avoid her gaze. 'I have nightmares. Often.' His voice was faint, little more than a whisper.

Dorothy's heart contracted. He'd never made such an admission before. The trust he must have in her to even mention such a thing stopped her breath. 'That's common.' She kept her voice steady. 'It's usual, in fact, with war trauma.' Freddie's nightmares and the screams of the men at the Cadbury's hospital were with her still.

'I wake in shame. The bed is often a wreck. Sometimes the furniture. I can make a good fist of it during the day, if I'm not confronted with an unexpected explosion.' He raised his eyes to hers. She knew he was thinking of the day of the factory tour as well as the car backfiring outside the meeting house. 'But such things are out of my control. I'm at the mercy of the world.'

'You've said that talking about it helps. Seek me out whenever you need to.'

He shook his head. 'I can't. You must understand—'

'Whenever you need to.' Dorothy held firm.

'But I'm married. You must know how it would look.' She saw a flash of fear in his eyes.

Despite the churning in her stomach at the thought of his wife, Dorothy remained steady. 'We'll be careful, as we have been today. Your wellbeing comes first. You're not alone. I'm always on your side,' she repeated. 'Always.' The persuasive techniques being used in Devon underlined the power of the mind. She must help him believe he was capable of improving his lot.

When it was time to return to work, Thomas left by the back door, checking first to make sure no one would see him leave. Dorothy stayed to clear away the lunch things. Sarah might be curious about the number of chocolate tarts missing but Dorothy would make an excuse about the cold weather making her hungry. She took one last look around to make sure everything was as it should be with a wistful smile. Thomas may have baulked at some of her suggestions but even so the day had been a success. He was beginning to trust her on a deeper level. She wasn't going to rush him. There was plenty of time. Dorothy couldn't help the small voice that rose in her mind – the longer it took, the more time she'd have with him before his wife arrived to claim him.

21

Dorothy

The afternoon passed with small problems to be rectified and some of the girls' work to be corrected. Dorothy dealt with it all with a sense of optimism. Production was on target and her next stop was the enrobing department for her usual daily inspection. Dorothy was pleased the suggestions she'd made to Maisie were working and her young protégée was much happier in her position of supervisor. However, this afternoon she found Maisie distracted and taciturn.

Dorothy took her aside. 'Whatever is the matter, Maisie? I thought we'd sorted your problems with the girls.'

'We have. Your suggestions have worked well, thank you.' Maisie dropped her head. 'It's a personal matter. I know I shouldn't let it affect my work but it's upset me so. I'm sorry, Mrs Adwell.'

'Is your mother unwell? Your sister?'

'Oh, nothing like that. I didn't mean to alarm you.' Her cheeks coloured.

Dorothy pursed her lips. It must be boy trouble. She'd seen Maisie and Frank together on too many occasions for it to be coincidence. 'This is about Mr Sutton, isn't it?'

Maisie's head snapped up, a stricken look in her eyes. 'Yes it is. How did you know?'

'Mr Sutton is a fine man. I'm sure if he's hurt your feelings it will have been a case of crossed wires.' She'd have words with Frank later. Knowing him he'd be totally unaware that he'd led the girl on even though she'd warned him to tread carefully. He would've been his usual friendly self and Maisie had mistaken his intentions.

'Is he a fine man though?' Maisie blurted. 'I thought so but I've been told differently.'

Dorothy's skin prickled. 'Really? Who by?'

'I don't like to say.' Maisie hung her head.

'Then tell me what was said.'

Maisie twisted her hands together. 'I was told he was a coward. That he didn't fight in the war.'

Dorothy clenched her jaw in irritation. She'd hoped such meanness was behind them but the war lingered on in many different ways. 'Are you still on good terms with Mr Sutton? Or have you accused him of this as well?'

'I haven't said a word to him but I'll have to soon. We're supposed to go on an outing this Sunday. I don't know what to do.' Maisie was on the verge of tears.

That put a different complexion on it. Maisie and Frank were stepping out. He should have informed her – she was responsible for Maisie's wellbeing at work. She'd be having words with him herself, but not about cowardice. 'I suggest you keep your appointment with Mr Sutton and ask him to his face before believing scurrilous gossip. I think you'll be surprised by what you hear.'

'I don't know if I dare.'

'Come now, Maisie. It's clear that the two of you have formed a bond of some sort. You owe him the chance to explain.'

'Yes, Mrs Adwell.' Maisie looked far from convinced.

'Back to work now and try not to look quite so downcast.' Dorothy gave her a quick smile. It was so often the case that the girls' emotions got the better of them, which led to a drop in productivity. When Freddie was killed, her response was to work even harder and put in more hours volunteering at the hospital. A busy mind had no time to linger and a tired body slept better at night. Dorothy rubbed the ever-present ache above her heart. It hadn't worked.

On her way to the fork and bowl section Dorothy was intercepted by the man himself. Frank's face was flushed and his hair awry. 'Speak of the devil,' Dorothy said. 'You have some explaining to do, Frank Sutton.'

'It's not just the covering department. It's the entire factory.'

'Pardon?' Dorothy was baffled not only by his words but by his sense of urgency.

'All work has to stop. Now.'

'But we have two hours of production ahead of us.'

'I thought you'd have heard. There's a problem. A big one. The steam pipes aren't working and in this weather it won't be long before the chocolate solidifies.'

'What's happened with the pipes?'

'It's not just the pipes. The boilers are shut down. The confectionery department is in chaos. And as for Pascall's—' He threw up his hands. 'It's a disaster.'

Dorothy was still none the wiser. 'Frank, please. Tell me what's happened.'

Frank ran a hand through his hair. 'The water was turned off to the works, all of it, without a moment's notice. Nobody knows why. Now every batch in every department is ruined.'

Dorothy's thoughts went immediately to Margaret. The waste and loss would be considerable and, as Chief Forewoman, Margaret would have to deal with the aftermath. 'I'll tell the girls to stop work immediately and send them to the dining hall until we know the outcome.'

'You might as well send them home. It'll take some time to sort this mess out.'

'Right then.' She gritted her teeth and got to work, racing through the chocolate department shutting down the workstations as she went. As there was plenty of time before knock-off she instructed the girls to give their areas an especially thorough clean. Once their duties were done and the girls had left for home, Dorothy sought out Margaret. Every floor of the factory was still and hushed. Even the conches, usually in motion twenty-four hours a day, were silent – they were useless without the steam coils beneath them to keep the chocolate warm. Water was crucial to almost all the Firm's operations. She found Margaret alone in the confectionery department, sitting at one of the workbenches, her shoulders hunched.

Dorothy pulled up a wooden stool. 'What a day.'

Margaret shook her head slowly. Her eyes were blank. 'It's ruined. Ruined. A whole day's work, not to mention the raw materials. So much waste.'

Dorothy sympathised. Bournville employees were taught to abhor waste. The popular Flake had come about when a worker noticed that the excess chocolate spilling over the edge of the moulds cooled into folds of thin layers. Potential waste became profit. However, the day's wastage wouldn't be remedied by the invention of a new chocolate line.

Margaret took off her spectacles and pinched the bridge of her nose. 'It's just one thing after another.'

As Chief Forewoman, Margaret had borne the brunt of all the problems they'd encountered since arriving in Tasmania. The burden had weighed heavily. It was if a flame that had burnt brightly was slowly dimming. Dorothy had hoped the expertise of the new arrivals would ease Margaret's cares but there'd been no noticeable improvement in her demeanour. Dorothy's concern was that the flame might be snuffed out completely. 'What can I do to help?'

Margaret sighed. 'Unless you can conjure up an extra eight hours a day, I'm not sure there's anything to be done. The targets the Firm has set are hard enough to meet and then something like this happens ...' She gestured to indicate the eerie stillness of the confectionery room.

'The directors will have to take this into consideration with the monthly targets. They're reasonable men.'

Margaret humphed. 'Reasonable men who've never done a day's work on the factory floor.' She replaced her spectacles. 'We'd be better off with a worker as a director. At least Dorothy Cadbury had the wherewithal to start as a factory hand before she worked her way up to the position of director.'

Dorothy's heartbeat quickened. A worker on the board in Hobart was exactly what was needed. If Margaret thought this way others must too. She suppressed the excitement that rose in her chest. 'Sarah speaks very highly of Mr Cooper.' Dorothy kept her voice steady. 'I'm sure he'll do right by us.'

'Ah yes, Miss Harris. She's a funny one, isn't she?'

Dorothy stilled, not wanting to betray her reaction. She should rush to Sarah's defence but, much as she wished they didn't, Margaret's words had hit a chord.

'And that Esme is always stirring up trouble of some sort,' Margaret continued. 'You're better off out of the hostel. You wouldn't want to hear what she says about you and Miss Harris being given a cottage. It'd curl your hair. Needless to say she wants one for her and Ida. Thick as thieves they are now.'

Dorothy pressed her lips together. She wouldn't be drawn into that discussion. 'And what about yourself, Miss Stanton? How are you faring?'

Margaret splayed her hands on the workbench. 'To be honest, my mother back home is failing. I hope to return for a visit as soon as is practicable but I'd have to pay my own way and that's not possible as yet.'

'I'm sorry to hear about your mother.' Poor Margaret. Yet another burden to add to her troubles. 'I hope she recovers soon.'

'Thank you, Dorothy.' Margaret patted her hand. 'You're one of the good ones.'

Margaret's earlier comment about Sarah niggled. Dorothy smoothed the hair behind her right ear. 'May I ask, what did you mean about Sarah?'

'What's that?'

'You said Sarah was a funny one.'

Margaret blinked. 'I did, didn't I?' She cleared her throat. 'Well, she's different to us, isn't she? With her airs and graces. I can't make her out.'

Sarah did have a mystery about her that tended to keep people at arm's length, including Dorothy at times. She had hoped for a clue from Miss Stanton but it was clear the Chief Forewoman had nothing more than a vague feeling. 'She's always been kind and considerate to me.'

'Oh, don't mind me.' Margaret stood wearily. 'What does it matter in the face of a calamity such as today? I need to see Mr Cooper and give him an estimate of the wastage and loss. Lord give me strength.'

'If you need any help, please let me know.'

'Thank you. Like I said, you're one of the good ones.'

Dorothy watched Margaret walk away. The woman's shoulders were hunched and she seemed to have developed a slight limp. Never mind about her mother's health, Dorothy worried about Margaret's.

After tea that evening, Dorothy settled by the fire reading Sarah's copy of *The Home* magazine in an attempt to distract herself from the day's events. With a crack the front door was flung back on its hinges, announcing Sarah's late return. She stormed into the room and threw herself into one of the armchairs without bothering to remove her coat. 'What a day.' She snatched her hat from her head, tossed it aside then pulled off her gloves and let them fall to the floor.

'It was a disaster.' Dorothy put the journal aside. 'I thought it'd be the undoing of Margaret.'

'Poor woman. She is struggling.' Sarah threw her head back and stared at the ceiling. 'I can't believe the incompetence.'

'Of Margaret?'

'What?' Sarah frowned at Dorothy. 'No.' She stood, took off her coat, picked up her hat and gloves and threw them all on the dining table. 'Can you believe it? Some idiot from the Glenorchy council turned a valve the wrong way.' She lit a cigarette and began to pace, frustration radiating from her. 'He thought he was turning on the water when in fact he was turning it off. To make matters worse, it was impossible to discover the mistake until the flushes were viewed to see if the water was flowing or not. That's what the inspector said, not that I know what it means exactly. The bottom line is that there was a delay fixing the problem and the Firm has to pay the price. But that's not all.' The pacing stopped abruptly. 'Some of the valves are right-handed and others are left but there's nothing on the plans to indicate which is which!' Sarah sucked hard on her cigarette and expelled the smoke through her nose. 'Cadbury's has spent hundreds of thousands of pounds to establish this factory and the council's stupidity brings it crashing down with the turn of a valve.'

'Was it incompetence?'

'What do you mean? Of course it was.' Sarah glared at her. 'Weren't you listening? The valves aren't marked on the plans.'

Dorothy didn't take Sarah's anger personally. It had been a trying day for everyone. One that had become even more trying when Dorothy had arrived home to find a letter – not in the letterbox where she mightn't have found it until tomorrow, but pushed under the front door where there was no chance she'd miss it. 'I'm wondering if it was deliberate.'

'Why on earth would you think that?'

Dorothy took the letter from the side table next to her chair and held it out. 'Read this.' She felt remarkably calm as she handed it to Sarah, having had time to get used to its content. What did unnerve her was that whoever delivered it knew she no longer lived at the hostel but here, in this cottage. She'd felt safer at the hostel with a bedroom on the first floor and there always being someone else around. Here, on the estate, anyone could peer in their windows and there'd be times, like this evening, when she was home alone. After reading the letter, she'd pulled down the blinds and drawn the curtains. She'd also bolted every window and made sure both the back and front doors were locked.

Sarah stabbed out her cigarette and scanned the letter. 'He's saying it was deliberate?'

'Not exactly. It's always so cryptic. He's *implying* it was deliberate. He might be taking advantage of what you've said is incompetence for his own purposes.'

Sarah remained focused on the letter. 'And what does this line mean: *The power to save the factory is in your hands*?'

'From what I can gather, he thinks I'm the key to stopping any further sabotage. Although I have no idea why.'

Sarah sat down, the letter clutched in her hand. 'He keeps harping on about this thing of great value. What on earth is it?'

Dorothy glanced away with a shrug, avoiding Sarah's eyes. 'He must have me confused with someone else.'

Sarah tapped the letter with a fingernail. 'For the letter to arrive this evening, whoever wrote it must have known what happened this afternoon, almost as soon as it occurred. Which means they most probably work at the factory.'

A chill snaked up Dorothy's spine. If this man worked in the factory he could be close by at any time. 'Could it be one of the men living here on the estate?'

'If any of those men were spies they'd have shown their true colours back home. I don't think they'd have risked coming out here, some with families, just to hand over information they could've been paid for from the comfort of Bournville.'

'So, you definitely think he's a spy? Not an admirer after all?' Dorothy felt vindicated although she would've preferred to be wrong.

'He'll have to make a move soon. He's been undermining you, trying to shake your confidence, all the better to achieve his goal of getting what he wants from you. We need to gain the upper hand before that happens.'

They sat in silence for a moment, the only sounds the crackling of the fire and the lonely call of a plover.

Dorothy leant forward. 'If he does work at the factory, his details will be on file.'

'But we don't know his name.'

'No.' Dorothy indicated the letter. 'But we know what his handwriting looks like.'

Sarah smiled slowly. 'Very clever, Mrs Adwell. Very clever indeed.'

22

Maisie

It was the perfect Sunday afternoon for a young courting couple to take a trip to Sandy Bay. Even though the winter air had a bite to it, the sun was bright and the blue of the sky a dazzling sapphire. Maisie would have preferred it to be sleeting and blowing a gale, then she'd have an excuse not to go. Sadly, the weather remained resolutely cheerful. She put on a brave face when Frank came to collect her and they left with Mother's usual insistence that she be home by five. Mother had warmed to him, Lily adored him with his tales of England and Bournville, even Andrew had grudgingly admitted he was a good chap, but Maisie had nothing but misgivings.

She allowed Frank to take her arm on the short walk to the tram stop but when they reached Maisie's favourite seats on the top level she kept her hands firmly folded in her lap. Frank reached to take a hand in his but she kept her head turned and pretended not to notice. She met his attempts at conversation with one-word answers, if that, and they lapsed into an uncomfortable silence. Maisie had no

228

intention of bringing up the subject that weighed so heavily on her mind where others could overhear.

At the final stop by the beach at Sandy Bay, the River Derwent mirrored the brilliant blue of the sky. Seagulls dipped and swooped, hoping for scraps from the many picnickers making the most of this picture-perfect day. If she and Frank had been here even a week earlier, Maisie would have been blissfully happy with her beau beside her and the world at her feet, but all she felt was a heaviness of body and mind. Frank kept a cautious distance as they walked to the foreshore.

'A penny for your thoughts,' he said.

Maisie dared not look at him. Part of her wanted him to hold her close, to put an end to the cruel thoughts Percy had put in her mind, and, more disturbingly, Mrs Adwell had not denied. This treacherous part of her wanted him to kiss her, to feel the warmth of his lips on hers, and to dissolve into his arms. Instead she kept her body rigid and pushed the thoughts aside. 'There's a bench up ahead. Shall we sit?' It was set back from the beach, beneath a tree and away from the path. They'd have some privacy there.

Once seated, Frank turned towards her. 'What's wrong, Maisie? Are you worried about your mother? I know her health has been suffering. Or is it Lily? You two are so close.'

Maisie shook her head. The concern in his voice threatened to undo her. Already her eyes burnt with unshed tears.

'Is there a problem at work?'

'No.'

'Then what is it? Please tell me. I hate to see you like this.'

Maisie pulled a handkerchief from her coat pocket. She knew she couldn't hold back her tears much longer. 'I've been told something about you.' The tightness in her throat prevented her from saying more.

'About me?'

She nodded. A tear escaped and she wiped it away with her handkerchief.

'Dear Maisie. Please tell me what it is. I'd never hurt you; you must know that.'

'It was about the war.' Her words were little more than a whisper but even so they burnt her throat, her tongue, her lips.

'The war?'

Maisie dared look at him and saw the confusion and concern on his face. Hope bloomed in her heart. Maybe Percy had been lying. Maybe it wasn't true. But if that was the case why didn't Mrs Adwell deny it? 'I was told you didn't fight.' She couldn't say the word 'coward'. The slur that had tainted her feelings for him had kept her awake every night since the conversation with Percy.

Frank frowned. 'I don't understand. You're upset because I didn't fight in the war? But I thought you knew.'

Shock resonated through her. 'Knew? How would I know?' He wasn't denying it, but more than that, all this time he must have thought she condoned his cowardice.

'At the pictures, when I told you I was a Quaker, you were so hesitant. I thought it must have been because you knew that pacifism is one of the cornerstones of our beliefs.'

Maisie wrung her handkerchief in her hands. She'd hoped he would at least deny it. She'd even imagined him becoming angry when she brought up the subject, threatening to confront anyone who called him a coward. She'd run scenarios in her head of why he mightn't have fought – a medical problem, an exemption of some description – but not this. He was an able-bodied young man, like so many others who'd signed up and done their duty, and yet he had stayed home, safe from the guns and blood, safe from the bombs and bayonets, safe from the fate that had taken her father. Pacifism was just another word for cowardice. Percy was right. Frank was a coward.

'Please understand, Maisie.'

She hated the pathetic wheedling tone of his voice. She didn't want to hear another word.

'Quakers believe there is something of God in everyone,' he persisted. 'Every one of us is a being of unique worth.'

Maisie screwed her eyes shut. If she could close her ears as well she would. Was there anything of God in the men who killed her father? Frank went on and on about Quakers valuing all people equally and why they were against anything, *anything,* that might harm or threaten them. If he truly believed it he would stop talking right now. Couldn't he see he was harming her with his justifications and holier-than-thou beliefs? They were trumped-up excuses to enable him to hide safely tucked away, while other men bravely went to fight. And die. Her tears of sadness became hot tears of rage.

She held up her hands to stop his words. 'Are you saying that all the brave men who fought and died were actually evil in God's eyes because they were ordered to kill the enemy and therefore the God inside them? Do you think my father is in hell right now because he took up arms against our enemies?' Maisie stood, anger pulsing through her. 'Are you saying my mother and I were wrong to knit socks and scarves and donate what little we could to send care packages to our men at the front? Do you believe we were all duped into doing the devil's work?' Tears flooded down her cheeks, falling on to her coat, and she let them run unchecked.

'No, Maisie, I—'

'Stop. I don't want to hear another word. Not from you. Not now, not ever.' Maisie couldn't look at him. She despised everything about him – his sad eyes; his pathetic, puzzled expression; his justifications.

She clenched her fists in frustration. 'Goodbye, Mr Sutton, and good riddance.'

She didn't turn when he called her name, nor did she wait for the tram to take her back to town. She walked away and kept walking. She didn't notice the blister on her heel, or the pain on the soles of her feet where the shoe leather was thin, until she arrived home, tired and breathless but still angry.

'You're home early, dear,' Mother called out from the kitchen.

'Yes.' Maisie went into the bedroom she shared with Lily, grateful that her little sister wasn't there. She closed the door behind her, took off her coat and shoes, and climbed into bed. She pulled the coverlet up over her head, to block out the light. How she wished it could block out the world. If only she could disappear and never see Frank, Mrs Adwell or Cadbury's again. As she lay there, listening to the sound of her breathing as it slowed and steadied, rational thought returned. Cadbury's wasn't the problem and neither was Mrs Adwell. Frank was the problem. She'd allowed him to distract her with his charm and good looks but she was better off without him, without any man. Frank had served as a warning.

Maisie threw the coverlet back and swung her legs over the edge of the bed. She stared into the empty air, thinking. Far from being the problem, Cadbury's was the solution. All the forewomen were single except Mrs Adwell, who was widowed. All of them were competent, accomplished women with fine careers. Maisie was already a supervisor and Mrs Adwell had faith that she could be a forewoman in time. Maisie's purpose was to look after her family. Her duty was to take care of her mother and help Lily become everything she was capable of. She was never going to achieve that if she went down the path of courtship, marriage and children. She'd had a lucky escape. Romance and marriage were a trap and Frank had been the bait; she recognised that now. What would getting married accomplish other than cooking and cleaning every day without pay? No. She was much better off as she was, working for a firm that truly appreciated her and supporting the family she already had. She didn't need anything else and she certainly didn't need Frank.

Maisie stood and uttered a 'hah' of defiance. She should thank Percy when she next saw him for telling her about Frank. It had set her back on the right path. She opened the door and made her way to the kitchen where Mother sat in her chair by the lamp, the ever-present pile of mending beside her.

'Pass me over that shirt, Mother,' Maisie said as she sat beside her. 'What needs fixing here?'

'How was your afternoon?' Mother didn't look up from her careful stitches but there was curiosity in her tone.

'Illuminating.'

'Oh, how so?' Still she didn't raise her eyes.

'I'll just say, we won't be seeing Frank Sutton again.'

At that Mother lifted her head. 'Never?'

'Never.' Maisie licked the end of the cotton and threaded it through her needle.

The next day at the factory Maisie found it difficult to keep to her resolve. She was on edge, worried she'd see Frank, that he'd walk by on his way to fix something and instead of stopping to say hello as he usually did, he'd go straight past. Even though she wanted nothing to do with him, coward that he was, it would still break her heart. And what if one of the enrobers broke down with a problem she couldn't fix with her little spanner? She couldn't call on Frank. She'd have to get Mrs Adwell, and Maisie wasn't keen on seeing her either. Why hadn't Mrs Adwell warned her? How could she remain so friendly with a coward after her own husband had died in the war? Maisie's stomach was a tight knot that showed no signs of unravelling.

When it was time to take the tray of chocolates to the office it was a relief to get out of the factory, but once free of the endless hum of machinery and the warmth of the chocolate section, the cold rushed in and chilled her heart. She'd thought Frank was the one. She'd dared to think they were in love. The tears welled up but there was no place to put the tray down and reach for her handkerchief. She had no choice but to let them fall.

'Maisie?' Percy emerged from the shadows, a look of concern on his face. 'Are you all right?'

Maisie ducked her head in an attempt to hide her tears.

'Here, let me take that.' He held out his hands for the tray. Gratefully she passed it to him and dug her handkerchief from her pocket. 'I'm sorry to see you so sad. Will you tell me what's troubling you?'

His voice carried so much concern that the brittle wall she'd constructed around the subject of Frank Sutton crumbled. She'd been too ashamed to tell anyone, even Gertie, that she'd been courted by a coward. But Percy already knew. 'It's Mr Sutton.' Her voice was little more than a whisper.

Percy nodded slowly, the tray of chocolates in his hands. 'So you asked him.'

'Yes.' Maisie turned her head to hide her shame.

'I'm sorry, Maisie, but it's best you know the truth. You probably hate me for being the one to shatter your dreams.'

'No, no.' Maisie fiddled with her handkerchief. 'I don't hate you. I'm glad I found out when I did. Before things …'

'Before things went too far?'

Maisie bit her lip. She'd nursed dreams of a little cottage, a garden, a baby or two with Frank protecting them all. But now she knew he was incapable of protecting anyone from anything. A shudder ran through her.

'Not all of us are like Frank, Maisie. Most of us did our duty. Hell, if I wasn't carrying this,' he lifted the chocolate tray slightly, 'I could show you my shrapnel scars. Lucky to escape with my life, I was.' His face fell. 'I had mates who weren't so lucky.'

'My father ...' Maisie shivered.

'I know, Maisie, I know. And I'm sorry. So many of us lost a father, a brother, a mate, a sweetheart. None of us were left unscathed. Except for the likes of Frank Sutton, that is.'

Maisie took in a shaky breath. 'I'm grateful you told me. Really I am. But I must go.' She reached for the tray of chocolates but Percy moved them just out of her grasp.

'If you'd like to show how grateful you are, how about saving a dance for me next Saturday?'

Percy's sudden change confused her. She shook her head. 'The dance? I don't think I'll be going.' She'd been looking forward to showing everyone that she and Frank were a couple but Percy was right, that dream was shattered.

'Can I change your mind?' Percy smiled. His teeth were so very white and straight. He could be in the movies. Frank's lower front teeth were crammed together and one of his upper front teeth was slightly crooked. She'd found it endearing, once.

Maisie sniffed and resolutely tucked her handkerchief away. She wouldn't cry over Frank ever again but she wouldn't tempt fate by going to the dance. 'I don't think so, no.'

Percy shrugged as if it was water off his back. 'If you decide to come, I do hope you'll save a dance for me.' He handed her back the tray. 'Until then.' He gave a small salute and sauntered away.

Maisie watched him leave. What would it be like to be so sure of oneself? She couldn't work him out. But then she'd never met a man quite as handsome as he. Perhaps that kind of self-confidence came with good looks. Then there was that other side to him – concerned, thoughtful and funny. He'd often made her laugh in their brief encounters. She realised she was still staring after him and was ashamed to have such thoughts with her heart so recently broken. She lifted her chin. It was Frank Sutton who should be ashamed, not her. She would go to the dance and she would dance with Percy, and if Frank was there, so much the better.

23

Dorothy

July 1922

'Dorothy, wait.'

Dorothy turned at the sound of Sarah's voice.

'Are you heading home?' Sarah asked as she approached.

Sarah usually ate lunch with the other clerical staff – Dorothy had counted on it. 'Yes, I am.' She fiddled nervously with her scarf.

'Wonderful. We can have lunch together.' She put her arm through Dorothy's. 'Let's keep each other warm until we get there. I don't know whether I'll ever get used to it being cold in July when back home it would be midsummer.'

Dorothy's mind raced to Thomas. It was too late to tell him not to come. 'You don't usually have lunch at home.'

'I needed to talk with you. I've finished going through the employee files.'

Dorothy dropped Sarah's arm and slowed to a stop. 'And?'

'Nothing, I'm afraid. I couldn't find anything that matches the handwriting.'

Disappointment hit hard. Dorothy had been so sure the files would reveal the identity of the letter writer. 'That's a shame.'

'I was certain he must work here.' Sarah gave a little shrug of annoyance. 'I've been wrong before but not often.'

'Then we're no closer to finding him than we were before.' Dorothy started walking again. She had a more pressing problem. Thomas would arrive at the cottage at any moment. How on earth was she going to explain him to Sarah? And how would Thomas react? This was the very thing he had feared.

Sarah matched her gait. 'It's been an aggravating morning all round. I need a break from the office and the latest palaver. A brisk walk by the river would probably do me good, but honestly it's too chilly. And this wind!' She tightened her coat around her. 'All I want is a hot cup of cocoa, a thin piece of toast and the comforts of our cottage.'

'What is it now? Another visit by dignitaries? The Royal Melbourne Show?' The Firm had plans to showcase their wares at the show in September. Sarah had told her it was turning into quite the production.

Sarah shook her head. 'We all knew there would be trials and troubles when we came to Tasmania. The first factory outside of Britain? It was never going to be a simple task, but I don't think anyone saw this debacle coming.'

Dorothy's thoughts immediately went to Margaret. The poor woman wouldn't be able to bear much more. 'You have me worried.'

'Then let's hurry home out of this weather and I'll tell you all about it over lunch.'

Dorothy took a furtive look towards the riverbank, wondering if she'd spot Thomas heading towards the back of the cottage. There was no sign of him. She'd have to warn him, but how? What would happen when he turned up at the back door? She increased her pace. The back door. That was the answer.

When they reached the cottage Dorothy ducked into her bedroom. 'I'll join you in a moment.' She wrote a quick note for Thomas and hid it in her pocket.

In the kitchen Sarah had put the kettle on to boil and was slicing the bread. 'There are some rather delicious things in the ice chest. Cheese and ham. Were you saving them for tea or shall we indulge ourselves now?'

The ham and cheese were for Thomas's lunch. Dorothy thought quickly. 'I'm going to make pea and ham soup for tea. That's why I bought the ham on the bone.'

'Well, you'd better get the peas on to soak or else we won't be eating the soup until tomorrow.'

'Silly me, I meant to do it this morning. I'll prepare something else tonight and we can have the soup tomorrow.'

Sarah looked at Dorothy with a quizzical smile. 'You're usually so organised.'

Dorothy forced a brightness into her voice. 'I'm keen to hear your news, but first I need to use the WC.' The lavatory was next to the laundry, outside but under a covered way, and right by the back door. Dorothy closed the door behind her and stepped into the weather. She tried to wedge the note in the doorframe but the wind threatened to whip it away. She could tack the note to the door to keep it in place, but the hammering would make too much noise. In the laundry she picked out a screwdriver and a small screw from her toolbox. It would take longer but she could affix the note almost silently. She turned at the sound of a footfall on the steps behind her.

Thomas's eyebrows arched in a query. 'What are you doing?'

239

She put a finger to her lips and handed him the note. A mixture of longing and fear flooded through her body. He read it quickly and nodded. They stood awkwardly for a moment, together but apart. She yearned to touch him, to hold his hands in hers, to ask him how he was faring – if his sleep was improving or whether the nightmares still plagued him, if he'd made use of her suggestions and if so had they worked – but instead she stood mute.

'Dorothy?' Sarah called out from the kitchen. 'Have you fallen in? Lunch is ready.'

Thomas stepped away to leave and without thinking Dorothy leant forward and kissed him. Not on the lips, she would never dare, but on his cheek. A quick, light kiss. She regretted it immediately. A look she couldn't interpret clouded his eyes – fear, pain, surprise, longing? He turned and hurried away, leaving her off-balance.

'Dorothy?' Sarah stood in the back door, a puzzled frown on her face. 'What's going on? I thought I heard someone.'

A rush of fear seized Dorothy. How long had Sarah been there? What had she seen? 'The door was rattling. It's this wind.' She held up the screwdriver. 'I was tightening the hinges and grumbling to myself about it.'

'Of course you were.' Sarah shivered as another gust battered the cottage. 'Much as I appreciate knowing the cottage won't tumble down around our ears, let's get inside where it's warm.'

Dorothy followed her with a shaky sense of relief.

They sat at the dining table while Sarah told her, between bites of toast, about the latest fiasco enveloping the Firm.

'It's just as I predicted,' she said. 'The local confectioners are fighting back, with the indomitable Mr Macpherson Robertson as their general. He's put a million and a half pounds into his enterprise and will do anything, and I mean anything, to protect it. The situation is developing into a war. On one side there's Cadbury-Fry-Pascall, seen as the invading force. On the other side are the allied resources of MacRobertson's, Hoadley and Allen's, defending their companies on their home soil.'

Goosebumps rose on Dorothy's skin. 'Are you saying they're responsible for the troubles the factory has had? Did one of their "soldiers" turn off the water, set fire to the sawmill, and somehow engineer Mr Crosswell's fall from the scaffolding?'

Sarah dabbed her mouth with her napkin and sat back in her chair. 'I don't know who was responsible for those incidents, if anyone, but I think we've underestimated Mr Robertson.'

'In what way?'

'Here's a man who started work at the age of nine. He set up a confectionery manufacturing operation in the bathroom of the family home when he was nineteen. With sheer hard work his business became the largest confectionery works in Australia. The man lets nothing stand in his way.'

Dorothy couldn't help but be impressed. She'd started working at about the same age as Macpherson Robertson. 'He's defending everything he's worked hard for. You can't blame him for that.'

Sarah tapped her fingernails on the table. 'Don't you understand? He's telling everyone we're the enemy and treating us as such. And you haven't heard the worst of it.'

'Then tell me.'

'In this war, Macpherson Robertson holds the winning card. Glucose. He's spent a lot of time and money to ensure he controls the entire supply. It's a deliberate move to starve Cadbury-Fry-Pascall of the ability to produce confectionery. His aim is to force us to combine with MacRobertson's with him having the controlling interest. Any sign of dissent and he'd cut our supply of glucose like that.' She snapped her fingers.

'We can make chocolate without glucose but nothing else. There'd be no centres for our chocolates, no creams or fondants, and as for Pascall's – it would be the end of them.'

'Exactly.'

'Now I understand why there's so much concern in the office.'

'Speaking of which, I'd better go.' Sarah stood. 'I'm sure there'll be more dictation from Mr Cooper this afternoon and in the coming days. Letters and wires are flying endlessly back and forth.' She began clearing the table. 'Let's leave the washing up until this evening.'

'I'll put the dishes in the sink. I have a little more time.' Dorothy took the plates to the kitchen. When she returned, Sarah was by the front door pulling on her coat.

'I hope I haven't worried you too much with my talk,' Sarah said. 'It seems you have other things to worry about.'

Dorothy hesitated, unsure of what she meant. 'Does Margaret know about the problems? Has she taken it badly?' If Margaret faltered it was Dorothy who'd have to pick up the slack.

'I'm not referring to Margaret.' Sarah put on her hat and checked her appearance in the hall mirror. 'You were already worried before I even mentioned the Firm's troubles. Does it have anything to do with the man at the back door?'

Dorothy froze. 'What man?'

'Oh, come now, Dot. Are you going to tell me he was a travelling salesman? They always come to the front door.' Sarah removed a compact from her handbag and smoothed powder on her nose. 'Perhaps you'll explain him away by saying he'd mistakenly come to the wrong cottage, or he was a potential robber and you were warding him off with your screwdriver.' She placed her compact back in her handbag and studied Dorothy.

Dorothy straightened. Yes, Thomas was married and they had to be careful, but they'd done nothing wrong. 'He's a friend.'

242

'A friend. I see. And you were planning a secret lunchtime assignation until I ruined it for you.'

'Assignation?' Sarah made the word sound so dirty. 'No. Nothing like that. As I said, he's a friend, that's all.'

'Then why was he sneaking in the back door and why did you warn him off?'

'You know what the Firm's like. Everything has to be above board and proper.'

Sarah pulled on her gloves. 'Please, Dot, be careful. You say he's just a friend and it's completely innocent—'

'It is.'

'And I believe you but others won't. We both know there are those who would use something like this against you.'

Dorothy's thoughts immediately went to the mysterious letter writer. From the start he'd made it clear he'd been watching her.

Sarah checked her appearance once more. 'I have no doubt that if there was the slightest whiff of scandal, Esme would be shouting it loud and clear across the factory.'

Esme? Dorothy hadn't even thought of her. 'I'm sure she would.'

'Your personal life is none of my business and I hope it doesn't become other people's business.' Sarah stepped towards her and placed a gloved hand on Dorothy's arm. 'You have a certain amount of latitude being a widow, but still there are standards. Think carefully about what you're doing. Is he worth it?'

The image of Thomas's troubled eyes, the fear and pain there, the tremble in his hands and the knowledge of his nightmares rose to mind. 'Yes. He's worth it.'

'Well, then.' Sarah's smile was gentle but tinged with sadness. 'I don't want to encourage you but I will do this: I'll give you fair warning if I plan to come home for lunch at any time.'

'Thank you, but—'

'Your life is your own and you must live it as you see fit.' Sarah's grip tightened slightly on her arm. 'Just be sure of his intentions.'

Dorothy pulled away. 'His intentions are honourable. I can assure you of that.' It was her own intentions she was more worried about. Why had she kissed him, if only on the cheek?

'Good. I'm sorry to have ruined your lunch.'

'I'm relieved in a way, that you know.'

Sarah tilted her head with a smile. 'Yes, well, meeting him will be easier for you from now on.'

'That's not what I meant. I don't like us having secrets.'

A cloud passed over Sarah's eyes and there was a tiny shift in her features, then her smile returned. 'Indeed.' She opened the door. 'I must get on.' The door closed behind her.

24

Maisie

Gertie's house was a sprawling tumbledown weatherboard in Montrose. Maisie took in the peeling paint and the broken struts on the verandah. It was big enough for his seven children but clearly Mr Thompson didn't have many pennies left after feeding them to spend on maintaining the place.

Gertie led Maisie to a sleep-out at one end of the verandah. 'This is my bedroom. It used to be Linda's, my big sister, but since she got married it's all mine.' Gertie opened the door. The room was small and furnished sparsely with a single bed, bedside table and a wardrobe. Even so the pride on Gertie's face was obvious. 'I have my own entrance, see. I can come and go as I please. Put your things by the wardrobe and come meet the rest of the rabble.'

When Maisie had decided to go to the dance after all, Gertie had insisted she come to her house after work to get ready. It made sense – Cadbury's was a short ten-minute train ride away from Gertie's. Maisie had been loath to leave her mother with an afternoon's worth of work but Lily had assured her she'd do her best to help. Now Gertie introduced Maisie to a tangle of children whose names she would never remember, various cats, at least two dogs and a flock of chickens.

Mrs Thompson flustered about in the kitchen, her hair piled up in a messy bun and flour smudged on one cheek. 'I'm always baking something for this lot,' she said as she smacked a pair of small hands away from the mixing bowl. 'I'm making a spiff chocolate pudding for tea tonight. Since Gertie's started working at Cadbury's we've no shortage of cocoa.'

'Sounds scrumptious, Mum,' Gertie said. 'What a shame Maisie and me won't be able to help with the washing up.' She grinned. 'We have to rush off after pudding to go to the dance.'

'Don't you worry, my girl, Sunday dinner's washing up is all yours.'

Gertie groaned and pulled Maisie back to her room. 'We'll get some quiet in here, at least for a little while.' She knelt and pulled a small stack of magazines from underneath her bed and arranged them carefully on the quilt. The covers were of glamorous men and women, all perfectly coiffured and dressed. 'I adore *Motion Picture* magazine.' Gertie picked one up and held it lovingly. 'Come sit beside me.' She patted the bed.

As they flicked through the pages, Maisie was dazzled by the pictures and tales of movie stars – their clothes, their lives, their films. It was a different world. The pages also displayed advertisements for make-up and lingerie. The underwear ads made Maisie feel awkward and when she saw one for sanitary napkins she had to suppress a gasp. Gertie was oblivious to her discomfort as she swooned over a photograph of Conrad Nagel.

'Here he is in *Saturday Night*.' She pointed to the article. 'Isn't he handsome? And look at Leatrice Joy's dresses. This one is practically backless and the other one plunges at the sides. It looks more daring than it is though; see the cunning panels.'

Maisie examined the photo. The dress made it look as though her sides were naked to the waist.

'Imagine if we wore something like this tonight.' Gertie giggled. 'It's Saturday night, after all.'

'They're not exactly practical. Look at the trains. How could anyone dance in something like that?'

'Oh, the trains have special loops at the end. You put it over your wrist to keep the train out of the way.' Gertie extended her wrist gracefully and tilted her head in a pose not unlike the ones in the magazine.

Maisie shook her head in disbelief. 'How do you know these things?'

'I watch and learn. The moving pictures are very educational.' Gertie smiled in her cheeky way. 'I've learnt more from going to the pictures than I ever did from school.' She ran a finger along the photograph of the dress. 'I dream about wearing gowns like these.'

'Do you really want to look as though you're half naked?'

'Maybe. Maybe not. But I would love to wear lovely dresses that show off my figure. These days the dresses are like boxes, there's no shape to them at all.' She shuddered. 'The fashion would have us flat chested and with no waist. Why do they want us to look like boys?' Gertie thumbed through a magazine and landed on one of the underwear advertisements. 'Look here. Brassieres that flatten your chest. Can you imagine? In some ways I long for the old days when a woman could show off her bosom.'

'Gertie!' Maisie blushed at the mention of the word.

'What? It's better than walking around looking like a box. How are we ever supposed to attract a husband?'

'Is that what you want? A husband?' Maisie was surprised. Gertie was younger than her. Were her thoughts really of matrimony?

'I'm not going to work in a factory for the rest of my life. It's all right for some. You have Frank wrapped around your finger.' She cosied up to Maisie until their arms pressed together. 'When will we be hearing the sound of wedding bells?'

Maisie almost pulled away but stopped herself. She didn't want anyone, not Mother or Lily or even Gertie, knowing what had happened with Frank. Gertie was sharp. She'd guess if Maisie wasn't careful. 'I think that's a long way off.' She tried to keep her voice light and hoped Gertie didn't notice the slight tremor.

'At least you know it'll happen.' Gertie stood. 'As for me, I need to bait the trap.' She opened the small wardrobe and removed a shimmering dress of pale blue. 'Isn't it beautiful? The material looks like silk but it's actually viscose.' She held it up. It was more of a slip than a dress. The neckline was cut straight across but it hung from tiny beaded straps. It was simple but Maisie could imagine it would be transformed once Gertie was wearing it.

'Yes, it is beautiful. But won't you be cold? It's the middle of winter.'

Gertie shrugged. 'I'll have to wear my boring old coat but once we get there I'll reveal the real me underneath. Besides, the dancing will warm me up. I expect I'll have plenty of attention from the boys.' Gertie laid the dress lovingly over the bed. 'It's a pity the Bournville spinsters will be on hand to stop anyone having any fun.'

Maisie disliked the term 'Bournville spinsters' but it had become common usage with the girls. She could understand why. The British women were always keeping an eye on them – on the train, at lunchtime, and they'd be at the dance tonight to make sure there was no hanky-panky. 'I'm sure we'll still be able to have fun.' She forced herself to sound bright. Before she'd discovered the truth about Frank she'd been looking forward to the dance, but now she was just going through the motions.

Gertie turned to her. 'And what about you? What are you wearing tonight?'

Maisie took her best dress from the bag she'd brought with her. It needed a light press but being made of wool it hadn't crushed too badly.

Gertie's face fell. 'Surely not.'

'Why, what's wrong with it?' Maisie only wore the dress once a week, to church, and it was still in good condition despite being a few years old. It was a shame it itched her so badly.

'I'm sorry, Maisie, but it looks like something Miss Stanton would wear. It must be as old as her too. I know you've already found the love of your life but it doesn't mean you have to go to the dance dressed like a frump.'

Maisie bit down her objections. It was true – next to Gertie she'd look dowdy but then anyone would.

Gertie returned to her wardrobe. 'Because you're my friend, I'm going to lend you my second-best dress.' She pulled out a sleeveless number in deep crimson with a modestly scooped neckline and a tiered skirt falling from the dropped waist. She held it against herself. 'It'll look lovely on you, and as you're a bit shorter than me you won't find the length too scandalous.' She was joking, but as the dress fell only slightly below Gertie's knees, Maisie would be glad of a lower hemline. 'Most of the new fashions are very easy to sew, but something like this with the tiered panels of different lengths is a little trickier.'

'You made this?' Maisie looked more closely at the stitching and construction. 'It's beautifully done.'

Gertie glowed with the praise. 'I make all my own clothes. Here, try it on.'

As the dress settled over her shoulders and down her hips, Maisie thrilled with delight. She'd never worn such a beautiful thing. The dress was a magical combination of loose but shapely and the tiered ruffles swished in a satisfying manner around her calves. It would be lovely to dance in. Her heart contracted. Who would she dance with? Not Frank. Not now. Percy had asked her to save a dance for him but one look at Gertie in her slip of a dress and she knew a man like him would ditch her in a flat second to take up with her prettier friend.

Gertie stood back and surveyed her with delight. 'Golly! You carry it off better than I do.'

Maisie waved her compliment away. 'I'm sure I don't, but I would like to have a dress like this.'

'Then why don't you? I'll lend you the pattern. It won't take much adjusting, if any.'

Maisie blanched. She couldn't justify spending money on material for a new dress when there were so many other expenses. 'Gertie, can I ask you something?'

'Anything.'

'It's a bit personal.'

'My favourite kind of question.' Gertie grinned.

'I don't mean to pry, but how do you afford going to the pictures, the movie magazines and material for new dresses?' Maisie winced with the audacity of her question but Gertie seemed unaffected.

'I'm earning better money than I did in my last job. I pay board, but after that my money is my own.'

'I see.' Maisie guessed that was the difference in having a father who was still alive and bringing home a wage.

'After I'm married I plan to sew dresses for other women as well as for myself. For some pocket money, you know. I couldn't stand having to ask my husband for money every time I wanted to go to the movies or buy a magazine.'

Maisie smoothed the material of the crimson dress over her hips. If she could afford it, she'd pay Gertie to make her a dress like this. 'I'm sure you'll have women lining up. You're a very good seamstress.'

'Mum taught me to sew and to knit. I can make just about anything, but I usually spend my time mending and darning. There are endless piles of it in this house.'

Maisie knew how that felt.

'We've fixed the dress problem, now we need to do something about your hair.' Gertie picked up a small jar from the bedside table. 'This should do the trick.'

Maisie nervously touched her wild locks. 'What is it?'

'Pomade. It will help keep your hair in place. Just a little bit, mind. Here, I'll show you.' Gertie undid Maisie's hair and carefully laid the pins on the bed. She scooped out a tiny amount of pomade from the jar, spread it on her fingers and smoothed it gently over Maisie's hair. 'There. I guarantee you'll have a much easier time of it and won't have bits sticking out everywhere. Give it a go.'

Maisie pulled her hair back into her usual bun. The smoothness of her locks and the ease with which she was able to contain them amazed her. She'd even be able to keep her hair neatly under her cap at work. Mrs Adwell would be pleased. She shook her head in amazement. Her hair stayed in place. 'Thank you. This is wonderful.' It felt more like a miracle.

'Keep it.' Gertie pressed the jar of pomade into Maisie's hands with one of her cheeky grins. 'Your need is greater than mine.' She stood back and looked Maisie up and down. 'How about some rouge and a little lipstick to really make the most of your beautiful hair and that fabulous dress.'

Maisie might be feeling a little more adventurous but make-up was a step too far. 'I don't think so.'

'Fair enough. You're probably more of a Mary Pickford than a Theda Bara.'

Maisie laughed, pleased to be compared to Mary Pickford rather than the alternative. She'd never admit to it, but she found Theda Bara terrifying.

25

Maisie

At lunchtime the following Monday, Maisie sat with the other supervisors, as she had since Mrs Adwell had organised it. The arrangement worked well. The supervisors could call each other by their first names and often talked over any problems and concerns. But today there was only one topic of conversation – the dance.

'You looked lovely, Maisie,' Daphne said. 'Your dress was divine.'

'I wish it was mine. It belongs to Gertie. She very kindly lent it to me.'

'Oh, Gertie,' Daphne said in a tone that had every girl at the table nodding. At the dance, as soon as Gertie had taken off her coat, all eyes had turned to her just as she'd hoped. The dress had shimmered as she'd walked, accentuating her curves, and she'd worn a sequinned headband that sparkled with a light to match her eyes. The young men had clamoured round her while Maisie followed, feeling more like an older sister or spinster aunt than her friend. Gertie had lapped it up, danced with everyone who asked, laughed too loudly, and attempted to slip out the side door with one particularly keen young man before being stopped by one of the Bournville chaperones. By the end of the night she'd been asked out by three of her dance partners and had whispered to Maisie, a little too loudly, that at least two of them were in with a chance, before collapsing in a fit of giggles. Maisie suspected one of her prospective beaus might have slipped a little something into Gertie's glass of punch.

Maisie had kept an eye out for Frank so she could avoid him at all costs. She needn't have worried. He'd spent most of the night as a wallflower, if a man could be described as such. He'd danced with Mrs Adwell but it was clear his heart wasn't in it. Mrs Adwell had been a surprise. She'd worn a lovely dress with a dropped waist and beading around the neckline. Maisie thought she and the other British women would be as thick as thieves but when Mrs Adwell approached them, they'd given her the cold shoulder. Instead she'd spent her time with Miss Harris, who looked rather dashing in a stylish emerald-coloured dress.

'Wasn't the band smashing?' Alice sighed. 'I could have danced all night.'

The girls smiled in agreement. O'Callaghan's Jazz Orchestra had done a sterling job of keeping couples on the dance floor. Maisie had enjoyed a foxtrot with Percy, who, unsurprisingly, was a superb dancer and led her around the floor with confidence and ease. Later in the evening, when Gertie was catching her breath, she'd teased Maisie about playing hard to get with Frank. 'You haven't danced with him once,' she'd said. Maisie knew she'd have to tell Gertie at some stage, but she couldn't, not yet. The pain that nestled under her breastbone niggled still. The shame was there too, that she'd fancied herself in love with a coward, a man who deserved nothing but disdain.

The other supervisors chatted on about who had danced with who and what that might mean, the decorations, the supper, and the fact that the Cadbury's social committee was planning more dances.

'You know what worries me?' Jane was a serious young woman, only a little older than Maisie. 'The girls are trained to an acceptable standard and then what happens? They go to one of these dances, meet a fella and then that's that. They're married and gone. All that effort wasted.'

'It's true,' Daphne agreed. 'It's such a shame we can't work once we're married.'

'Why is it a shame?' Alice asked. 'A wife should be at home looking after her husband and children.'

'It's a shame,' Daphne replied, 'because so many of the girls aren't interested in bettering themselves. They say they work hard enough as it is and won't take up the offer of evening classes.'

'I enjoy the evening classes.' Maisie laughed lightly. 'Who needs to go to the pictures when you can learn algebra and economics?'

'That's right,' Jane agreed, failing to see the joke. 'I'd much prefer to improve my mind than step out with a young man who'd trap me with a wedding ring.'

'Before marriage a woman is a queen; after marriage, a subject,' Daphne said. Alice glared at her. Daphne shrugged. 'I read that somewhere.'

'I don't think I'll ever get married.' Maisie regretted the words as soon as she'd said them. Alice looked at her with such a shocked expression she felt as though she'd admitted to treason. 'Well, at least not for a good long while,' she backtracked.

'That's very sensible,' Jane said. 'A woman can't have a career if she plans to marry and that's the end of it.'

'I'd like to be a forewoman,' Daphne said with a determined glint in her eye.

'Me too,' agreed Jane. 'And I have no shame in saying so.' She flashed a look at Alice.

This time Maisie kept her thoughts to herself. If she was a forewoman Lily could definitely attend university. She'd happily be a spinster to see her little sister shine. But there was still that pull. She remembered her hand in Frank's, the way he looked at her, her arm in his, how they'd talked and laughed and fitted so well together. She'd had a taste of, if not love, then something very close. She couldn't imagine it happening again. She'd learnt her lesson. Lily was more important than any man.

The next morning Percy was waiting for her in the shadows outside the office when she approached with the tray of chocolates. 'Did you enjoy the dance?' he asked, flashing his teeth in a disarming smile.

'I did, thank you.'

'I enjoyed dancing with you.' He moved closer.

'You dance very well.'

'As do you.' He looked down at the ground then raised his eyes to gaze at her from under his lashes. The effect was mesmerising and at the same time slightly off-putting, as though he'd practised it. 'I would've liked to dance with you more but didn't want to send tongues wagging.'

'That was very thoughtful of you.' Maisie felt as though they were dancing now. It was as if he were circling her.

'I was wondering ...' He paused and lifted his chin, not looking directly at her but giving her a three-quarter view of his fine jawline, his perfectly proportioned nose and the angle of his cheekbone. 'When you're inside the office, where do you put the chocolates?'

Maisie frowned. What an odd question. There was something in his manner that kept her off-balance. 'On the filing cabinet near Mr Cooper's office. Why?'

'Oh, nothing.' He flashed that smile again and moved closer. His hand hovered over the chocolates but all the while he kept his eyes locked on hers. Without looking he selected a chocolate and put it in his mouth. 'Mmm,' he murmured as he devoured the chocolate and then slowly licked his lips. 'Delicious.'

'That's a relief.' Maisie laughed nervously. 'I'd hate to think we were making chocolates that tasted horrible.' Her hands trembled. She wasn't quite sure what was happening.

Percy leant closer still, the sweet scent of chocolate on his breath. 'Just one more.' He picked up another chocolate. 'I can never resist.' His eyes gazed into hers. He moved the chocolate to his mouth. Her eyes followed as his lips parted and he placed the chocolate on his tongue. Slowly he closed his mouth and hummed in a kind of ecstasy. His eyes closed as he sucked on the tasty morsel, the low humming in his throat growing in intensity. Maisie's head began to spin, the earth tilted under her feet and the tray shifted in her hands.

'Steady there, Maisie.' Percy put his hands on hers. A charge went through her, sending sensations to places she didn't dare name. 'You carry precious cargo. You need to deliver this tray safely and place it on top of the filing cabinet outside Mr Cooper's office.' His eyes were locked on hers. 'Have you ever wondered what's inside the filing cabinet?'

Maisie blinked in confusion. The mist that clouded her mind slowly lifted. Percy stood in front of her, the tray of chocolates between them. He cocked his head to one side and studied her, a slight smile dancing on his lips. 'You have an important job to do,' he said. 'I mustn't keep you any longer.'

'No.' Her mouth was dry.

Inside the office Maisie made her way to the filing cabinet as if in a dream. To unnerve her even more, there was a tray of chocolates already there. She stared at it and then back to the tray she carried.

She always removed the tray at the end of the working day just in case any remaining chocolates attracted vermin. There were never any left over but she did it just the same. She looked again at the tray on the filing cabinet. It was almost full. It didn't make sense. Not much had made sense in the last fifteen minutes.

One of the clerical staff bustled by but stopped when he saw her. 'More chocolates. We are spoilt. Here, I'll make a space for your tray.' He cleared some papers from the top of the adjacent filing cabinet.

'Thank you.' Maisie slid her tray in place. 'There must have been a mix-up.'

'Mrs Adwell brought the first tray. She said she might bring us extras from time to time.' He examined the chocolates, picked out a maple caramel and ate it with delight.

Maisie frowned and tried to clear her head. 'But why?' she blurted. 'Why would Mrs Adwell bring a tray of chocolates?'

'Maybe it's because she and Miss Harris share a cottage on the estate. That's her desk right there.' He nodded to the desk outside Mr Cooper's office. There was no sign of Miss Harris. 'Mrs Adwell probably does it out of friendship. Bringing a tray of chocolates would be a good excuse for them to catch up.'

That made no sense. If they shared a cottage they could see each other at home anytime.

The clerk picked out another chocolate, hesitated and then chose another to add to it. 'For later.' He bustled off. No wonder there were never any chocolates left at the end of the day.

Had the office staff complained that there weren't enough chocolates? Perhaps that's why Mrs Adwell had brought in another tray. But why hadn't she told her? Maisie could easily bring two trays, one stacked on the other. They weren't heavy. The beginning of a headache bloomed at her temples.

The train ride home that evening was especially trying. To leave the warm factory for the bitter chill of the evening was hard enough, but to wait for a train with all the other factory workers knowing there might be standing room only was dispiriting. Maisie had been on her feet all day and longed for a seat. When the train finally arrived, belching steam and smoke, the workers surged forward. Being a supervisor, Maisie felt the need to set a good example and refused to elbow others out of the way. As a result she stood almost all the way into town.

When Maisie finally arrived home, she was greeted with a big hug from Lily.

'I love the way you smell.' Lily inhaled deeply. 'Like a box of chocolates.'

Maisie always smelt of chocolate – her hair, her skin, and it permeated every fold and crease of her clothes. Even after her Saturday evening bath she was still aware of the faint aroma as she walked to church on a Sunday morning.

'Andrew always smells so awful and you always smell delicious.' Lily held her hand as they walked up the hall to their bedroom.

'How was school today?' Maisie took off her shoes and rubbed the balls of her feet before putting on her slippers.

'A bit dull. I've finished all the extra work Miss Bracey gave me and she doesn't have anything else. She's told me to go back over old work but I don't see the point.'

Maisie smiled and tapped her forefinger on her little sister's forehead. 'You're too clever by half.' If there was another grade at the school Lily would have been promoted months earlier. 'Don't worry. You'll be going to The Friends' School next year and I'm sure they won't run out of things to teach you.' They'd both rejoiced the day the news arrived that Lily had won a scholarship. Mother professed to be uncertain but her pride was obvious. Since her heartbreak with

Frank, Maisie's enthusiasm for the Quaker school had waned, but she didn't let her doubts affect Lily. No matter the Quakers' views on war, their reputation for education was second to none.

Lily faltered. 'I'm not so sure.'

'What do you mean?'

'I overheard Mother and Andrew. I don't know whether I'll be able to stay in school, not even with a scholarship.'

'I don't understand.' Cold dread gripped Maisie's heart. 'What's happened?' She took Lily's hand and pressed it between her own.

Lily began to sniffle. 'I wasn't supposed to be listening. They didn't know I was there.'

'What did they say?'

Lily bowed her head. 'They're in the kitchen. Don't tell them I said anything.'

Maisie held her sister close and smoothed her hair. 'Don't worry. Everything will be all right.'

Lily nodded and pressed into Maisie's arms. 'At least you still have your job. I'd rather have your smell than Andrew's.'

Maisie blinked as nausea threatened to overcome her. Andrew had lost his job. How? Gently she untangled herself from Lily. 'You stay here with Blackie.' The cat was, as usual, curled up on Lily's bed. Oh, to sleep the day away as he did. 'I'll have a talk with Mother and Andrew and find out what's going on.' She pulled her handkerchief out of her pocket and handed it to Lily. 'Here. Dry your eyes and blow your nose.'

Maisie watched as Lily cuddled up with Blackie. She closed the door behind her and made her way to the kitchen.

Mother looked up from her usual spot under the lamp. Andrew sat next to her, his head in his hands. A pot of stew bubbled on the range, the steam carrying the scent of rosemary and thyme.

Maisie pulled out a kitchen chair and sat opposite her brother. 'Andrew?'

He raised his head. His exhausted face said it all. His eyes were bloodshot and he looked older than a boy his age ever should. 'I'm sorry, Maisie, I've let you down. I've let you all down.'

She leant over and touched one of his stained and callused hands. 'What happened?'

'They sacked him, that's what.' Mother's voice contained a bitterness rarely heard.

Andrew flinched. 'They've given me my notice. Two weeks.'

'Why?'

'He's done nothing wrong. Your brother's a good worker. He's worked hard for that lot and this is the thanks he gets.'

Andrew shot Mother a look. 'The owner had no choice.'

Mother humphed and went back to the mending.

Andrew pressed his lips together. 'The owner's brother was working at a mine in the west. More money than working in a tannery. Until now. The mines are closing. The sawmills too. All the workers are coming to town looking for work. Unemployment was bad before, but now ...' He shrugged his shoulders in defeat. 'The Returned Soldiers' League is scouring every workplace for jobs for our war heroes. I probably would've lost my position anyway, given I'm not one of them.'

'Through no fault of your own.' Maisie couldn't help think of Frank, a coward and yet secure in his job at Cadbury's. 'You were no more than a child during the war.'

'Not only is the new man the owner's brother but he's a returned soldier to boot.' Andrew shook his head. 'I never had a hope.'

'Oh, Andrew. I'm so sorry. What about the zinc works? You have a friend there.'

'He's in the same boat. Hanging onto his job by his fingernails. Now the construction is done there's not much demand for unskilled labour. Anything that comes up goes straight to a returned soldier. Fair enough, so many of them have families to feed.'

'And here I am a war widow with a family to feed, but do the powers that be ever think about women like me?' Mother scowled at the mending.

'And IXL?' The jam factory was just down the road at the Old Wharf. When the wind blew in a certain direction the whole of the Glebe was bathed in the scent of boiling fruit. Andrew had worked there when he was younger during the summer holidays when the berry season was in full swing.

'The fruit season is over, even apples. There's no work at the docks either. Not that I could get a job without a ticket.'

'I'll ask at Cadbury's.'

'It's probably the same there, but thanks.'

'There'll be no scholarship for Lily now.' Mother picked up the next piece of mending. 'When she turns fourteen, she'll have to get a job and that's the end of it.'

Disappointment hollowed out Maisie's stomach. Without a proper education Lily would be doomed to repetitive menial tasks that would drive her to despair. Her fine mind would be wasted. Maisie shifted to face her mother. 'I'll stop going to evening classes. I'll come straight home and help with the ironing and mending. And no more dances. I'll spend every spare moment working here with you.'

Mother shook her head. 'That'll help but it won't be enough. Not with your brother's wage gone. Lily will have to go to work.'

'But—'

'But nothing. It's decided.' Mother's mouth was set in a grim line.

Her brother's face wore an expression of such guilt and sorrow it was all Maisie could do not to weep. Weep for her brother, for her mother whose husband's body lay in the mud of France, for Lily whose brilliant future had been snuffed out, and for herself. Without the evening classes she'd be overlooked for promotion. Her dream of becoming a forewoman was over. All their hopes had turned to dust.

26

Dorothy

Dorothy

During the morning break Dorothy noticed Maisie hovering nearby. Maisie was doing well as a supervisor and, combined with her attendance at evening classes, was top in line for a promotion to deputy forewoman when the time came. Dorothy was also pleased to note that Maisie had managed to tame her wild hair. It remained neatly restrained under her cap. However, Maisie was still a little unsure of herself when dealing with management. While Dorothy waited for Maisie to get her courage up to approach her, the few minutes remaining of the morning break trickled away.

'Mrs Adwell?'

At last. 'Yes, Maisie, how can I help?'

Maisie gripped her hands together. The poor girl looked as though she wished the floor would swallow her whole. 'It's about my brother.'

Dorothy knew where this conversation was headed.

'His position at the tannery was given to the owner's brother and so he's lost his job.' Maisie's expression was pitiful. 'He's a good worker. A hard worker. The owner has given him an excellent reference. I wondered ...'

'You'd like me to see if there's any work for him here.'

'If you could, Mrs Adwell, I'd be most grateful. It's my little sister, you see, and her schooling. It's my evening classes and my mother— Oh!' She clamped her lips together as if to stop herself from saying any more. Her cheeks coloured with embarrassment, or was it shame.

'I'll ask, Maisie, but don't get your hopes up. The construction work is mostly finished and the other departments are fully staffed, but I'll see if anything can be done.' If Maisie's little sister wanted a job, it would be a different matter. Men stayed in jobs to build a future for themselves and to take care of their families. Most young women saw a job as a more temporary arrangement. In the seven months since the first girls had walked through the factory gates, quite a few had already left.

'Thank you, Mrs Adwell.' Maisie almost curtseyed in her gratitude before she rushed back to the enrobers.

It would be a shame if Maisie had to stop attending the evening classes. Dorothy had kept a close eye on all the students' marks. She took a professional interest, of course, but also it gave her an excuse to talk with Thomas in the office. He'd told her Maisie was keen and industrious, which was reflected in her marks. Dorothy would do her best to find her brother a job but she wasn't at all confident.

At lunchtime Dorothy sought out Frank. She found him by the river, staring into the waters of the Derwent. He turned to her with eyes that reflected the low, grey clouds.

'Maisie Greenwood approached me this morning,' she said, keeping her voice neutral.

Frank stiffened and returned his focus to the river. 'I see.'

'I said I'd come and talk to you.' Dorothy kept her words purposefully vague. She hoped he might volunteer some information about what had happened between them without her prying.

'What did she say? I expect she blamed you for introducing her to me in the first place.' His laugh was short and bitter. 'She has quite a temper, as I've discovered.'

That was that, then. Maisie's chat with Frank had not gone the way she'd hoped. 'I'm sorry it didn't work out.'

'Well, we can't have the daughter of a brave man who gave his life for King and Country consorting with a coward now, can we?'

'A coward?' Dorothy was shocked by his words. 'You? Of all people!'

'What? Maisie didn't tell you? I thought she would've shouted it from the rooftops. I'm surprised she hasn't presented me with a bouquet of white feathers.'

'No, she never mentioned it.'

'That's a blessing at least. I wondered if she'd keep it to herself. I expect she's ashamed of being connected to me in any way.'

'Where on earth did she get the idea that you were a coward?'

Frank rubbed his forehead as if trying to find an answer there. 'I don't know, but in a way I'm grateful. At least she knows the truth.'

'But it's not the truth, is it? I've got a good mind to give her a talking-to and find out who's been spreading these lies.'

'Please don't. For many people it is the truth.'

'But—'

Frank raised a hand. 'Please. I appreciate your concern but I'd prefer to leave it be.'

Dorothy scowled. 'If that's what you want. I can't pretend it hasn't made me cross though.'

Frank managed a small grin. 'I can see that.' He tilted his head and studied her. 'Maisie didn't mention any of this?' It was less of a question and more of a realisation.

Dorothy avoided his accusing gaze. 'No.'

Frank gave a quiet huff. 'I think you might have hoodwinked me, Mrs Adwell.'

'I knew something was going on between you and Maisie. Would you have told me off your own bat?'

'Probably not.' Frank shoved his hands in his pockets. 'Especially not now.'

'Well, then.' Dorothy's guilt evaporated with a sense of justification.

'What did Maisie approach you about then?'

'Her brother needs a job.'

'Ah.' Frank rocked slowly back on his heels.

'Would you give him one, if there was one available?'

'Of course. But any job that comes up is already promised to a returned soldier. I'm sorry, but there's nothing for Maisie's brother.'

Dorothy nodded. 'I thought that'd be the case. No harm in asking.'

'Please explain it to her. I'd hate her to think I refused out of spite.'

'Anyone who knows you, Frank Sutton, knows you never do anything out of spite. I'll tell her I asked at the office.'

'Thank you.'

'You really do care for her, don't you?'

Frank shifted his gaze to the river. 'Not that it matters now.'

The cottage was dark and quiet when Dorothy returned home. Sarah had thoughtfully laid a fire before she'd left for the mainland earlier in the day. Mr Cooper was joining the Chairman of Directors on the mainland in an attempt to secure an alternative source of glucose. No stone was being left unturned in their bid to keep Cadbury's out of the clutches of the local confectioners. Sarah was accompanying them on the important mission, 'to keep them on track and out of trouble', as she'd said.

Dorothy lit a taper and touched the flame to the kindling. Building a fire was one of Sarah's many skills and the wood took in a matter of moments. Satisfied it needed no further attention, Dorothy placed the screen in front of the fireplace. In the kitchen she investigated the contents of the ice chest. Even though she really should eat the leftover stew, she settled for a cup of cocoa and toast. Back by the fire she rested her supper on the side table and picked up the book she'd ordered recently from a catalogue – *The Maintenance and Repair of Clocks*. Dorothy studied the illustrations, admiring the way every cog and spring was perfectly designed for a purpose. She planned to set up a small bench in her bedroom and practise on an old clock she'd bought from a rag-and-bone man in nearby Glenorchy. All she was waiting on were the specialised tools she'd ordered from Melbourne. The fire burnt low in the grate as she spent a pleasurable hour reading about the inner machinations of clockwork. Her fingers itched to take apart the movement of the old clock, clean it and check the escapements and bushings, to experience a sense of accomplishment when it was operational again and keeping perfect time. She missed the satisfaction of bringing something broken back to life. There was little use for her mechanical skills in the new factory.

Dorothy stood to fetch a log for the fire and was startled by what sounded like a soft knock at the back door. She checked her watch, taken by the thought that if it ever broke one day she'd be able to repair it, and wondered who on earth would be visiting at this hour.

She eyed the poker and considered taking it with her. Could the mysterious and threatening letter writer finally be making a move? She decided against the poker, switched on the portico light and opened the back door.

'Thomas!' Dorothy quickly switched off the light again in case one of the neighbours saw, and ushered him inside. 'What are you doing here?'

'I was heading home after class. I fully intended to walk to Claremont and catch the train but ...' The tremble in his hands was fearsome. His jaw was almost locked with tension. 'I saw a flash in the sky. Well, I thought I saw a flash. I couldn't ...' Thomas gritted his teeth. 'I know Miss Harris is on the mainland but even so I'm taking a terrible liberty. I'll understand if you turn me away.'

'There'll be none of that.' Dorothy helped him into the kitchen, took his hat and lowered him onto a chair. His body was stiff and unyielding as if trying to ward off danger by becoming a shield. 'I'll make you a cup of tea with lots of sugar.' Something hot and sweet would help.

'I can't stay long. I'll miss the last train.' His eyes darted around the room, unable to alight on anything.

Dorothy spoke in soothing tones while she made the tea, making sure to take the kettle off the hob as soon as the water started to boil so the whistling wouldn't alarm him. 'Here.' She put the cup in front of him before realising her mistake. The tea would spill in his trembling hands. 'Wait a second.' Dorothy took the cup to the sink and poured a third of it down the drain. If he held the cup with both hands he should be able to manage.

As she put the cup back down in front of him he looked at her with a stricken expression. 'I'm sorry to burden you but I'm at my wit's end. I can't catch a train in this state – the smoke, the steam, the noise.' Thomas had been offered a room in one of the new cottages with other clerical staff last month but he'd turned it down and still lived in town. He'd told her it suited him, to live apart from the men he worked with. He needed distance when his affliction struck. Once his wife and son arrived it would be different. He'd gladly take up a cottage on the estate then. Dorothy had smiled and agreed, despite a hollowness inside her.

Dorothy sat beside him now. 'You can stay as long as you need. There's no hurry.'

'But I will have to get back.' He went to stand but collapsed back on the chair. 'I'm not the man I used to be.' He looked at her with pitiful eyes. 'That man is a stranger to me now.' He reached into his jacket for his cigarettes and matches but his shaking hands made striking a match impossible. Dorothy took them from him, lit a cigarette and placed it between his lips. He inhaled a deep lungful of smoke and expelled it slowly. 'I started smoking in the army. They told me it would help.' He frowned at the cigarette held tightly in his trembling fingers. 'It didn't. It still doesn't.'

Dorothy pushed one of Sarah's ashtrays towards him. 'I'm here to help you, Thomas, no matter what it takes.'

'I can't do this to you.' His eyes darted from the ice box to the gas cooker to the pantry. 'I don't know what I was thinking, to be in your house at night, alone with you. Your reputation. I'm sorry I came.'

'I'm not. I'm glad you trust me.'

He crushed out his cigarette. 'All those years of orders. Of being told what to do at every moment. Of being sent to certain death. Except I didn't die, not all of me, just the parts that were good. I wanted to run, every day. All of us were all half out of our minds with fear. To be shot as a coward would've been a relief, of a sort.' He dropped his head into his hands. 'I'm so tired. I'm just so tired.'

'You need to rest. The living room is nice and warm. Come.' She helped him stand and take off his coat then led him, like a child, to a cosy spot in front of the fireplace. 'I'll get another log for the fire and we'll sit together for a while. There's no need to do anything or go anywhere. There's not even any need to talk. Just rest.' Dorothy watched as he began to relax and the tremor in his hands lessened. The deeply etched lines on his face and the dark shadows under his eyes spoke of many sleepless nights. The poor, poor man. To be so haunted by a past he couldn't escape.

Outside, she chose two hefty logs that would burn long and slow. The sky was clear and deep with a thousand pricks of light dancing in the heavens. She'd heard that on rare winter nights the Southern Lights sent sheets of green and purple shooting into the sky from the horizon. Could that have been what Thomas saw? She turned to the south, past the looming bulk of Mount Wellington black against the dark sky. A deep longing gripped her for the skies she knew, the familiar stars, the snow in December and the jonquils in March promising warmer days to come; all that she had known for most of her twenty-five years. It wasn't often she was homesick, but tonight, with a man she cared for in her living room reminding her of what she'd had for a brief moment in time, the ache for home grew like frost on a windowpane, spreading through her chest. She rubbed the place above her heart where the pain always lingered.

When she returned with the firewood, Thomas was sleeping. Dorothy lay a blanket over him and returned to her armchair by the standard lamp. It was hard to concentrate on the technicalities of clock springs and cogs with him so close. Invariably her eyes were drawn to him sleeping there – the fall of his hair, the shape of his mouth, the line of his jaw. It was a luxury to gaze upon his face without any fear of reproach or repercussion. In time her own eyelids began to droop. She rose, giving only a moment's thought to her dilemma. Gently she kissed the top of his head and made her way to bed.

It was the noise that woke her. The sound of something smashing. Dorothy threw back the covers and rushed to the living room. Thomas wasn't on the couch, the blanket was on the floor and the fire only embers. Clearly many hours had passed. A muffled sob came from the kitchen. Dorothy found him curled in a ball under the kitchen table, moaning and crying. His hands gripped his head as he rocked. The crash she'd heard had come from the vase that had been on the table and was now in shards on the floor. Sarah's vase. She'd think about that later.

Was Thomas dreaming or was he awake? She couldn't tell. While she was volunteering during the war she'd been told it was best not to wake a shell-shock victim when they were having a nightmare, but she couldn't leave him in such a state. Slowly she lowered herself to the floor next to the table, avoiding the broken vase. 'Thomas, it's me. You're safe. Nothing will hurt you here.' Dorothy kept her voice low and soft as if he were a frightened dog capable of snapping at her at any time.

'No, no, no.' Thomas's voice was a long howl. He clawed at his face, creating welts where his fingernails dug into the skin.

Dorothy caught her breath at the damage he was inflicting on himself. She crawled closer to him and slowly, carefully, placed a hand on his arm. He flinched but didn't strike out. Encouraged, she moved closer. There wasn't much room to manoeuvre. Her only option was to press her body against his until she was almost encircling him. In an effort to calm him she began to sing the first song that came to mind – a lullaby. A faint memory rose in her mind of her mother smelling of bread and milk, rocking Dorothy in her arms. Dorothy rocked with Thomas now, her body in time with his. His moans grew louder but she didn't pull back, instead she held him closer and sang of home and peace, of safety and love. Their bodies warmed each other's as they huddled under the table. Dorothy's face was wet from the longing she had for Freddie, the old yearning for her mother so long dead. There were threads inside her that were still tightly bound to home, to Birmingham, to Bournville, to all the joy she'd known there and all the sorrow. Both she and Thomas had hoped to outrun the pain and grief, only to end up here, moaning and crying on the kitchen floor. Slowly the rocking stopped. Dorothy gently pulled his hands away from his face. 'You're safe. Nothing will harm you here.'

Thomas opened his eyes in bewilderment. As he took in his surroundings – the tabletop above him, the floor, Dorothy – his expression turned to confusion and then horror. 'What happened?'

'It's all right. You're safe,' Dorothy repeated.

'No. This can't be.' Thomas pulled away.

Dorothy moved slowly to give him room. 'There's nothing to be ashamed of.'

Thomas scrambled out from under the table. 'I can't believe I let this happen.'

Dorothy followed him. 'You didn't have a choice. Thomas, it's not your fault. It's part of the condition.'

'I should never have come here.' He began to pace but was distracted by a fragment of vase crushed under his shoe. 'Did I do this? Did I break it?'

'It doesn't matter. All that's important is that you're safe.' Dorothy noticed a trembling in her own hands as the shock of what had happened caught up with her.

Thomas picked up a chair and righted it. He began to search the kitchen. 'Where's the broom? I'll sweep it up.'

'In the laundry beside the mop.' While he was gone she sat at the table and exhaled slowly to help calm her racing heart.

He returned with the dustpan and broom and began sweeping up the debris. 'I'll replace it. I'll repay you.' His face fell. 'How can I ever repay you? What have I done?'

'No harm's been done.' Dorothy shook her head gently. Her nerves were beginning to settle.

Silently Thomas swept up the remainder of the vase. He wrapped the shards in newspaper and took the bundle outside to the rubbish bin. When he returned he was a little calmer. 'I'm sorry I subjected you to this ... this weakness.'

Her heart ached for him. He blamed himself. 'It's not a weakness. It's a result of war.'

Thomas shook his head. 'I've taken an enormous liberty.'

'Because I encouraged you to. I meant it when I said I was on your side, always.' She leant towards him, trying to convince him with both words and actions.

'You couldn't have possibly expected what happened here tonight.'

'I experienced far worse in the Cadbury's hospital.'

Thomas finally sat down, perched on the kitchen chair opposite her. 'Nothing shocks you, does it, Dorothy?'

She gave him a wistful smile. 'I think the war accustomed us to a great many things. Most of which we thought we'd never see or experience. We were fortunate to survive it.'

'Survive it, yes, but not unscathed.'

'No. Not unscathed.'

Lightly, Thomas touched her hand. 'I am grateful.'

Dorothy watched a mix of emotions cross his face – embarrassment, humiliation, sadness and gratitude – knowing she would do the same for him again at any time, without a moment's thought to her status or reputation. 'You're welcome.'

He checked his watch. 'I have to go.'

'But there are no trains until morning.' It was past midnight.

'I'll walk. I've been told exercise is good for what ails me.' His mouth twisted in a strange lopsided way.

'But it'll take hours and it's so late.' Dorothy was aware of the risk but was happy to take it for Thomas. 'You might as well stay. You can sleep on the couch.'

'And be here when the sun comes up and the neighbours start rousing? No. I've done enough harm already. There's still time to get home for breakfast and a change of clothes, then my usual train ride to the office.'

'I expect it's for the best.' She collected his hat and coat and saw him to the back door.

He moved closer, as if to kiss her cheek. She hovered for a moment, almost weightless, daring to hope, then he pulled back, tipped his hat and was gone.

27

Maisie

August 1922

The morning was brittle with cold. Jack Frost nipped at Maisie's nose as she waited for the Cadbury's train. The other girls crowding in at each stop brought with them a comforting warmth. She'd had yet another sleepless night worrying about Andrew losing his job and Lily having to find one. When the train arrived at Cadbury's the air was thick with fog. The usual chat and laughter of the girls was subdued with every sound swallowed up by the heavy air. It was like walking through a cloud with the factory looming out of the mist, swathed in the white of the Bridgewater Jerry. On days like this Maisie had learnt it could be a bright day in Hobart but by the time the train reached Glenorchy they'd be surrounded by the fog. Sometimes it wouldn't lift until lunchtime, leaving them in a strange kind of limbo, as if time had stopped. It suited her mood – heavy, thick and dull. She couldn't see a way forward.

When it came time to deliver the tray of chocolates she hoped Percy wouldn't be waiting. Over the past weeks she'd sent one or other of the girls, using the excuse of sharing the responsibility, but Mary had grown restive without her small allotment of time as acting supervisor, so Maisie had resumed the task. The truth was she hadn't wanted to see Percy. He had a way of persuading her to talk about the most personal of things, but the falling of her family into an even deeper poverty was a private shame she didn't want to share.

Despite her hopes for avoiding him, Percy emerged out of the fog, like a handsome wraith. 'There you are, Miss Greenwood. I've missed you. I've seen the other girls walking by with the chocolates but none of them have tempted me.'

Maisie had expected Percy would approach them the way he did her and was surprised when none of the girls had mentioned the charming Mr Bates. It seemed he waited just for her. 'I've been otherwise engaged.'

Percy moved closer. 'What's wrong, Maisie?'

'Why should anything be wrong?' She set her jaw, trying desperately to keep the tremor out of her voice. It had been a miserable month. Not even her birthday had raised her spirits. Gertie had done her best to jolly her along and given her a small bottle of cheap perfume. Maisie treasured it despite knowing she would never wear it.

'I know you, Maisie, and I can tell when you're upset.' The concern in Percy's voice was in danger of disarming her.

'I can't dilly-dally. I have a busy day.'

Percy's expression showed a hint of worry. 'You work so hard. I hope they're paying you what you're worth.'

'I can't complain.' She went to move on but his hand on her arm stopped her.

'A trouble shared is a trouble halved. Anything that's troubling you, you can tell me.'

Maisie ducked her head to hide the tears that threatened. This was just what she'd feared. 'Honestly, I can't stop. Not today.'

'I tell you what. Deliver the chocolates and I'll wait for you here. We can talk about what's troubling you then, without a tray of chocolates between us.'

The concern and warmth in his voice almost undid her. Unable to trust herself if she spoke, Maisie hurried towards the office.

Even though she'd wished he wouldn't be, Percy was waiting for her on her return. He guided her to a corner tucked out of the way. 'For privacy,' he said. 'Now, tell me, what's on your mind?'

Maisie tried to hide her distress, to no avail. Hesitant as she was to tell him her problems, the worry weighed on her heart like a millstone. Percy was so sympathetic, so kind and thoughtful. She could trust him, couldn't she? 'My brother lost his job through no fault of his own. Since Father died it's been tough to make ends meet.' Her cheeks burnt with the shame of it. 'My job here has helped, especially since I was promoted to supervisor, but now my brother's income is gone …' She turned her head away, determined not to cry. 'He's looked everywhere for work but there's nothing.'

Percy sighed. 'I understand. The likelihood that he'll find a new job is small, very small indeed. There aren't enough jobs for men as it is.'

'I was hoping my little sister could stay in school – she's so bright, you see. But those dreams have been dashed.' Maisie hung her head, aware she was talking too much.

'My poor, dear Maisie. I'm sorry about your hopes for your little sister.' His voice was gentle.

'Lily will have to get a job now, next month as soon as she turns fourteen. I had hoped …' Disappointment, frustration and sadness threatened to overwhelm her.

Percy stepped forward and took her hands in his. She trembled at his touch. 'Have you asked Mrs Adwell if she can help? She might be able to find a position for your brother.'

Maisie almost growled in frustration. 'She says there's nothing to be done. She asked at the office but there are no jobs.'

He tsked in disapproval. 'I thought if anyone would help you, it'd be her.'

Maisie took a breath to steady her anger. She'd thought the same thing and had been bitterly disappointed.

Percy sucked his teeth as if deep in thought. 'I might be able to help.'

'How?' If Mrs Adwell with all her connections couldn't help, what could Percy do?

'Not to be indelicate, but you need money. I'm in a position to make sure you have enough to see your family well cared for.'

Maisie pulled away. 'I don't understand.' It was true she'd never been sure of what Percy actually did at the factory but this sounded way beyond his means.

'I can supply you with money for services rendered.'

Maisie's cheeks flamed. 'Mr Bates, I am not that kind of girl.'

'I wasn't suggesting you were. But you are the kind of girl with nous and determination. You wouldn't have got where you are if you weren't. I reckon you're up to the task.'

Maisie eyed him suspiciously. 'What task?'

Percy looked around to make sure there was no one nearby. The fog was finally beginning to lift and they were more exposed. He leant in, his mouth close to Maisie's ear. His breath was warm against her cheek, the nearness of him sending sparks through her body. The memory of his lips, of his mouth, as he ate the chocolates rose in her mind. She clenched her hands to steady herself.

'If you can supply certain information, I can guarantee your sister will never have to work. She can stay in school for as long as she fancies. Your mother will be taken care of too, for the rest of her life. Imagine it, Maisie, your struggles will be over once and for all. And all you need to do is one simple thing.'

Maisie knew she should leave that second, turn on her heels and disentangle herself from the web Percy was weaving. But her thoughts were consumed by Lily's future, her mother's health and Andrew – a good man discarded by a society that had no use for him. She'd thought she could save them all if she just worked hard enough, but she realised she'd been living in a fool's paradise. Percy was offering her freedom from the grinding poverty that had haunted her family every day since her father had died. But she knew the kind of money he was hinting at was not something gained by orthodox means. There would be consequences if she did what he wanted. But there was also the possibility that the loss of her moral compass would be a price worth paying.

'I'm listening,' she said.

28

Dorothy

September 1922

Dorothy placed the tray on Sarah's bedside table. 'This will do you the world of good – my homemade chicken soup and there's some plain toast to go with it.'

Sarah blew her reddened nose. 'Of all the rotten luck,' she moaned. 'To get a nasty head cold now, of all times. I was looking forward to visiting Melbourne again.'

'At least you were able to go last month with Mr Cooper. And a successful mission it was too.' Cadbury's had negotiated with a small manufacturer and obtained enough glucose to satisfy the Firm's requirements. MacRobertson's stranglehold on supply was finished and the Glucose War was over.

'That trip was relentless – all business and endless negotiations.' Sarah sniffled. 'The Royal Melbourne Show would be a different kettle of fish entirely.'

'It is a shame, but it can't be helped.' There was much excitement surrounding the Firm's presence at the Royal Melbourne Show this year. Cadbury's was staging an exhibition called Ye Olde English Inn, where instead of ale patrons would be given delicious cups of Bournville cocoa. Fry's pure breakfast cocoa would be doing a similar service at another stand in the pavilion. The display of Cadbury-Fry-Pascall's confections in front of a large wall-sized picture of the factory, 'By Mountain and Sea', would surely attract much attention. Dorothy plumped the pillows and made sure Sarah was comfortable.

'Take someone in my place.' Sarah's voice was husky, altered as it was by her illness. 'The fare is paid for. It would be such a shame for it to go to waste. What about your protégée, Martha? Or is it Madeline? I'm sorry. My head is so clogged I can't think clearly.'

'Maisie.'

'Yes, that's it. Maisie. Why not take her along? From your description she'd be well up to the task of representing Cadbury's.'

Dorothy paused. Local Melbourne girls were being employed to serve cocoa and take care of sales, but as a representative of the Firm Maisie would be expected to answer questions from the public about all aspects of the factory and chocolate making. She'd proved she was a quick study and with some coaching she'd be up to the task. 'That's a good idea. Maisie is one of our longest-serving local girls.'

'That's just what the Firm needs after the slurs about us bringing out all our employees from England. Maisie can answer questions about production in her wonderful Australian accent and prove to all comers that Cadbury's does employ locals.'

'And I could do with an ally, now you're not coming.' A few of the British women were going, including Esme, but not Ida, which was odd – the two were rarely apart. Margaret was staying put at the factory to make sure production maintained its targets. Dorothy wondered if it was the only reason. Their Chief Forewoman had lost enthusiasm for anything outside of her usual routine. It was as if her capacity had reached its limits after the enormous effort to get the factory operational and all the problems they'd encountered along the way. Dorothy helped as much as she could, taking on extra duties, while Esme turned a blind eye and kept to her own domain.

'That's settled then.' Sarah took another sip of the soup. 'Ah, this is just the ticket, thank you.'

'Maisie's mother will have to give permission.'

'I'm sure any mother would be proud to see her daughter given such an opportunity. And you'll be there to chaperone. I think it will be splendid. Don't forget to tell Mr Cooper it was my idea.' She managed a smile before she placed the soup bowl back on the bedside table and leant back into the pillows. 'Being brilliant has quite worn me out.'

'I'll leave you to rest.' Dorothy picked up the tray and took it back to the kitchen. The idea of Maisie accompanying them to Melbourne had merit and if questioned – Dorothy's thoughts immediately went to Esme – she could say it was the office's idea to bring Maisie, which was true in a way. The other local supervisors might be envious but Dorothy could use it as an incentive for the Sydney Royal Easter Show next year. She'd ask Maisie tomorrow and set the wheels in motion.

'Mr Moreland, what a pleasant surprise. What are you doing aboard the *Nairana*?' Dorothy feigned ignorance when she saw Thomas on deck. He'd told her he was coming to Melbourne to interview prospective teachers, not only for the evening classes but for the proposed Day Continuation School. He was also taking advantage of the trip to visit his sister who'd immigrated to Melbourne several years earlier.

Thomas tipped his hat. 'Good morning, Mrs Adwell. Lovely weather. The last time I crossed Bass Strait the seas were fearsome.'

'I believe you know Miss Maisie Greenwood.' Dorothy gestured to Maisie. 'Maisie is part of our group representing Cadbury's at the Royal Melbourne Show.'

'Delighted to see you again, Miss Greenwood. I'm sorry you weren't able to continue with the evening classes.'

'Mr Moreland.' Maisie bobbed her head in greeting but kept her eyes down.

'Have you been to Melbourne before?' Thomas asked.

'No. The furthest I've ever been from home until now is Claremont.'

Thomas nodded with a kind smile. 'Now your horizons are being expanded even further. I hope you enjoy your time on the mainland.'

'Thank you, Mr Moreland. I'm sure I will.'

'Maisie, this sea air is making me thirsty,' Dorothy said. 'Could you fetch me a bottle of lemonade, please?' Dorothy opened her purse and extracted some coins. 'And one for yourself.' She looked up at Thomas. 'Would you like some lemonade, Mr Moreland?'

'Not for me, thank you.'

After Maisie departed, Dorothy moved closer. 'This reminds me of how we first met. Do you remember?'

'How could I not?' He gazed out over the grey sea. 'The many miles we travelled on the *Ormonde*. What a journey it was.'

Dorothy glanced around to ensure there was no one close by and placed her gloved hand next to his on the railing. 'We know each other so much better now.'

His jaw tensed for a moment and then relaxed. 'I hope you don't think me ungrateful. It's just sometimes I think it's hopeless.'

'I'm here – to give you hope when you have none of your own.'

He shook his head. 'I'm not sure why you haven't given up on me. I have nothing to offer you.'

'I made you a promise. Any time the trouble comes, you can rely on me.'

Finally he turned to her. 'You are too good to me, Mrs Adwell.'

'Thomas,' she whispered, edging her hand even closer. Her little finger brushed against his. There was still no talk of his wife joining him in Tasmania. The thought filled her with both hope and sorrow. His son had grown a year older without him. It wasn't fair of Dorothy to wish that Thomas would never be reunited with his wife.

At the sound of approaching footsteps, he broke away abruptly, forcing a smile. 'There are several promising candidates for the new position. I'm sure we'll find just the right fit.'

Maisie was at Dorothy's side then, offering a bottle of lemonade. 'Thank you, Maisie.' Dorothy cleared her throat. 'I was just talking with Mr Moreland about the plans for extending the education program at Cadbury's.'

Maisie turned her full attention to Thomas. 'Mrs Adwell has told me about the Day Continuation School. It's for the younger employees?'

'Yes, it's based on the system at Bournville, but there are no guarantees when it will be up and running. I'm going to Melbourne to interview prospects but they'll have to be content with teaching evening classes for some time.'

'I see.' Maisie's eyes dulled.

Dorothy placed a comforting hand on her arm. 'Maisie has a younger sister. Very bright by all accounts. If she can't stay in school when she turns fourteen, the Day Continuation School would be perfect for her.'

'I'm sorry our plans are taking so long,' Thomas said. 'But there are always the evening classes. I'm sure you'd agree, from personal experience, how beneficial they are. Perhaps you'll be able to join us again at some time.'

'I hope so, Mr Moreland.' Maisie's smile was tight.

Dorothy regretted that Maisie could no longer attend classes. If she could have found her brother a job she would have but there were none to be had. 'Well, we must get on, Thom—' Dorothy bit her tongue at the slip. 'Mr Moreland. Enjoy the rest of the trip.'

Thomas touched a finger to the rim of his hat. 'Mrs Adwell. Miss Greenwood.'

Dorothy and Maisie continued their promenade around the deck. When she spied Esme at the bow Dorothy was glad of the young woman's company. Dorothy and Esme exchanged the barest of greetings before Esme turned her back with a sneer. Honestly, the woman was insufferable.

The noise and bustle of the Royal Melbourne Show kept Dorothy on her toes from morning till night. More than once she was grateful for a fortifying cup of Bournville cocoa. At first she'd been concerned for Maisie – the sheer number of people from all walks of life; the women dressed in the latest fashions, some of the hemlines positively scandalous; the traffic; and the constant din were all things Maisie wouldn't have experienced before. Dorothy kept a close eye on her but within two days it was clear Maisie was taking the hustle and bustle in her stride. When the crowds pressed in, eager to taste the free offerings, Maisie answered their questions with a growing confidence.

The Fry's breakfast cocoa stand was some distance from the Cadbury's exhibits, which was a blessing. Even during tea at the hotel, Esme snubbed her. Lizzie apologised, well out of earshot of

Esme, but in the end it was easier for Dorothy to take dinner at a table for two with Maisie.

Dorothy raised a glass of lemonade in a toast. 'Here's to you, Maisie, and another successful day.'

Maisie dropped her eyes demurely. 'Thank you, Mrs Adwell.'

'We'll be heading back home the day after tomorrow. Hopefully your brother will have secured a job while you've been away.'

Maisie's expression hardened. 'One can only hope.'

Dorothy folded her serviette. It was clear she hadn't quite been forgiven. 'I'm going to give you an hour or so off tomorrow afternoon, to explore all the show has to offer.'

Maisie looked at her in surprise. 'But we're so busy. I think the Cadbury's exhibit must be the most popular of the entire show.'

'And tomorrow you'll get the chance to find out. Call it a reconnaissance mission. Have a look at the other exhibits and tell me what you think.'

'I've been to the Hobart Show but it doesn't hold a candle to this one.'

'We'll be exhibiting at the Royal Hobart Show next month. The experience you've gained here will be very useful.'

Maisie rewarded her with a smile. 'Thank you.'

Dorothy rose from the table. 'Another busy day tomorrow. It's time we retired.'

Dorothy was roused from her slumber by a soft but insistent knock on the door. Half asleep, she stumbled to open it. Thomas stood in the dim light of the hotel hallway, his body hunched and his eyes wild.

'I'm in desperate need.' His voice was a hoarse whisper. 'I daren't fall asleep. I can't trust myself. I fear the damage I might do.'

Dorothy took a quick look at Maisie's sleeping form. Thankfully she hadn't stirred. 'I'll meet you in the hotel foyer in five minutes.'

Thomas shook his head. 'The night porter, the night manager. I would prefer …' He pressed something into her hand.

The cold metal of his room key against her palm sent a shock through her body. It was one thing to invite him into her home at night when she was there alone, but to go to his hotel room? She'd have to sneak in and out like a trollop. He must be in dire straits to resort to such a request.

'I wouldn't ask it of you, but …' He twisted his shaking hands as his eyes darted down the hallway then back to her. 'Please.'

She'd promised she would help him whenever he was in need. That time was now. She pushed down her misgivings and nodded once. 'I'll be there.'

Dorothy closed the door and dressed with a quiet stealth.

Maisie rolled over and sleepily opened her eyes. 'Mrs Adwell? Is everything all right?'

Dorothy stood perfectly still, hardly daring to breathe. It was dark. Hopefully Maisie couldn't see she was fully dressed. 'Everything is fine, Maisie. Go back to sleep.'

'Yes, Mrs Adwell.' Maisie's eyes closed again and her breathing settled.

Slowly, carefully, Dorothy opened the door and closed it behind her.

29

Maisie

The other supervisors gathered around Maisie at lunchtime, eager to hear about her adventures in Melbourne. They hung off her every word as she told them about the crowds and the fashions, the success of the Cadbury-Fry-Pascall exhibits and the other pavilions she'd visited in the hours Mrs Adwell had given her to explore.

'I tasted the strangest thing,' she said. 'It was like a big ball of pink cotton wool on a stick. It was only tuppence and there was so much of it.'

'What was it made of?' Jane asked.

'Just sugar and colouring from what I could tell. The man poured the sugar in the top of a machine that he turned by hand. It heated and spun at the same time making a cloud of pink fluff. He called it Fairy Floss.'

'How odd,' Daphne said.

'It was hard to know how to eat it but I pulled pieces off and they melted in my mouth.'

'What was your most favourite thing of all?' Alice leant forward.

Maisie knew they'd expect her to talk about the fashion parade, the newest automobiles on display, or the Grand Parade. 'I know it sounds silly,' she said, 'but it was the Poultry Pavilion.'

'What?' Alice burst out in peals of laughter. 'Chooks? You can come and look at chickens anytime in my backyard if you like.'

'The Poultry Pavilion?' Daphne looked at her askance. 'Truly?'

'I know, I know.' Maisie waved their incredulity aside. 'But the chickens were nothing like the backyard variety, sorry, Alice. They were all so puffed up and proud of themselves, especially the roosters. They tried to outdo each other with their crowing as they strutted about in their cages. They made me laugh so much.' Her smile faltered as she remembered why she was in such need of cheering up. The night before Mrs Adwell had answered a knock on their hotel room door in the middle of the night. It was a man. Mrs Adwell had dressed and gone. She hadn't returned for hours. Maisie had pretended to be asleep but the worry had kept her awake. The next morning Mrs Adwell made no explanation, in fact she pretended nothing had happened. Shock, disappointment and confusion had worried at Maisie all that day, until she'd visited the Poultry Pavilion. After a morning of pretending to be happy for the public, the roosters with all their posturing had put a genuine smile on her face.

'You are a strange one, Maisie Greenwood,' Jane said. 'Nevertheless, I think Mrs Adwell must have you in mind as a deputy forewoman to take you with her to Melbourne.'

There was a murmur of agreement around the table.

'If that's the case,' Maisie said, 'it won't be long until we're all promoted.' She pushed her sandwiches aside. Her appetite was gone. Thoughts of Mrs Adwell and that night in Melbourne made her restless and irritable. Fresh air and views of water and mountain would soothe her nerves. 'I'm going to get some air. I'll see you tomorrow.'

'Until then, Deputy Forewoman.' Alice gave her a mischievous smile.

Outside the hint of spring on the air lifted Maisie's spirits. The grounds around the factory were finally clear of the debris from the construction that had surrounded them when she'd started work here. Gardens had replaced the rubble and the first of the spring bulbs happily bobbed in the light breeze. A selection of freesias beckoned her to bend down and inhale their heady fragrance. She had to almost bury her nose in their blooms to offset the ever-present aroma of chocolate and cocoa.

By the river, the water's steady, eternal presence calmed her. The river didn't worry about who said what to whom, or the latest fashions, or if a boy liked it, or if Mrs Adwell had a secret assignation with a man. The river just was. Like the mountain. She lifted her head to take in the strange sideways view of Mount Wellington that still surprised her. Odd how a shift in perspective could completely change how you felt about something, or someone. Like Frank. Like Mrs Adwell. There was a time when Maisie had wanted to be more like her – confident, clever, in control. Now she wasn't sure of Mrs Adwell at all, or what her true nature was.

Maisie wandered in the direction of the big rock by the riverbank but as she drew near she was disappointed to see two figures already there, a man and a woman. She went to turn back but a snatch of conversation drifted towards her on the breeze and she recognised Mrs Adwell's voice. Maisie approached slowly. She knew she shouldn't spy but after Melbourne she wanted to know more. Mrs Adwell and the man seemed cosy, sitting on the rock together. His voice was little more than a low undertone, impossible to recognise, and his back was towards her. Was he the one who'd come to their hotel room in the middle of the night? Cautiously she edged closer, hardly daring to breathe. Her next step landed on a twig and the snap of it resounded through the empty air. She flinched. The man stood abruptly, pulling his hat down low and his collar up so that Maisie couldn't see his face. She turned on her heel and rushed back to the factory.

Maisie watched on in a daze as the enrobers started up and her girls busied themselves lining up the centres for the journey through the waterfall of chocolate. A nagging feeling kept tugging at her. There was something vaguely familiar about the man by the river but she couldn't put her finger on exactly what.

Later that afternoon, when Mrs Adwell came to check their work, Maisie stood by nervously. After she was done, Mrs Adwell beckoned her away to a quieter spot. Maisie's stomach dropped.

'Are you quite well, Maisie?' Mrs Adwell asked. 'You don't seem yourself.'

'Is there a problem with the work, Mrs Adwell?'

'Not at all. It's very much up to standard, thanks to your diligence.'

Maisie bobbed her head in thanks.

'I'm concerned about you though. I wondered if the trip to Melbourne had taken something out of you. You were awfully quiet on the voyage home.'

Maisie looked away. 'It was rather overwhelming, Melbourne and the show and all. Not that I'm not grateful.' Maisie was flustered. She'd been glad when the trip was over. She'd hardly known how to speak to Mrs Adwell during their remaining time together. It had been a relief to get home to the Glebe, but the sight of Mrs Adwell by the river with a man had brought it all back.

'And you're perfectly all right then?' Mrs Adwell's voice was insistent.

Did Mrs Adwell suspect she'd been aware of what happened that night at the hotel? Did she know it was her by the river? It was clear that Mrs Adwell was expecting an explanation of some sort. 'You mentioned my brother might have found work by the time I arrived home but he hasn't. Are you sure there isn't a position for him here?'

'I'm sorry, Maisie. I've asked everyone and in every department. There's no work available for your brother.'

Maisie bit her lip as much out of frustration as annoyance. She was sure Mrs Adwell, with her position of responsibility and all her contacts, could find something for Andrew, even if it were only temporary. 'I understand.' She tried to keep the bitterness out of her voice.

'You did well in Melbourne. If you keep your head down and work hard, good things will come your way, I'm sure.' Mrs Adwell nodded in farewell and headed off.

Maisie stood, steadying her breath. Mrs Adwell's words echoed in her mind – if she kept her head down. It felt like a threat. A slow burning anger rose in her chest. She was struck with a vicious desire to return the threat – her silence about that night in Melbourne in return for a job for Andrew. The thought was repugnant but she was desperate. The last of Andrew's pay was gone. He'd worn out his shoe leather tramping the streets of Hobart trying to find work only to come home exhausted, dispirited and famished. Lily's birthday was less than a week away, hovering like an axe over her hopes. Even if Maisie worked every spare minute ironing and mending it wouldn't be enough. Lily would have to get a job and that was the end of it. Unless … her thoughts turned to Percy. Previously his suggestion had been unthinkable. Now it might be her only way out.

Lily blew out the fourteen candles on her birthday cake as Mother, Maisie and Andrew sang a falsely cheerful round of 'Happy

Birthday'. After Lily made the first cut, careful not to touch the plate lest her wish not come true, Maisie cut thick slices and loaded up their plates. She'd returned home from work with very special chocolates, but not even the beautifully decorated box had raised their spirits. 'Should have saved your money,' Mother had grumbled.

Now Maisie turned to them with a tight smile. 'I have good news.'

All of them looked up from their plates.

'I don't know what you wished for, Lily, but there is one wish that can come true.'

'What's that?' Lily's eyes brightened. It hadn't been the happiest of birthdays for her so far but Maisie planned to change that right now.

'I have an extra special birthday present for you.' Maisie avoided Mother's gaze but even so could sense her agitation. She clenched her hands under the table to strengthen her resolve. 'You won't have to leave school after all.'

Mother scowled. 'No, Maisie. We agreed.'

Andrew's mouth dropped open. 'Does Cadbury's have a job for me?'

'No, but—'

'How dare you get your sister's hopes up.' Mother's face flushed with anger.

Andrew's expression darkened. 'What are you playing at, Maisie?'

Maisie jutted out her chin in defiance. When she'd arrived home from work, she'd told Mother the story she'd rehearsed so carefully. She'd thought her mother would be overjoyed but instead she'd questioned every aspect and refused to let Maisie mention it until the proof was in her hands. That was the end of it, Mother had said, Lily would start work as planned. She'd looked into positions and, although there was no work for Andrew, there were jobs available for Lily as a domestic or shop girl. Maisie had fumed, knowing the pittance Lily would be paid for the loss of a better future, but had stayed silent on the matter, until now. 'I'm getting a bonus, the first of many. Lily can stay in school.' Percy had promised a sum so large she knew she could never admit to it. Instead she planned to hide the money and dole it out at regular intervals.

'A bonus?' Andrew frowned. 'Nobody's giving bonuses. Businesses are struggling as it is.'

'That's what I said.' Mother glared at Maisie.

'Cadbury's is doing well now that production is at full capacity. The bonus is a way of thanking me and the other supervisors for all our hard work.' She laughed, a thin, false sound. 'We think it's a bribe to stop us from marrying.' She was appalled at how easily lying came to her now.

'I can stay in school?' Lily jumped up and raced around the table to give Maisie a hug.

Maisie squeezed her back. 'Yes, you can.' She caught Mother's eye over Lily's shoulder and the anger seething there. She'd crossed a line, she knew it, but it was far from the most dangerous line she was yet to cross.

Late the next afternoon, when the enrobers were silent and the girls had cleaned their section until everything gleamed, Maisie said her farewells.

'Aren't you coming to the train with us, Miss Greenwood?'

'I've left the chocolate tray in the office and I don't want them complaining of mice in the morning.' Maisie had discovered that on the rare occasions there were any chocolates left the clerical staff took them home, but the girls weren't to know. 'Goodnight. I'll see you bright and early tomorrow.'

The long shadows of twilight reached for her as she made her way to the office. The sun was slipping below the hills to the west, its faint glow lighting her way. As she'd hoped, the door was still unlocked. The clerical staff had left for the day but the cleaners would be coming soon to do their part. Maisie had minutes at best. Hurrying to the filing cabinet, she was surprised to see two trays there again. Mrs Adwell had made another of her deliveries. There'd been so much going on that the mystery of Mrs Adwell's extra tray had fallen into insignificance and Maisie hadn't thought to ask her. She couldn't afford to be distracted now. Already her nerves were brittle and in danger of snapping. Slowly she opened the filing cabinet and began the search, her trembling fingers making the task more difficult. The rustle of paper and the sound of the cabinet drawers sliding open set her teeth on edge. Every sound was dangerous. Maisie worked fast, aware of the ticking clock on the wall and time running away. File after file revealed nothing. Tears of frustration pricked her eyes as she skimmed the last of the papers. It wasn't there. She had to stop herself from slamming the drawer shut in frustration. Mother was right, she should never have made that promise to Lily. Maisie clenched her fists. She wouldn't give up. She had to find it.

Percy had said what he needed might be in Mr Cooper's office. Fear flickered through her like a flame. She had an excuse to be near the filing cabinets but to be in Mr Cooper's office without permission would mean instant dismissal. She thought of Lily and how she'd thrown her arms around her when Maisie had told her she could stay in school. Resolved, she stepped towards Mr Cooper's office. Her hand was on the doorknob when she heard the main door open. She tried turning the handle. Perhaps she could hide inside. The door was locked. Quickly she scuttled back to the filing cabinets, her heart pounding.

'Maisie? Is that you?' Mrs Adwell approached her. 'What are you doing here at this hour?'

Maisie swallowed hard, trying to collect her wits. 'I forgot to collect the chocolate tray. I was worried about mice.'

'That's conscientious of you but I hardly think it would matter. There are never any chocolates left by the end of the day.'

'Is that why you've started bringing in another tray?' Maisie regretted her words as Mrs Adwell's face closed.

'Well, I, yes … ' Maisie had never seen her lost for words. Mrs Adwell smiled tightly. 'Now there are more office staff, I thought they'd appreciate an extra tray from time to time.'

'I could always bring two. They're not heavy.'

'That's kind of you, Maisie, but it's not an everyday thing.'

Maisie's eyes were drawn to an envelope in Mrs Adwell's hand. Mrs Adwell followed her gaze. 'I was just leaving this for procurements. Some extra supplies we need.' She quickly put the envelope in her pocket as if to hide it.

Mrs Adwell's behaviour seemed a little odd or was it just that Maisie's nerves were heightened? Either way she needed to leave. 'Well then, I'll say goodnight.' Maisie picked up the trays.

'Goodnight, Maisie.'

Maisie hurried back to Block 1 and slid the trays into a rack. She leant against one of the tall, white columns and squeezed her eyes tight in frustration. She'd done what Percy had asked and come up empty-handed. Her promise to Lily burnt in her stomach and bile rose in her throat. She had failed and in doing so she'd let down everyone she loved. Mother's anger had been justified. Lily would have to take on one of those poorly paid positions after all. Any dreams of university were shattered. Exhausted by fear and grief Maisie walked with heavy steps to the change room.

The last train from Cadbury's had left. It was a long walk to the nearest station at Claremont. The only consolation was that the nights were a little warmer now and the weather fair. Footsteps on the gravel path behind her set the back of her neck tingling. She sped up slightly. The footsteps matched her pace. Maisie thought of running but instead turned to face her pursuer rather than be taken by surprise.

'Hello there, Maisie.'

'Percy?' What was he doing here? She'd thought she'd have until tomorrow to tell him the bad news.

'The one and only. I've been keeping an eye on you but I thought I'd wait until we were alone. Do you have something for me?' He moved closer. His smile was devilish. 'You were in the office for some time. I hope you were successful.'

Maisie slowly shook her head. 'I found nothing. And then Mrs Adwell came in.'

'Nothing?' His smile turned to a frown.

'I looked through all the filing cabinets. Mr Cooper's office was locked.'

'Are you sure, Maisie? I mean, you have a lot at stake here.'

'I know. My brother—' She stopped herself from saying more. Percy already knew her woes. It's why she'd agreed to his plan.

'It would be such a shame if you were out of a job too.' Percy's voice had an edge she hadn't heard before.

'What do you mean?'

'I mean,' he leant in, 'you've been rummaging through the filing cabinets where you have no right to be.'

Maisie took a step back. 'Only because you asked me to.'

'And how are you going to prove that?'

The world fell away as a rushing sensation threatened to overcome her. Only Percy's eyes remained, burning into hers. He'd told her it would be a simple thing to find the information he wanted, then he'd give her the money and that would be the end of it. She'd been a fool – gullible and naive – and now she was trapped. 'You wouldn't.'

'Not if I don't have to.' Percy examined her as if she were a specimen to be dissected. 'There is that other matter we discussed.'

Maisie's stomach clenched. Finding information in the filing cabinets was one thing but his other request was sordid.

'Well?' He cocked an eyebrow, waiting for her reply.

How had she ever thought he was handsome? His face was shadowed with cruelty and greed. She faltered. 'I don't know.'

'I disagree. I think you do. Remember what's at stake here, Maisie.' He turned up his right palm. 'On one hand you can save your family and have all your dreams for your sister come true.' He turned up his left palm. 'On the other hand you lose your job and destroy Lily's future as well as your own. The shame would probably kill your mother.' He shrugged with a chilling nonchalance. 'The choice is yours.'

Ice ran through Maisie's veins. The man was a monster. There was nowhere to run, no one to ask for help and no one to blame but herself. He'd baited the trap and she'd willingly walked right in. She took a breath.

30

Dorothy
October 1922

There were two letters in the box when Dorothy and Sarah returned home from their half-day Saturday. Dorothy's heart stuttered when she saw the distinctive cursive on the envelope addressed to her. It had been a while since the last one and she'd hoped there'd be no more. She stood in the entrance and quickly scanned the contents then put the letter back in its envelope and hid it in her pocket. Although it was spring, the evenings were still cool. She'd set a fire and use the letter as kindling. That's all it was good for.

'What's wrong?' asked Sarah. 'You're dreadfully pale.' She'd begun to set out the lunch things on the table. 'Not bad news, I hope.'

Dorothy set her features into a bland expression. 'A letter from my cousin. My aunt is unwell. It seems she won't be with us for much longer.' Dorothy hated lying to Sarah but didn't want her poring over the contents of this letter as she had with the others. No one could see the accusations written there.

'I'm sorry to hear that. It's hard, isn't it, being so far from family at times like these.' Sarah's eyes were sharp with inquiry. Dorothy had never mentioned her brothers or any other kin. Why would she? Bournville had been her family, and Freddie.

'The other letter is for you.' Dorothy avoided her eyes while handing it to Sarah.

'Thank you.' Sarah turned the envelope to read the address on the back. 'It's from a woman I met in Sydney while there with Mr Cooper.'

'I'll heat up the soup and put on some toast while you read it.' Dorothy was glad of the excuse to retreat to the kitchen. She needed to settle her nerves. A cold finger of fear traced down her spine as the words of this latest letter swirled in her mind – *I know what happened in Melbourne*, and once again that familiar refrain, *You have something of great value*. This letter was different to the others. Instead of vague threats, this threat was real. The writer would tell the Firm about her behaviour unless she gave him what he wanted. Her career would be in tatters if she refused.

Dorothy could hardly swallow the soup and the toast stuck in her throat. She managed a superficial conversation with Sarah, who enthused about her letter and reminisced about her time in Sydney. Dorothy nodded at all the right moments but her mind was spinning. How on earth had anyone seen her go to Thomas's room in Melbourne? She'd been so careful. It was one thing for her reputation to be dragged through the mud but she couldn't allow any harm to come to Thomas. He was too fragile as it was. This would destroy him. There was a small glimmer of hope. The letter didn't mention him by name.

Sarah had always said she'd be by her side when this evil man made his move. Until now Dorothy had found solace in her friend's support, but with the arrival of this letter she was on her own. She had to be. The contents of this letter must remain a secret. Sarah could never know.

'Dorothy?' Sarah's voice registered through her turbulent thoughts.

'Sorry.' Dorothy forced herself to focus. She cast about for a reason for her distraction. 'I was thinking about George Cadbury Junior's upcoming visit.' It was a valid excuse. Excitement was mounting about his arrival in two months' time. There was speculation that he was coming to personally oversee production of the Firm's most famous chocolate, Dairy Milk. The Australian market had been crying out for its return through the war years and the embargoes, and now, finally, it might begin production here in Tasmania.

'Oh, the extra work it's causing me!' Sarah exclaimed. 'I know it's terribly exciting, but you can't imagine the paperwork and organisational effort involved. The Chocolate Prince arriving on our shores. What a ballyhoo.'

'You're right, I can't imagine.' What Dorothy could imagine was the amount of work it would take to make the changes to the chocolate section for Dairy Milk production. Changes she'd be happy to oversee. But would she? Or would she be gone, forced out by this malicious blackmailer. She pushed back her chair and began collecting their plates and bowls. 'I'm going for a walk. I'll do the washing up when I get back.'

Sarah waved her hand in dismissal. 'Leave them. You made lunch. I'll do the dishes.'

The unexpected sound of a round of explosive bangs made Dorothy wince. Empire Day was long gone with its bonfires and crackers but Guy Fawkes was early next month. Dorothy enjoyed the excitement of fireworks but the crackers that just went bang seemed pointless.

'Those local boys,' Sarah said. 'They do love their double bungers. I wouldn't be surprised if we heard a volley of tom thumbs next.'

'Let's hope they leave the rest for Guy Fawkes night.' Dorothy pulled on her coat, hat and gloves, the incriminating letter crinkling in her pocket. How she longed to rip it up and toss it in the river.

Gravel crunched under her feet as Dorothy strode past the other cottages and towards the water. Frustration and anguish built at the base of her throat. She'd come to Tasmania with plans and ambitions but now it was not only her dreams that were threatened, but the man she cared so much about. The Derwent stretched out to the hills of the eastern shore under a cloud-scattered sky. Her thoughts went to the stench, smoke and noise of Birmingham and the hovel her family called home. She'd escaped her mother's fate of marrying a drunkard, bearing his children and dying young. She'd pulled herself out of the slums through her own hard work and determination. Was she to lose it all now? The breeze lifted and carried with it the sound of splashing. When she heard a small cry of distress she began to run.

The boy was struggling, out of his depth and fully clothed. His head sunk below the water, a circle of bubbles the only sign. Dorothy pulled off her shoes and discarded her coat, hat and gloves as she rushed towards the riverbank. A picnic blanket, plates and food were scattered on the ground and a tumbler lay discarded closer to the bank. Where were his parents? She focused her attention on the boy. He'd managed to get his head above the water but within seconds he'd sunk again. Dorothy pushed into the river, the cold of it biting through her stockings, soaking her dress. The water was heavy with silt. She dove into the murk where a dark form loomed. She found his arm and pulled the boy towards the surface, both of them gasping and coughing. The boy grabbed at her, arms flailing, and dragged them down again. Dorothy spun him around, pinned his arms to his chest, and kicked up towards the light. They broke through the surface again and she sucked precious air into her lungs.

'It's all right. It's all right,' Dorothy said, her mouth against his ear. 'You're safe now. Relax. I'll get us back to shore.'

He was limp, a dead weight in her arms. Holding him against her side she headed for the riverbank, but with the boy unresponsive and the weight of him and her clothes, the water was like treacle. Finally the river bed was beneath her feet. She struggled up the slope with the boy in her arms. He was unconscious. Dread pooled in her stomach. Dorothy put him on his side, checked his mouth, then laid him on his front with his head to one side. She pushed on his lower ribs, two seconds on, two seconds off as she'd been taught at Bournville. He coughed and a spume of water gushed from his mouth. The boy's eyes slowly opened.

'Thank God,' Dorothy whispered. She helped him roll over and into a sitting position. His face was ashen, as pale as death.

Dorothy kept her voice gentle and calm. 'I'm Mrs Adwell. You're safe now.'

'I want m-my m-mummy.' His teeth chattered from shock and cold. He was young, probably only six years old. What were his parents doing, leaving him alone by the river? She looked towards the ruined picnic. What had happened?

A breeze picked up, sending a shiver through her. 'Let's get you out of your wet clothes and wrap you in the picnic blanket.' She kept her voice light. 'Your mother will be back in a moment. Sit here, next to me.' She knelt and patted the ground beside her. The trembling in his body increased as she eased off his little knitted vest and shirt. She pulled at one corner of the picnic blanket, not caring as the plates and food tumbled into a heap on the ground. The picnic had been in ruins before she'd arrived. Gathering the blanket, she wrapped it tightly around the boy. 'There, that's better.'

He looked at her with uncertain eyes. If she hadn't been walking by the river this young boy might now be floating, dead in the water. Dorothy forced a smile. 'You know my name, but what's yours?'

'Edward.' His voice was so soft she had to lower her head to hear him. Their faces were almost touching.

'Edward is a fine name.' Dorothy looked around, hoping his parents would return. She longed to take the boy back to the cottage, sit him by a warm fire and give him a hot cocoa, but if she did, his parents wouldn't know how to find him. Her clothes were dripping wet and the afternoon breeze was on the rise. If they didn't get warm and dry soon they'd both catch their death. 'Edward, I'm going to pick up the rest of my clothes. Can you see them?' She pointed towards her coat, hat, gloves and shoes on the ground further along the riverbank. He nodded. 'I'll be back in a moment.'

Her heart broke a little as she left him wrapped in the blanket surrounded by the wreckage of what should have been a happy picnic. After collecting her things, Dorothy wrung the water from the skirt of her dress as best she could, slipped her damp feet into her shoes and wrapped her coat around her wet clothes. Within seconds the coat was damp as well.

'Edward. Edward, where are you?'

Dorothy turned at the sound of a woman's voice. She was lean to the point of thinness, her hair had come undone and was falling in untidy waves around her face. If she'd been wearing a hat it had been lost. Her cheeks were mottled and her eyes red.

'Mummy?' Edward stood on unsteady legs.

Edwards's mother rushed to his side and fell to her knees to hold him. 'I'm sorry, my darling boy.' She pulled back. 'Why are you wrapped in the picnic blanket?'

'I fell in the water, Mummy.' Edward began to cry. 'I didn't mean to.'

Edward looked at Dorothy and his mother's eyes followed.

Dorothy moved closer and gave Edward a reassuring smile. 'You went for a little swim, didn't you, Edward?'

'A swim?' The woman's eyes widened in horror. 'But he can't swim.'

Dorothy was sorely tempted to scold this woman for leaving her young son alone so close to the river when she knew he couldn't swim. 'Edward mightn't be able to swim, but I can.' She tried to hide the accusation in her voice.

'I was under the water, Mummy. I couldn't breathe.' Edward's words jagged between his sobs.

The woman held him tight and looked up at Dorothy with tear-filled eyes. 'You saved my son's life. I'm forever in your debt.'

Her face was such a picture of despair – her hair wild, her face streaked with tears – Dorothy's anger and blame were replaced by a surge of concern. Three plates lay scattered on the ground along with three tumblers. Something had happened at the picnic, something that had caused this woman great distress even before she found out about her son's brush with death. 'I'm just glad Edward is all right.' She shivered with the cold and with the thought of what might have been.

'You're soaking wet.' The woman began to unbutton her cardigan. 'Please, put this on.'

'It's not necessary. I live nearby.'

The woman held her son closer. 'We were having a picnic. We're planning to move here, to the estate.' Her face crumpled with an expression of anguish so intense that Dorothy had to look away.

'Edward is safe now. I'll be on my way.' Whatever had happened here was none of Dorothy's business. She began to walk towards the cottage.

'What's happened? Is everything all right?' A man appeared, his jacket askew and his brow creased in confusion. Then he saw Dorothy.

A wave of panic rose in her throat. She jammed her hands in her coat pockets and flinched when her fingers touched the letter.

'Please, stay,' the woman called out. 'You saved my son's life.'

Dorothy faltered.

'Yes,' the man said. 'Please. Stay.'

Dorothy shifted to face them – the woman holding her son, the man standing behind them. The family resemblance between man and boy was uncanny. She shouldn't be here, not with them, not like this. 'I ...' She was unable to put her thoughts together in any way that made sense. The first lesson she'd learnt on the streets of Birmingham came back to her in a rush of adrenaline. When faced with danger, run. That fierce desire to flee overcame her now. She gritted her teeth, turned her back and headed towards the cottage, the warmth of the fire, and the safety of home.

31

Maisie

A pall of despair hung over the breakfast table. Andrew's bag sat by the front door, a reminder of his imminent departure. Maisie was determined not to cry. Lily showed no such restraint – her tears threatened to water down the bowl of porridge sitting untouched in front of her. Misery was etched into Mother's face. She'd seen her husband off to war and now her only son was going off to a battle of another kind.

'Are you sure you need to go to the mainland?' Mother asked yet again. 'Couldn't you find work in the Midlands? Even Launceston would be closer. You could catch the train down to see us.'

'I've tried everything. There's no work.' Andrew looked down at his hands. 'The only answer is to go to Melbourne. If I can't find anything there I'll head north to Sydney.'

'But it's so far away,' Mother pleaded.

'I know. But the wages are better. Better wages for shorter hours. The workforce is unionised there, you see. All being well, I'll be able to send money home soon.' He stood. 'I'd best be on my way.'

It was a sad procession that followed him to the front door.

'My boy, my boy.' Mother clung to him while Lily wrapped her arms around them both. Maisie stood close by, biting back the tears. 'You'll write and let us know how you're getting on.'

'I will.' He ruffled Lily's hair. 'And I'll send you books.' He turned to Maisie. 'And I shall expect letters in return telling me how well you're doing in your job. Feel free to include some chocolate.' He winked.

It was the wink that undid her. The false bravado of her little brother pierced her heart. He was barely seventeen. Maisie clutched at her handkerchief. 'Goodbye, brother, and good luck.'

He gave a wave at the gate and headed down the steep street. Mother's knees buckled and she would have collapsed if Maisie hadn't had a firm arm around her waist. It was only the three of them now, a household of women.

'At least we won't have to put up with his terrible smell any more,' Lily sniffled, as they walked back to their breakfast. Her attempt to cheer them up was appreciated but failed to lighten the weight of their grief. They sat at the kitchen table, their porridge cold, all of them staring at Andrew's empty chair.

Word of Mrs Adwell's heroics on the weekend spread like wildfire through the factory. Maisie had trouble keeping her girls focused on their tasks. At lunchtime Mrs Adwell was the only topic of conversation at the supervisors' table.

'She saved the little boy's life. She deserves a medal.' Alice's cheeks were flushed with excitement. 'We have our very own heroine here in the chocolate section.'

'All Cadbury's employees learn to swim at Bournville,' Daphne said. 'They should bring in the same rule here, given we're surrounded by water.'

'He wasn't an employee though, was he? He was a young boy,' Jane said.

'It was lucky it was Mrs Adwell who found him then, half-drowned in the river.' Daphne sat up a little straighter. 'I can swim, of course.'

The other supervisors exchanged glances. Maisie had never had the time nor the inclination to swim. At best her rare visits to the beaches along the river involved paddling no deeper than her ankles and the water was always dreadfully cold, even on a summer's day. She suspected the other girls felt the same.

'I think Cadbury's ought to give her some kind of award,' Jane said.

'My point exactly,' Alice nodded.

'You're awfully quiet, Maisie.' Jane looked at her with inquisitive eyes. 'I'd have thought you'd be shouting her praises from the rooftops.'

Maisie forced a smile. 'It was quite the feat, from all accounts.'

'I heard she didn't want a fuss.' Daphne stood, bringing the conversation to a halt. 'I'd say Maisie understands that and respects Mrs Adwell's wishes, as should we all. Time to get back to work.'

On her way to the enrobers a familiar figure waved at Maisie, beckoning her over.

'Gertie. Hello.' Maisie was genuinely pleased. Since Andrew had lost his job every spare moment of her days had been busy helping Mother and she'd hardly had time to spend with her friend.

'Did you hear about Mrs Adwell?' Gertie gushed. 'Isn't she amazing?'

'I think all of Hobart has heard about Mrs Adwell by now.'

Gertie put her arm through Maisie's and leant in close. 'I have news that's even more exciting.' Her eyes shone and was that a touch of lipstick on her lips? Make-up was forbidden in the factory. Gertie giggled and whispered in Maisie's ear. 'I'm in love.' She pulled back and waited for Maisie's response with a wide smile.

'In love?' Maisie didn't doubt it for a second. The way the boys had flocked around her at the dance, Gertie had her choice of beaus.

'He wants to marry me. He's just waiting for the money. He says his ship is coming in soon. When it does, he'll buy me the biggest diamond ring.' Gertie wiggled the fingers of her left hand.

Maisie suppressed her surprise. Gertie was only sixteen. A beau was one thing but surely she was too young for marriage. 'Where did you meet him?'

'He's such a good dancer and so handsome.' There was a touch of smugness in her smile. 'I made another new dress for the latest dance just to impress him and it worked. It made the Bournville spinsters raise their eyebrows but I don't care.'

Maisie could only imagine. If the dress was even more daring than the one she'd worn to the first Cadbury's dance Maisie would have raised her eyebrows too. 'And does this young man have a name?'

'He's sworn me to secrecy until he puts the ring on my finger.' Gertie made a buttoning motion in front of her lips. 'I'm sorry I can't tell you yet, but I hope you're happy for me. Once I'm married I won't be working here any more.' She gestured at the factory. 'I expect I'll be living in a mansion in Sandy Bay. I'll have you over for posh afternoon teas.'

Her joy was infectious and Maisie wished her all the luck in the world. To be free of the tumbledown house at Montrose would be quite a step up for Gertie.

When Maisie arrived back at the enrobers the girls were in a huddle, still talking about Mrs Adwell and her heroic feat. Every time Maisie heard the tale it had grown by epic proportions. She was surprised no one had her fighting off man-eating sharks to save the boy, although it might only be a matter of time. With some difficulty she wrangled them back to work but when Mrs Adwell arrived for her regular inspection the whispers and giggles began again in earnest.

'Come now, girls, concentrate,' Mrs Adwell announced. 'I know what you've heard but I didn't do anything extraordinary. Anyone else would have done exactly the same thing given the circumstances and that's an end to it. Back to work.'

Maisie watched as Mrs Adwell went along the line checking the centres and the flow of chocolate from the enrobers. It was as if it were just another day and Mrs Adwell was the same person as she was last week. But she wasn't, not in Maisie's eyes. Mrs Adwell had saved a boy from drowning and even though she refused to take any credit, it didn't take away from the fact that she'd put her life at risk to save another. Cold guilt niggled in Maisie's chest. Had she judged Mrs Adwell for being the worst kind of woman when in fact she was the best?

Maisie steadied her nerves. 'Mrs Adwell?'

Mrs Adwell raised her head. 'Yes, Maisie.'

'Could we meet after work, please?'

'We can't talk here and now?'

'I'm sorry. It needs to be after the girls have gone.'

Mrs Adwell regarded her. 'Very well. I'll be here at five thirty.' She opened her mouth as if to say something, then stopped. Instead she turned and left.

Maisie clenched her hands to stop them from trembling. She was trapped between two choices, neither of them good. She would lose her job if she failed to do what Percy demanded, and if she told Mrs Adwell the truth her position here would be forfeit. She couldn't win. With Andrew gone she needed this job more than ever. She paused for a moment and thought of her father. He would want her to be brave and loyal, to do what was right and to be proud of her actions. Maisie lifted her chin. She knew what she must do.

It was strange being in the factory without the rumbling of machines and the chatter and laughter of the girls. The enrobing room was cavernous, much bigger than it seemed in daylight when it was full of busyness and bustle. Only one constant remained, the aroma of chocolate. Maisie would miss the delicious smell if she had to go, as would Lily. Throughout the afternoon the doubts had surfaced time and time again, but Maisie had thought of her father and steeled herself for what was to come.

Footsteps heralded Mrs Adwell's arrival. As always, her hair was pulled back in a neat bun at the base of her neck, gleaming dark against the white surroundings.

'Well, Maisie,' Mrs Adwell said. 'What's all this about?'

Maisie wrung her hands. This had been so much easier in her imagination but with Mrs Adwell facing her, fear threatened to engulf her. 'I, ah, that is ...'

Mrs Adwell studied her, waiting patiently.

Maisie turned her head away. It would be easier if she didn't look at Mrs Adwell. 'When I started delivering the trays of chocolates to the office there was a man who'd always be waiting for me.'

Mrs Adwell stiffened. 'Did he do something he shouldn't?' The fierce tone in Mrs Adwell's voice made Maisie feel even more ashamed. 'Did he touch you, Maisie?' It was clear her forewoman would defend her against any harm and yet Maisie had betrayed her.

'No, nothing like that. He asked me questions about myself, about my position here.' She braved a glance at Mrs Adwell. 'He was the one who told me about Frank Sutton.'

Mrs Adwell pressed her lips together then nodded once. 'Go on.'

'When my brother lost his job, the man, Percy – that's his name, Percy Bates – told me he could help. He'd give me money, a lot of money, if I'd do something for him.'

'And what was that?' Mrs Adwell's voice had a knowing tone.

'He wanted me to go through the filing cabinets and to search Mr Cooper's office.'

'Oh.' Mrs Adwell straightened her shoulders. 'Not what I was expecting. So, that's what you were doing when I disturbed you.'

'Yes.' Maisie hung her head.

'What were you looking for?'

Maisie hesitated. She thought of her father – *brave and loyal* – and clasped her hands together even more tightly. 'Recipes.'

'Ah.' There was no sense of surprise in Mrs Adwell's voice. 'And did you find any recipes? Did this Percy Bates give you the money he promised?'

'No.'

Mrs Adwell sighed. 'I understand you were desperate when your brother lost his job and I'm sorry I wasn't able to help, but, Maisie, this is very disappointing.'

Tears welled in Maisie's eyes. 'I'm sorry. I was angry and upset, and you're right, desperate. I should never have done it.'

'You wouldn't have found them anyway. The recipes are tightly guarded.' Mrs Adwell paused.

Maisie waited as if at the edge of a high cliff, expecting to fall.

'You've been extremely foolish,' Mrs Adwell continued. 'But I can see you're sorry. You've done the right thing in coming to me, I just wish you'd done it sooner.' She held Maisie with her gaze. 'I think you've learnt your lesson. You're a good worker, Maisie, with much promise. We'll say nothing more of this but, without incriminating you, I will alert management to the actions of Mr Bates.'

'You can't,' Maisie blurted.

Mrs Adwell stiffened. 'Miss Greenwood. I'm doing you an enormous favour. Most girls would be grateful. I hardly think it's your place to say what I can and cannot do.'

'I am grateful, I am, but you see, when I couldn't find what Percy wanted I thought it was all over but it wasn't.'

Mrs Adwell's eyes were steely. 'Go on.'

'He threatened to get me sacked. He said he'd tell everyone I'd gone through the filing cabinets if I didn't do something else.' Maisie's pulse raced. The hardest part was just ahead.

'And what was that?' Mrs Adwell stood perfectly still.

Maisie lowered her eyes. She couldn't bear to look at Mrs Adwell. 'He wanted information on you.'

There was a chilling silence. Maisie dared to look up. Mrs Adwell's face was a mask. Nervously Maisie picked at her uniform. Flecks of dried chocolate smudged her fingers. The silence stretched out.

At last Mrs Adwell broke the silence. 'What did he want to know?'

Maisie concentrated on the smear of chocolate between her thumb and forefinger. She wished she'd never said anything but it was too late to take it back. 'He asked me to tell him anything I might know that paints you in a bad light.'

'What did you say?' Every word was cold and solid as if carved from stone.

'That I've seen you with a man by the river.'

'With Frank? I mean, Mr Sutton.'

'Not Mr Sutton. Another man.'

'Did you recognise him?'

'No. He kept his hat tilted down and his collar up. I could give Percy a rough height but that was all.'

Mrs Adwell smoothed the hair behind her right ear. 'Good. An accidental meeting with a man by the river, there's no harm in that.' It was as if she was talking to herself.

'Then there was that night in Melbourne ...' Maisie held her breath.

Mrs Adwell froze, her hand still to her hair. 'What night?'

Maisie thought she would die of shame. 'A man came to our hotel room. I didn't hear what was said but soon after you dressed and left. You didn't return until almost dawn.'

Mrs Adwell's frown deepened. 'Are you wanting money from me, Maisie?'

Maisie's mouth dropped open in horror. 'No.'

'But you told him about that night.'

'Yes. I had to. The threats he was making ...' She wished the floor would open and swallow her whole. Her nerves were so tight it was as if the flesh was being flayed from her bones. And there was the horrid thought that kept prodding her conscience. Before Percy had inveigled her into this web she'd had the idea of threatening Mrs Adwell herself, in return for a job for Andrew. Percy must have picked up on how far she'd debase herself. She'd brought this on herself.

'Does this Percy Bates want money from me?'

'I'm not sure, but he said you have something of great value.'

Mrs Adwell flinched. 'Is that the exact phrase he used? Something of great value?'

'Yes. That exact phrase.' Every word he'd said was burnt into Maisie's memory.

'I see.' Mrs Adwell stood deep in thought while Maisie hovered anxiously, wishing none of this had ever happened. Finally Mrs Adwell raised her chin, a look of determination on her face. 'Maisie, we are going to keep all of this to ourselves.'

'Yes, Mrs Adwell.' A small hope dared to bloom within her. She hadn't lost her job. She might yet be safe.

'And you will do something for me.'

'Anything, anything at all.'

'I need Percy Bates to write you a note. I haven't the slightest interest in its contents, but I want something handwritten by him. Can you arrange that?'

Maisie nodded dumbly. This was unexpected. 'I will try. I will. I'll do my best.'

Mrs Adwell's eyes burnt into Maisie's. 'The only thing I want to hear from you right now is, "Yes, Mrs Adwell, I can do it".'

Maisie took a deep breath. 'Yes, Mrs Adwell, I can do it.' Her voice sounded far from confident. She had no idea how to get Percy to write her a note. But Mrs Adwell didn't want to hear excuses.

'Good. When you have it, bring it directly to me.'

Maisie fidgeted nervously. 'Please, Mrs Adwell, what do I do about Percy Bates? He keeps threatening to get me sacked unless I give him more information.'

'You're safe now that you've told me. Nobody's going to give you the sack with me in your corner but I want you to keep stringing him along. At least until we have that letter.' She stopped. 'You haven't told him who the man was who came to our hotel room, have you?'

'I don't know who he was. Percy wants me to find out though.'

'Right. Tell him you're spying on me and that you'll have more information for him soon.' Mrs Adwell glanced around the factory then back at Maisie. 'For the time being I want you to keep in close contact and get that note to me as soon as possible. There's no time to waste.'

'Yes, Mrs Adwell.' Maisie's head spun with a mixture of relief and despair. She might still have a job but she'd been presented with an almost impossible task.

'Get it done, Maisie.' Mrs Adwell turned and walked towards the exit, her footsteps echoing through the cavernous space.

32

Dorothy

Dorothy arrived home to the sound of Sarah in the kitchen, busy with pots and pans.

'You're late,' Sarah called out. 'I know it's your turn to cook but I thought I'd make a start.'

Dorothy took off her hat and coat and made her way to the kitchen. 'Pardon?' She was still dazed from her conversation with Maisie. She'd thought their meeting would be easily resolved – a matter of a work problem or more trouble with a boy. Never had she imagined the nasty scheme the girl was involved in and how it would affect her personally.

Sarah wiped her hands on a tea towel. 'Are you quite all right?' She scrutinised Dorothy with a keen eye. 'You look a bit peaky.'

'There's something I need to discuss with you. We can talk during tea.'

'From your expression, I don't think it can wait. Besides, I won't be able to eat a single bite until I know what's wrong. Let me take care of this.' She gestured to the cooker and the gently steaming saucepans. 'I'll turn off the heat. There's nothing here that will be ruined for the waiting. I won't be a moment.'

Dorothy walked slowly to the living room, sank into an armchair and closed her eyes. Much as she appreciated Sarah's friendship and support, she needed to tread carefully. There were some facts she'd have to withhold.

Within minutes Sarah joined her. 'Tell me what's going on.'

'Do you know of an employee by the name of Percy Bates?'

Sarah thought for a moment. 'The name's not ringing any bells, but we have over two hundred employees now. Why?'

'I'm late home because Maisie Greenwood wanted to meet with me.'

'Ah, your protégée. What did she have to say?'

'She told me she's being blackmailed by a Percy Bates.'

'Blackmailed?' Sarah looked genuinely shocked. 'Why on earth would anyone want to blackmail Maisie?'

'This Percy Bates promised her money if she'd search through the filing cabinets and Mr Cooper's office.'

'Oh.' Sarah nodded slowly. 'Trying to find the recipes.' She reached for her cigarettes, tapped one against the case and lit it.

'Yes. She did what he asked but didn't find anything.'

Sarah settled back in her chair and crossed her legs. 'Well, we've been expecting this, haven't we? If not from the local confectioners then from the British manufacturers trying to take advantage of the newness of our operation and the naivety of our local staff. Fortunately, all our secrets are well protected. We learnt that lesson back at Bournville. The spies there were relentless.' She drew on her cigarette. 'It's clear he's after the Dairy Milk recipe. They all are, these parasites. The other recipes would be a prize but that recipe is the real goal. Once production starts here we'll need to be extremely vigilant.'

'Percy Bates offered to pay Maisie to get the recipe for him.'

'I'm not surprised she failed. What does surprise me is the blackmail.'

'He's threatening to expose her as a thief, or an attempted thief, if she doesn't do what he wants.'

'And so she told you.' Sarah ashed her cigarette. 'Case closed, I would say. How can he blackmail her when she has negated his trump card? You're clearly not going to fire her even though that's what she deserves. You're too fond of that girl, Dot.'

'There's more. He's asked her to find information about me.'

'You? Why?'

'He's blackmailing her. I expect he wants to try to blackmail me as well.'

'He thinks you have a better chance of accessing the recipes.'

Dorothy nodded. When Maisie had tearfully told Dorothy her story, a disturbing thought had formed in her mind. Percy Bates had always known the girl wouldn't succeed. He'd set Maisie up from the start with the aim of using her to get to Dorothy. 'He told her I had something of great value.'

Sarah sat forward, bright-eyed, and crushed out her cigarette. 'The same phrase as in the letters. At last. We have our man. I thought he'd given up. You've had no letters now for, how long?'

'A while.' Dorothy avoided Sarah's eyes. She could never tell her about the last letter and the threats it contained.

'He must've been holding off to see what happened with the Glucose War. If the Firm was forced to combine with the Australian manufacturers there'd be no point in their agents trying to steal our recipes. They could just sit back and wait for them to fall into their laps. Now the Glucose War has come to nothing, our ratbag spy is back in action.'

'And threatening my staff.'

'This is great news.'

'It is?' Dorothy frowned.

'Maisie has given us the key to exposing him. I have to give her credit for that. Most girls would be too terrified to come forward.'

'Exposing him?' Dorothy's hand touched the base of her throat. Percy Bates reminded her of many of the men she knew back in the slums – vicious types with low morals, if any. When cornered he was sure to bite. Percy knew about the hotel in Melbourne. If news of that night was made public, Dorothy would have to resign. She may have a little more leeway as a widowed woman, but a liaison with a married man would be impossible to justify. Sarah had warned her but Dorothy had never thought it would come to this. 'We can't. Not yet.'

'I think he's done enough to warrant prosecution, don't you? Or at least being sacked.'

'All we have at the moment is Maisie's word. However, I've told her to get me a sample of his handwriting. She'll ask him to write her a note or some such. I'm almost certain his handwriting will match the letters.'

Sarah studied Dorothy. 'That's clever. Once we have the evidence we can avoid getting Maisie involved, well, to any further degree.' She tapped her fingernails on her skirt. 'There is another way that will avoid Maisie entirely. We know for certain he's an employee now, don't we?'

'That's what Maisie says.'

'Well then, we may not have to wait for the letter. Now I know his name, his details will be easy to find in the personnel files. His application should be there, written in his own fair hand. Bingo!' Sarah clapped her hands together as if Percy was a mosquito she'd just killed between her palms.

Dorothy realised too late she'd made a mistake telling Sarah. She should have kept quiet, waited for the evidence of his handwriting and then blackmailed the blackmailer – if he kept his mouth shut about what may or may not have happened in Melbourne then she wouldn't tell management about his threats to herself and Maisie, or the fact he'd compelled Maisie to steal. She'd been a fool to include Sarah in this mess.

'Dot?' Sarah slid off her chair and knelt beside Dorothy. 'I know this is a burden on top of everything else. You haven't been yourself since the near-drowning. I've told you how brave you were. Not only that, management and the directors have been singing your praises. The young boy would be dead—' She stopped herself. 'Enough of that. You've heard it all a thousand times.' Sarah touched Dorothy's hand. 'You're the heroine of Cadbury's. I can't imagine why Percy Bates would think he could blackmail you.' She waited, her head slightly tilted to one side, for Dorothy to say something.

Dorothy was back on the riverbank, sodden, dripping and cold with the boy limp in her arms. She shivered. It could have been so different. Part of her regretted running away that day, the part that thought she was owed an explanation. Why hadn't Thomas told her his wife and child were joining him? How could he let her discover it for herself like that? Did she mean so little to him? In her heart though, she knew if she'd stayed she'd be the one to have had to explain. Since that day she'd avoided Thomas. She'd stopped going to the meeting house on Sundays and no longer left an extra tray of chocolates in the office. There were no more lunches at the cottage or talks by the river. His absence left a jagged hole in her life – one she was familiar with. She'd been a fool to think he could fill it.

'Please, Sarah, it's been a long day.' Dorothy closed her eyes. She yearned to disappear. Talking with Sarah had seemed like the right idea when she'd arrived home, but Dorothy had painted herself into a corner. If she said anything more she'd have to lie her way out.

Sarah patted her hand and stood. 'You relax by the fire and I'll get tea sorted.'

After she left the room, Dorothy buried her face in her hands. She had no one to blame but herself.

When Dorothy made her inspections over the next few days, Maisie always hung back a little. It could only mean she'd had no luck with the note as yet. Impatience and anxiety made Dorothy jittery. At home she attempted to settle her nerves in the kitchen. Baking was a way of creating certainty in an uncertain world. Weighing and measuring, mixing and stirring often helped soothe her. That night Yorkshire puddings instead of potatoes would be a treat with the lamb chops, peas and carrots, and a steamed chocolate pudding with custard was just the thing for afters.

She was shelling peas when Sarah came rushing in, pulling off her coat and gloves. She flung her hat onto the kitchen table and grabbed Dorothy by the hands. 'Dot, I have some wonderful news. I've been bursting to tell you all day but couldn't risk anyone overhearing at work.'

'Is it about Percy Bates?'

Sarah's face creased in a frown. 'No. In fact there is no Percy Bates in the personnel records. He must have given Maisie a fake name, which makes me think he's smarter than I gave him credit for. We'll have to wait for Maisie's note after all.'

Dorothy hid her relief. The way was now clear. When Maisie gave her the note she'd manage Percy Bates without getting Sarah involved. 'Tell me then, what's this exciting news of yours?'

'Margaret is returning to Britain.'

Dorothy stepped back in surprise. 'Margaret? Why?'

'Come. Sit.' Sarah pulled out a chair from the kitchen table and motioned to Dorothy to join her. 'You must have noticed Margaret wasn't coping with the pressures of being Chief Forewoman.'

'I've been worried about her.' Margaret had become increasingly short-tempered and irritable lately. 'But to return to Britain?'

Sarah waved her words away. 'Margaret has made a rod for her own back. She's too rigid, too set in doing everything the way it was done at Bournville – not taking into account how different this factory is and has to be. We've created a factory for the modern age while Margaret is still stuck in her pre-war ways.'

Dorothy thought it unfair to have Margaret's efforts dismissed. 'It's been an enormous undertaking.'

Sarah leant forward, her eyes bright and excited. 'An undertaking that will soon be yours.'

'Mine?'

'I really shouldn't tell you this before the official notification, but the local directors are in agreement. I typed Mr Cooper's letter and sent it to Bournville this afternoon. It's all official. I've known this was in the works for a while but couldn't say anything until it was confirmed.' Sarah sat back and beamed at her. 'You, Mrs Adwell, are the new Chief Forewoman of Cadbury-Fry-Pascall.'

Time slowed. Dorothy had planned and worked for this opportunity. It was what she'd hoped for but hadn't expected so soon. It had been only a little over a year since she'd arrived in Tasmania. 'Chief Forewoman.' The words sent a thrill through her. Surely now her ultimate ambition of being on the board couldn't be too far away.

'Yes. And richly deserved. It's been noted that you'd already taken on many of Margaret's responsibilities without ever taking credit. The board has been impressed with your selflessness, not to mention the quality of your work.'

Dorothy's thoughts flew to Ida. She'd be so proud. Or would she? Ida's loyalties lay with Esme now. Oh, Esme. A heaviness deadened her joy. Dorothy could only imagine her reaction to this news. 'But what about Esme? She's next in line for the position along with me and she's more senior than I am.'

'Tosh. She's her own worst enemy. She's done nothing but complain since she's been here. All that recent fuss with her threatening to resign was the last straw.' Esme had flabbergasted everyone with her latest manoeuvres – demanding another pay rise and a cottage or she'd resign. 'The Firm would be glad to be shot of her, I think, despite the expenses they've incurred in bringing her out here. Hopefully she'll make good on her threats when she hears you're the new Chief Forewoman.'

'Who'll be taking up my role of Forewoman A?' Dorothy hoped it would be Ida. They may have drifted apart but Ida would always hold a place in her heart.

'All things in time. For now we're celebrating your success, very quietly so no one can hear us, until the official announcement is made. Make sure to act surprised when it is.'

'I do worry about Margaret.' The responsibility had taken its toll. Dorothy hoped she wouldn't suffer the same fate. 'Along with everything else, she told me her mother back in Birmingham is ailing.'

'Margaret missed home more than any of us. I think the Firm is doing her a favour by letting her out of her contract. Her fare back to England will be paid for too, even though there's no obligation. When the announcement is made, Cadbury's will say she's taking up a new position as a liaison between the Firm's base at Bournville and its outpost here in the colonies. There'll be no loss of face.'

'Is it true? Will she have a new position?'

'Her knowledge will be invaluable.' Sarah tapped her fingers lightly on the table. 'Now stop worrying about everyone else and take a moment to enjoy your success. If I had a bottle of champagne I'd pop the cork right now. There's some of that delicious apple juice in the ice chest. That'll do. I'll get some glasses. You sit there and bask in the glory of your promotion.'

Sarah radiated an excitement that Dorothy didn't dare feel. She should be over the moon, but her thoughts kept returning to Percy Bates. Everything she'd worked towards for so long was teetering like a house of cards and he had the power to bring all of it crashing down.

33

Maisie

Maisie closed the front door behind her and began the steep descent to the railway station. She scarcely registered her neighbour's hello as she walked past. Mrs Perkins would only ask, as she always did, about Andrew and whether he'd found work in Melbourne. There'd be no need to tell anyone else in their street, or in the whole of the Glebe, once Mrs Perkins got wind of it, but Maisie had nothing to tell. No news was supposed to be good news but not in this case. Lily was still attending school but Maisie couldn't keep pretending for much longer. Every evening when she returned from work Mother asked her about the bonus. Every time Maisie had to lie. 'Soon,' she kept saying.

The previous night, after Lily had gone to bed, Mother had confronted her. 'It's time you stopped this nonsense. I'm going to write to The Friends' School and tell them Lily won't be able to take up the scholarship.' When Maisie objected her mother stopped her with a glare. 'It's the decent thing to do. Another child will be able to take advantage of the school's generosity.'

Maisie had begged for more time but with no word from Andrew and despite her and Lily's efforts with the mending and ironing, she'd begun to despair. They were behind with the rent and sometimes there was barely enough for a meal on the table.

The Cadbury's train pulled into Hobart station in a plume of coal smoke and steam. During the journey the noise of the engine, the clatter of the wheels on the tracks and the incessant chatter of the other girls pressed in on her. Maisie's mind was like this train, always on the same track, the wheels circling endlessly and her thoughts chattering on and on about the predicament she was in. Every idea she had about persuading Percy to write a note was either too ludicrous or too transparent. If she didn't succeed she'd be out of a job, no matter Mrs Adwell's assurances. Why was a note from Percy so vital? She didn't know, only that it was. Not even the news that George Cadbury Junior was coming to the factory and the accompanying rumour that he'd be overseeing the production of Dairy Milk cheered her up. What was the point of her favourite chocolate being available again if she was no longer working at Cadbury's and couldn't afford to buy it? It was a bitter joke.

The train shuddered to a stop. The crush of the other girls jostled Maisie out of the carriage and onto the Cadbury's platform. There were over a hundred women and girls working at the factory now, each of them in a hurry to get to the change rooms, don their whites and scrub their hands before being at their stations at precisely eight am. If she did lose her job she wouldn't be missed in this throng. Mrs Adwell might think of her as an opportunity lost but her attention would focus on another girl soon enough. She had to get a note from Percy somehow. It was her only hope.

'Maisie, oh, Maisie.'

Maisie searched for the familiar face in the crowd. Despite the relentlessness of her thoughts she smiled in anticipation. Gertie was always like a ray of sunshine on a gloomy day. When she finally spotted her, Maisie gasped. 'Your hair!' Gertie's golden tresses were gone, cut in a line just below her ears, and a sharp fringe framed her face.

Gertie grinned and smoothed her hair. 'Isn't it just the thing? It's called a Dutch bob. Mary Thurman has made it famous. I love it.'

Of course Gertie had modelled herself on an actress. 'It's ... very different.' Maisie had envied Gertie's beautiful long hair. This haircut was almost brutal.

'My mother's not happy and my father, well, let's just say Daddy doesn't approve, but it's my hair, not theirs.' Gertie put her arm through Maisie's as they walked along. 'Are you coming to the dance on Saturday? Please say yes. You can come to my place after work again. That was such fun.' Her eyes sparkled with the mischief that Gertie was so well known for.

'I wish I could, but I have to help Mother.'

'Again?' Gertie pouted. 'You haven't been to a dance in such a long time. Hasn't your brother found a job yet?'

'Not yet.' Maisie restrained herself from saying more.

Gertie pressed closer. 'If you were coming on Saturday it would be all too obvious who my special someone is. I'll be dancing every dance with him.'

'I'll just have to wait.' Maisie played along, swept up in Gertie's effervescent joy. 'I expect to read the engagement notice in the *Mercury* any day now.'

Gertie grinned conspiratorially. 'I think you already know him.'

'I do?'

'You danced with him at the first Cadbury's dance. The one we went to together. I don't think you could ever forget him. His smile.' She put her hand to her cheek. 'Blinding.'

Maisie's breath caught in her throat. Surely she couldn't mean Percy? 'I danced with a few different men that night.'

'But only one as handsome as him.' Gertie pulled Maisie away from the crowd to duck around the corner of the change rooms. She pressed a finger to her lips. 'If I tell you, you must promise not to breathe a word. He wants to keep it a secret until his ship comes in.'

Dread pooled in Maisie's stomach. If it was Percy then the ship he was depending on was her. The information she was supposed to give him about Mrs Adwell was how he planned to get the money, not only to pay Maisie so Lily could stay in school but also to marry Gertie. 'I promise.' She waited, her nerves stretched taut.

Gertie pressed her hands to her heart. 'He's the most handsome man in the world and it's me he loves. Me! Gertie Thompson. But I won't be Gertie Thompson for much longer. Remember, you've promised not to tell a soul.'

Maisie nodded, not trusting her voice.

'Goodbye, Miss Gertie Thompson, hello, Mrs Percy Bates.' Gertie giggled in delight. 'Doesn't that sound divine?'

'Percy Bates?' The earth fell away. 'You're going to marry Percy Bates?' Maisie's head spun.

Gertie frowned. 'You could sound a little happier for me.'

'Oh, Gertie, I wish I could be, but I'm not sure. He's …' Maisie thought desperately for any reason she could give Gertie but came up with nothing. 'I just don't know if he's the right one for you.'

Gertie's face turned to stone. 'Oh, fiddle-faddle. All the girls want to be with Percy Bates but only one of us will actually marry him, and that's me.'

'I wish you well, I really do. I just think you could do better.' Better than a blackmailing, lying, smooth-talking bully.

'He's the most handsome man in town and he's going to be rich. What could be better than that?' Gertie tossed her head, her short bob falling neatly back into place.

Maisie's jaw tensed. She wanted to say something, to tell her the truth about Percy Bates, but how could she possibly explain – and even if she did, she doubted Gertie would believe her.

Gertie stuck out her bottom lip. 'I thought better of you, Maisie. I didn't think you'd be jealous like the other girls.'

'Jealous?' Maisie took a step back. That was the last thing on her mind.

'Yes. I saw the way you looked at him at the dance. You were all moon-eyed.'

Maisie blinked in surprise. 'Was I?' He'd been very charming, that was certain, until he'd shown his true colours.

'He only danced with you the once. I could tell you were miffed. And now you're jealous instead of being pleased for me.' Gertie pouted. 'Please be happy for me. He's so devastatingly handsome, don't you think? Of course you do. You'd have to be blind not to. He could be a movie star.'

Maisie desperately wanted to be happy for her friend but she could see nothing good coming from their marriage. A sudden thought stopped her short. Did Percy mean to marry Gertie or was he just stringing her along? She was a pretty girl with a happy nature and loved a bit of fun. Was he angling to take advantage of her? From what she knew of the man it was entirely possible. She had to warn Gertie. Maisie opened her mouth to speak but an insidious thought stopped her. She hesitated, hardly able to believe she was capable of thinking such a thing, let alone of acting on it. She could be forgiven though, couldn't she? These were desperate times. Steeling herself, she smiled at Gertie, her face stiff with the falseness of it. 'I am happy for you. And you're right, he's very handsome. I'm sure many girls would love to be the one on his arm.'

Gertie flushed with pride. 'You bet they would. I have to fight them off, but it's me he wants.'

'How do you know?'

'How do I know?' Gertie's eyes opened wide in indignation. 'Because he's told me, more than once.'

'In writing?'

Gertie faltered for a moment. 'You mean, like a love letter?'

'Yes, or a little note, just something that says how he feels about you. It's so romantic, don't you think, to receive a love letter from your beau?' Maisie kept smiling, her cheeks aching with the strain.

'I don't need a letter to prove he loves me.' Gertie fiddled with her hair.

'Of course not.' Maisie feigned nonchalance. 'But wouldn't it be lovely to have some words from him written in a letter. You could keep it under your pillow and read it whenever you want.' Her palms grew clammy. This was her chance to save herself as well as Mrs Adwell and bring this whole nasty business to an end.

'It would be nice.' Gertie's eyes grew dreamy.

'A love letter from the most handsome man in the world, the man who's going to be your husband.' Maisie almost choked on her words. 'It would be just like in the movies.'

Gertie nodded. 'Yes, it would.'

Maisie glanced towards the factory. She had to convince Gertie now or they'd be late. 'I hope you'll keep me in mind when you're choosing your bridesmaids.'

'Of course I will.' Gertie clasped Maisie's hands in hers. 'I can't imagine walking up the aisle without you there.'

'What a wonderful day it will be. And what a wonderful love letter I'm sure he'll write you.' She leant closer, their heads almost touching. 'I'd love to read it if you'll let me, being your bridesmaid and all.'

'You'll be the only other person who'll ever see it. I'll keep it tucked in here.' Gertie gestured to her bosom. 'Right next to my heart.'

'He's a lucky man.' Maisie squeezed Gertie's hand. It was done. 'Now, we really must get ready for work.'

Together they rushed into the change room, smiling and giggling. Maisie detested herself for deceiving her friend but there was one thought uppermost in her mind – the end would justify the means. It had to.

34

Dorothy

DEATH OF MR. CADBURY.

LONDON, 24 October 1922

Mr George Cadbury, chairman of Cadbury Brothers, and founder of Bournville Model Village, died today, aged 83. Cadbury's is a name that has been in the mouths of the people for a lifetime. The extent of the cocoa industry under Mr George Cadbury's control and that of other firms whose names are as household words need not be emphasised, but one point stands out in this connection, viz., that business men, when animated by sound principles, do an amount of good which active propaganda cannot accomplish.

Dorothy sat at the kitchen table, her head in her hands, oblivious to the tears falling on the tablecloth. Without George Cadbury she would still be trapped in the slums of Birmingham. She wouldn't have received an education, or learnt how to swim or play cricket, and she certainly would never have learnt how machinery worked and how to fix it. Without George Cadbury she would have believed her father and brothers who'd told her she was a waste of food and breath, not worth spitting on. Instead, George Cadbury had taken a chance on her. She'd never taken his faith in her for granted and had worked hard, been promoted, and travelled across the world. Now she was Chief Forewoman of the Claremont factory. None of this would have been possible without his vision and belief. And he was dead.

Sarah placed a cup of tea in front of her and handed her a clean handkerchief. Dorothy received it gratefully, wiped her eyes and blew her nose. 'I'm sorry. I can't seem to stop crying.'

'I understand.' Sarah sat beside her and slowly sipped her tea. Dorothy was yet to see her shed a tear but Sarah very rarely let her emotions overcome her.

When the news had been announced at the factory earlier in the day, Dorothy had immediately sought out Ida. They'd clung to each other like the children they'd been when they'd first started working at Cadbury's. Sadly it had taken Mr Cadbury's death to mend the rift between them, but even so she was grateful. Dorothy had sent a silent prayer his way thanking him for doing good works even after he'd passed away.

'Remember the morning Bible readings and prayers?' Dorothy said to Sarah. Like so many others, she'd arrived at work early for the free breakfast rather than the prayers. 'Mr Cadbury, standing up there with his beard and his Bible. When I was young I thought he was like God but as I grew older he was more like a father.'

Sarah nodded. 'He thought of his employees as children and considered it his duty to look after them as a father would.'

'Part of me thought he'd live forever.' Dorothy gazed out the window towards the factory. 'I guess, in a way, he will, through his work and his legacy.'

'No one we love ever truly dies. They're always with us in our memories and in the patterns of our lives.'

'True. Freddie is still in my heart.' Dorothy crumpled her borrowed handkerchief into a ball. 'There were times I regretted we'd never had children. If we had, part of him would live on in our child. We were only just married before he went to war and when he came back on leave … well, he wasn't himself. And then it was too late.' Dorothy dashed away yet another tear. 'Listen to me, babbling on. I'm sorry, it's just that today's news …'

'I understand. The shock of loss tends to bring back all griefs. We keep them locked away then a blow like this springs the lock and there they are, demanding our attention.'

Dorothy met Sarah's eyes. Her friend was always secretive about her personal life. 'Have you lost someone you loved?'

'I don't know anyone who hasn't.' Sarah gave her a sad smile and looked away.

'You mentioned a man called Arthur …'

Sarah stood. 'I'll freshen the tea.'

Her avoidance cemented Dorothy's view that Arthur had been special to Sarah, otherwise why would she be so reticent to talk about him? 'Sarah? You know about Freddie. You know all about my life at Bournville. We're friends and yet I hardly know anything about you. Please. Who was Arthur?'

Sarah remained at the sink, filling the kettle. 'What difference does it make? He's dead.'

Dorothy flinched at the coldness in her voice. 'It makes a difference to me. To our friendship.'

Sarah put down the kettle and turned towards her. 'Why is this so important to you?'

'He was clearly important to you and you are important to me. You said yourself, the shock of grief brings back all our losses. I've been thinking of Freddie today. Have you been thinking about Arthur?'

Sarah looked away. 'Yes, I have.'

'Please tell me about him. He must have been a very special man to win your heart.'

'All right. But it goes no further than this room.'

'I promise.'

Sarah returned to her seat. She smoothed the tablecloth in front of her. 'Arthur was my match in every way – smart, curious about the world and how it worked, quick-witted and kind. He was also a secret I dare not tell anyone.' Dorothy saw a sadness in Sarah's eyes she'd never seen before.

'Why was that?'

'Oh, people knew we were sweethearts, but they didn't know the rest. We met before the war. Then, like it is again now, when a woman married she had to give up her career. I had a lot more at stake than he did, but I didn't hesitate.' A faint smile played on Sarah's lips. 'We found a little cottage tucked away.'

'You never married?' A weak flame of shock flickered in Dorothy's chest then sputtered out just as quickly. Sarah had never been one to play by the rules.

'Not in the eyes of the law, but for us it was the perfect marriage.'

'But what would have happened if you'd had children?'

'Some women aren't built to be mothers.' Sarah cleared her throat and took a sip of her tea. 'All our secrecy was for nought. He died behind enemy lines.' She brushed invisible crumbs from the table. 'One more week and the war would have been over.'

Dorothy wanted to ask what Arthur was doing behind enemy lines. Was he lost, had he been taken prisoner, or was he on a secret mission of some sort? Instead she held her tongue and waited.

'Sometimes I'd forget he was gone.' Sarah's eyes grew distant. 'I'd wait for him to come into the room or expect him to be sitting by the fire when I came home. Then the reality would come rushing back, almost crushing me. I couldn't stay there, not in that cottage, and, as it turns out, not even in England. I thought a change would do me good.' She smiled in a tight, pinched way. 'Hence this ...' She gestured to their cottage and the factory beyond.

'I understand.' Dorothy reached for Sarah's hand. 'Part of the reason I agreed to travel twelve thousand miles was to escape all the memories. Not of Freddie himself, you understand, I would never want to be free of his memory and the times we spent together, but I needed to break free of a certain ... I don't know, a way of being, I suppose.'

'And you've found that here?' Sarah's eyes searched hers.

Dorothy sat back and placed her hands in her lap, aware her cup of tea had grown cold and that the night was drawing in around them. A few days earlier she'd found a letter from Thomas in the laundry. He'd hidden it in her toolbox, knowing Sarah would never find it there. The letter might have languished among the wrenches and screwdrivers for some time if Dorothy hadn't decided to fill her empty days without Thomas by building a lattice along the back fence for passionfruit and beans. He'd written to say that he'd hoped to see her in private but the opportunity hadn't arisen and he hadn't wanted to compromise her by approaching her at the factory, hence the letter. He'd moved to the estate with Vera and Edward. Dorothy had taken a sharp breath. Thomas had never mentioned them by name before and she'd never asked. It would make them seem more real. But now she'd met them and knew their names there could be no more pretending. The letter continued by Thomas saying Vera wanted to thank her properly for saving Edward's life. Would Dorothy please visit? As she'd read his words about their heartfelt gratitude and how they owed her a debt they could never repay, Dorothy had allowed herself a few hot tears before burning the letter in a small pile of offcuts, dead leaves and prunings.

Sarah had trusted her with her secret – perhaps it was time she shared her own. She'd been alone with it for so long it had left her exhausted and bereft. There was already too much sadness. A pressure released in her chest, as if her heart had been constricted by bands of iron and now they were loosened. She took a slow breath to steady herself and began. 'I met a man on the voyage to Tasmania. He was like my Freddie in so many ways. It was as if fate had put him in my path. When he told me he was bound for Hobart I was certain of it. He was damaged, you see, and I thought I could help him.' An unbidden sob rose in her throat. 'He reminded me so much of Freddie.'

'The man on the ship?' Sarah encouraged her to continue.

'He had the same haunted look, the same tremors, the same desperation. The same shame.' Dorothy shivered and wrapped her arms around herself. 'It broke my heart all over again but I felt as though I'd been given a second chance. I was determined to do anything I could for him.'

'This is the man who came to our cottage that day at lunchtime.'

'Yes.' Dorothy bit her lip.

'And you've been seeing him regularly.'

Dorothy looked away. 'I never thought it would become so complicated.'

'Because Percy Bates knows.'

The shock of Sarah's words made her gasp. 'But, how … I …' Dorothy's mind went blank with confusion.

'There had to be more to this story with Maisie. Once she'd told you what was going on and you didn't fire her, he had no ammunition. But that wasn't the end of it.' Sarah's voice was gentle but insistent. 'I understand the need for absolute proof in the form of a sample of his handwriting but there was something else. Something you weren't telling me. And it had to do with him wanting information about you. Of him planning to blackmail you.'

'I was ashamed,' Dorothy whispered.

'For trying to help someone who reminded you of the man you loved? There's no shame in that.' Sarah sat back slightly. 'Maisie went to Melbourne with you. My guess is something incriminating happened there. Is Percy Bates using that knowledge to threaten you?'

Dorothy shook her head, desperately regretting she'd ever mentioned any of this to Sarah. It was bad enough that Maisie knew, but Sarah?

'I'm on your side, Dot. I always have been. But I can't help you if I don't know the truth.'

'I can't.' She couldn't betray Thomas. He had a wife and child. She had no claim on him.

Sarah moved closer and made sure Dorothy was looking at her before she spoke again. 'Dot, please. Tell me everything that's happened and together we will stop Percy Bates, I promise.'

Shame, confusion and a desperate need to be free of this chaos battled in Dorothy's heart and mind. 'I'm not sure ...'

Sarah took both her hands in hers. 'In loving memory of Mr George Cadbury, let's stop Percy Bates from doing any further harm.'

Dorothy paused. Her future depended on what she said next. If she went along with Sarah's plan it may well be the last thing she ever did for Cadbury's – but at least it would be on her own terms, not Percy's. If she had to leave the Firm and all it meant to her, she'd make it worth it. But she couldn't blacken Thomas's reputation along with her own, especially now his wife and child had joined him. 'All right. I'll tell you everything.' And she would. Everything, except Thomas's name.

35

Dorothy opened the envelope. Her heart leapt. The handwriting was the same. This proved Percy Bates's guilt.

'Well done, Maisie. Very well done indeed.' Dorothy continued to scan the letter. It was a mild declaration of love from Percy to Gertie Thompson. 'How did you get hold of it?'

Maisie fidgeted. 'Gertie was boasting about Percy being in love with her and that he was going to marry her. I challenged her to prove it and ...'

'Gertie could never refuse a challenge like that.' Her admiration for Maisie was only tempered by the fact that Maisie was the reason they were in this situation.

'But I have to return it.' Maisie worried at her lower lip. 'Gertie doesn't know I have it. If she finds out I took it she'll kill me.'

'Tell her she must have misplaced it and you're sure it'll turn up. I doubt she'll want it back though when she finds out the truth.' Poor Gertie. She was destined to be left heartbroken no matter what happened. Dorothy was sure Percy Bates was not the marrying kind.

'I still don't understand why you need it,' Maisie said.

'No need for you to worry about that. You've done your part.' Dorothy folded the letter and placed it in her pocket, making sure it was safely tucked away.

'But my part isn't over yet. Percy expects to meet me. He wants the name of the man—' Maisie winced. 'I'm sorry, Mrs Adwell. I've done what you told me. I've been stringing him along, saying I've been spying on you. I told him I'd give him the information he wants.'

'And he'll give you the money.' Dorothy narrowed her eyes. Maisie might have kept her job, but with her brother out of work her family would still need funds.

Maisie's face crumpled. 'I don't want the money. Not any more. I wish I'd never gone along with him. I'm grateful you didn't sack me on the spot. I know I deserved it.'

Satisfied by the girl's remorse, Dorothy smiled. 'On the contrary. We think you've been very brave, and clever.'

'We?' Maisie blanched. 'Does someone else know about this?'

'Only Miss Harris. We have a plan. Mr Bates won't be worrying you for much longer.' Dorothy had the upper hand now. There'd be no more waiting and fretting until the next threat from this vile man. She and Sarah were going to lay a trap. She noticed the fear on Maisie's face and hurried to reassure her. 'We can trust Miss Harris. We're going to deal with this and make sure no one else ever knows. You said he expects to meet with you.'

'He wants to meet at a pub in town on Saturday afternoon. Down by the wharf.' Maisie's brow furrowed. 'Do I have to, Mrs Adwell? If my mother found out there'd be hell to pay.'

After everything that had happened, the fact that Maisie was still worried about how her mother would react if she was seen in a pub endeared the girl to her further. 'Tell him you can't meet him there. Besides, most pubs won't let a woman in the door.' She suspected Percy wanted Maisie to feel out of her depth. Meeting at a pub would put him at an advantage.

'What if he insists?'

'Then he doesn't get his information. You've told him you have exactly what he wants. Believe me, he'll want to meet wherever you suggest.'

'But where?'

'The boiler house.' Dorothy and Sarah had discussed it at length. They needed a place with no one else around. There had to be no doubt that the man who turned up at the designated time was Percy Bates. The spacious factory grounds were perfect and known to all of them. Of all the possible meeting places, the boiler house was the safest. If they met on the river side of the building no one would spot them. By Saturday afternoon the factory workers would have left for the day. One of the sporting teams might have a game at the Cadbury's grounds but the fields were at a considerable distance from the boiler house.

Maisie hesitated. 'You want me to meet with him there? Alone?'

'No. As I said, you've done your part. All we need is a time and place for the meeting. He'll be expecting you but he'll get more than he bargained for.'

The furrows on Maisie's brow deepened. 'There's just one thing. What if you confront him and he says he's innocent, that you have him mistaken for someone else?'

'Why would anyone else be lurking around the boiler house on a Saturday afternoon with a lot of money?'

'I don't know – he could say he was just out for a walk. And how are you going to know he has the money with him? I'm sure he'll keep it well hidden. You'll have no proof he's the man you want.' She took a breath. 'Without me.'

'No, Maisie, it's too dangerous.' Dorothy remained firm.

Maisie's eyes brimmed with tears. 'I'm to blame for all of this. If I'd never gone along with him in the first place none of this would have happened. Let me help. Please.'

'If it hadn't been you, he'd have picked someone else.' Dorothy wanted to reassure the girl, even though she was sure Percy had targeted her deliberately. Maisie had access to the office and she was closer to Dorothy than most employees.

'But he did pick on me and I went along with him.' Maisie's hands were clenched. 'This is my mistake. Let me fix it. I'd hate for him to slip through your hands.'

Maisie had a point. Percy was cunning. He could easily pretend to be someone else when she and Sarah confronted him. If Maisie was there he couldn't deny it.

Maisie jutted out her chin in defiance. 'Even if you say no, I'm going to be there at the boiler house. I want to see Percy Bates taken down a peg or two. He's a horrible man.'

Dorothy had to hide her smile. The girl certainly had grit. She nodded once. 'Very well. Come to our cottage after work on Saturday.'

'Thank you, Mrs Adwell.' The look of gratitude on Maisie's face was worth the trepidation that knotted in Dorothy's stomach.

36

Dorothy

After work on Saturday Dorothy kept Maisie back on a pretence. When the other girls left, she reminded Maisie of her address. 'It's best if we don't walk there together. Percy might be keeping an eye on you. Head along the riverbank and then make sure you come to the back door. The fewer people who see you the better.'

Maisie nodded and made her way to the change room.

At the cottage, Sarah greeted Dorothy with a fierce expression. 'I'm looking forward to catching this cad,' she growled.

Dorothy was glad she'd never crossed Sarah – she'd be a fearsome opponent. 'Percy Bates will get his comeuppance today.' She tried to match Sarah's bravado but fell short.

A tentative knock at the back door announced Maisie's arrival. They ushered her inside and sat her down, reassuring her all the while as they laid out their plan.

'And you'll be there? Close by?' Maisie's eyes darted anxiously from Sarah to Dorothy.

Dorothy would rather not use Maisie as bait, but it was what the girl wanted and Sarah had agreed it made their plan watertight. 'We'll be just around the corner listening to every word he says. As soon as he shows you the money we'll move in.'

Sarah checked her watch and then held Maisie with a steady gaze. 'Dorothy and I will leave now. We'll approach the boiler house from the direction of the bean store. In ten minutes, walk around the factory to the river and follow the railway line to the river side of the boiler house.' She stood and smoothed her skirt. 'Are we ready?'

Nerves twinged in Dorothy's stomach. It felt good to take action but there was still the possibility of danger. They had no idea what Percy Bates was capable of.

Dorothy and Sarah pressed against the eastern wall of the boiler house. Dorothy hardly dared to breathe. It seemed like an age before footsteps approached, heavier than a woman's. They heard the sound of a match being struck and the smell of cigarette smoke wafted towards them, then a jaunty whistle. Dorothy gritted her teeth. The man was so confident he was whistling 'Ain't We Got Fun'.

More footsteps. This time lighter and more tentative. Maisie.

'You got what I want?' It was a male voice. No pleasantries, just straight to it.

'Yes.' Maisie's voice contained a trace of fear.

'Then give. What's the dirt on Mrs Adwell? Remember, it's worth your while.'

Dorothy shuddered at the sound of her name in his mouth. A curl of anger rose in her belly.

'I have what you want. But first you have to prove you have what I want.'

Good girl. Maisie had said the words just as they'd rehearsed.

'Oh, I see.'

The sound of his footsteps moving, but where? Was he trying to intimidate Maisie?

'Your negotiation skills have improved.' His voice was a jeer. Dorothy's hand formed a fist.

'I won't tell you a thing until I see the money.' Maisie remained firm.

The sound of a foot crushing into the gravel. Dorothy guessed he'd extinguished his cigarette.

'It's all here. See?'

Dorothy shifted, ready to make her move. Sarah held her back and shook her head. 'Wait,' she mouthed.

'Let me count it.'

'Jeez, you have become a cool customer. There's no way I'm handing you this money without the information. I'll count it for you.' He began.

'That's all right. I can see it's all there.' Maisie's voice was a little higher than usual, and a little louder.

Sarah gave Dorothy a quick nod and they parted ways. Sarah headed around one side of the boiler house and Dorothy the other. Dorothy arrived as Percy Bates quickly shoved an envelope inside his jacket pocket. She could see now why the girls were dazzled by him. His suit was more expensive than his wage would allow, his hat sat at a jaunty angle and he had the striking good looks of a film star. They wouldn't think so highly of him if they could see the ugly snarl on his face.

'What's going on?' he barked, staring at Dorothy.

Sarah arrived, cool as a cucumber, and sized him up. Percy's head swivelled from Dorothy to Sarah.

Dorothy rushed to Maisie's side and pulled her out of harm's way. 'Well done,' she whispered. Maisie's hands were shaking but her smile was brave.

'That's a lot of money you have there, Percy Bates.' Sarah emphasised his name.

'What's it to you?'

'Who's paying you, Mr Bates?' Sarah's eyes burnt with a cool anger.

'I don't know what you mean.'

Sarah looked him up and down. 'Such a fancy suit, such a lot of money in your pocket. Clearly we're paying you too much.'

'We?' Confusion turned to understanding. 'Oh, I get it. You work for Cadbury's.'

Dorothy stepped forward. 'You know I do.'

He looked her up and down. 'Never seen you before in my life.'

He was lying. The first letter had said he'd seen her in the bean store. The anger grew, rising up through her chest. 'I'm Mrs Adwell.' She'd force him to confront the woman he'd been threatening for months, the woman whose life he was willing to destroy.

There was no flicker of recognition in his eyes even though he knew exactly who she was. He'd mentioned her by name only moments ago. His self-possession chilled her. He doffed his hat. 'Pleased to meet you, Mrs Adwell. I'm Mr Percy Bates.'

'No, you're not.' Sarah moved closer. She hovered, like a snake ready to strike.

'What?' For the first time Percy looked rattled.

'I've asked questions of the men.' Sarah's voice was steady with a note of menace. 'Questions like who always leaves his post at a particular time in the morning, the time when the tray of chocolates is delivered to the office? Who's been flashing money around? Who's been talking about his ship coming in?' She smiled a chilling smile. 'But my favourite question was, who do the men detest the most? Everyone agreed on that one and it certainly wasn't Percy Bates. In fact, there is no Percy Bates employed at Cadbury-Fry-Pascall.'

Percy was startled for a moment but quickly recovered. 'It's got a good ring to it though, doesn't it? The girls like it.' He winked at Maisie, who looked as though he'd slapped her.

'Unlike Cecil Bottom.' Sarah's smile twisted in scorn.

Percy's face turned to stone. A furtive gleam of rage flickered in his eyes.

Maisie gasped. 'Cecil Bottom?'

Dorothy stifled a laugh. 'Not so attractive now, is he, Maisie?'

'I can't imagine Gertie would want to be known as Mrs Bottom,' Maisie whispered. Dorothy was glad to see the amusement in her eyes. She'd worried how the day's events would affect Maisie but it was clear the girl had backbone.

'Right,' Dorothy kept her voice businesslike. 'I have the threatening letters you sent to me. The handwriting matches the note you gave Gertie Thompson.'

'Gertie?' His eyes darted from Sarah to Dorothy. 'What's she got to do with this?'

'Nothing. Except for the note you wrote to her and the fact you plan to marry her.'

'Gertie knows nothing about this,' Maisie butted in. 'I tricked her.'

'Interesting.' Percy appraised her. 'You're smarter than I thought.'

'So you don't deny this is your handwriting?' Dorothy held the letter in front of him, careful lest he try to snatch it away.

Percy gave it a cursory glance and shook his head. 'As we've established, my name isn't Percy and this letter is written by someone of that name, not me.'

'But you gave this letter to Gertie,' Maisie said.

'Maybe I did, maybe I didn't.' Percy's casual shrug set Dorothy's teeth on edge. 'Either way, that doesn't mean I wrote it.' He puffed out his cheeks and looked up the river towards the mountain. 'Let's just say I was sweet on a girl and wanted to impress her. She wanted a love note but I knew once she saw my handwriting she'd think less of me.' He tilted his head towards Sarah. 'My handwriting is atrocious. That's why my personnel forms are typed, but you already knew that.'

Sarah's face was like thunder.

'So,' Percy continued, 'I paid someone to write a love letter for me. I figure by the time she finds out my own writing is a scrawl, I'll be long gone.'

Maisie gasped and lunged forward but Dorothy held her back.

Percy looked from Sarah to Dorothy to Maisie with a smug smile on his lips. 'Is that all you've got, ladies? If so, it's been lovely, but I really must press on.'

'What about the money?' Dorothy demanded. They were not done yet.

'I have enormous luck with horses.' He smirked.

This cad made Dorothy's blood boil. 'We have threatening letters in a hand that may or may not be yours. We have proof that you claim the letter to Miss Gertie Thompson was, if not written by you, then by the same person who wrote the letters to me, meaning you must know that person. We have proof you have money beyond your means, and we know you were blackmailing Maisie with an eye to blackmailing me.'

'And what are you doing with all that proof?' Percy looked about with an expression of feigned concern. 'Have you called the police? Will they arrive at any moment?' He paused for effect. 'No. I didn't think so. Have you hauled me up in front of management? Nope.' Percy thrust his hands into his pockets and rocked back on his heels. 'Suppose I did write those letters and say I did get Maisie so twisted up she'd do anything for me.' He winked at Maisie again and once more Dorothy had to restrain her. 'I know something that could destroy you both. Something you clearly don't want anyone else to know, otherwise you'd have the authorities on to me in a flash.' He sauntered towards Dorothy. 'What did you expect would happen here today? Did you think I'd admit to being a blackmailer. Did you think I'd throw up my hands and say, "You got me, I've been trying to steal your recipes."'

'We never mentioned recipes.' Sarah's voice was cold.

Percy flinched but recovered in an instant. 'What does it matter? You have no proof of anything. Circumstantial evidence at best. If you try to take this further I'll deny everything. And who's going to believe a gaggle of women? No one's going to take a woman's word against a man's. No one.'

The anger surged through Dorothy. She clenched her fist, pulled back her arm and punched him. The crack of his nose gave her instant satisfaction. He stumbled back against the wall clutching his face, blood streaming between his fingers.

'Mrs Adwell!' Maisie exclaimed.

'Mrs Adwell indeed,' Sarah said, nodding in approval.

Dorothy shook out her hand. The impact of the blow resonated through her knuckles. 'You can take the girl out of the slums, but you can't take the slums out of the girl.' Her accent was pure Brummie. She'd never thought the skills she'd learnt to protect herself when she was young would come in handy again and yet here she was, and it felt good.

'That nose is definitely broken,' Sarah gloated. 'You won't be so pretty now.'

'You'll pay for this,' Percy mumbled between blood-covered fingers. 'I'll get you.'

Sarah stepped up close beside him. 'No, you won't, because if you lay one finger on Dot, or Maisie, we'll be straight to the police with all the evidence we need.' Her voice held a chilling tone of menace.

Back at the cottage, Dorothy, Sarah and Maisie sat in the living room sipping on steaming mugs of hot cocoa. Maisie eyed Dorothy with a combination of wariness and admiration. Dorothy's hand ached and the cool compress she'd applied only eased the pain a little, but it had felt good to punch Percy Bate's smug face. Sadly it had achieved little, except to make him more likely to lash out and take them all down with him. 'I'm sorry, Sarah,' Dorothy said.

'For what?'

'He riled me up so badly I lost my temper.'

'If you hadn't punched him, I would have. What a loathsome little toad. But I underestimated him. He's definitely done this kind of thing before. The fake name, the typed personnel records making sure nothing can be traced to him, and to top it all off to be so cool in the face of our accusations.' Sarah tapped her fingernails on the table. 'If I didn't despise him I'd actually be impressed. But I have the measure of him now.'

Dorothy turned to Maisie. 'You'll need to be especially careful. Ask one of the other girls to take the chocolates to the office. Don't walk along the riverbank on your own and when you leave for the day make sure you're always surrounded by people.' She didn't want to worry Maisie unnecessarily but if anything happened to her, Dorothy would never forgive herself.

'For once I'm glad the train carriages are segregated,' Sarah said. 'At least he can't get at you there.'

Maisie's eyes widened. 'But he's not going to try anything, is he? Not after what you said.'

'No, of course not.' Sarah's tone was assured. 'It's best to be careful though.'

'When you've finished your cocoa I'll accompany you home on the train, just to be sure,' Dorothy said.

'We'll all go, but not by train.' Sarah had a mischievous glint in her eyes. 'I have access to the keys for the Cadbury's vans. After the events of this afternoon I think we deserve to travel in style.'

Sarah was a competent driver – even so, Dorothy was pleased to make it back without incident. The street Maisie lived on was so steep she'd thought the van would topple over. Once it was safely back in its designated parking spot and they'd returned to the cottage, Dorothy and Sarah collapsed on the couch.

Sarah kicked off her shoes and eased her neck. 'I'd forgotten what fun driving is. I must do more of it.'

'You could teach me. If I lose my job I could become a chauffeur.' Dorothy's attempt at mirth failed to raise a smile.

'You are not going to lose your job.' Sarah was emphatic.

For all her wiles and contacts, Dorothy knew Sarah couldn't guarantee it. Percy Bates had outsmarted even her. Their plan to get rid of him without having to involve anyone else, least of all the authorities, had failed. Dorothy had to face facts. Her days at the Firm could well be numbered. 'I've never told anyone this, but my aim in coming to Tasmania was to be on the Board of Directors.' She looked away, embarrassed by her bold admission. 'I knew it would be impossible at Bournville but here …' She'd held this, her greatest ambition, so tight it made her ache, but now she knew it would never happen she was finally free to voice it.

'You wanted to be our very own Dorothy Cadbury, without the advantages of being a Cadbury.' To Dorothy's surprise Sarah seemed unfazed by her revelation. 'That's why you were so keen to change your accent.'

'I didn't want to be labelled as soon as I opened my mouth. I thought I'd have more of a chance, be taken more seriously, if I sounded like you.'

'That's ironic. If you were going to make it to the Board of Directors it'd be because they need factory representation and there's no greater proof of a factory background than a broad Birmingham accent. All the directors are from sales. They need a staff voice on the board.'

Margaret had said the same thing. Dorothy eyed Sarah, her curiosity piqued. 'It sounds as though it's been discussed.'

Sarah tapped her fingernails on the arm of the couch. 'You might as well know, the Australian Commission at Bournville was considering appointing you to the board.'

'Really?' Dorothy sat up straight, her heart beating fast. 'Why didn't you say?'

'Because I didn't want to give you false hope. And I was right. They've decided to bring out a factory man from Bournville.'

The excitement vanished as quickly as it had arisen, leaving Dorothy with a sense of dull resentment. 'So, rather than appoint their Chief Forewoman, with a working knowledge of the factory here in Tasmania, they've chosen a man.'

'Actually, it was your position as Chief Forewoman that was seen as a problem. It would've put the Chief Foreman's nose out of joint.' She smiled. 'A little like Percy Bates's nose. And you wouldn't even have to punch him.'

'I'd never break Dicky Corbett's nose but to be honest I wouldn't mind putting it out of joint to be on the board.' Dorothy seethed. 'I'll bet if they were considering Dicky for the position they'd never have worried about my nose.'

'He was never an option.'

'But I was.'

'Yes, but like I said, it's not to be.'

Dorothy gritted her teeth. Everything she'd worked towards for so long would be denied her. All the miles from home and the tribulations she'd been through had been for nothing. And why? So one man wouldn't be upset and another man could take a place on the board that rightly belonged to her. Percy's jeering face came to mind and her irritation grew. He was certain he was going to get away with his lies and threats because he would be believed over them, just because he was a man.

An audacious idea hit Dorothy with such force it sucked the breath from her lungs. Her mind reeled. Could she do it? Did she dare? If she did there'd be no going back. Ever. It would mean the end of her career with the Firm. Could she let go of being Chief Forewoman? Could she walk away from everything the Cadburys had given her? Her cherished ambition of being on the board – an ambition she had worked towards for years, that she'd studied for and bettered herself to gain – had been snatched away from her. Even so, she had a lot to lose. She would have to start again, somewhere else. Her mind raced. She could move to Sydney, get a job at the fancy department store Sarah liked so much and, in time, rise to the top. Her new accent would certainly come in handy then. But, most importantly, before she left, she'd take Percy Bates down with her. She pressed a hand to her chest. Was she willing to give up everything to achieve it?

Sarah gave her a quizzical look. 'What are you thinking?'

'I was thinking about David Jones in Sydney.'

Sarah shook her head in bemusement. 'Not what I was expecting, but I approve. I have their latest catalogue if you want to look through it, but for now how about we have the last of the chocolate scones for tea? I really can't be bothered cooking.'

'Sounds marvellous.' Dorothy watched Sarah as she headed for the kitchen. After all they'd been through, she hated hiding anything from her friend, but this was one last secret she had to keep. At least until Monday.

37

Maisie

Maisie spent Saturday night and the whole of Sunday restlessly going over the events in her mind. She was glad, for once, for the piles of ironing and mending that kept her busy until exhaustion robbed her fingers of any usefulness. Even so, sleep eluded her. She was desperately afraid Percy might retaliate. Both Mrs Adwell and the impressive Miss Harris were on her side, but still the worry lingered. Their plan to trap Percy – she couldn't think of him as Cecil – had been an abject failure and Mrs Adwell's instructions to stay close to the other girls had her worried. Clearly both she and Miss Harris thought Percy Bates was a dangerous man. Maisie kept conversation with Mother and Lily to a minimum, worried she might blurt out what had happened. She'd given up the lie of the bonus once she'd admitted everything to Mrs Adwell, and Mother had stopped asking.

On Monday morning, when Mrs Adwell didn't appear for her usual inspection, Maisie began to fret. Since Mrs Adwell had become

Chief Forewoman she had delegated all of her former responsibilities as Forewoman A to her successor. All except the enrobers. She'd maintained her daily visits to the machines she was so enamoured of. What on earth could have kept her away? Lunchtime arrived and the other girls hurried off to the dining hall. Despite Mrs Adwell's warning, instead of joining the other supervisors Maisie searched through the factory. There was no sign of her. If Percy had hurt Mrs Adwell, she'd never forgive herself. None of this mess would have happened if she'd only said no to him at the start.

Maisie decided to risk going to the cottage. As she walked along the river she couldn't help but keep looking behind her, afraid that Percy would appear at any moment. By the time she reached Mrs Adwell's back door she was a tumble of nerves. To her relief Mrs Adwell opened the door, unharmed and wearing a suit of dark blue wool, buttoned high at the neck. Her hair was perfectly coiffed in a smooth chignon and the overall effect was of formality and respectability.

'Maisie. I wasn't expecting to see you.'

'Sorry, Mrs Adwell. When you didn't turn up at the enrobers I was worried. I see you're all right though, so I'll go.' Maisie made to leave.

'No, come in. You'll hear the news soon enough, I expect.'

Maisie followed her to the living room. 'What news?'

'Have a seat.' Mrs Adwell sat in one of the armchairs and indicated to the one opposite.

Maisie sat, hands in her lap, a sense of foreboding creeping over her.

'You won't see me at the factory again, Maisie. I resigned this morning.'

Maisie gasped. Percy must have got at her. Without Mrs Adwell to stand up for her, he'd be free to terrorise her until she was forced to resign herself. 'Please don't go. You're the best manager I've ever had.'

'Thank you, Maisie, and you've been one of my best girls. I have high hopes for you, Miss Greenwood.'

'But Percy—' She stopped. He would bring her undone.

'You needn't worry about him. Despite all his bluster, I had the trump card when it came to making sure Percy Bates, or Cecil Bottom, got his comeuppance. I couldn't let a man like that get away with what he's done. If he was allowed to go free, who knows what else he'd do.' Mrs Adwell smoothed the hair behind her right ear. 'I had to ensure he was stopped.'

'What have you done?'

'I'm sure the gossip will be all over the factory in no time, and then there'll be the court case. It's important, you see, that Cecil Bottom is put behind bars.' Mrs Adwell looked towards the garden. 'I went to Mr Cooper's office this morning and told him a Cadbury's employee was blackmailing me and I wanted to press charges. I tendered my resignation effective immediately, given the circumstances.'

'The circumstances?' Maisie felt as light as an echo. She couldn't believe what she was hearing.

Mrs Adwell turned back to Maisie with a melancholy smile. 'I told Mr Cooper that Cecil Bottom had procured unsavoury information about me and was using it in an attempt to get his hands on the Cadbury's recipes. I also told him that with Mr George Cadbury Junior arriving soon and the production of Dairy Milk being imminent, the blackmailer had become especially dangerous. To cement my case, I told Mr Cooper something no woman would ever admit to if it wasn't true.' Mrs Adwell paused. 'I admitted I was being blackmailed because I was having an affair with a married man.'

Maisie recoiled. She knew Mrs Adwell was seeing someone and wanted to keep it secret – the incident at the hotel in Melbourne had disturbed her deeply, but she never expected him to be married. Adultery was a mortal sin. Maisie gripped the arms of her chair as the room tilted around her. 'I don't believe it.'

'I kept your name out of it, naturally. The way I explained it to Mr Cooper, the matter is between myself and Mr Bottom, no one else. Percy, I mean Cecil, may want to tell a different story but after this morning I don't think anyone will believe him.' Mrs Adwell folded her hands in her lap. She was the picture of calm.

A tangle of emotions raged through Maisie. 'But this was all my fault. I have to speak up. I—' She was about to say *I will defend you* but realised she couldn't defend an adulteress. She put her head in her hands, unsure of what was right, of what she should do.

'You're young. Your entire career is ahead of you. You have a mother and younger sister to look after. That's where your responsibilities lie. Not with me. This cad targeted you because of me. There's no blame here except mine.'

'But a married man ...' Maisie blurted. Her high regard of Mrs Adwell was based on a lie.

'Oh, Maisie.' Mrs Adwell sighed. 'There's always more to any situation than meets the eye. Take Frank Sutton, for example.'

'Mr Sutton?' What did he have to do with any of this? For a moment Maisie feared that Frank was the man Mrs Adwell was involved with. Was he married? Had he lied to her about that too?

'The man you knew as Percy Bates told you Frank was a coward. I think we've established that Mr Bates cannot be trusted. Frank Sutton may be a Quaker and a pacifist but he was braver than many others during the Great War.'

'I don't understand.' Maisie's head was spinning. Nothing made sense.

'Go and find Frank. Ask him what he did during the war.' Mrs Adwell's voice softened. 'Give him a second chance, Maisie. He really is very fond of you.'

'I don't think I could.' Maisie shook her head in doubt and confusion. 'I was awful to him the last time we spoke. And so angry. With due cause, so I thought.'

'Because of what Percy Bates told you. I suggest you listen to Frank Sutton instead and then make your decision.'

Memories of Frank flooded back. She'd thought he was the one for her until he'd broken her heart. Or had he? He'd tried to explain and she'd refused to listen. 'I don't know.' Her voice cracked.

'Nobody's perfect, you've made mistakes like everybody else. You admitted them to me and that took courage. Admitting our mistakes is important but being willing to make amends is valiant.' She glanced at her watch. 'You still have time to talk with him before the lunch break is over. You'll probably find him by the river.'

'Do you think he'll want to talk to me, after what I said to him?'

'I'm sure of it.'

Maisie rose to her feet. 'I really am sorry. Thank you, Mrs Adwell, thank you for everything.'

'Off you go and find Frank.' Mrs Adwell accompanied her to the back door. 'You have a bright future ahead of you, Miss Greenwood.'

Maisie glanced back once on her way to the river. Mrs Adwell was still standing under the portico outside the back door, looking out across the estate, the river and the hills as if for the last time.

He was there alone, where the riverbank dipped low, skimming stones across the water. There was no breeze and the river was still. The stone skipped once, twice, three times before it sunk beneath a circle of ripples.

'Frank?' Her voice was weak, faltering. Maisie cleared her throat. 'Frank.'

He turned. Surprise flittered across his face then he contained his expression to one of polite neutrality. It was more than she deserved.

'Miss Greenwood. To what do I owe the pleasure?'

He was so polite. Too polite. Her courage melted and threatened to run away entirely. She pressed her hands together and felt the warmth and strength there. Mrs Adwell believed in her. She could do this. 'Can we sit?' She nodded towards the low flat rock where they had spent so much time together in the past.

He frowned slightly, more perplexed than displeased, she hoped. 'Of course.' Frank dusted off the rock and waited for Maisie to settle before he sat, at the greatest distance possible.

Maisie willed her nerves to steady. 'I'm sorry for how I acted when we last saw each other. Since then I've discovered I didn't have the full picture. If it's not too much to ask, would you tell me what you did in the Great War? Please?' She lowered her head, afraid of what he might say and also afraid that he'd say nothing, get up and walk away.

'Mrs Adwell's been talking to you, hasn't she?'

Maisie looked at him in surprise. 'Yes, but how did you know?'

'She's always had a soft spot for you. She was pretty cut up when it didn't work out between us. If anyone could change your mind, it would be her. She's an exceptional woman.'

Maisie glanced away. She wondered what Frank would think of Mrs Adwell when he heard about her resignation. 'So, will you? Tell me what you did during the war?'

Frank stretched his hands in front of him as if looking for the answer there. He rested them on his knees and stared out over the river. Maisie's stomach gurgled in hunger but she had no appetite except for the story she hoped Frank would tell.

'I was just a boy when the war broke out,' he began, his voice low and uncertain. 'Not quite fifteen years old.' He smiled wryly. 'Well, perhaps not a boy, I'd been working for three years by then. Even though Cadbury's was a Quaker firm they never stopped their employees from signing up. Thousands did. Some of the younger lads even lied about their age but ...' He looked up at the sky. Maisie followed his gaze. A few small clouds floated above them in the spring-blue sky. 'Lying is something I was never good at. Not in my nature, I guess. I was brought up to always tell the truth.'

Maisie cringed, fully aware of how imperfect she was. She too had been brought up not to lie or steal and to obey the Commandments, but she'd failed.

'Anyway.' Frank rubbed his hands on his knees. 'Because so many Cadbury's workers enlisted they needed able-bodied young men to keep the factory going. Women, like Mrs Adwell, took up some of the jobs the men would normally do but they weren't capable of the heavier work, not all day and night, at any rate. I was given a lot more responsibility and, along with Mrs Adwell, learnt to fix just about every machine in the factory. Engineers were hard to come by, what with the war in need of their skills. Cadbury's changed during those years. The government ordered the production of essential foods at Bournville including butter, milk powder and cheese, even dried vegetables and fruit pulp. All of this was vital for the war effort. Don't get me wrong, we still made chocolate. Most of it went to our troops. We were proud that our chocolate was destined for soldiers protecting our country.'

Maisie sensed him tense. 'I turned eighteen in August 1917 and signed up immediately.' Maisie gasped and he turned to her with some urgency. 'Not to fight, you understand, I couldn't do that. I could never kill another man.'

Maisie shook her head in confusion. 'But you signed up?' Then the realisation hit. He'd signed up for a cushy office job, or more likely as an engineer fixing equipment far from the battle front. He was still a coward.

'I became a stretcher bearer with The Friends' Ambulance Unit, along with many other Quakers who refused to bear arms. George Cadbury's son Laurence was one of the first to volunteer. I was sent to the front, which I fully expected – that's where stretcher bearers were needed.' He shuddered. 'What I didn't expect, or should I say wasn't fully prepared for, was the carnage – the endless barrage of guns and mortar, the stench, the mud, the despairing cries of dying men, their blood soaking into my clothing.' He wiped his hands down his face as if trying to wipe it from his memory.

Maisie sat stunned, her breath shallow.

He shifted his body to face her. 'I'm sorry, Maisie, I didn't mean to shock you. I don't talk about it much. I guess this is why. I've told you about my younger brother back at Bournville but I didn't mention my older brother.' He looked away. 'He was in the ambulance unit too.'

'You have an older brother?'

'I *had* an older brother. Now all we have are memories and his name on a plaque.'

A choked sob escaped Maisie's throat. She'd read about the bravery of the stretcher bearers, risking their lives every day on the front lines – dodging bullets, shells and mines in no-man's land to rescue the injured. She reached for his hand, not caring about the tears streaking her cheeks. 'You're a hero, Frank Sutton.'

He shook his head. 'I spent less than a year doing my duty. My brother and others like him gave their all, year after year, never faltering in doing what was needed. Like him, many of them didn't make it home. They're the true heroes.'

'But you.' Maisie was fully aware of what a fool she'd been. 'You are my hero.'

Frank smiled at her with kind and gentle eyes. Maisie knew then that the hurt she'd caused had been forgiven. He stood and helped Maisie to her feet. 'I'd like to stay here with you, but we'd better get back. May I walk you to the factory?'

'I'd be honoured.' And she meant it. She'd been a fool to have believed anything Percy Bates had told her.

Frank linked his arm with hers and hope blossomed in her chest. He was a good man and, if he was still willing, he would be her man again.

38

Dorothy

It was a beautiful day to say goodbye to the job she had loved for over half her life. The best of spring was upon them. Earlier that morning when Dorothy had left the cottage the sunrise had tinged the peninsula with pink and gold. The colours had reflected on the river, in the shallows and the inlets. The hazy mist that had decorated the hills had dissolved now the sun was high in the pale sky. For the second time that day, Dorothy pulled on her gloves and took her hat from the hallstand. The afternoon was warm enough not to need a coat, besides, she wasn't going far. What would the weather be like further north in Sydney? The shock on Mr Cooper's face this morning and Maisie's response at lunchtime had cemented her decision not only to resign but to leave Hobart. She couldn't stay. She'd have to return for the trial but hopefully it would be brief. The Firm would try to keep the story quiet but there was no doubt it would be in the papers. The court case would cement her humiliation.

She made her way to the row of newer cottages where the verges were stippled with grass shoots yet to become the lush lawn of the more established areas. The cottages themselves shone with the bright smugness of the new. A scent of fresh paint and timber mingled with the ever-present waft of cocoa and chocolate. Families would live and grow here. A small part of her envied them but it wasn't her path. Still, there was one family who'd been constantly in her thoughts.

She knocked on the door of number sixteen and waited with a sense of dread. The door opened. The woman from the riverbank startled when she saw Dorothy on her doorstep.

'I'm sorry to arrive uninvited. I'm Mrs Adwell. Dorothy Adwell.' Dorothy stumbled over her words. She hadn't expected this sudden rush of apprehension.

'Of course. Dorothy. I recognise you. How could I not.' Her wide smile overshadowed the tired and careworn lines around her eyes. 'I've been longing for this day. Thomas said he'd written you a letter expressing my gratitude and asking if we could meet in person.'

Apart from burning it, Dorothy'd had no idea of how to respond to the letter. She had no intention of subjecting herself to the agony of seeing Thomas and his wife together, even now. She'd come to their cottage at this time of day, while Thomas was at work, because she was a coward.

The woman reached for Dorothy's hands. 'I'm so grateful. So very, very grateful. Please come in. And do call me Vera. Excuse the mess.'

Dorothy followed her into the living room. There were a few toys by the window and a pile of washing waiting to be ironed on the dining table but apart from that the place was spotless. She searched for signs of Thomas in this domestic scene and noticed an ashtray by an armchair, a pile of marking from the evening classes on the table.

'I can't bear to think what would have happened if you hadn't been there that day.' Vera shuddered.

Dorothy gave a small shake of her head. 'Anyone would have done the same.'

Vera's eyebrows pinched together. 'If Edward had drowned, we would have blamed ourselves and we would have been right. To leave him alone like that ...'

Dorothy didn't know what she would have done, given the choice. The poor woman had no idea her boy would fall in the river. Even so, she realised she still harboured some blame towards her. 'You were between a rock and a hard place. Thomas was in distress and needed your help.'

Vera's mouth dropped. 'How did you know?' Then a look of understanding transformed her features. 'Oh, of course, you know about Thomas's ...' she hesitated, 'his condition, better than most. It was the fireworks that day. The crackers. They had a dreadful effect on him.' Vera moved like a restless bird. 'Shall we sit?' She offered Dorothy an overstuffed armchair in a patch of sun and took another chair for herself. 'Words can't express how grateful I am, Dorothy.' Vera's eyes glistened with tears. She pulled a handkerchief from her apron pocket. 'My life wouldn't have been worth living if Edward had been taken from me too.' She dabbed her eyes. 'Thomas told me your husband was killed at the Western Front. So many lost. So many of us bound by grief.'

Dorothy smoothed the hair behind her right ear. How much of her life had Thomas shared with Vera?

'I do hope we can be friends.' Vera's eyes searched Dorothy's with a keen-edged need. 'I've met some of the wives here at the estate. They're perfectly nice, but with you I feel as though we already have a bond. Thomas had mentioned you to me but after that day by the river I'm afraid I was relentless with my questions. I think he told me everything just to stop the barrage.' Her hands fluttered. 'But where are my manners? Would you like a cup of tea? I have some chocolate tartlets just out of the oven.'

Vera knew everything? The sooner she said what she'd come here to say and left, the better. 'No, but thank you. I don't want to be any bother.'

'Oh, Dorothy. You saved my son. You could never be a bother.' Vera's mouth twisted as if holding back a dam of sadness. 'When I was told my husband had been killed ...' She took a shaky breath. 'Well, you know what that's like.' Her fingers plucked at the embroidery on her handkerchief. 'I don't know how much Thomas told you about my circumstances.'

'I'm sorry. Your husband was killed?' Dorothy baulked. Was Thomas her second husband? He'd never mentioned it. And if so, who was Edward's father?

Vera shook her head with a wan smile. 'I thought my brother would have told you.'

Dorothy was completely adrift. 'Your brother. Why would your brother have told me?' Who was her brother? Did he work at the Firm as well? Another thing Thomas hadn't told her.

'Why indeed. Thomas can be rather daft sometimes when it comes to things of importance.'

'Thomas?'

'Yes, my brother.'

'Thomas is your brother?'

Vera looked at her with startled eyes. 'Yes, of course.'

Vera's words hit Dorothy with a mix of astonishment and mortification. Vera wasn't his wife, as she'd assumed that day on the riverbank, but his sister, and Edward wasn't his son but his nephew. Thomas had mentioned his sister before they'd sailed for Melbourne but only that she lived there. He hadn't volunteered any other information and she hadn't pursued it, worried that he might talk more about his family, in particular his wife. Until now Dorothy had thought his sister was still in Melbourne. She clenched her hands together as a rush of shame coursed through her. She'd made assumptions, stupid assumptions. All those weeks she could have spent with Thomas wasted. And now it was too late.

A slow realisation suffused Vera's features. 'Did you think I was his wife?'

Dorothy looked away, aware of the flush of embarrassment creeping up her neck.

'Oh, my stupid brother. I can't believe he was so thick as to not tell you.'

'To be fair, I didn't give him a chance.' If only she hadn't run away that day by the river. If only she'd asked him questions about his family, his sister. She'd never even known their names.

'The fault is not yours. Thomas is completely to blame. I'll have words with him when he comes home, believe you me.'

Vera sounded just like a sister cranky with her brother. The truth that Vera was Thomas's sister and not his wife reached Dorothy's heart. A lightness unfurled in her bones, straightening her spine. She'd been hunched, protecting herself from expected blows and now those blows would never fall. Not from Vera.

Vera gave her head a small shake. 'But I can't stay cross with him. Not when he gave me refuge.'

'What do you mean?'

'I met Robert, my husband, at a dance.' Vera's eyes grew misty. 'A handsome Australian soldier on leave. He swept me off my feet, quite literally. When we danced he picked me up and swung me round. I was smitten. We were married as soon as possible. Edward arrived nine months later.' Her mouth trembled. 'Robert only met him once.'

Dorothy nodded in sympathy. It was an all-too-familiar wartime tale – a whirlwind romance, a marriage, a baby, a heartbroken widow, a fatherless child.

'Robert was gone but at least I had Edward,' Vera continued. 'Even though the thought of raising him without a father was heartbreaking. That's why we moved to Australia. To be with his grandparents. At first it was lovely. My mother-in-law was warm and welcoming and she doted on Edward. But in time it became clear that my father-in-law was resentful, not only of his son's death, but of the fact his boy had married a Pom, as he called me.' Vera winced. 'He was the head of the household and it's hard to live in a house where you're not welcome. Oh, he was very keen to have Edward as a replacement for his son but he'd rather not have me there.'

'I'm sorry to hear it.'

Vera smiled wistfully. 'That's when Thomas came to my rescue. He suggested Edward and I move to Tasmania and share a cottage with him at the Cadbury Estate. It sounded like a dream come true both to me and Edward. Who wouldn't want to live in the land of chocolate?'

Dorothy said nothing, not trusting her voice. She was leaving it behind forever.

'I'm glad you and I have finally met. I'm sure we're going to be the best of friends.' Vera's pale cheeks coloured slightly. 'It's just that, with everything Thomas has told me, I feel as though I already know you.' Vera leant forward and briefly touched Dorothy's hand. 'And our friendship will give you the perfect excuse to spend time with Thomas. No one could object, knowing I'm here.' She dropped her voice. 'He told me how worried you are about him being married and how it could damage both your reputations. I'm the perfect cover.'

'I can't …' Dorothy wavered. Vera was offering her something she longed for but which could never be.

'This is forward of me, but I was hoping, when the weather warms up, that you might teach Edward to swim.' Vera's hands fluttered at her throat. 'I worry every day, you see, being so close to the water, and you're such a strong swimmer, thank goodness.'

Dorothy was aware of a pain in her jaw and realised she'd been clenching her teeth. 'I'm sorry but that won't be possible.'

Vera's shoulders dropped. 'Oh, I have been too forward, I knew it. I'm asking you for favours when you've already done so much. Forgive me.'

'It's not that. The thing is, I'm leaving.'

'Leaving the estate? But why?' Vera's forehead creased in confusion. 'It's such a lovely place to live and so convenient to your work.'

Dorothy took a breath. 'Not just the estate. I handed in my resignation this morning. I'm leaving Cadbury's. And Tasmania.'

'I don't understand. Thomas told me you're Chief Forewoman, a very prestigious position. Why would you give it up?'

Dorothy smoothed the hair behind her right ear. 'When I came to Tasmania, my aim was to be on the Board of Directors.' She was glad to have a handy excuse for her resignation, one that didn't involve the ongoing trials Percy Bates had brought to her life. 'I was considered for the board. Unfortunately the idea was dismissed. A Bournville man will be taking up the position, so …' She shrugged with what she hoped was careless ease. 'I have reached the pinnacle of my career with Cadbury's. There are no more mountains to climb here. I must go looking for a new Mount Everest.'

'Oh, Dorothy. I had such hopes of getting to know you.' There was a note of longing in her voice. 'You've been so good to Thomas.'

'I don't know how much good I've been.' Dorothy shook her head. 'I thought I could fix Thomas, as if he were a broken clock, but I fear I've just made things worse.'

'No.' Vera's tone was emphatic. 'Don't ever think that.'

Dorothy considered telling her the truth about Percy Bates, his blackmail attempt and the drastic action she'd taken to put an end to it, but what good would it do? If all went to plan Vera need never know. Even so, Dorothy's guilt remained. 'I hope you'll forgive me for any harm I might have brought on your family.'

'There's no need to ask for forgiveness. You've been a blessing, in all our lives.'

'I had ideas above my station. I may be able to fix machinery but I had no business trying to mend Thomas's mind. I was a meddling fool and I'm deeply sorry.'

Vera settled back in her chair and shifted her gaze to the light-filled window. 'When Thomas first told me about you and that you thought you could help with his troubles, I was unsure. I was also suspicious. What did this woman want with my brother?'

Dorothy looked away in shame. What indeed?

'I hadn't realised until I got here just how bad it was. The nightmares, the shaking ... as you well know. He told me he'd tried every cure back home. He was doubtful there was anything you could do, but he was desperate. I was doubtful too, until you saved my son. Edward lives and breathes only because of you. You might have wanted to save Thomas but you did save my son. I owe you a debt I can never repay.'

'Your words are payment enough.' Dorothy stood, suddenly restless. 'I must go. I have to pack and arrange passage to Sydney.'

Vera remained sitting. She looked up at Dorothy with sadness. 'He'll miss you. You did help him, despite what you think.'

'For the most part all I did was listen.'

Vera's face clouded. 'Something his wife lost the capacity for some time ago.' She stood and held Dorothy's gaze. 'He won't have told you, Thomas is nothing if not loyal, but it was never a happy marriage.' She shook her head. 'Well, maybe it was at first, but not for long. After he returned from the war I think she would have preferred to see him locked up in an asylum.'

Dorothy took a ragged breath. How could any woman want that for her husband?

'I'm sorry. I sound callous, I know.' Vera pursed her lips. 'But it's true. Thomas made the right decision, coming to Tasmania, even though it means he's far away from his son. He misses him dreadfully and feels guilty for leaving him. His wife made him think they'd join him as soon as he was settled. Time will tell, but I never trusted that woman.'

Dorothy had assumed the marriage had been a happy one. That was one of the reasons she'd never asked about it. To hear such vitriol about Thomas's wife was a shock. 'I really must get on.'

'Thomas has the afternoons off when he takes a class in the evening. He'll be home any minute. Won't you stay, just for a little while?'

Dorothy wavered. Like a milksop she'd come here this afternoon hoping Vera would pass on the news of her departure to Thomas without having to do it herself. But Thomas deserved the truth. Once news broke of Percy's arrest, Thomas would know exactly who the third party was, even though he'd never be named. She had to be the one to tell him. Dorothy hoped to choose the time and place but the front door opened and the decision was made for her.

Thomas's eyes widened when he saw Dorothy. He removed his hat and placed it on a hook in the entryway, never taking his gaze from her.

'Thomas.' Vera moved to greet him. 'Look who's here.'

'Good afternoon, Mr Moreland.' Dorothy's skin warmed under his attention.

'Mrs Adwell. I wasn't expecting to see you here.' His voice carried a trace of concern.

'Dorothy was saying goodbye. She's leaving Cadbury's.'

Thomas took a slight step back. 'But why?'

Dorothy's heart contracted, knowing this was the last time she'd see him. 'Career reasons.' She kept her voice steady.

'Dorothy will explain it all to you,' Vera said, reaching for her hat. 'I'm going for a walk. It's such a beautiful day.' Vera was gone before either Dorothy or Thomas could say a word.

Silently Dorothy and Thomas stood in the bright, sunny room. The toys on the floor and the pile of clean washing on the table reminded Dorothy of the life she and Freddie would have had if the war hadn't destroyed all their plans.

'Dorothy? Are you all right?' Thomas took a step towards her.

'Sorry.' She blinked to clear the tears that gathered at the corners of her eyes. 'It's been a strange time. It's over now.'

'Why are you leaving Cadbury's?' The furrow deepened between his eyes.

Dorothy took in a deep breath and let it out slowly in an effort to ease her aching heart. She couldn't bear to tell him the details of how she'd got everything so horribly wrong and the drastic actions she'd taken to make amends, but she knew she must.

He moved closer. The sunlight shone on his hair, smooth with brilliantine. 'I'm not going to lie. I will miss you. You've been a sanctuary.'

Dorothy saw the sadness in his eyes and had to break away. She moved to the window overlooking the backyard. 'It's peaceful here on the estate, now the major construction work is complete. So much fresh air and space. Just what you need.' She dared to look at him for a second, saw the worry on his face and turned away again. 'The latest research from England shows outdoor physical labour can work wonders. Many shell-shock victims have improved enormously after working on farms. Here you have your own garden. And there's the jam-tin golf course some of the workers have cobbled together now the quarry is no longer in use. There'll always be something to keep you busy.' She was aware she was talking too much.

'Dorothy.' He stepped closer again. She ached with the nearness of him. 'I can't believe you're leaving. I know how much the Firm means to you. And your career.'

Dorothy hesitated, not sure where to begin. Anyone who didn't know about the industrial espionage that plagued the chocolate firms in England would find it hard to fathom. She steeled herself. 'I've been the target of a blackmail attempt.'

Thomas blanched. 'Blackmail? But why?'

She turned towards him. 'The blackmailer was after certain trade secrets that he thought or, more likely, was told I had. One of Cadbury's recipes in particular. He was determined to get what he wanted, no matter how long it took and how many people he'd destroy on the way. To stop him I had to fall on my own sword, so to speak.'

'I don't understand. Why should you be forced to give up everything you've worked so hard for?'

'If I didn't give him what he wanted I'm certain he would have targeted someone else. He had to be stopped. So, to make sure he'd be imprisoned, I admitted to what no woman would, unless it were true.'

Thomas became very still. 'What was that?'

Dorothy's throat was dry. She swallowed. 'I told Mr Cooper I was being blackmailed because I was having an affair with a married man.'

Thomas nodded slowly. 'I see.' The air around him was charged with tension.

Dorothy was desperate to reassure him. 'I didn't mention a name to Mr Cooper, there was no need. Neither the blackmailer nor his informant know who the man is. You're safe.'

A look of dismay crossed Thomas's face. 'I'm not worried for myself. But you, you're losing everything – your job, your home and your reputation – for something that's not even true. An affair?'

'It's worth it to know this cad will be arrested, if he hasn't been already. I expect he'll try to weasel his way out of it, but I have trumped him.' Dorothy stood a little straighter. 'Why would any woman admit to adultery if it wasn't true? He'll go to gaol and whoever was employing him to steal secrets from the Firm will think twice before attempting it again.'

'Is there no other way?'

'It's done. I must face the consequences.' Dorothy clenched her hands in an attempt to quell the grief welling inside her. 'And you must pretend you never knew me.'

Thomas bridged the gap between them. They'd been physically closer before but only when he'd been in a state and she had soothed and comforted him. Today he was perfectly himself. Perfectly Thomas. 'I'll never forget you. How could I? Thank you, Dorothy, for everything.'

'I've done nothing.' His closeness threatened to bring her undone.

'You've never judged me when so many others have and that has been the greatest of gifts.'

A sob escaped Dorothy's lips. 'I'm sorry, Thomas. I'm so dreadfully sorry.'

He looked into her eyes. 'For what?'

She avoided his gaze. 'At first I wanted to help you because you reminded me of my Freddie.'

'I know.'

'You knew?' During their time together Thomas had often asked her questions about herself. At first she'd resisted, thinking he was trying to deflect attention away from his problems. However, in time she'd noticed that sometimes taking the focus off his predicament helped him relax. She'd told him about her marriage, the cottage at Bournville and Freddie's death but she'd never mentioned his shell shock, afraid that Thomas would think her motivation to help him was tainted somehow. He would have been right. 'How?'

'Sometimes when you looked at me it was as if you were seeing someone else. At first I thought it was an idealised version of me, a version that you hoped I was, but I began to realise there was more to it. I reminded you of Freddie. He suffered from the same affliction, didn't he?'

Dorothy dropped her head, ashamed of the truth. If Freddie had lived she would have spent her life, to her last breath, trying to mend his broken mind. Thomas had taken Freddie's place in many ways. She nodded. 'But then ... I didn't mean to or want to, but I've fallen in love with you.'

'I know that too.' Gently he reached up and smoothed the hair behind her right ear. 'And I, a little, with you.'

She closed her eyes and leant into his hand. His touch and his warmth were all she yearned for. A fierce need overcame her in a rush of heat. She opened her eyes to meet his. 'Our friendship has been beyond reproach, but now that I'm about to leave, I wonder—'

Before she could finish Thomas enfolded her in his arms and pressed his lips against hers, warm and pliant, yet firm. Memories came rushing back of her kisses with Freddie on those summer days when life was full of promise, and cares were far away – his body against hers, the endearments they whispered to each other, the times that were theirs alone with no one else to hear or see, a complete world that belonged just to the two of them. Her body flooded with sensations that threatened to overwhelm her. She could stay forever, with him, just as they were.

Thomas pulled away, leaving Dorothy swaying as if she were back on the *Ormonde* where they'd first met. 'Goodbye, Mrs Adwell, it's been an honour to know you.' His smile belied the sadness in his eyes. He held out his hand.

Dorothy indulged in the warm familiarity of his touch for the last time. She would never see him again. 'Goodbye, Mr Moreland. I wish you only good things.'

She left without a backward glance, her hand clutched to her heart.

39

Dorothy

Sarah jumped up as soon as Dorothy walked in. 'What on earth have you done?' Her face was flushed and a vein pulsed at her temple.

Dorothy had managed to compose herself on the way back to the cottage. She'd dried her tears and turned her face to the sky and the gentle sunlight. By the time she'd arrived home, the sharp pain in her heart had diminished to a dull ache. Even so, she could still taste Thomas on her lips and knew she'd never forget how it felt to be in his arms. In the wake of Sarah's angry greeting, Dorothy took off her hat and gloves and smiled with a serenity that didn't match her emotions. 'I've done what I had to.'

Sarah flung herself onto the couch. 'But you didn't have to, you little idiot. I know you believe Cadbury's saved your life but that doesn't mean you had to sacrifice yourself to save Cadbury's. I had a plan, which I would have told you if you hadn't left so early this morning.'

Dorothy couldn't have sat through breakfast with Sarah then walked with her to the factory without letting slip what she was planning. The sunrise this morning had been worth the early start. She took a seat in one of the armchairs and regarded Sarah with all the calm she could muster.

Sarah leant forward, her elbows on her thighs, and glared at her. 'And then you weasel Frank into doing your dirty work by getting him to send me on a wild goose chase so that I was away from my desk when you went to see Mr Cooper. Of all the low-handed—' Sarah narrowed her eyes to slits. 'You knew I'd stop you. And I would have. If you'd given me half a chance.'

Dorothy smoothed a crease on her skirt. 'Well, it's done now.'

'No, it's not. I've undone it.'

Panic fluttered in Dorothy's chest. 'What? How?'

'I couldn't have you sacrifice yourself because of Cecil Bottom, or Percy Bates, or whatever he might choose to call himself next. Actually, I'll always think of him as Percy Bates. I'm sure Cecil was a nice young boy once but Percy has always been an awful, awful man.'

'Tell me what you've done.'

'As soon as I returned from Frank's bogus mission,' she shot Dorothy a deathly stare, 'Mr Cooper called me in to his office to tell me you'd resigned. Resigned! He was reluctant to tell me why but told me it involved blackmail and – as the details would come out in court anyway – adultery.' Sarah slapped her hands on her knees. 'You could have knocked me over with a feather. And then I got angry. At you. Luckily I do my best work when I'm angry.'

Dorothy saw the rage in Sarah's eyes and didn't disbelieve it for a second. It troubled her, though, that she was the reason and the target. She knew her friend would be upset but she never suspected Sarah would be this angry.

'I'd been stewing over what to do since Saturday afternoon and last night it came to me. A brilliant scheme even if I do say so myself.

But you, Dorothy Adwell,' she stabbed a finger at Dorothy, 'had to go and ruin it with your confession and sacrifice. Trust you to be the martyr when what was really needed was the swift demise of Percy Bates.'

'Demise?'

'Figuratively speaking. Although if I could get away with it, I'd gladly kill him.' She raised an eyebrow at Dorothy. 'Fortunately for you, I figured out Frank's ruse and returned to Mr Cooper's office in good time. He was so shocked by your admission he hadn't had the wherewithal to call the police. I managed to convince him that because of your stupidity, well, that's not the exact word I used, we should forget your overwrought confession and stick to the facts.'

'Which are?'

'Percy Bates was threatening to spread lies about you, hence the mention of adultery, in order to force you into giving him the Dairy Milk recipe. That, of course, none of his accusations were true, which was of great relief to Mr Cooper, I must say. I told him you were afraid Mr Bates would continue to harass not only you but your staff and thought the only way you could protect them and the Firm was to do what you did. I also told him that not only was Percy Bates a spy trying to get his grubby hands on the Dairy Milk recipe, but he was a thief, stealing from the Firm, and should be arrested immediately. I must say he was a lot happier with a charge of petty theft rather than blackmail.' Sarah sat back looking very pleased with herself.

'And Mr Cooper believed you?'

'It's easy to turn a silk purse into a sow's ear. It's just a matter of mud. I told Mr Cooper I'd have the proof on his desk by tomorrow morning. It means I'll have to go back to the office and work late tonight, but I'm happy to do it to see Mr Bates gone.'

'What proof?'

'I have my ways.'

Dorothy stilled. 'Do your ways involve framing him?'

'The man is a spy, which will be hard to prove. And a blackmailer, even harder to prove without dire consequences. Theft though? That's easy. Percy Bates will be given his marching orders today. He'll be arrested as soon as I provide the evidence and he will be convicted.' Sarah crossed her legs and waited, as if expecting praise.

Dorothy was aware of the tension in her jaw, her hands, her chest. She shook her head slowly. 'I appreciate that you're prepared to do whatever it is you're planning, fiddle the books, I expect, but I can't let you do it. What if your deception is discovered? I won't let you put yourself at risk. Not to save me.' Anger towards Percy rose in her throat. He was to blame for Sarah putting herself on the line, for the anguish Maisie had gone through and for Dorothy leaving the job she loved in disgrace. 'I'm going to go ahead with the blackmail charges.'

Sarah jumped to her feet, hands on her hips, and glared at Dorothy. 'Don't underestimate me. The evidence will be watertight. But as for your blackmail charges, what concrete proof do you have? Letters Percy claims he didn't write. The word of a young employee whose loyalties belong to you – any decent lawyer would shoot down her testimony in a second.'

'I've promised Maisie she won't be involved.'

'You may not have a choice. What if Percy's lawyer decides he wants her on the witness stand?'

A sickening feeling rose in Dorothy's stomach. 'Why would a defence lawyer do that?'

'Why does a defence lawyer do anything?' Sarah threw up her hands. 'To get his client off the hook. Imagine Maisie on the stand being subjected to a barrage of questions, her character discredited, her testimony shredded to pieces. Is that what you want?'

'No. Of course not.' Dorothy desperately tried to think of something that would hold up in court. 'There's you. If you're willing to testify.'

'Of course, but once again, his defence lawyer will state that I'm compromised. We're friends. We share a cottage, for goodness sake. My testimony would be thrown out as hearsay and doubtful at best. Honestly, Dot, your case might fail and then where will you be? Ruined for nothing and Percy Bates goes free.'

'There's my testimony. Why would any woman destroy her reputation to bring a blackmailer to justice? Why would any woman admit to adultery if it wasn't true? That's my trump card. The court will have to believe me.'

Sarah sighed. 'But it's not true, is it?'

'What?'

'You weren't having an affair with a married man.'

'Why would I admit to it if it wasn't true?'

'To send Percy Bates to gaol. To see justice done. He's got you so worked up you'd do or say anything to see him in prison.' Sarah studied Dorothy with a steady gaze. 'I admire you, Dot, for the strength of your convictions, I really do, but what do you expect me to say when I'm called to the stand and asked about your alleged affair with a married man? Remember, I've sworn on the Bible. I have to tell the truth or be gaoled for perjury. Your whole case depends on this supposed adulterous affair and being blackmailed because of it. What happens when I tell the court you were not having an affair, but instead were doing your Christian duty by helping a brave soldier whose mind had been damaged by the war? You've told me everything about your liaisons with the man who reminded you of Freddie. There was no adultery involved. And what happens when they put Thomas Moreland on the stand? What will that do to him?'

Dorothy gasped. 'I never told you his name.'

'Oh, Dot.' Sarah shook her head as if Dorothy was a foolish child. 'I've known it was Thomas Moreland for a long time. We live in the same cottage, remember? But even before then, I knew. And those extra trays of chocolates you'd bring into the office? You might have fooled everyone else, but not me. They were a ruse to see Thomas. Not only that, but you'd also leave a hidden note with the tray to arrange meetings. He'd put two chocolates on a saucer on his desk for a yes and one for a no. Nobody else noticed, but I did.'

'And you never said anything?'

'It was none of my business. I was worried for your reputation but you were careful.' Her smile was brief and unconvincing. 'Be that as it may, even your own testimony won't stand up in court. Do you really want to get Thomas involved? You've confessed to an affair. Everyone from the press to the judge is going to want to know who it was with.'

'I couldn't see any other way. I had to do something.' Dorothy put a hand to her forehead. She had thought it would be an open and shut case. 'Percy can't go free. It's not fair.'

'We've been through a war, Dot. Good people died. Evil people went free. Life is not fair.'

Dorothy inhaled a shuddering breath. 'But I want the evil people to be punished. I want there to be justice.' She sounded naive, she knew it, but part of her truly believed the world should be a just place.

'I know, I know. We all do. That's why we went to war. But sometimes the results are different to what we expected, what we hoped.'

'I did what I had to do. Percy would have dragged us all down.'

'If you go through with your plan you'll drag yourself down. You know how to swim, Dot, there's still time to save yourself from drowning.' Sarah leant towards her. 'Please.'

The entreaty in her friend's voice caused her to hesitate. Her desire to see Percy punished was great but the damage she might inflict on the innocent could be even greater. 'I'll have to think about it.'

'Then think quickly.' Sarah's voice held a note of frustration. 'As soon as I have the proof on Mr Cooper's desk you must retract your accusation and your resignation.'

'Must I?' It had been hard to tell Mr Cooper that her resignation was effective immediately. She hated to let the Firm down but in the circumstances Mr Cooper had been relieved.

'Yes, you must. If not for yourself then for the rest of us. Think of the consequences if you leave.' Sarah's eyes widened in mock horror. 'Esme will be Chief Forewoman!'

'Then at least one person will be happy with the result of all this mess.'

'Esme? Happy? Nothing would ever make that woman happy. She even keeps moaning about the arrival of George Cadbury Junior this week. Everyone else is thrilled and all she can say is, "Why do they call him the Chocolate Prince when Fry's has been making chocolate far longer than Cadbury's?" Honestly, that woman is impossible.'

'I thought Mr Cadbury wasn't due until next week.' After everything that had happened, Dorothy had hoped to be gone by the time he arrived.

'He's keen to see the new factory so he's cutting his time in Sydney short. He'll be here in a matter of days.' Sarah stood. 'I must get back to the office. Don't expect to see me home for tea. I'll survive on chocolates.' She fixed Dorothy with a stern look. 'Retract your accusation, Dot, and your resignation. Save yourself and the rest of us.'

Dorothy followed Sarah to the door and waited while Sarah fixed her hair, touched up her lipstick and put on her hat and gloves.

Before she left she laid a gentle hand on Dorothy's arm. 'I mean it. Retract your resignation. If not for your sake, then for mine. I couldn't possibly bear to deal with Miss Esme Abbott as our Chief Forewoman.'

Dorothy smiled, as she knew Sarah expected her to, but said nothing. She closed the door and leant against it. All she'd wanted to do was to fix what was broken, to mend it so that it worked again. That way everything ran smoothly and everyone was happy. But it hadn't worked. Instead, she'd been wrong. Again. And then there was Sarah, who'd so coolly announced her plan to frame Percy as if it were the easiest thing in the world. Dorothy had found it chilling but it was as if it meant nothing to Sarah. Plus she'd known Thomas's name, even though Dorothy had done her best to keep it a secret. Sarah had always been Dorothy's staunchest ally but she dreaded to think what would happen if that ever changed. Sarah would be a formidable opponent.

The memory of Thomas's kiss still lingered. She may not have had an affair with a married man but Lord knows she'd wanted to. She couldn't stay at the estate knowing Thomas was so close – the pain was too great. It was an impossible situation. She couldn't stay at the Firm either, not after what she'd told Mr Cooper this morning. She'd never forget the horrified expression on his face. How could he keep the woman who'd admitted to having an affair with a married man in his employ, especially as Chief Forewoman? Sarah had told him it wasn't true, but Dorothy knew he'd always harbour doubts. She could never hold her head up at the factory again. Her mind was made up. She might retract her accusations against Percy Bates – as Sarah had so brutally pointed out, the case would do much harm and potentially very little good – but her resignation? No. The best thing for her to do was to leave Cadbury's, and the life she loved, behind.

40

Maisie

A gentle breeze drifted down the valley and the blue waters of the Derwent sparkled like a string of diamonds. Maisie and Frank sat on their favourite rock by the river, hands entwined. To an outsider they might appear to be a young courting couple happily in love, but the assumption would be at odds with their sombre expressions.

'So you see, Frank, I can't marry you,' Maisie said, a quaver in her voice. 'Not yet, anyway. And not for some time. I'm the main breadwinner in the family. Now he has a job, Andrew sends some money home but everything's more expensive in Melbourne so it's not a lot. With Mother's failing health and the doctor's fees, we're still only scraping by. There's talk I might be promoted, but even so it may not be enough for Lily to stay in school.' She knew Mrs Adwell was behind the mooted promotion, a parting gift following the shocking news of her resignation. Yesterday's events had left Maisie dizzy but Frank's hand encircling hers was a source of reassurance.

'I can't say I'm not disappointed, but I understand,' Frank said. 'Your love for your sister is one of the many things I find endearing about you. And that's why I have another kind of proposal for you.'

'What kind of proposal?' Maisie shifted to face him.

'I don't want our marriage to deprive you of your income, so I suggest a long engagement. As long as you need. Say you'll marry me, Maisie, please?' His eyes implored her. 'I know I want to spend the rest of my life with you but I'm prepared to wait. In the meantime, as your fiancé, I'll contribute to Lily's education. I'll do whatever I can to ensure she stays in school and has a good chance of being accepted into the university.'

Maisie hesitated. A faint echo of shame still haunted her over how she'd treated Frank and yet not only had he forgiven her but he was also offering to grant her dearest wish. 'But university is years away, and she'll need support even then. Are you sure?'

'All of us who knew him admired George Cadbury.' Frank's face grew solemn. 'He was a strong believer in giving his employees every chance to have an education. He put that belief into action with the classes and facilities at Bournville. Back home the Firm even provides scholarships to attend university. Allow me to follow in his footsteps. Let me, in my own humble way, provide the way forward for Lily's education.'

Maisie chewed her bottom lip. 'I'm not sure.'

'I left school at twelve, Maisie, it's just the way it was back then.'

'You're not that much older than me.' Maisie lightly nudged his shoulder with her own.

'I'm four years older. Those years and a war have seen a great many things change. The point is, I would've been thrilled to stay in school. Imagine the things I could've learnt. Even so, the one day a week of Day Continuation School was a blessing. Then, after I got back from the war, I took evening classes. Learning is something I wouldn't deny anyone if I had a chance. I want Lily to have that chance. I've done the sums. I can afford to contribute the same amount of money Lily would earn if she gets a job.'

Even with the pittance a fourteen-year-old was paid, Maisie baulked. 'But that's too much. I can't accept it.'

'Then accept it for Lily's sake. Can you do that?'

Maisie's mind raced. Mother had written to The Friends' School as she said she would. Lily's scholarship was gone. But this money meant Lily could still attend and apply for a scholarship for the next year. 'Mother will object.' Maisie shook her head. 'She's too proud to take charity.'

'How can she object to her future son-in-law helping to support the family? Isn't that what sons-in-law are supposed to do?' Frank looked at her earnestly.

'You really have thought all of this through, haven't you?'

'To be honest, Maisie, I'm being selfish.' He squeezed her hand. 'I want us to be married, whatever it takes and whenever that might be.'

'A long engagement, you say?'

'As long as is needed.'

'Then there's only one answer I can give.' She gave him a shy smile.

Frank reached into his pocket and was down on one knee before she could blink. He opened a small blue velvet pouch and took out a plain silver ring with a single tiny sapphire reflecting the blue of the sky above them. It was the most beautiful thing Maisie had ever seen.

'Maisie Greenwood, will you be my wife?' Frank looked up at her with shining eyes.

She paused to savour the moment, one she thought she'd never experience because of her blind stubbornness. She thanked God that

Frank was the better person and had forgiven her completely. 'Yes. Yes, I will.' He slipped the ring onto her finger. The warmth of his touch and the coolness of the ring made her shiver with a strange delight. She spread her fingers and admired the ring as it sparkled there. 'Such a pity I'll have to take it off again when it's time to go back to work.'

Frank handed her the velvet pouch. 'Keep it safe in here and put it back on as soon as the shift is over. I want the world to know you're mine.' He stood and held his hands out to Maisie. She grasped them and he lifted her to her feet with ease. His smile was wide, showing off the slightly irregular teeth she loved so much. 'Here's to the future Mrs Frank Sutton.'

Maisie dipped her chin, overcome. In another time he would have asked her father's permission before slipping a ring on her finger. She lifted her gaze to the sky. *He's a good man, Father. You'd approve of him. I think you'd even like him.* A pair of white cockatoos flew past. She traced their flight with her eyes. A good omen, she was sure of it. A sign from her father? She smiled wistfully. Perhaps.

'What are you smiling about?'

'I think there's just one thing missing.' Maisie scuffed the grass with the toe of her shoe.

'What's that?'

Her stomach fluttered at the brazenness of what she was about to say. 'I think you're supposed to kiss me.'

A slow smile spread across Frank's face. He leant closer. 'A good husband always obeys his wife.'

His face grew close and his features blurred. Maisie had never kissed anyone before. What if she did it wrong? She closed her eyes like they did in the movies. Frank's warm lips lightly settled on hers, soft as a butterfly. Her worries fell away as he held her tighter in his arms. All thoughts disappeared as his kiss deepened. A fever swept through her body, making her dizzy and breathless. Slowly he pulled away but her lips followed his, drawn to them like a magnet. He chuckled deep in his throat and the vibrations rippled through her. It was as if he was a pebble and she was water.

'Oh, sorry. I didn't mean to interrupt.' A high tense voice broke them apart. Gertie stood a small distance away frowning at them, her face blotched and her eyes puffy.

In her joy it didn't register that Gertie was upset. 'Gertie.' Maisie held out her left hand for inspection. 'You can be the first to congratulate us.' She beamed. 'We're engaged.'

Gertie burst into tears. 'I was supposed to be getting married.'

Maisie pulled away from Frank. The conversation with Mrs Adwell came back in sharp focus. Poor Gertie. Percy, Cecil, whatever his name was, would've been arrested by now. 'What's happened?' she asked, not wanting to hear.

'Percy and I were supposed to meet last night.' Gertie clutched her sodden handkerchief. 'He didn't turn up. Then today I tried to find him but he wasn't anywhere. He's avoiding me, I know it,' she sobbed.

Frank stepped forward. 'Miss Thompson, forgive me, but are you talking about the man known as Percy Bates?'

She glared at him with wild reddened eyes. 'What do you mean "known as"? He's my Percy and I am going to be Mrs Percy Bates. He promised.'

'I'm very sorry to be the one to inform you, but Cecil Bottom, known as Percy Bates, was let go.'

'Cecil Bottom?' Gertie screwed up her face in confusion. 'No. Percy Bates.'

'Percy Bates was sacked and ...' Frank hesitated. 'I'm sorry, he was taken into police custody.'

Gertie's mouth fell open. 'But why?'

'I'm not sure of the details but theft was mentioned.'

Maisie stared at Frank. 'Theft?' It wasn't what she was expecting.

'That can't possibly be true,' Gertie wailed. 'Not Percy. Someone called Cecil Bottom perhaps, but not my Percy.'

'They're one and the same, I'm afraid.'

Gertie swayed as if to faint. Maisie and Frank rushed to her side. They settled her on the rock. Maisie sat beside her, her mind a tumble of questions. Mrs Adwell had said Percy would be arrested for blackmail, not theft. Did this mean Mrs Adwell had lied to her? But why would any woman lie about a thing like that? Perhaps she'd wanted to prove a point to Maisie and look where that point had led – Maisie was now engaged to Frank. A confusion of emotions swirled in her stomach. She was with the man she loved. Percy had been arrested. Gertie, however, was in a dreadful state. 'Gertie,' she said gently. 'Percy is not a good man. His being arrested is the proof of it. I know it hurts now, but you're better off without him.'

Gertie sniffled. 'You don't understand. He promised to marry me.'

Maisie studied Gertie's face. There was a trace of forbidden rouge on her cheeks and lipstick on her mouth. She'd probably applied it in anticipation of seeing Percy. A vision of Gertie in her daring dress, the boys trailing around her like ants, danced in Maisie's mind. A cold certainty spread through her as she remembered Gertie's bedroom, with its own entrance. She looked up at Frank. 'I'm sorry. I need to talk to Gertie alone.'

Frank nodded. 'I'll see you tomorrow.' He blew her a kiss out of Gertie's eyesight and walked away.

Maisie adopted a calm expression, the same one she used with Lily when she'd been in trouble at school. 'What's going on, Gertie? You can tell me. I'm your friend and always will be, no matter what.'

Gertie moaned and tears raced unchecked down her cheeks. 'He told me he loved me. He promised to marry me.' She gripped Maisie's hands. 'I'm ruined. Ruined! My father caught us. He's thrown me out of the house. Percy barely escaped with his life. I told my dad we're getting married and he said we'd better make it quick. Percy has to marry me, you see? He has to.' The last words were a howl of pain.

Guilt clutched at Maisie's throat. She'd known Percy was no good but instead of warning Gertie, she'd used her. She'd tricked her into providing a letter that had turned out to be useless. If she'd told Gertie the truth about Percy all of this might never have happened. But would Gertie have believed her? To her great shame, Maisie had been quick to believe Percy's lies about Frank, but other women were disinclined to think ill of the one they loved. Either way, some of the blame for Gertie's pain was hers.

'Gertie, listen carefully. I want you to go to sick bay and tell Nurse you're unwell. Ask for a headache powder and to lie down for a bit. After a while say you need to go home.'

'I can't go home.' Gertie sniffled.

'Your father will still be at work and your mother will be too busy to notice. Pack a few of your things then go to the station and wait for the Cadbury's train. I'll be on it after my shift, waiting for you.' A chilling thought made Maisie pause. 'Gertie, I'm sorry to ask you this, but could you be ... are you ...'

'No.' Gertie snorted. 'I'm not that stupid. I stole my sister's French cap. She's married now, you know. I gave it a good clean and it was as good as new.'

Maisie didn't know what a French cap was but it sounded distasteful.

'And besides.' Gertie looked away. 'When my father barged into my room Percy hadn't, you know ...'

Maisie frowned in puzzlement. 'Hadn't what?'

Gertie rolled her eyes. 'Blimey, Maisie. He hadn't finished the business, so there's no way I can be expecting.'

'Oh. I see.' Maisie's cheeks flamed. She coughed to cover her embarrassment. 'Right. Well then, I'll be waiting for you on the train and you'll come home with me.'

'But what about Percy? How will he know how to find me?'

'Percy will be in the lock-up. After that he'll be in gaol. If you want to, you can find him, but I strongly advise against it.'

Gertie burst into heaving sobs. Maisie rubbed her back and murmured reassuring words, as much for herself as for Gertie – how on earth was she going to convince Mother to agree to this plan?

41

Maisie

'Golly, this road is steep.' Gertie struggled with her suitcase as they headed up the hill to Maisie's home. 'You could never play street cricket here.' She stopped to catch her breath. 'You'd spend the entire time running down the hill after the ball and then struggling back up.'

'Here, I'll take your suitcase for a while.' Maisie sagged under its weight. When she'd told Gertie to bring a few things she'd been expecting a small bag, not a large suitcase. 'Now remember the plan. You're just going to stay for a couple of nights.' The size of the suitcase would say otherwise but it couldn't be helped.

'But I've got nowhere else to go. I can't go home. Not with Percy in gaol,' Gertie sobbed.

'Let's not mention any of that to Mother. There's no need for her to know.' Maisie didn't want to lie but she also wanted her friend to have a bed to sleep in tonight. Over the past few months she'd become used to keeping things from her mother. The deceit had weighed heavily, but now that the horrid debacle with Percy was over she had room for a few new secrets.

Finally Maisie and Gertie struggled through the gate, lugging the suitcase between them. 'Mother, Lily,' Maisie called out as she opened the door. She was grateful Gertie's tears had stopped. The climb meant Gertie couldn't cry and walk at the same time.

Lily came racing down the hallway, plaits flying behind her. 'Maisie, I learnt about birds and migration today. I have so much to tell you. Did you know—' She stopped short when she saw Gertie and the suitcase. 'Hello, are you going on a trip?'

'This is a friend of mine, Gertie. Gertie, this is Lily.'

'Hello, Lily. Nice to meet you. I have a little sister about your age and several younger than that.' Gertie smiled her brightest smile. It was clear she wanted to make a good impression.

'You must have a big family.'

'Huge.' She spread her arms out wide and Maisie glimpsed the cheeky, fun-loving Gertie she knew so well.

Lily giggled and Gertie gave her a wink.

'Maisie?' Mother called from the kitchen. 'Do you have someone with you? Come and introduce us.'

'Coming, Mother.' Maisie steeled herself and gave Gertie a warning look. 'Let's leave your suitcase in the bedroom for now. One thing at a time.'

'That's a big suitcase,' Lily said, as Maisie manoeuvred it down the hall and into the bedroom she shared with Lily.

'What a beautiful cat,' Gertie said, going to Lily's bed and giving Blackie a stroke under the chin. He started purring immediately, lifting his chin for more.

'His name's Blackie. He came for the mice but stayed for me. He likes you, which means I like you,' Lily said with a definitive nod.

Gertie's face crumpled for a moment. Maisie held her breath, afraid she'd start crying again, but Gertie rallied and her smile reappeared. 'And I like you. I have the feeling we'll be the best of friends.'

'Maisie?' her mother's tremulous voice called out again. Maisie took Gertie's arm and guided her down the hall, rearranging her face into an expression of calm and ease, neither of which she felt.

As always Mother was hunched over the mending. Maisie's heart lurched at the sight. Summer was on the way. If her mother could spend some time outdoors in the fresh air and sunshine instead of cooped up in the stuffy kitchen she was sure it would do her the world of good.

'This is my friend, Gertie Thompson. We work together at Cadbury's. Gertie, this is my mother, Mrs Greenwood.'

'Please excuse me not getting up,' Mother said, indicating the skirt she was working on draped over her lap. 'You're Maisie's friend. You went to the Cadbury's dance together.'

'I am, Mrs Greenwood. We started at Cadbury's on the same day and we've been friends ever since.'

'We're going to be best friends too,' Lily chirped as she joined them.

'Is that so?' Mother gave Gertie an inquiring look.

'We both love cats,' Lily said. 'And Gertie has a sister my age and several younger too.'

'That's very interesting, thank you, Lily, but perhaps you could let Miss Thompson speak for herself. Please, take a seat.' Mother nodded her head towards one of the kitchen chairs. 'Would you like a cup of tea? Maisie, could you put the kettle on, please? And Lily, I believe you were doing the vegetables. The carrots won't peel themselves.'

Tentatively Gertie took the proffered chair while Maisie got the tea things ready, keeping a nervous eye on her friend all the while. Lily took her place at the sink where the carrots lay half peeled.

'From memory, you live at Montrose, is that right, Miss Thompson?'

'Please, call me Gertie, Mrs Greenwood.' Gertie hesitated. 'Yes. My family live at Montrose.'

'That's quite a distance, but handy to the factory.'

'Gertie's going on a trip,' Lily said, smiling over from the sink.

Maisie tensed but her mother's face remained calmly interested. 'Are you travelling far?'

'Well ... I ...' Gertie faltered.

Maisie returned to the table and stood beside Gertie. 'I was hoping Gertie could stop with us for a few days, if that's all right, Mother. Andrew's room is empty and Gertie needs a place to stay.'

'Have you left Cadbury's, Gertie? Is that why you're going on a trip?'

Maisie cleared her throat nervously. 'Gertie's not going on a trip. Lily leapt to that conclusion.'

'Because of Gertie's big suitcase, I presume.' Mother raised an eyebrow.

'How did you know?' Maisie asked.

'I may be old but I'm not deaf, not yet anyway.'

The kettle came to the boil and Maisie dragged herself away to make the tea, concerned at the turn the conversation was taking.

'I'm not leaving Cadbury's, Mrs Greenwood,' Gertie said. 'I love working there.'

'Did you bring home any chocolate?' Lily asked excitedly.

'Not today. Sorry.' Maisie usually brought something home, even if it was just a few rejected chocolates for Lily and Mother, but once again the day had taken so many turns she hadn't thought of it.

'Lily,' Mother said. 'Leave the carrots and go to your room. I'm sure you have some homework to do.'

'I've done all my homework and I still have some carrots to peel.' Lily waved a carrot as proof.

'You can finish that later. Go to your room and read a book.'

Lily frowned then slowly trailed up the hallway.

Maisie's stomach clenched. Usually Mother was telling Lily to get her nose out of her books. She brought the tea things to the table.

'Leave that for the moment, Maisie.' Her mother put aside the mending. 'Sit down and tell me what's really going on.'

Maisie sat. 'It's as I said,' she began nervously. 'I'm hoping my friend Gertie can stay here with us for a few nights.' She glanced at Gertie, whose bottom lip was starting to quiver. She willed her friend to stay calm.

'During the working week? When Gertie lives so much closer to the factory?' Mother shook her head. 'It doesn't add up.'

Horrified, Maisie watched Gertie grasp her chest and emit a choking sob. 'I'm sorry, Mrs Greenwood. I can't go home. I have nowhere else to go.' She began to cry.

Mother took a deep breath and nodded. 'It's as I thought. Trouble with a boy?'

Gertie's head whipped up, her face streaked with tears. 'He said he was going to marry me.'

'Mother, please,' Maisie said, desperate to right the situation. 'It's not what you think.'

'On the contrary. It's exactly what I thought.' Mother glowered at her. 'What do you think you're doing, Maisie? A fallen woman, in our home. What kind of influence is this on Lily?'

'Would you turn her out on the street? Gertie has been the victim of the vilest of men, I know from experience.'

Mother's mouth fell open in horror. 'Not you too?'

'No, nothing like that. I know the man and he's a liar, a thief and a blackmailer and will stop at nothing to get what he wants. He's the worst kind of man.'

'He's been arrested,' Gertie cried.

'Oh, my Lord.' Mother closed her eyes as if to shut out what she was hearing.

'Please, Mother. Gertie is the innocent here.' Maisie was stretching the truth but she couldn't see her friend thrown out in the street. 'She's learnt her lesson in a most heartbreaking and humiliating way.'

'I have.' Gertie nodded, dabbing at her eyes with her handkerchief. 'I swear.'

Mother frowned at Gertie. 'Leave Maisie and I to discuss this please, Miss Thompson. You can bide your time in my son's room. It's the lean-to through there.' She pointed to the back door.

'Yes, Mrs Greenwood.' Gertie obediently left the room.

When she was gone, Mother faced Maisie. 'Whatever has possessed you? This is a respectable household. She will bring shame on our house.'

'She's a good girl, Mother, really she is.' Maisie could justify the fib. She truly believed the experience with Percy had woken Gertie from her besotted movie-star dreams. 'And she's a good worker.' That much was true. Gertie was one of the few girls who was willing to work harder to take advantage of the incentive scheme. It might be only so she could buy pretty things, but even so she earned them. 'She'll pull her weight around the house, cooking and cleaning. She'll help with the mending too. She's a much better seamstress than I am. And she'll pay board, more than Andrew was paying.'

'Board? Were you planning on this being a long-term situation?'

'If you agree, then yes.' Maisie had nothing to lose. 'Andrew's room is vacant. He's not coming back.' They missed him but knew his move to the mainland was for the best. He had a future there. 'Doesn't it make sense to take in a boarder? Even Mrs Perkins would have to agree with that.'

'But Gertie is a fallen woman.'

'And so was Mary Magdalene and yet Jesus didn't send her away. Isn't it our Christian duty to take her in?'

Mother huffed. 'But the shame. I couldn't have an unwed mother in the house.'

'Gertie is not in the family way, I promise.' Maisie couldn't believe she was talking about such things with her mother.

'How can you be sure?'

Maisie dare not mention the hideous-sounding French cap – that in itself was testament to Gertie's guilt, and she certainly wasn't going to tell her mother that Percy hadn't 'finished the business'. 'I'm sure. Please, give her a chance.'

Mother wiped a work-worn hand over her eyes. 'We could do with the extra income.'

Maisie relaxed slightly.

'But Lily is not to know why she's here, ever, and if I think she's influencing your sister in an undue fashion, Miss Thompson is out the door.'

'Agreed.' Maisie dared to breathe again. 'You won't regret it, Mother. I promise.'

Mother frowned. 'We'll see. Call your friend back in.'

Maisie knocked on the lean-to door. Gertie's tear-stained face looked up from where she sat on Andrew's bed. 'I could be comfortable here, I know it.' Gertie smiled at her hopefully. 'A few nice touches to make it pretty and I'd be happy as a lamb in clover.'

'Come inside. Mother wants to talk with you.'

Gertie's face fell. 'She's going to throw me out, isn't she?' Her bottom lip began to tremble.

'No, I don't think she is.'

Mother scrutinised Gertie as she came back in. 'Maisie tells me you're a fine seamstress.'

'Oh, yes, Mrs Greenwood. I sew all my own clothes as well as dresses for my younger sisters and I'm forever patching and darning.'

'See that pile there.' Mother nodded towards a basket of mending waiting for the needle. 'Make a start on that while Maisie and Lily make the tea. We've only three lamb chops but I'm sure Maisie will share hers with you, won't you, Maisie?' She tilted her head, a small smile on her lips. 'After all, it is the Christian thing to do.'

Maisie called Lily back in to finish peeling the carrots while she started on the potatoes. Gertie settled in, sharing the lamplight with Mother, and began sewing in fine neat stitches.

Lily eyed Gertie with curiosity. 'Are you staying for tea?'

'It would appear that I am.' Gertie smiled at her.

'Goodie. I'd better peel an extra carrot.' Lily happily turned back to the sink.

After a few minutes of strained silence, Mother reached for the garment Gertie was working on and examined it. She turned it over to look at the stitching from the other side. 'She'll be staying for longer than just tea.' She handed it back to Gertie with a nod. 'Gertie will be boarding with us for a while.'

The tension dropped from Maisie's shoulders and she allowed herself to breathe deeply for the first time since she'd arrived home with Gertie.

'Does this mean with both of you working at Cadbury's you'll bring home double the amount of chocolate?' Lily asked.

Gertie laughed and the sound warmed Maisie's heart. 'I suppose it does. Now, what was that you were saying about bird migration earlier?'

Mother stifled a groan and Maisie couldn't blame her. Gertie was yet to learn the deluge of information Lily was capable of imparting. As Lily began talking about swallows and shearwaters, and the routes they took each year, Gertie listened with rapt attention, asking questions at just the right time, but always keeping her eye on her mending. Mother settled back in her chair, a slight smile on her lips. Maisie finished with the potatoes and took over peeling the last of the carrots as Lily had become distracted with her dissertation on migration. She took in the cosy picture in front of her. Her news about Frank and their long engagement could wait – the ring remained nestled in its small velvet pouch – but she knew both Mother and Lily would be overjoyed. Lily liked him and Mother had always thought he was a good man. Maisie was the one who had wobbled. She'd ask Frank over for Sunday dinner. She, Lily and Gertie would prepare a special meal while Mother relaxed for a change. With Lily staying in school and Mother able to take it a bit easier, the coming year would be a good one. And, to top it all off, if the rumours were true, this Christmas would mark the return of Cadbury's Dairy Milk. Maisie smiled in anticipation. It would be a very good year indeed.

42

Dorothy

Dorothy snapped closed the locks on her suitcase and set it by the front door. It had only been a few days since she'd resigned but each of them had been a kind of agony – knowing Thomas was close but not daring to see him, thinking of Esme as Chief Forewoman, seeing the factory outside the window but no longer having a place there. She would have left sooner but the *Nairana* had been fully booked. Instead she'd hidden away in the cottage waiting for this moment. Dorothy walked slowly from room to room, trailing her fingers over the dining table, the back of the couch, the kitchen benches and the gas cooker. She opened the back door and stepped outside to look over the garden. 'Good luck,' she said to the vegetable patch. 'You're going to need it.' She hoped whoever shared the cottage after she left was a better gardener than Sarah. Sarah hadn't made the decision yet, but her new housemate certainly wouldn't be Esme.

A cheeky blackbird hopped about the garden, his yellow beak poking around the silverbeet and tomato seedlings. With a pang

Dorothy realised she wouldn't be around when the vegetables were ready to harvest. She closed her eyes and inhaled deeply. As always the aroma of chocolate and cocoa wafted on the air. The scent was woven into her working days and even her dreams. How long would it be until it finally faded from her clothes? It would never leave her memory or her heart. Cadbury's was part of her very being. Thoughts of George Cadbury rose in her mind – his vision and his generosity. 'Thank you,' she whispered, 'for everything.'

A knock on the front door startled her. She stepped inside and went to answer it. Ida stood on the front verandah. 'What a lovely surprise.'

'Are you sure?' Ida asked tentatively. 'I didn't know if I should come or not.'

Dorothy ushered her inside, chagrined that she hadn't thought of seeking out Ida herself. She'd had so much on her mind. 'I'm glad you came.' She beckoned her to sit in the living room. 'Would you like a cup of tea?'

'I can't stay long.' Ida perched on the edge on an armchair. 'I just ducked over to say goodbye.' Her eyes betrayed confusion and a touch of sadness. 'I don't understand why you're leaving. None of us do.'

Dorothy steadied herself. She was grateful there'd been no gossip linking her to Percy Bates, let alone Thomas. She was glad now that she'd never told Ida about the letters. It made her reason for leaving much easier to explain, even though it wasn't the truth. 'It's time for a change. I've come as far as I can with the Firm and I'm in search of new horizons.'

'You've always been ambitious, but you're Chief Forewoman. Isn't that enough?'

Her disappointment at not being invited to join the Board of Directors was on the tip of her tongue but the truth was, it still hurt. Even now she couldn't bear the thought of Ida telling Esme, knowing how much the woman would gloat. 'I've done what I set out to do. The girls are doing a marvellous job, and the success of Cadbury's is assured. Anything more is treading water.'

'George Cadbury Junior is here today though. If the rumours are true, he'll be overseeing the production of Dairy Milk. Don't you want to stay for that?'

Dorothy brushed her question aside. 'Esme is Chief Forewoman now. She must be very pleased.'

Ida laughed. 'Ar, she's over the moon. Thinks it's her birthright to hear her talk.'

'And you'll be next in line.' Dorothy was relieved and pleased that Ida had been promoted to Forewoman A. It was only right.

'She ain't ever giving that position up.' Ida snorted. 'They'll have to carry her out in a box, and not a chocolate box neither.'

Dorothy smiled. 'That's probably true.'

'She's like a dog with a bone, that one. Try and take it off her and expect to get bit.'

Dorothy held her tongue. It would do her no good to criticise Esme in any way.

'It's a shame you and Esme never got on. She's been a good friend to me, especially when you ...' Ida looked away. 'Never mind.'

A heavy pain settled in Dorothy's chest. 'I couldn't compete with Esme for your friendship.'

'Oh, Dot.' Ida shook her head. 'You never even tried.'

Dorothy went to object. It had been impossible to break the bond Ida and Esme had formed after the terrifying sea voyage they'd endured together. Should she have tried harder? A jumble of complicated emotions swirled through her – remorse, grief, loneliness, regret, hurt and resentment. Esme had claimed Ida for her own and Dot had let her. She'd let Ida go.

Ida sighed. 'I didn't come here to rag on you. What's done's done. We had some good times, didn't we, back at Bournville?' Ida's smile was crooked and her eyes still carried a trace of hurt.

'Yes, we did.' It felt so long ago now.

'Nothing's turned out how I thought.' Ida looked around the room, avoiding Dorothy's eyes. 'I hope you're happy in Sydney and that you find what you're looking for.'

'You could come and visit.' The idea was appealing. She knew no one in Sydney.

'Sydney?' Ida shook her head. 'I ain't never getting on a ship again as long as I live. Didn't you ever wonder why I didn't go to the Melbourne Show?' She snorted. 'The voyage from home was more than enough for me. My stomach still lurches at the thought of it. I'm a landlubber through and through.' Ida stood. 'Work's awaiting.'

Dorothy walked her to the door. 'Thanks for dropping by.' She held out her arms, not knowing how Ida would respond. Ida stepped forward and they embraced, just for a moment. 'I'm sorry I hurt you,' Dorothy said. 'Believe me, I never meant to.'

Ida sniffled. 'You'll have me bawling if you're not careful.' Outside the front door she turned to Dorothy with a small grin. 'Tara-a-bit, Dot.'

Dorothy couldn't help but smile at the familiar Brummie farewell. 'Tara-a-bit, Ida.' Dorothy watched her walk towards the factory. Ida turned back once, waved and walked on.

The back door opened. Dorothy's heart leapt. Was it Thomas come to say one last goodbye? Sarah came into the living room. 'I spied you through the window with Ida,' Sarah said. 'I didn't want to interrupt so I snuck around the back until she'd gone. Is everything all right? She didn't know anything, did she?'

'Nothing, thanks to you and Mr Cooper.'

'Mr Cooper doesn't want a word of this getting out, believe me. You're in safe hands there.'

Dorothy flinched. She was grateful, but she'd be glad to be free of the constant reminders of humiliation and failure.

'Are you all set? Bags packed?'

'I'm ready. The taxicab should be here at any moment to take me to the station.'

'I cancelled it.'

'What? Why?'

'I'm going to take you to Hobart in one of the Cadbury's vans.' Sarah held her hands out to stop Dorothy's objection. 'It's all above board. I have permission. One last spin with my best friend.'

Dorothy laughed. 'Is there nothing you can't wrangle?'

'Nothing yet.' Sarah smiled.

'Sarah, may I ask a favour?'

'This sounds serious. We'd better sit down.' Sarah took a seat on the couch and Dorothy sat beside her. 'What is it?'

'Keep an eye on Maisie for me? She's a good girl and has so much potential.'

Sarah hesitated for a moment. 'I will, on one condition.'

'What's that?'

'That you give me permission to tell her the truth about you and Thomas.'

'What?' Dorothy glared at her. 'No. I never want Thomas dragged into this.'

'I won't mention his name. Look, she thinks you had an affair with a married man. I want to set the record straight. She needs to know that, instead of an affair, you were actually helping a man who'd gone through hell and was reliving it every day. She should know there was nothing else to it, that no matter what you admitted to, it wasn't true. You only said what you did to nail Percy. I don't want her to think badly of you, Dot, when all you wanted to do was good.'

Dorothy shuddered. What would Sarah think if she knew about the kiss?

'Please, Dot. Give the girl something to aspire to. She's always admired you. I'd hate for her faith in you to be destroyed. Percy Bates has done enough. Don't let him take this away as well.'

Dorothy nodded. 'All right,' she whispered. 'As long as you never tell her Thomas's name.'

'Agreed.' Sarah crossed her legs and studied her. 'There is something else I'll never tell her.'

'What's that?'

'Percy Bates was right. You do have something of great value.'

Dorothy froze. 'What do you mean?'

'The recipe for Dairy Milk. You've known it since the war.'

Dorothy's heart pounded in her ears. 'What makes you—?'

'During the war you worked in areas a woman wouldn't usually have access to, including the mélangeur and conching rooms. You'd know the ingredients and their exact proportions, as well as the time, temperature and pressure required for perfect results.'

'Not everyone who works in those areas knows the recipe for Dairy Milk. If that were the case it would've been stolen years ago.' Dorothy heard the note of defiance in her voice and tightened her lips.

'True. But Percy's insistence confirmed that whoever was paying him had done their homework. He played a long game and I don't think his backers would have continued to invest if they didn't think it was true.'

'Pure speculation.' Dorothy picked some imaginary lint from her skirt.

'I want you to know how much I admire you, Dot. This isn't the first time you've been enticed or threatened to divulge the recipe. No matter what though, you have never, ever succumbed.'

Dorothy faltered. 'How did you ... how could you know that?'

Sarah leant forward and lowered her voice. 'Because I'm a spy.'

Instinctively Dorothy jerked back to put distance between her and Sarah. 'A spy?' Margaret's words – 'she's a funny one, isn't she?' – echoed in her head. Sarah's sidesteps in their past conversations, the things she knew about the Firm's business and how she'd recently stitched up Percy Bates, all flooded her mind in a jumbled whirl. Dorothy had wondered about Sarah at times but had stupidly pushed her suspicions aside. Why? Because she'd come to rely on Sarah's friendship and support. She'd felt so alone once Ida had made her allegiance to Esme clear and it was Sarah's advice she had sought concerning the letters. She took a sharp breath. The letters. 'It was you.' Dorothy almost choked on the words. 'You sent the letters.' It all made sense now – Sarah's inside knowledge, the way the letters arrived so quickly. A spy would be able to disguise their handwriting. It added up. A growing anger burnt in her chest. Had Sarah and Percy Bates been in cahoots all that time, undermining and threatening her?

Sarah's laugh was more a bark of surprise. 'What? No. The letters were definitely Percy's work. I had nothing to do with him or his scheme. However, I was employed, in part, to keep an eye on you. I must say it was a lovely change. Usually I'm tasked with keeping tabs on men.' Sarah seemed remarkably relaxed.

A fine sweat gathered on Dorothy's brow. All this time she'd thought Sarah was her friend when in fact she was being paid to get close to her, to watch her. Dorothy could see now how Sarah had manipulated an ongoing friendship – arranging to share a room at the hostel, the elocution lessons, the luxury of their own cottage.

Her hands formed into fists as she tried to contain her anger. She'd been a fool. The secret of the Dairy Milk recipe had been a burden she'd been willing to carry despite the trouble it had caused her in the past. She should have known she could never trust anyone. Especially Sarah. 'Who's employing you?'

'Dorothy, I'm on your side, remember. I'm employed by Cadbury's. The Firm pays me to do many things, including help safeguard the recipes. Perhaps I was being overly dramatic calling myself a spy. Yes, I keep track of employees and watch for any sign of espionage – I guess that could be called spying, but perhaps "detective" is a better term.'

Dorothy grappled for words. 'I knew the Firm employed detectives and the like but why would they give you the job?'

Sarah touched the side of her nose with her index finger. 'A few tricks I picked up during the war.'

'But you were with the Voluntary Aid Detachment during the war.'

'Was I?' Sarah's eyebrows arched in surprise.

Dorothy hesitated. Sarah had never mentioned the VAD. Dorothy had assumed. 'You said you'd considered being a nurse after your experiences.'

'I also said we all did our bit. My bit happened to be mainly in the shadows.'

Sarah had always been elusive when questioned and vague about her past. Now Dorothy knew why. Sarah was a spy for Cadbury's and was hinting she'd also been a spy for the Allies during the war. This was a woman who knew how to keep secrets no matter the cost. Dorothy was mere collateral.

'Dot, I never wanted to mislead you – sadly it's part of the job.' Sarah's expression appeared to be genuinely remorseful but Dorothy didn't hold any faith in it. 'I didn't factor in how much this particular job would affect me though. I am genuinely fond of you, Dot. We're so much alike. I do hope we can remain friends.'

'Friends? How can we be friends? You lied to me the first day we met and you've been lying to me every day since.' Anger gave way to the deep, jagged pain of betrayal but she wouldn't cry. She refused to show how deeply Sarah had hurt her.

'And you've lied to me.'

'I—'

'You can't deny it.' Sarah's voice was calm. 'Thomas?' She paused and Dorothy felt a stab of shame. 'But more pertinent to this conversation is the fact that you knew all along what Percy Bates meant by you having something of great value and yet you never let on. Not even when I asked you.'

Dorothy smoothed the hair behind her right ear. There was no point in keeping up the pretence any longer. Sarah had known all along. In some ways it was a relief to finally let it go. 'I couldn't. It's the Firm's most precious recipe. I signed an agreement but even so I would never tell anyone.'

'I know. And that's why I admire you.'

'You admire me for being a liar?'

'I admire you for being loyal. You could have been wealthy, living a life of leisure, but no. You're a rare woman, Mrs Adwell. I respect you enormously. I do hope you can forgive me.'

Dorothy wanted to believe her but the hurt was too fresh. 'I'm not sure ...'

'We both know the truth about each other now. No more secrets. Not from each other. I'm afraid you'll have to keep what you've learnt about me today to yourself.' Sarah leant towards her. 'We'll keep each other's secrets, Dot. It will be another bond between us.'

Dorothy didn't know if that was the kind of bond she wanted. A bond of lies. 'What does it matter? I'm leaving.'

Sarah sighed. 'I wish you weren't.'

A knock on the front door startled Dorothy. What next?

Sarah checked her watch. 'Right on time. Good old Georgie.' She returned her focus to Dorothy. 'Please let me drive you to the train later. I know you're wary of me now, but I meant it when I said you were my best friend.'

The exchange with Sarah had left Dorothy drained. Her emotions were a confusion of anger, hurt and sadness. She had little fight left in her. She nodded.

'Thank you.' Sarah went to answer the door.

Dorothy was glad she was leaving. The kiss with Thomas, Sarah's lies, the look on Mr Cooper's face – she wanted to run away from them all.

'Here she is, sir.' Sarah ushered a man into the living room. 'Dot, there's someone here who'd like to talk to you.'

Dorothy gasped. 'Mr Cadbury.' The name came out half-strangled. She got to her feet. 'Good afternoon.' George Cadbury Junior stood in front of her, a bemused smile on his face.

'Mrs Adwell.' He doffed his hat in greeting. 'You've been the topic of much conversation today.'

'Oh dear.' Dorothy put her hand on her heart and sank back onto the couch. How much more could she take?

Sarah stepped forward. 'Please, Mr Cadbury, give me your hat and take a seat. Would you like a cup of tea?'

George Cadbury Junior chuckled as he sat. 'No, thank you. I've already drunk enough tea today to last the week.'

'Right then. I'll leave you to it.'

'Sarah?' Dorothy looked at her in consternation. Sarah had promised no more secrets and yet had clearly known of this visit.

'I'll be back a little later to take you into town.' Sarah retrieved her hat and gloves and left.

George Cadbury Junior cleared his throat. 'I was disappointed to hear of your resignation, Mrs Adwell. For personal reasons, I believe.'

Dorothy nodded, unsure if she could trust her own voice.

'You've been a valuable and loyal worker through the years. Miss Harris has told me just how loyal.'

'Thank you, sir.'

'I've had a few interesting conversations today, not the least being with Thomas Moreland's sister.'

'Vera?' Fear clutched at Dorothy's stomach. Why on earth would Vera want to talk with George Cadbury Junior?

'She insisted on an appointment. She was concerned that you'd resigned under false pretences and was quick to assure me that you had only been assisting her brother with his condition. I must admit to being rather confused by what she said and why she was telling me but one thing came through clearly. She's a strong admirer of yours, Mrs Adwell.'

Dorothy ducked her head to hide her shame. Thomas must have told Vera the real reason for her resignation. The poor woman had rushed to her defence, not knowing that since then all talk of adultery had been swept under the carpet.

'She also mentioned you'd saved her son from drowning. I'd have thought we would have given you a commendation for your actions.'

'It wasn't necessary, Mr Cadbury. I did what anyone else would have done under the circumstances.' She'd begged Sarah to make the proposed commendation go away. At the time she'd thought Vera was Thomas's wife and couldn't have borne a ceremony with him, Vera and little Edward present. Her error still mortified her.

'Hmm.' He stroked his moustache. 'Loyal, brave, generous and humble. You're just the type of employee the Cadbury family treasures.' He looked out the window towards the factory. 'I've seen the photos and depictions, naturally, but nothing prepares one for the actual sight of this grand and modern factory between the mountain and the sea.' He turned back to her. 'And you've been a vital part of it. Chief Forewoman, no less.'

'Thank you, it's been an honour.' Dorothy didn't know what else to say. Platitudes would have to do.

'Miss Harris has informed me that you're unable to remain here at Claremont, no matter how much we implore you. It would be such a waste to lose your expertise and the knowledge you've gained through your years of service with the Firm. I wonder if you might give thought to another option.' He paused. 'Mrs Adwell, would you consider returning to Bournville?'

'Bournville?' She'd been hand-chosen and promoted to be one of the chocolate pioneers. How could she return to her old job after being Chief Forewoman here? There'd be too many questions, too much shame.

'Cadbury's Dairy Milk is the most popular chocolate in the world.' He gave a smug smile, and she couldn't begrudge him – he was, after all, the man who'd invented it. 'Demand is constantly increasing and production is struggling to keep up. I find myself in need of an overseer who knows the recipe and the processes, someone who's an expert at solving problems and whose loyalty is beyond reproach. There's only one person I can think of who fits the bill. Mrs Adwell, I am offering you the position of Chief Forewoman of Dairy Milk production.'

'Oh, my.' Dorothy's pulse raced. It was one thing to be Chief Forewoman here in the colonies but to be a Chief Forewoman at Bournville – it was an enormous honour and a significant promotion.

'I'll give you some time to think about it. Miss Harris tells me you're planning to relocate to Sydney and begin a new career there. May I suggest, if you accept my proposal, that you enjoy a short holiday in Sydney? I can attest to it being a beautiful city. We can book your passage back to Bournville from there.'

'I don't know what to say, sir. It's a very generous offer.'

'Not generous. Well deserved.' He stood and Dorothy rose also. He took a step towards the front door and then turned back. 'There is one other thing.'

Dorothy's heart sank. Here it came – the proviso.

'I do hope you accept the offer, not only for your expertise in the factory, but for your skill on the pitch. I'm sad to say, the Cadbury's women's cricket team has floundered without you.'

Dorothy couldn't help but smile. She'd read in the *Bournville Works Magazine* that her old team had failed to make the finals this season. 'I have missed the willow and leather,' she said. 'I haven't had the chance to play while I've been here.' It would be summer soon in this land where the seasons were upside down. She had hoped to be recruiting a team by now but the sordid business with Percy Bates and her position as Chief Forewoman had taken all her time and resources. There had been nothing left for the game she loved.

'You haven't been playing cricket?' Mr Cadbury raised his eyebrows in mock outrage. 'That in itself is a travesty and one I hope we can rectify.'

She accompanied him to the front door. 'Thank you. I'll let you know before the end of the week.'

He took his hat from the hallstand. 'I hope you return to Bournville. It will be our loss if you decide to stay in Sydney.' He tipped his hat and stepped outside.

Dorothy closed the door and leant against it. Her Sydney plan had been an escape route but she had no work lined up, only a room in a boarding house to use as a base until she did. Nothing would be lost if she didn't stay there. Cadbury's was in her blood and in her bones. The Firm had given her a life she could never have imagined as a child. She belonged with the Firm and always would. But could she return to Bournville? She'd left, in part, to be free of her sadness and grief. It hadn't worked, at least not in the way she'd hoped it would. Dorothy had wished for so long that Freddie had come home to her, damaged though he was. She would have nursed him, comforted him, and she'd once believed she could have restored him to the man he used to be. Meeting Thomas had been both a gift and a heartbreak, but now she realised it had also set her free. No matter how much she'd read about theories and practices, she hadn't been able to fix Thomas, just as she would never have been able to mend Freddie's broken mind. The heavy burden of guilt and remorse, of grief and sorrow, fell away. She would always love Freddie but she need feel no regret for failing at something she could never have achieved.

Grabbing her hat and gloves, Dorothy rushed from the cottage. She didn't need to wait until the end of the week.

George Cadbury Junior hadn't walked far. He was standing admiring the cottages and the view.

'Mr Cadbury,' she called.

He turned.

Dorothy stepped towards him. She was going home.

43

Dorothy

July 1926

Dorothy pulled a tray of perfectly cooked, perfectly round chocolate biscuits from the oven. Once they were cool she'd sandwich them together with a chocolate butter-cream filling. She imagined how Michael's eyes would light up when he saw them. He'd been wary of her at first and not sure how to respond. She'd won him over with her cooking and with her prowess as a cricketer. His bowling skills had improved under her gentle tutelage and although batting wasn't her main strength, she'd managed to improve his technique in that regard as well. When he visited they practised in the field behind the cottage with only a few sheep as curious onlookers.

She checked the mantel clock and fanned the biscuits to help them cool. He'd be arriving soon with smuts on his cheeks from the train. Michael could never resist sticking his head out the window to feel the air rushing by. Although he was twelve years old now, he was still a boy in so many ways.

Dorothy's return to Bournville almost four years earlier had been bittersweet. Memories of Freddie and of her times with Ida had haunted the streets of Bournville and the factory. Her grief and regret had faded with time but there were some things she neither wanted nor needed to forget. Both of them would always hold a special place in her heart. She'd lived back on the estate for some of that time and relished her position as Chief Forewoman of Dairy Milk production. George Cadbury Junior had been right. The world's appetite for Dairy Milk kept growing exponentially. Her work was fulfilling and exhausting. In some ways she envied Margaret, whose position was less demanding. Being the liaison between Bournville and Claremont agreed with her and she'd returned to full health. She and Dorothy would often meet for lunch in the newly constructed dining room with the enormous windows that were left wide open in the warmer months. The Cadburys' passion for light, air and space continued.

She often thought of Sarah. In a way Sarah's duplicity had made it easier for Dorothy to leave Tasmania. She would never know how much of their friendship had been real. Sarah had stayed in Tasmania to protect the Dairy Milk recipe. Ironically production had been delayed time and time again for a multitude of reasons and the world's favourite chocolate was still not rolling off the line. They corresponded occasionally. Sarah's letters informed her that Percy Bates had been released from prison and had disappeared. He was probably skulking around on the mainland somewhere. *Good riddance to bad rubbish*, Sarah had written. She also wrote that Esme had finally managed to wrangle a cottage for herself and Ida, while Sarah shared her cottage with Lizzie, who was now a Forewoman A. Dorothy replied carefully, giving nothing away.

Dorothy gazed out the window to the green fields ringed with familiar oaks and elms. Her time in Tasmania had been more of an adventure than she could have ever imagined. Sometimes she wondered how her life would be now if she was still on the chocolate peninsula with the screeching cockatoos, silent black swans and the ever-flowing river. She shook herself from her reverie. Life back home had become more fulfilling than she'd ever imagined. Indeed, it was a life she never would have dared to live if she hadn't made that journey to Hobart five years earlier.

While the biscuits cooled she wandered outside into the garden. The sun warmed her as she gathered deep pink scented stocks, delicate sweet peas and vibrant blue cornflowers. The apples were colouring up on the tree at the bottom of the yard. The sweet and juicy fruit would be a more than adequate consolation when the weather turned cold and the nights began to close in. But now the summer days stretched out before her with the promise of another grand final for the Cadbury's women's cricket team and a full two weeks with Michael.

Inside, she inhaled the sweet scent of the blooms as she arranged them in a vase. Although the garden had needed much loving care when she'd first moved to this cottage, the soil was deep and rich and the plants had responded with enthusiasm to her attention. She'd been rewarded with an abundance of produce and beauty for her table.

Dorothy glanced at the clock once more. Nervous excitement built in her chest. Today Thomas would not only be bringing Michael home with him for the summer holidays, he'd also be bringing news. News she had waited years for. When it had become clear that his wife was never going to join him in Tasmania, Thomas had resolved to return to England. It was the only way he would be able to see his son. His loyalties were torn though, between his son and his sister and nephew who were reliant on him in Claremont. Vera had been a regular correspondent, keeping Dorothy up to date with Edward's continued good health, all thanks to Dorothy, as Vera never failed to mention, and the developments in their lives at the estate. Reading between the lines of Vera's letters, Dorothy had wondered about Vera's romance with a member of Cadbury's clerical staff. Within a year they were married and the three of them happily ensconced in one of the Firm's cottages. Needless to say, it had the result of freeing Thomas, a result Dorothy was sure Vera had intended.

When Thomas had returned to England, Dorothy had lived on tenterhooks, wondering if he and his wife would settle back into domestic life together with their son. The answer came on an autumn day with the oaks ablaze and a slight mist in the air. Thomas had knocked on her door at Bournville with a mix of sadness, love and hope on his face.

'I know I have no right to ask this of you,' he'd said. 'But could we possibly resume where we left off in Claremont?'

Dorothy had hesitated for a moment, unsure of what he meant, longing and desire pounding at her ribs, in her throat and on her lips. She was left in no doubt as he stepped forward and enfolded her in his arms. His mouth on hers left her breathless. This was not a kiss goodbye. This was the beginning of a new life.

Thomas's wife had other ideas. She would not grant him a divorce. Thomas had despaired until Dorothy had found a little cottage within walking distance of Bournville, tucked away from prying eyes and gossiping tongues. Thomas had baulked at first, concerned for Dorothy's reputation. Dorothy had smiled. 'I admitted to adultery back in Tasmania – why not make it true?'

She didn't tell him she'd learnt a few tricks from Sarah and was sure their secret would be safe. With Dorothy working day shifts at the factory and Thomas teaching evening classes it was simple to avoid detection. On the occasions when they were seen together at social events and cricket matches it was natural for them to spend time talking. Everyone knew they'd both worked for the Firm at Claremont and assumed that was their connection.

It had been almost two years since Thomas's return. In the quiet of the countryside, with Dorothy's care and with the understanding support of the Firm, who'd seen many of their employees return from the Great War with wounds both visible and invisible, the shell shock had improved slightly. The nightmares continued but weren't as violent and he'd learnt to avoid situations where his condition might be brought on by a loud noise or flash of light. Birmingham, with its constant clamour, smoke and stench from the factories and forges, was somewhere he would never venture.

Dorothy took a mixing bowl from the cupboard and beat butter to a cream. She added cocoa and sugar and beat it again until the chocolate butter filling was thoroughly mixed. A good cook always tastes as she goes. She dipped a finger into the mix and licked it. Delicious. The biscuits were cool enough now to sandwich together and she piled a plate high with the chocolatey treats. The sound of the gate opening announced Thomas and Michael's arrival. She untied her apron and smoothed her hair. The anxious anticipation that had been her companion all day rose in her throat. Today might be the day everything changed.

She opened the front door and watched Thomas and Michael walking up the path lined with roses and vibrant dahlias. The scent of summer wafted towards her along with the busy drone of the bees.

Michael looked up with a grin. 'I scored forty-eight runs in the final.'

'Congratulations. What a mighty effort.' Of course his first words to her would be about cricket, their common ground. Next he'd be asking her what there was to eat. She pre-empted him. 'I've just finished making your favourite biscuits. Come inside, you must be hungry after the train.'

'I'm starving.' Michael lugged his suitcase up the front steps and into the cottage. Dorothy resisted the urge to kiss his cheek. They weren't quite there yet and, besides, he was of an age where her affections might embarrass him.

Thomas was close behind him. It was hard to judge his expression under the brim of his hat. She waited, her stomach clenched in a tight knot. Thomas had hoped to return from collecting Michael with news. His wife had mentioned a male friend a few times, which had given Thomas cause to be optimistic. He thought she might finally be ready to accept the scandal of a divorce and move forward with her life. Dorothy had briefly entertained thoughts of a future where their love was no longer a secret – a wedding, a cottage at Bournville, and in time a child or two of their own. She'd pushed away the fantasy. It had been wrenched from her before. She didn't trust that it wouldn't again.

Now she searched Thomas's face for a sign. Divorce wasn't something they wanted to talk about in front of Michael. Not yet. He was used to his parents not living together, they'd been apart for so long, but a permanent change would need to be handled gently. She knew Michael would be in the kitchen scoffing biscuits and well out of earshot. Thomas took off his hat and stood on the step below her. His eyes looked directly into hers.

Dorothy licked her lips in nervous anticipation. 'Welcome home, Mr Moreland. Any news?'

A slow smile gathered at the corners of his mouth. The lines around his eyes crinkled.

Her heart stopped for a beat. 'Did she say yes?'

Thomas's smile deepened. He nodded.

Relief flowed through Dorothy with such strength she could hardly draw breath. His wife had finally agreed to a divorce.

'And now I have a question for you and I hope the answer is also a yes.' Thomas took her hands in his and lifted them to his lips. His warm breath on her skin sent a delicious quiver through her body. 'Mrs Adwell, will you marry me?'

Dorothy took him in, the man she had hoped to fix but had come to realise she never could, the man who had reminded her of Freddie but had become his own man in her heart and mind, the man she loved body and soul. Freddie would always have a place in her heart but over the years her heart had grown. There was room for grief and sadness, love and joy, and all that life could throw at her in between. Today was a day for love and joy. Today was a day for happiness.

'Ar,' she said, in the accent she'd been proud to reclaim since her return to Bournville. 'Ar, Mr Moreland. I will.'

AUTHOR'S NOTE

I'm delighted that *The Chocolate Factory*'s release coincides with Cadbury's 200th anniversary. In 1824 John Cadbury opened a grocer's shop at 93 Bull Street in Birmingham. He started producing his own products shortly afterwards. When his sons, George and Richard, took over the business they became so successful (after some tough and trying times) they built the factory in the park at Bournville where Cadbury remains to this day.

During the time in which *The Chocolate Factory* is set industrial espionage was rife between the chocolate companies. They often sent spies, posing as employees, to steal each other's trade secrets. They would also employ detectives within their own factories in an attempt to catch these spies. As Dairy Milk was the most popular chocolate in the world at the time, the recipe was in constant danger of being stolen. If you think this scenario is reminiscent of *Charlie and the Chocolate Factory*, you're right. Roald Dahl went to a boarding school not far from Bournville. Cadbury's would send samples of new products to the boys to taste test. This instilled a lifelong love of chocolate in Roald Dahl and also a fascination with how it was made, its history and the machinations of the chocolate spies.

While Cadbury is known as Cadbury today, for a long time it was known as Cadbury's, hence the use of that nomenclature in this novel. The name gradually became Cadbury from the 1970s onwards but many, including myself, still refer to it as Cadbury's. Old habits die hard. I grew up in Hobart where the most anticipated school excursion of the year was a visit to the Cadbury's factory at Claremont. The smell in some sections was overpowering but the delights of being in a chocolate factory and seeing where the magic happened, not to mention the treats we were given, outweighed any olfactory concerns.

I took a trip down memory lane to visit the chocolate peninsula as part of my research. Sadly factory tours are no longer allowed, but I'm forever grateful to Caz Mitchell, Site Administration, Cadbury, for being so generous with her time and knowledge. We sat together on one of the many benches dotted around the factory grounds and pored over an enormous folder filled with Cadbury's history and photographs. She also provided me with photos of areas I couldn't access. The original bean store is still there and the railway tracks, although the trains have not run for many years. Tony Sansom from the Claremont Golf Club and I sat in the club room with a fabulous view over the course and the river. He took me through the early days of the club and how it evolved from the employees' original jam-tin course. In a beautiful case of happenstance, I was walking along Bournville Crescent just as Warren O'Rourke was getting into his car outside his house. His home is one of the original cottages on the estate and he invited me back for a tour. Warren has done a beautiful job of restoring the cottage as much as possible to its original state. I could imagine Dorothy and Sarah living there and what their daily routines would have been like. I was also able to stay at the Cadbury estate on MacRobertsons Terrace which made me chuckle given the animosity between Cadbury's and MacRobertson's in those early days.

There are many mentions of the Quaker beliefs of the Cadburys and of other characters in this novel. Indeed, the impetus to write *The Chocolate Factory* came from my interest in Quakerism. My grandparents were Quakers and I attended the world's largest Quaker school – The Friends' School in Hobart. As I've grown older my beliefs have aligned more and more with the Quaker values of simplicity, social justice, equality, pacifism and stewardship of the earth. I hope you've enjoyed finding out why so many of the best-known chocolate companies were founded by Quakers.

It took more than a love of chocolate and an interest in Quakerism to bring to life the early years of the Cadbury factory in Tasmania and Dorothy's time living and working at Bournville. *Chocolate Wars – From Cadbury to Kraft: 200 Years of Sweet Success and Bitter Rivalry* by Deborah Cadbury (HarperPress 2010) and *A History of Cadbury* by Diane Wordsworth (Pen and Sword Books 2018) provided excellent information about the Cadburys, Bournville and the success of Dairy Milk chocolate.

To research the Claremont factory and the women who travelled from Bournville I found vital insights in '"Belles from Bristol and Bournville in New Surroundings": female confectionery workers as transnational agents, 1918–1928' by Emma Robertson (*Women's History Review*, 25:4, 563–583) and 'Gender, Skill and Trade-Unionism: Women Workers at Cadbury in Tasmania 1920–51' by Ruth Barton (*HSIR*, Autumn 2001). I am grateful to both Emma and Ruth for making their work available to me. I also found Ruth's theses *Cooperation and Labour Management at Electrolytic and Cadbury-Fry-Pascall Between 1918 and 1939* (University of Tasmania, March 1989) and *Cadburys at Claremont:*

an Antipodean Bournville? (University of Tasmania, 1981) both useful and fascinating. *Venturing Overseas: Geography and the Cadbury Chocolate Factory at Claremont, Tasmania, 1921–67* by Peter Wilde and Elissa Sutherland (Tasmanian Historical Studies, 2010) also provided relevant details, while Robert Crawford's book *More Than a Glass and a Half: A History of Cadbury in Australia* (Halstead Press, 2022) delved into the marketing and advertising of Cadbury's products as well as the history.

Bruce Smith, Archivist, Mondelez Heritage Collection, Melbourne, patiently answered my many questions and also supplied a digital copy of the October 1922 edition of *Bournville Works Magazine* from the Cadbury archive at Bournville. The articles and photos in the magazine shone a light on the building of the new factory and the staff who worked there in such a way I almost felt as if I were there.

It would be much more difficult to write an Australian historical novel without the help of the National Library of Australia and Trove. I know I'm not the only one who was thrilled when the Federal Government pledged ongoing funding for Trove in 2023. I will continue to donate to the National Library but happily the government's pockets are much deeper than mine.

I spent many days at the State Library of Tasmania in the Hobart Reading Room studying reports, examining maps and investigating product lines, various tariffs and embargoes, and many other details that never made it into the novel but all informed the writing. My heartfelt thanks go to the librarians and archivists there, with special mention to Janine Tan of the State Library and Archive Service, Libraries Tasmania. I had a hell of a time finding out the location of the hostel where the Cadbury's women lived and it was Janine who finally tracked it down. The building is now the Connewarre Clinic and has changed greatly since 1921, as has Main Road.

I must make special mention of two Facebook groups – Tasmanian History and Claremont–Windemere History. The members never failed to answer my questions with their in-depth knowledge and often wonderful conversations would ensue. Through the Claremont–Windemere History group I was put in touch not only with Tony Sansom but also Robert Rayner, who generously talked to me about his days working at Cadbury's back in the 1950s.

Most of the events and incidents in *The Chocolate Factory* are based on fact; however, I fictionalised George Cadbury Junior's visit to Australia. I expect he was much too busy at Bournville to take the long trip to Tasmania. His cousin, William A Cadbury, did visit the factory in March 1923. William was one of the directors of Cadbury Brothers, Limited and Richard Cadbury's second son.

I have thoroughly enjoyed researching and writing about the early days of the Cadbury Factory at Claremont. An essential part of that was taste testing a lot of different varieties of Dairy Milk. As I did I often wondered what George Cadbury Junior would make of his most famous invention being used in such a myriad of ways. I like to think he'd be very pleased indeed. I know I am.

ACKNOWLEDGEMENTS

Thank you to Nicola Robinson, Johanna Baker and Suzanne O'Sullivan at HQ for guiding this novel through the process of publication. A massive debt of gratitude to Annabel Blay who did such a marvellous job of editing *The Last of the Apple Blossom* that I begged to have her back to edit *The Chocolate Factory*. My writing is better for her insights, questions and suggestions.

Thank you to Annabel Adair for finding all those niggly things with your eagle-eyed proofreading skills.

The gorgeous cover was designed by Debra Bilson. I was filled with joy when I first saw it and haven't been able to stop looking at it since. It's beautiful, evocative and a little bit mysterious.

Thank you to Natika Palka for your publicity nous and for your marketing prowess.

To the HQ and HarperCollins sales team, a massive thank you for getting *The Chocolate Factory* out into the world. And to our beloved booksellers, thank you for putting books into the hands of readers. That's when our words truly come alive. You are worth your weight in chocolate.

To my early readers Jodie Miller, Sara Hartland and Leanne Lovegrove – thank you for pointing out plot holes and inconsistencies. Your feedback and encouragement was invaluable.

I wish Sue Goldstiver was still on this earthly plane to hold this book in her hands and read the final version. Sue, Jodie and I were in a writing group together for fourteen years and supported each other through our writing ups and downs as well as the vicissitudes of our personal lives. Sue's sudden death was a shock and a huge sadness to all who knew her. Her spirit has been with me, urging me on through the many stages of drafting and editing. I miss her smile, her wit and her quirky ways.

To my crew in Tasmania, thank you. Ian Salisbury for being the best chauffeur a girl could ask for and for all your suggestions and encouragement. Penny McDonald for friendship, fun, food and freezing cold walks. Lisa-Ann Gershwin, the Jellyfish Goddess, for your amazing generosity and gorgeous sense of humour. And Jacq Ellem for being my Huon Valley angel.

Also to Karen Brooks, writer extraordinaire and an inspiration to me and many others, thank you for chocolate chip cookies, apple slice and one of the best views in Hobart.

And to my husband, Ken, thank you for your abiding patience as I've prattled on about obscure chocolate facts and characters you've never met. There's no one else I'd rather travel through this life and this world with. Here's to many more adventures ahead.

talk about it

Let's talk about books.

Join the conversation:

f @harlequinaustralia

♪ @hqanz

◉ @harlequinaus

harpercollins.com.au/hq

If you love reading and want to know about our
authors and titles, then let's talk about it.